R 2

BEHOLD A PALE HORSE

BEHOLD A PALE HORSE

PETER TREMAYNE

headline

First published in 2011 by
HEADLINE PUBLISHING GROUP

Cataloguing in Publication Data is available from the British Library

ISBN 978 0 7553 7747 3

Typeset in Times New Roman PS by Palimpsest Book Production Limited,
Falkirk, Stirlingshire

Printed and bound in Great Britain by
Clays Ltd, St Ives plc

Headline's policy is to use papers that are natural, renewable and recyclable
products and made from wood grown in sustainable forests. The logging
and manufacturing processes are expected to conform to the environmental
regulations of the country of origin.

HEADLINE PUBLISHING GROUP
An Hachette UK Company
338 Euston Road
London NW1 3BH

www.headline.co.uk
www.hachette.co.uk

For the wonderful Sister Fidelma enthusiasts
that I met in the Abbey of Bobbio, who suggested
that she travel there –
Bobbio in noir, perché no?

Et ecce equus pallidus et qui sedebat desuper nomen illi Mors et Inferus sequebatur eum . . .
And I looked, and behold a pale horse: and the name that sat on him was Death, and Hell followed with him . . .

Revelation 6:8
Vulgate Latin translation of Jerome 4th century

PRINCIPAL CHARACTERS

Sister Fidelma of Cashel, a *dálaigh* or advocate of the law courts of seventh-century Ireland

At Genua in the kingdom of the Longobards
Magister Ado of Bobium
Brother Faro
Sister Gisa

In the Trebbia Valley
Radoald, Lord of Trebbia
Wulfoald, commander of Radoald's warriors
Suidur the Wise, physician to Radoald
Aistulf the Hermit

At the Abbey of Bobium
Abbot Servillius
Venerable Ionas, a scholar
Brother Wulfila, steward
Brother Hnikar, apothecary
Brother Ruadán, formerly of Inis Celtra
Brother Lonán, herbalist

Brother Eolann, *scriptor* or librarian
Brother Waldipert, cook
Brother Bladulf, gatekeeper
Romuald of Benevento, Prince of the Longobards
Lady Gunora, his nurse
Bishop Britmund, of Placentia, leader of the Arians
Brother Godomar, his steward

On Mount Pénas
Wamba, a goatherd
Hawisa, mother of Wamba
Odo, her nephew, a goatherd
Ratchis, a merchant

At Vars
Grasulf, son of Gisulf, Lord of Vars
Kakko, his steward

AUTHOR'S NOTE

May 2008 found me in Northern Italy promoting the Sister Fidelma Mysteries. One of the most exciting events was being invited to the famous Abbey of Bobbio to talk to a gathering in the ancient cloisters. The Abbey of Bobbio was one of the few places that I had long wanted to visit, but never before found the opportunity.

Bobbio, or Bobium as it was originally called, had been established in AD612 by the celebrated Irish saint and missionary Columbanus (AD540–615). He was from Leinster but had become Abbot of Bangor, Co. Down, before beginning his travels abroad. The original Irish form of his name, Colm Bán, meant 'white dove', but he is often confused with his Donegal namesake Colm Cille (AD521–97), meaning 'dove of the church', popularly known as Columba. Colm Cille's most famous foundation was on Iona, a tiny island off the coast of Scotland. Bobbio became equally renowned in Europe for its great library and its scholars.

It was a privilege for me to be talking about Sister Fidelma in such a setting as the ancient cloisters of Bobbio. A member of the audience asked me why I couldn't bring Fidelma to Bobbio, solving some mystery during a visit to this great

Irish establishment in the Val de Trebbia, in the Apennine Mountains.

In *Shroud for the Archbishop*, Fidelma had already visited Rome where she solved the mystery of the death of Wighard, the Archbishop-designate of Canterbury, which took place there in AD664. It was a real event around which I had created a story. So, I replied, 'Why not?' The major Northern Italian daily newspaper *Libertà*, reporting the event, carried the story under the headline *Bobbio in noir, perché no?* The idea for the story took two years to germinate and came out in this form, but not before I made further trips to the Trebbia Valley.

The Sister Fidelma Mysteries, with the exception of the two short-story collections, follow a strict chronological order, analogous to the date of their publication. For example, the first novel, *Absolution by Murder* (1994) was set in May AD664. The subsequent novels cover the years through to AD670, the year in which *The Chalice of Blood* (2010) is set. *Behold A Pale Horse* becomes an exception. This story follows immediately on from the action in *Shroud for the Archbishop*, which was set in Rome during the summer of AD664. Readers may recall that Fidelma left her new friend, Brother Eadulf of Seaxmund's Ham, in the Eternal City to return home to Ireland. She took a ship from Ostia, the port at the mouth of the Tiber, with the intention of disembarking at Massilia (Marseilles) and following the pilgrims' route overland.

Peter Tremayne

The Trebbia Valley

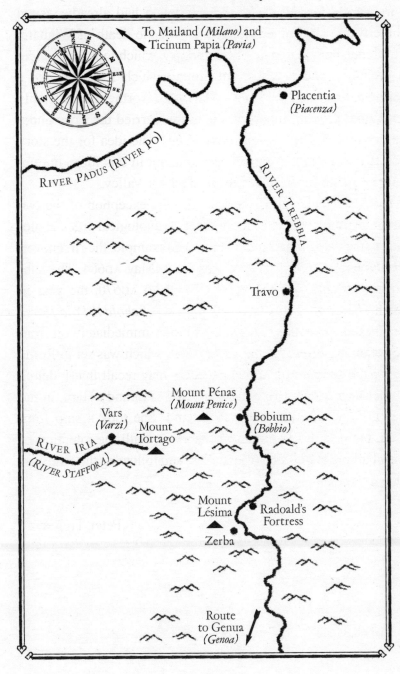

CHAPTER ONE

The elderly man was obviously a religieux. He wore the *corona spina*, the tonsure of St Peter, and a long brown woollen homespun cloak over a robe of similar material, with leather sandals on his feet. Marking him as being above the lower orders of religious brethren, he carried a staff of office topped with a small silver hook as if it were a crozier of the type a bishop might use.

He hurried by Sister Fidelma without a glance, the soles of his sandals slapping on the cobbles of the narrow street. Fidelma was sheltering under the thatch cover of a little house in the crowded section of the old seaport where she had found lodgings. She barely glanced up as the man passed her, registering the details only subconsciously. In truth, she was bored and her mind preoccupied with the question of how she could pass the time; pass another day in this dreary harbour town where she had been stranded for several days.

It seemed a lifetime ago since she had left Rome to travel down the Tiber to the seaport of Ostia and thence obtain a passage for Massilia. Everything appeared to go well at first. The ship set sail with a blustery wind from the south-east, and the captain was confident of an easy voyage. Before the day was out, however, everything had gone wrong. The wind suddenly changed direction, a storm came out of nowhere and a sail was ripped, a spar cracked and the ship was driven against some rocks, splintering the planking around the keel. Fidelma could not blame the captain for poor seamanship. In fact, he had saved the lives of his passengers and crew by being able to bring the crippled vessel into the nearby natural harbour of Genua before it sank. The sailors seemed to consider this as a blessing from the old gods. When Fidelma inquired why, she was told that Genua was named from the two-headed god Giano, who was the protector of ships. The superstitious sailors felt the god had reached out to save them.

The fact remained that the ship was beyond immediate repair. Fidelma was assured that the seaport of Genua was the crossroad of commerce and that she should easily be able to secure a new passage to Massilia. However, the assurances proved wrong. There were few ships in the harbour and none heading for Massilia nor to any adjacent port. There was some rumour that a Frankish fleet might be heading for the seaport and talk of war in the air, but she took no notice. Fidelma had wandered the back streets around the harbour until she was directed to a small hostel which catered for religious pilgrims. She had no complaints about the hospitality, but the days were long in passing and there was no sign of any ship on which she might continue her journey.

Genua was not a place which held her attention. The old woman who ran the hostel had related the general history of the area within one brief conversation. In recent years, various conquerors had seized the seaport for strategic reasons and it was here the ships of the ruling Byzantines had once harboured while they tried to stop the invading Germanic tribes, the Longobards, who now held sway and had mixed their culture in this centre of commerce. Alboin and his Longobards had swept down the entire Italian peninsula during the previous century and conquered it, with the exception of isolated territories such as the lands around Rome itself, which clung to their independence. Some thirty-six powerful Longobard dukes now ruled under their King.

Among the languages of the seaport, she could hear various tongues, and Fidelma could now distinguish the harsh gutturals of the language of the Longobards from the others. However, she was thankful that Latin was still the language of general communication, for at least she was able to make herself understood.

She was dwelling on these matters when the elderly religieux had hurried by. Some part of her mind registered this fact but would have dismissed it, had it not been for the two men following in his footsteps. It was their manner that caused her to glance up and give her full attention. They were hooded, their dark cloaks covering their tall figures, and they were bent forward, giving the impression of serious intent; one, at least, carried a cudgel in his right hand. Fidelma realised that this was what had caught her attention. The man's cloak had flapped back as he passed, thus momentarily revealing the weapon. They both seemed to be treading carefully, as if to avoid making the same noise on the cobbles that had marked the passage of their quarry.

Fidelma did not think about consequences. If there was some knavery here, then her training as a *dálaigh* – an advocate of the laws of her own land, now part of her very being – caused her to move automatically. Quietly, she followed the two men as they shadowed the elderly religieux along the narrow street. There were only two or three people moving along in the opposite direction and no one took any notice of them. Then they approached a stretch which was devoid of people. One of the men began to increase his stride, and some instinct caused Fidelma to slip into the shelter of a tiny recess between the buildings – just as the second man turned his head and glanced back, as if to check whether anyone else was on the street. When she peered cautiously out again, she saw that both men were closing rapidly on the elderly man. He seemed unaware of their presence. The leading pursuer had already raised his cudgel to strike.

Fidelma found herself throwing caution to the wind and running after them.

'*Caveo! Caveo!*' she cried loudly in Latin.

The elderly religieux turned at her cry and met the downward strike of the cudgel with a dexterous movement of his staff, fending off the blow.

The second attacker turned immediately to face Fidelma and she realised that he also held a cudgel. He raised it as he ran back towards her. What happened next was over in a few seconds. Still running forward, she suddenly ducked and halted. Her antagonist had no time to stop his forward momentum. He went flying across her crouched body and came down heavily on the cobbles, his cudgel spinning from his hand. Fidelma swung round and kicked the weapon further from him as he lay momentarily winded on the ground.

She had only used the art of the *troid-sciathagid* a few times before. She had used it once in Rome not so long ago when she had been attacked. It was a traditional technique of her people, called 'battle through defence' which had been taught in ancient times by those wise teachers who felt it wrong to carry arms to protect themselves. In these violent times, lonely missionaries were often attacked, robbed and sometimes killed. Now, many of the *peregrinatio pro Christo*, the missionaries who went abroad, learned how to defend themselves in this manner without the use of weapons.

Fidelma adopted a defensive posture, ready to confront her attacker again. His cloak had fallen open and her eyes caught an embroidered symbol on his right shoulder. It was a curious design, like a flaming sword surrounded by a laurel wreath. She was still looking at it when there was a shouted instruction from behind her. The next moment, the first attacker brushed roughly by her, running down the street. His companion rolled over, came to his feet and joined him. Both of them disappeared swiftly into some side alley. Fidelma hesitated, not knowing what to do next, when a voice behind her called in Latin: 'Let them go, Sister. Let us not take chances.'

She turned back to the elderly man, who stood leaning on his staff. There was a slight abrasion on his forehead and a trickle of blood.

'Are you hurt?' she demanded, moving forward.

The elderly man smiled. 'It could have been worse, but thanks to you, Sister, I was warned in time to deflect the blow. And you? I have seen that trick done before by an Hibernian Brother. Are you of that country?'

'I am,' Fidelma agreed solemnly. 'I am Fidelma of Hibernia.'

'Then well met, Sister Fidelma. I am Ado of Bobium.'

Fidelma glanced at the silver shepherd's hook on the end of his staff. 'Abbot Ado?' she ventured.

He chuckled with a shake of his head. He was a handsome, intelligent-looking man, in spite of his advancing years. He had blue eyes and his hair was white and almost to his shoulders but well-tended. He gave the impression of a man of some strength, and the way he had handled his staff to disarm his attacker showed that he had not only strength but dexterity.

'An abbot? No, although some address me as Magister Ado as a token of respect for my scholarship and advancing years.' He glanced quickly around. 'However, I would advise that we do not tarry here in case our friends return. My destination is not far away. Come, let me offer you some hospitality for your timely assistance against those . . . er, robbers.'

Fidelma felt that the elderly man had been going to use another word to describe his attackers, but she did not press him. Here was some distraction from the boredom she had been faced with just moments ago. She fell in step with him as they continued across the narrow street and, after her new companion asked a few prompting questions, she explained how she had come to be in Genua.

Magister Ado eventually came to a halt before a door.

'Here we are,' he said, raising his staff and knocking on it in a curious pattern which indicated a code. Almost at once, the door was opened by a young man with an anxious look on his dark, handsome features. He was also dressed in religious robes but seemed alert and muscular, as though designed to be a warrior rather than a man of the cloth. His expression became one of dismay as he saw the drying blood on the old man's forehead.

'Magister Ado! Are you hurt?'

Again the elderly religieux smiled and shook his head.

'Nothing serious,' he replied. 'But my companion and I will be the better for a cup of wine, Brother Faro.'

The young man looked curiously from Magister Ado to Fidelma. Then he forced a smile.

'I am sorry for my hesitation. Please enter; come in quickly.'

He held the door wide open and Fidelma noticed that, once they had passed in, he had gone out into the street and glanced up and down as if to ensure that no one had observed their entrance into the house.

Magister Ado waited until the young man closed the door and led them through the stuffy interior to a small courtyard at the centre of the building. The air was still warm here but seemingly cooled by a tinkling small fountain in the centre. A moment later a young woman emerged from another doorway.

'Ah, Sister Gisa,' greeted Magister Ado. 'My companion and I are in need of wine. This is Sister Fidelma of Hibernia.'

The young woman – she was scarcely more than a girl – was examining the elderly religieux with concern.

'You have blood on your forehead, *Magister* . . .' she began.

'I am fine. Do not worry.' He turned to Fidelma. 'These are good comrades of mine – Sister Gisa and Brother Faro. They tend to fuss over me. Now, Sister Gisa, fetch that wine.'

The girl, with a quick, worried nod of greeting at Fidelma, moved to a side table and took up a flagon and clay beakers. Brother Faro's anxious expression did not diminish. 'What happened?'

'An attempt at robbery, that is all. Thankfully, Sister Fidelma was near since, without her help, things might have been worse.'

'You mean that they know you are here?' demanded Brother Faro.

Fidelma noticed that the older man glanced with a frown at his young companion before resuming his pleasant expression. 'Hurry with that wine, my child. The dust of the street is still in my throat.'

Sister Gisa glanced shyly at Fidelma, as she poured the wine. She was quite attractive, Fidelma noted. Her eyes were dark, matching the colour of her hair which could be seen at the edges of her headdress. The skin of her face was an olive brown, but not tanned by the sun as Fidelma had noticed others were in this southern clime.

'How did you come to have a hand in this matter, Sister?' the girl asked. So far, everyone spoke in impeccable Latin and not the local language.

Fidelma gave a half-shrug. 'I saw two men sneaking up behind Magister Ado and was able to shout a warning to him. That is all.'

Magister Ado was shaking his head. The smile he had resumed had not left his features. It seemed his permanent expression.

'All? She did more than that, my friends. One of the brutes turned to attack her and she was able to throw the man to the ground. I have seen such a thing done only once before and that was by one of our Hibernian Brothers.'

Brother Faro seemed overcome with gratitude.

'Then you have saved the life of our master. I thank you, Sister.'

'I was Brother Faro's teacher,' explained Magister Ado. 'I still am, if youth will listen to age.'

Youth was a relative term, for Fidelma estimated Brother Faro to be in his twenties.

'One thing I would like to know is why you were attacked?' Fidelma asked, sipping slowly at the wine. 'They were obviously more than mere street robbers who were involved in this matter.'

'Your senses seem very sharp, Sister.' Magister Ado frowned slightly and she noticed that a note of suspicion rose in his voice.

'It is my nature. In my country, I am a trained advocate of our laws.'

'Sister Fidelma?' Sister Gisa suddenly turned. 'Have you recently come from Rome?' Before Fidelma could confirm it, the young sister said excitedly to Magister Ado, 'It was a week ago, just before we left the abbey to come to meet you, when one of our brethren returned with gossip from Rome. He spoke of a Sister Fidelma from a place called Cashel in Hibernia. She had solved the mystery of the murder of a Saxon bishop which had taken place there. Even the Holy Father praised her. Are you this Fidelma of Hibernia?' she added, seeking confirmation.

Fidelma made a slight embarrassed grimace. 'I do not deny it. My father was Failbe Flann, King of Muman, whose capital lies at Cashel in Hibernia. My brother is now the heir apparent to the kingship. But I am merely an advocate, as I have said, and was on a mission to Rome on behalf of the bishops of my country.'

Sister Gisa was almost clapping her hands in delight. 'Do you know Brother Ruadán of Eenish Keltrah?'

Fidelma took a moment or so before she realised the young girl meant 'Inis Celtra'. Her eyes widened in amazement. Memories of her childhood studying at the school run by Brother Ruadán came flooding into her mind.

'Brother Ruadán of Inis Celtra was my tutor before I reached the age of choice. What do you know of him?'

'Brother Ruadán serves our abbey,' smiled Sister Gisa. 'When your name was mentioned by our Brother from Rome, he said he knew you.'

Fidelma tried to hide her surprise. 'But Brother Ruadán . . . he must be very aged. Are you saying that he is dwelling in an abbey somewhere nearby here?'

'Not exactly near here,' Brother Faro intervened. 'He *is* very aged. Alas, when we left the abbey a week ago he was confined to his *cubiculum* with the ague.'

'But where is he? In what abbey?'

'He is at the Abbey of Bobium,' replied Sister Gisa. 'He spoke of you with great affection, saying that he had once taught the young daughter of his king. He was certain that the Sister Fidelma mentioned at Rome was the same person that he once knew.'

Magister Ado was regarding her with interest. 'And is this true? Are you the same person who has won such approbation at the Lateran Palace from the Holy Father himself?'

Fidelma was uncomfortable at the fuss and repeated: 'I am Fidelma of Cashel. Where is this Abbey of Bobium? I should like to see Brother Ruadán again.'

'It is up in the mountains, Sister. About three days' ride on a good horse.' It was Brother Faro who responded.

Fidelma's face fell a little with disappointment. Three days on horseback and, doubtless, she would need a guide in this unknown terrain. With little prospect of finding an immediate ship for Massilia, she could possibly afford the time, but where could she find a horse and guide? She still had a long journey before her to reach home.

'Ah, then time and means prohibit my journey to see him,' she said. 'I beg your pardon, Magister Ado. I was letting emotion rule my mind. What was I saying?'

Sister Gisa was refilling the clay goblets. 'You were saying that you did not think the attack on the *magister* was just some street robbers taking their chance.'

'What makes you think so?' the elderly religieux asked.

'Your demeanour for a start,' Fidelma said. 'Your hesitation about describing the men who attacked you. The way Brother Faro here was anxiously awaiting your coming and the words you exchanged. The fact that he waited while we entered this house before checking to see whether anyone was observing . . . There are many good reasons why this does not appear as some chance attempt at robbery. That is even before we get to the behaviour of the attackers themselves.'

Magister Ado suddenly snorted with amusement.

'I think that there is little that escapes your eye, Fidelma of Cashel.'

'Except the explanation for this drama,' she pressed.

There was a moment of quiet before Magister Ado responded.

'You say that you only intervened because you saw that I, a religieux, was about to be attacked? You never saw me before that moment in the street?'

'I am a stranger here. Why should I know you?'

'Do you know much about this land, Sister? I mean this land of the Longobards?'

'Very little,' she confessed, still puzzled.

'Did you know that our Abbey of Bobium was founded by a great teacher from your country called Columbanus?'

'Colm Bán?' She automatically corrected the name to Irish form. 'I know of him and his works. But I thought his missionary work lay mainly among the Franks of the north. Also, I thought that he had died many years ago.'

'He did die many years ago – for it was over fifty years ago that he crossed the great mountains and established our abbey. I entered it as a young man to study in the great library that he left us.'

'The Magister Ado is renowned among our people,' added Brother Faro in a tone of pride. 'He wrote the great *Vita Cummianus*.'

'Not great, my son,' reproved the elderly man. 'I was young. It was a work of poor quality at best. Do you know of Cummianus, Sister?'

'I only know that Cuimmíne is a common name among my people.'

'The man I speak of was also a bishop from your land who came to Bobium when he was elderly but lived with us for many years. He was a truly saintly man, worthy of a better hand than mine to transcribe his life and deeds.'

'My *magister* is modest,' insisted the young religieux. 'He has written several works and is known through the land of the Longobards as a great scholar.'

Fidelma was thoughtful. 'Yet this still does not explain why you should be attacked.'

'Quite right. Quite right,' acknowledged the elderly man. 'How learned are you, Fidelma of Hibernia?'

'It depends.'

'Depends?' He was surprised at the answer.

'It depends what subject that you are inquiring about, for is it not said that everyone is ignorant of things that they have yet to learn?'

Magister Ado chuckled. 'I see that you like precision in your language.'

'I am a lawyer and taught to be so.'

'Very well. Let us say that there are many discords among the people here. There are factions, talk of civil wars and intrigues. They manifest themselves not just in the civil life but even among those of the Faith.'

'So why the attack upon you?'

'Bobium has stood above these intrigues and recognises the authority of the Holy Father in Rome and the creed of the Faith adopted at Nicaea. For some, that is a position worthy of death.'

Fidelma looked shocked. 'I do not understand.'

'We, who declare our creed to be that given by the First

Council of Nicaea, tend to band together for protection in this land.'

'Protection?' queried Fidelma. 'From whom?'

Magister Ado hesitated before he answered her. 'The majority of the people of this territory either remain devoted to the old gods of their ancestors or they believe in the doctrines of Arius. Some are more fanatical in their belief than others.' He lowered his voice. 'Wanton destruction and tumult marks the path of their leaders, and their war bands desecrate this land.'

Fidelma tried to recall something about Arius. She knew that he had been declared a heretic at the First Council of Nicaea. She could not remember exactly why.

'I would appreciate some elucidation, Magister Ado,' she finally said.

'Arius was from Alexandria where he taught the Faith three hundred years ago. While we uphold the Holy Trinity, Arius taught that there could only be one God. While God the Father had existed eternally, God the Son, born as Jesus, did not and was therefore created by, and thus inferior, to God. He even argued that this meant, at one time, Christ did not exist.'

'But we are taught the Trinity, that God is three in one – God the Father, God the Son and God the Holy Spirit.'

'Indeed,' Magister Ado solemnly agreed. 'But Arius and his followers declare there is one God, always existing before time began, and creator of the world. God the Father created His Son, Who was subservient to the Father, Who also created the Holy Spirit, Who was similarly subservient to the Son.'

Fidelma saw a logic to the argument, which she had never heard before, and decided that she must look further into these teachings. However, she kept this thought to herself.

'I fail to see how such differences in interpretation can lead to bloodshed,' she finally observed.

Brother Faro shook his head sadly. 'It already has. An Arian nobleman, visiting Bobium only a short time ago, was so incensed when one of our brethren refused to acknowledge his arguments, that he drew his sword and cut him down.'

'We must apologise to you, Sister Fidelma,' Sister Gisa added. 'I think Brother Faro tried to save you any anguish by saying that Brother Ruadán was sick with ague. In fact, he is confined to his bed having been beaten by these same followers of Arius. It happened the day before we left to come to Genua.'

Before Fidelma could express her shock, Magister Ado turned to Brother Faro. 'You should have told me this at once.'

'As Sister Gisa said, it happened the day before we left Bobium to come and meet you,' admitted Brother Faro. 'I would have told you sooner but my mind was filled with your safe arrival.'

'And the details?' pressed the *magister*.

'Brother Ruadán was found outside the gates of the abbey early one morning. There was a piece of papyrus pinned to his bloodstained clothing with the word "heretic" scrawled on it.'

Fidelma was astounded. 'You say that he is injured and confined to his bed? How badly injured is he?'

Sister Gisa compressed her lips. 'He is bad, Sister. Our physician did not hold out any great hope. As you know, he is elderly and there is little strength left in him to fight.'

Fidelma turned to Magister Ado. 'And do you believe that these men who attacked you were also followers of Arius?

That they sought to attack you because they knew you were from Bobium?'

'The brethren of Bobium are known for their criticisms of Arius,' Brother Faro intervened quickly. 'Other than that, Bobium has no enemies.'

'I can only think the same,' Magister Ado agreed. 'There is no need to harm the brethren of Bobium other than by those who are enemies to the Nicene Creed. But how these Arians knew I was in Genua, I do not know. I only stepped ashore this morning.'

Sister Gisa nodded thoughtfully. 'Magister Ado has only just returned from Aquitània. We came to accompany him back to Bobium.'

Fidelma had the impression that Magister Ado shot Sister Gisa a glance of both disapproval and warning. 'I had heard that a ship had put in from Massilia today,' she said, 'and I was hoping that I would be able to return on it. However, the master of the vessel told me that he was on his way to Ostia. Indeed, you are right to raise the question as to how these people would know you were here and thus able to launch an attack on you.'

Magister Ado shrugged. 'Our Arian enemies are doubtless well-informed, Sister. Bishop Britmund of Placentia is our most implacable enemy. He could have heard that Brother Faro and Sister Gisa were coming to meet me.'

Brother Faro flushed and said: 'We were careful not to reveal the purpose of our journey to anyone outside the abbey.'

'I am not blaming you, my young friend,' Magister Ado replied. 'But sometimes an attentive enemy can make logical deductions.'

'And that being so, we should not tarry long in this place,' Sister Gisa said nervously.

'Then you plan to set out for the Abbey of Bobium soon?' asked Fidelma.

'Tomorrow at first light,' Brother Faro affirmed.

Fidelma hesitated. 'If what you tell me about Brother Ruadán is true, I feel it my duty to try to see him before . . . before . . .'

She did not want to finish the thought. Brother Ruadán held a special place in the affections of Fidelma. Her mother had died giving her birth and her father, King Failbe Flann, had died when she and her brother, Colgú, were still very young. When the time came for Fidelma's schooling, she had been sent to Brother Ruadán's tiny community on Inis Celtra. From the age of seven until the *aimsir togu*, the female age of choice, at fourteen years, Brother Ruadán had been charged with the care of her education. He had become almost the father figure she had barely known. It was in him that she had placed her childhood feelings before going to further her education at the law school of Brehon Morann of Tara. Therefore, it was no sense of duty but an emotional need that compelled her wish to see him.

'You could accompany us, Sister.' Sister Gisa's voice was eager.

'It is a long ride through the mountains,' pointed out Brother Faro, with a reproving look at the girl.

'That would not stop me if I could find a horse. But I do not have the means to do so.'

Magister Ado looked thoughtful for a moment or two. Then, as if he had come to a decision, he turned to Brother Faro. 'Did you bring a mule in case there was extra baggage to be carried?'

Brother Faro looked at him in surprise and then reluctantly nodded. 'We did. We brought a mule with us for the baggage.'

'Perhaps . . .' began the *magister*.

Sister Gisa cut him short. 'There is not much baggage and I can ride a mule.'

'Can you ride?' Magister Ado asked Fidelma.

'I can,' she answered immediately. She had ridden almost before she could walk.

'It is a long ride and the terrain may be difficult for you,' Brother Faro protested.

'I have travelled long distances over mountain terrain,' Fidelma assured him.

'I was impressed that Sister Fidelma was able to see beyond the fact that my attackers were not simply street robbers,' Magister Ado told the young man. 'I think she may be useful to us.'

Before Fidelma could ask in what way, Sister Gisa said enthusiastically, 'Then it is settled. It will be good to have you as our companion on the journey.'

Brother Faro sighed, apparently accepting the inevitable. 'I think you should collect whatever you need to accompany us, but do not bring more than is essential for your needs, and do not speak to anyone more than you can help. When you return here, ensure that no one follows you. We shall set off into the mountains at first light.'

'I shall try not to be a burden to you, Brother Faro,' she told him solemnly, but he did not notice the humour in her voice.

'After the attack on Magister Ado, there is no need to impress upon you that we should be vigilant.'

'Very well, Brother Faro,' Fidelma replied. 'I shall make my preparations. I can leave anything I do not need in the hostel where I am staying, and will return here before sun-up so that darkness will veil me from prying eyes.'

As she rose to her feet, so did Magister Ado.

'Perhaps it would be best not to mention at the hostel that you are even journeying to Bobium,' he suggested. 'It is not an impossibility that my erstwhile attackers could decide to ask questions at any hostel in this port, seeking information about you and, therefore, about me.'

Fidelma did not show her intrigue at her newfound companions' conspiratorial methods.

'I shall be back before first light,' she said. 'And shall look forward to our journey to Bobium.'

'It is a difficult route through the mountains, Fidelma,' Brother Faro repeated, still sceptical. 'Some three days in the saddle. So I trust you prove as good a horsewoman as you say.'

'I am good enough,' replied Fidelma, suppressing her irritation at not being taken at her word.

'Then we shall make good time to Bobium,' Magister Ado said soothingly.

CHAPTER TWO

The sun was very low, seeming to balance awhile on the black tops of the mountains behind them before sinking rapidly. It had been a slow but hard ride from the port of Genua, climbing up into the mountains along the winding tracks. Fidelma noticed that the route they followed was broad and well used. Now and then, they encountered little bands of merchants leading pack mules in the opposite direction. They passed with friendly greeting. Fidelma observed them with interest for she had not expected to see so many people on the track.

'This is part of the old Salt Road,' offered Magister Ado, who was riding alongside her. Behind them came Brother Faro on a grey, fiery-tempered horse, while Sister Gisa was seated on the pack mule. Fidelma, who was a keen judge of horses, had observed that the horses they rode were of a breed she had not encountered before, with high withers, short back, narrow croup, and tail hung low.

'The Salt Road?' she frowned. She had been going to ask about the breed when Master Ado's statement distracted her.

'The road leads to Ticinum Papia, a city beyond this mountain range and further to the north. Merchants bring goods,

19

such as wool, wine and olives, to the seaport. Then they pick up salt and transport it back to Ticinum Papia. Hence the name, the Salt Road.'

'And is it to Ticinum Papia that we are heading?'

He shook his head. 'We will stop tonight at a little hamlet where the Salt Road turns up through mountains due north. Our route will continue into a valley which is called the Valley of the Trebbia, and that leads to the Abbey of Bobium.'

Fidelma had been observing the countryside through which they were riding. She was fascinated by the fact that it bore certain resemblances to her own land. The mountains were not towering peaks but were of the softer curves and rose to heights with which she was familiar. The lower slopes of the mountains were covered in dense forests. Many of the trees she could recognise as beech, rowan and whitebeam. Even the ferns and bracken gave a familiar look to the country-side. She could almost pretend that she was in her own land, except for some indefinable quality. Perhaps it was the rich, reddish-brown soil.

Now and then, in the sky above, she also recognised wheeling kestrels and sparrow-hawks. Among the trees she could hear snatches of birdsong that she was unable to identify. Perhaps that was what alerted her to the fact that she was in a strange countryside. Then she caught sight of an oak tree. She recog-nised it as an oak and yet there was something different about the shape of the leaves.

Her companions, Magister Ado, Sister Gisa and even Brother Faro, were friendly and helpful whenever she asked a ques-tion about the terrain or the flora and fauna as they rode along.

It was Brother Faro who eventually pointed to a hill which began to emerge high above the others a little distance ahead to their left.

'That is Monte Antola. Tonight, we shall rest this side of it, and then leave the old Salt Road, and tomorrow we move into the Valley of Trebbia to the south of it. Our abbey overlooks the banks of the Trebbia.'

Magister Ado added: 'It is on that southern peak, called the Prela, that the Trebbia rises as a spring and flows down all the way to a giant river we call the Padus. But that is a long way to the north of Bobium.'

It was now that Fidelma realised that the mountains were rising considerably higher than those she was acquainted with in Ireland.

'Do we have to climb over those mountains?' she asked with some apprehension at their forbidding contours.

'There is a pass,' Brother Faro assured her. 'And it is in that pass we shall find shelter for the night.'

That night they shared a small inn with a few merchants heading south. They had a warm corner and sat exchanging information about their background and countries. Magister Ado was full of questions about the land from which Columbanus came. In turn, Fidelma discovered some of the background of her companions.

Sister Gisa was a Longobard and came from the Trebbia Valley. She was, as Fidelma noted before, gifted with good looks and intelligence, and her comments were carefully considered before being uttered. Fidelma put her age as no more than twenty-one or -two. She had gone to Bobium to study computus under Magister Ado. Brother Faro had come to the abbey only two years before but, apart from being told that he came from somewhere to the north, Fidelma learned little about him.

'Is Bobium a *conhospitae* – a mixed house?' Fidelma queried after they had told her that several religious from her own land still came to serve in the abbey.

'No,' Magister Ado replied immediately. 'It never was. Until twenty years ago our abbey maintained the Rule as handed down by our founder, Columbanus. Then Abbot Bobolen, with the support of the brethren, decided to adopt the *Regula Benedicti*.'

'The Rule of Benedict?' Fidelma knew of the disagreements that this Rule was causing among the abbeys of her own land. 'You forsook the Rule of your founder?'

'We have to move with the times,' replied Magister Ado. 'Columbanus' Rule was harsh and compromises had to be made.' He saw her puzzled expression. 'You remark on this? Indeed, many could not agree with the heavy discipline and punishment that Columbanus imposed. Even if a member of the abbey found no time to shave and presented himself at Mass in such a manner, he could receive six strokes of the scourge.'

'But that is not the way of the religious houses in Hibernia,' Fidelma protested. 'How can you claim that this was the Rule of Colm Bán?'

'A Rule that we have now rejected in favour of Benedict.' He gazed at her thoughtfully and added: 'Several of the religious who have joined us from Hibernia have also been amazed at being told about the harshness of Columbanus' Rule.'

'Indeed, they would. It bears no resemblance to the rules that govern our own abbeys. In fact, it sounds more like the Penitentials which some are trying to impose in our land. Do you mean to tell me that Colm Bán adopted the Penitentials here?'

It was Sister Gisa who proposed an answer. 'I have heard it said that Columbanus was faced with trying to discipline his Frankish and Longobard followers, who needed a firm hand, and thus he adopted harsher rules than those used in his own land.'

'You said that the abbey had adopted the *Regula Benedicti* – so that means that the abbey is segregated between the sexes?'

Magister Ado gave an affirmative nod. 'There is a house for women outside the main abbey, although we have not entirely banned the sexes from coming together in work and in worship, joining us in the evening meal before prayer. Many still argue that we should maintain a *conhospitae*, the mixed houses which are still prevalent in your country.'

'Does your current abbot support the segregation of the sexes?'

'He supports the aescetics who believe in celibacy,' added Sister Gisa, and then compressed her lips after she had spoken as if she regretted her comment.

'Abbot Servillius is an old friend of mine,' Magister Ado explained with a disapproving glance at the young Sister. 'I have known him since a young man. He is of an old patrician family of Rome and very proud of that fact. He is a firm supporter of the concept of celibacy and frequently reminds us that it is an ancient custom even with the priests of Bacchus in Rome, for it brings us nearer to religious fulfilment.'

'The concept is certainly gaining powerful adherents in Rome,' Fidelma remarked. 'Does that cause tension in Bobium?'

'Not within the abbey, for the brethren are of one mind,' Magister Ado replied quickly. 'The cause of tension is mainly from the outside.'

'You refer again to the followers of Arius?' Fidelma saw a quick exchange of troubled glances between Brother Faro and Sister Gisa.

'There is no need to worry,' Magister Ado returned. 'If you are thinking of the attack on me, I believe it might be retaliation because I have spoken out against the profligate bishops and nobles of this land who claim to be followers of Arius. They use the banner of Arius as an excuse for their attacks on the religious communities.'

'Isn't that a cause for concern? From what you tell me, you had barely stepped ashore at Genua when you were attacked. How long had you been away?'

His look was suddenly keen. 'You have an inquiring mind, Fidelma.'

'It is the nature of my training,' she admitted. 'I ask pardon if there is anything amiss in my question.'

The elderly religieux seemed to relax and smile. 'Not at all. I was away but a few weeks. I took the journey only to purchase an ancient text in the *scriptorium* of the abbey at Tolosa. Now we are nearly home. Tomorrow we shall enter the Valley of the Trebbia. There will be nothing to fear there.'

For someone who had so recently been attacked, Fidelma was surprised at the man's quiet confidence and dismissal of further dangers.

The next morning, leaving the main highway, they followed a smaller track across the hills and soon descended into a long winding valley through which a gushing river now flowed.

'The Trebbia,' announced Brother Faro, who was now riding alongside Fidelma. Magister Ado and Sister Gisa were a little way ahead of them. 'The river flows all the way past Bobium. We will spend one more night on our journey, near Mount Lésima, and then the following morning we shall see the holy place where Columbanus settled with his followers.'

The valley was even more reminiscent of some lush green valleys in parts of Fidelma's native land. It was little wonder that Colm Bán had felt at ease in choosing this country in which to establish his community. Perhaps it had reminded him of his home. On hills on either side of the river, the brilliant green of beech in full leaf, the elder trees with their massive, many-branched domes, were glorious – but little else grew around them, for the dense leaves threw out a protective canopy during the summer, denying light to the shrubs that needed it. The beeches rose on the high slopes. Lower down, the more compact whitebeams grew, now and then catching a breeze causing them to show silver-white as the thick felt of hairs on the underside of their leaves were suddenly displayed. Again, bracken and fern spread along the lower valley slopes where the trees thinned. From some of these trees she saw the thick, climbing stems of wild clematis with their white and greenish flowers, causing an odour of vanilla to permeate the air.

Brother Faro noticed her interest in her surroundings and unbent further from his usual air of distance.

'You recall the dish we ate last evening?' He pointed to some tall trees dominating areas of the lower reaches. 'That was sweet chestnuts, the fruit of those trees there.'

Fidelma had seen such trees in her journey to the Saxon kingdoms. An old sage had told her that the Romans had brought the tree into the country long ago.

'They are similar to trees I have seen in the lands of the Saxons, but the nuts there do not ripen for eating like they do here,' she observed.

Magister Ado and Sister Gisa had halted in order for them to catch up.

'The nuts on these trees are rich and succulent,' called

Sister Gisa over her shoulder, hearing the end of their conversation. 'You have merely to bend down and gather the spiky husks, split them open and harvest the nuts. They are often used in the dishes here.'

Magister Ado now dropped back to ride alongside Brother Faro in order that Sister Gisa and Fidelma could continue their conversation on local food. Sister Gisa and Brother Faro rode nearest to the riverbank while Fidelma and Magister Ado rode on the interior side of the path.

Ahead of them, Fidelma had noticed a bird with pointed wings and long tail rising abruptly from where it had been standing by the edge of the river which ran to their left. The bird rose with its strange chirping cry and Fidelma recognised a kestrel. A moment later from the woods came piercing cries and two large, dark birds with broad rounded wings and short necks suddenly soared from the treetops. Buzzards. There came a cacophony of bird noise, causing her to glance at the dark woodlands. She saw a shadow by a tree and turned back with a cry of warning.

Magister Ado had apparently already seen the shadow, for he leaned sharply across his horse's neck. There was a whistling sound and Brother Faro gave a cry of pain and fell from his horse, sprawling on his back on the track. Fidelma had only time to realise that the haft of an arrow was protruding from his shoulder and there was blood spurting from the wound. When she glanced back, Magister Ado had straightened up. It seemed that he had seen the archer loosening his bow and ducked. The arrow had passed over him and hit Brother Faro instead. Sister Gisa was screaming.

Fidelma turned back to the trees. Two men, bows ready, had emerged from cover and were moving deliberately towards them. She was undecided for a moment. If they fled, they would have to leave Brother Faro, wounded as he was, to the mercy of the attackers, for there was no time to dismount and put his unconscious body on horseback again. But if they stayed it would surely mean their own death.

It seemed, however, that Magister Ado had decided upon his own salvation and was urging his horse forward, passing her. He had gone but a short distance when another sound ahead of them caused him to halt. It was a blast on a hunter's horn, followed by a series of short warning blasts. It was all happening so fast that Fidelma could not keep up with events and sat undecided on her horse. Along the valley track around a bend ahead of them, emerged half a dozen mounted and armed men at the gallop. She now saw the two archers turning and heading rapidly into the cover of the trees.

The leader of the newcomers shouted orders and three of the riders detached themselves, dismounted and were scrambling up into the dense forests after the fleeing attackers.

Sister Gisa had swung down from the mule and was kneeling by the prone form of Brother Faro. Fidelma dismounted and went to help her. Brother Faro's eyes were opening and he groaned a little. She saw that the arrow had stuck into fatty tissue and missed the important muscles. Nevertheless, she knew that it had to be extracted immediately and the wound treated. It could still cause poisoning, and he could die of the result.

'Hold him,' she instructed Sister Gisa, then turning to Brother Faro added: 'I am afraid this will hurt a little.'

He nodded that he understood. She peered closely at the arrow which, without bone or muscle to block it, had penetrated the flesh so that the point stuck out the other side. The arrowhead itself was thankfully smooth and not barbed. She reached forward and snapped off the feathered end as close to the wound as possible. Then, taking hold of the head, she pulled the shaft rapidly through the flesh. Brother Faro gave a sharp cry and fainted.

'Quickly, Sister, some water to wash the wound,' Fidelma ordered.

Sister Gisa brought the water from the river and something from her saddlebag. As Fidelma washed the young man's wound, Sister Gisa said: 'This is a paste of crushed garlic. I have often seen my father use it. In these parts it is spread on wounds and has healing qualities and will prevent infections.'

Fidelma nodded silently and allowed the girl to apply the paste before she bound the wound tightly with strips of linen. By the time she had finished, Brother Faro had recovered consciousness again. They sat him up, back against a tree trunk, and he took a little wine which Sister Gisa also provided.

Fidelma finally rose and walked to where Magister Ado was talking earnestly to the leader of the horsemen, who was now standing by his horse. He was a tall warrior with long fair hair and bright blue eyes that were almost a violet shade. Magister Ado performed the introduction.

'This is Sister Fidelma of Hibernia who travels to Bobium with us.'

'I am Wulfoald, Sister. I am in the service of Radoald, son of Billo, Lord of Trebbia. You are welcome in our country.' He spoke to her in faultless Latin.

'It does not seem that everyone would share your welcome.' Fidelma could not help the cynical response.

Wulfoald's left eyebrow rose a little disdainfully. He gestured towards the woodland where the attackers had disappeared. 'Bandits, Sister. They will be caught and punished.'

She was about to make a further remark when Magister Ado seemed eager to intervene.

'We were lucky that you and your men came along, Wulfoald.'

The young warrior gave a brief shrug. 'We were on our way to pick up some goods that my lord was expecting from merchants at the junction of the Salt Road. We heard the warning of the birds and a cry, and so I ordered the horn to be sounded to let it be known that Radoald's men approached. How is your companion?'

'Brother Faro?' Magister Ado seemed to realise for the first time that his young companion had been hurt. He swung round but saw that Brother Faro was sitting up and being well attended by Sister Gisa.

There came a call from the hillside and the three warriors who had chased after the attackers were returning empty-handed.

'They escaped, Wulfoald,' their spokesman said at once. 'They had horses further up the hill and were away before we could close on them.'

'Did you recognise them?' demanded Wulfoald.

'We did not. They wore black cloaks and hoods and we could not discern their features.'

Sister Fidelma glanced at Magister Ado. 'Black cloaks and hoods?' She made the comment into a question.

Magister Ado gave an almost indiscernible shake of his head, a warning in his eyes.

'Bandits,' Wulfoald said again, with emphasis. 'Have no fear, Sister. They will put much distance between here and their lair. They will know that my lord Radoald's reach is long and his vengeance is swift. They will not be back. As guarantee, I shall instruct two of my men to see you safe to the walls of Bobium itself. Indeed, I suggest that this night you accept the hospitality of my lord, Radoald, at his fortress. Our physician, Suidur the Wise, will be pleased to attend to your young disciple there.'

Magister Ado was profuse in his thanks. And while Wulfoald went to instruct his men, he and Fidelma made their way to where Brother Faro was now sitting up. The young man smiled ruefully.

'It stings a little but is not too painful,' he admitted when asked how his wound felt. 'I have had worse.'

'Will you be able to ride as far as Radoald's fortress?' asked Magister Ado.

'I am sure of it,' Brother Faro replied at once.

'Then we will seek the hospitality of Lord Radoald.' Magister Ado glanced around quickly at the hillside forest, as if to assure himself that the attackers had truly gone, and added: 'As soon as you are ready, I suggest we move on.'

'Black cloaks and hoods?' Fidelma commented again in a low voice. 'Do you not think that the same men who attacked you in Genua are the same who tried to kill you just now?'

Magister Ado was defensive. 'That does not necessarily follow. Lots of people wear black cloaks with hoods.'

'Not many during the heat of summer,' Fidelma replied dryly, glancing up at the cloudless blue sky.

'But the nights are cold,' he responded, almost sarcastically, before turning back to where Wulfoald and his men were waiting.

'I have ordered two of my warriors to escort you to the fortress of Radoald,' he called, indicating two of his men. 'And now we must be off, to meet with the merchants on the Salt Road.'

'Then there is nothing more than to thank you again for

your timely help.' Magister Ado bowed his head. 'Our thanks and blessings.'

Wulfoald remounted his horse. For a moment Fidelma thought the warrior had mistaken his mount, for his pale grey looked the image of the steed ridden by Brother Faro. Then she realised that it was of the same breed. At a sign from him, the band of warriors soon disappeared along the track.

Brother Faro had risen cautiously to his feet, aided by the concerned-looking Sister Gisa. 'I am ready to move when you are, *Magister*,' he said.

Once mounted again, Fidelma joined Magister Ado while Sister Gisa rode anxiously alongside Brother Faro. Behind them came the two silent warriors. They were professional and now and then, when Fidelma glanced back at them, they seemed to be surveying the surrounding woodlands with eyes that were alert and never still.

Magister Ado was not forthcoming with any further thoughts about the attack and Fidelma only once again broached the subject of the identity of the attackers.

'You must have deeply offended these followers of Arius, for them to make such attempts on your life,' she said.

'You seem sure that this attack was by the same men as in Genua,' he replied stiffly. 'There are enough bandits in this country, especially so close to the merchant routes, to give me pause before I would make such accusations.'

She knew it was useless to press him further. For some reason he did not want to acknowledge the obvious logic. Instead she tried a more oblique approach.

'How is it that people here are so adamant in their adherence to the teachings of Arius?' she asked.

Magister Ado glanced at her suspiciously. Then he shrugged. 'When the philosophies of Arius were flourishing in

Constantinople, a Goth named Ulfilias, who had converted to Christianity but through the teachings of Arius, went as missionary to the Germanic peoples. His teachings spread among the Goths, Vandals, Visigoths, Burgundians and Longobards. Most accepted this form of the Faith and fought those who, like us, declared for the Nicene beliefs.'

'And they have clung to the argument of Arius in spite of attempts to dissuade them?'

Magister Ado sighed – a deep, sad sigh. 'My people, the Longobards, have been followers of Arius for centuries.' He paused. 'Let me explain. Over three centuries ago, Arius was denounced in Alexandria for his teachings. Emperor Constantine called an assembly in Nicaea to argue the matter. Arius, as I have said, argued that while Christ was divine, He was sent to us for the salvation of mankind, but He and the Holy Spirit were not equal to God the Father, Who must have created them, for God created all things. The debate at Nicaea was long and fierce, and finally Arius and his teachings were condemned. A creed, a set of orthodox beliefs, was agreed by the assembly of bishops, and its central teaching was that the Father, the Son and Holy Spirit were of the same substance; that they were One, being Three in One. Christ is no less than God.'

'So once the Council at Nicaea had agreed on this, what was the outcome?'

'Constantine, the Emperor, exiled all those who refused to abide by the decision and all those who refused to condemn Arius and his supporters. He ordered all copies of the *Thalia* to be burned.'

'*Thalia* – what is that?' queried Fidelma.

'It is the book in which Arius explained his teachings. It means "Festivity".'

'So that should have ended the argument.'

'It did not. Another Emperor, Constantius, the second Emperor of his name, became an adherent of Arius and used his authority to exile the Nicene bishops, even exiling Pope Liberius and installing the Arian, Felix, in his place.

'When Constantius died, Emperor Julian went back to pagan idolatry, but declared everyone had a right to believe whatever they wanted. So every sect in the Faith returned to follow their own philosophies. Finally, after many years, the Emperor Theodosius and his wife, Flacilla, came to power supporting the Nicene Creed. They exiled all Arian bishops and published an edict that every subject of the Roman Empire should profess and swear allegiance to the Nicene Creed of the bishops of Rome and Alexandria or be handed over for punishment for not doing so.'

Fidelma was shocked. 'It sounds more like the Faith developed as a matter of political power than an appeal to the spirituality, morals and logic of the people.'

Magister Ado sniffed in disapproval. 'Sometimes people have to be shown the way.'

'But not by force, surely?'

'Oh, come.' Magister Ado smiled broadly. 'You are a lawyer in your own land. What is law but telling people how they should behave? And if they do not, aren't they punished? Isn't that forcing them to proceed on a moral path in their lives? You cannot appeal to spirituality and morals with those who are greedy and will let nothing stand in their way.'

Fidelma acknowledged that the scholar had a point – although she would argue it was a point that was not without its own moral concerns. However, she decided that it was wise not to pursue the matter further. After all, the man had been attacked twice – apparently because of his adherence to his beliefs. He had a right to them. It was best to avoid being embroiled in theological argument. She was, after all, a stranger in a strange land. Her main desire was simply to see her former mentor, Brother Ruadán, and to bring comfort to the old man in his illness.

Privately, she felt that she could understand why Arius argued that if there was one God Who was everlasting, and Christ was His only begotten son, then Christ, being begotten, must have been created by God. And didn't the Gospel of John quote Christ as saying that His Father was 'greater than I'? She was confused. Her own culture had always viewed the ancient gods and goddesses as being triune deities, each having three personalities and three outward appearances. So the Nicene Creed sat more comfortably in her people's theology than monotheism. She wondered if she could find a copy of Arius' book, the *Thalia*, to understand its philosophy more. She rode on, silently musing on the subject.

Their journey proceeded without further incident for a while; through the beautiful valley, following the track alongside the river. Now and then they would stop to water the horses and the mule or take a drink themselves from the pure river waters, or taste some fruit recommended by Sister Gisa from the bushes or trees. Sister Gisa would check occasionally on Brother Faro's wound. Albeit only a flesh wound, Fidelma knew that harm inflicted by an arrow could be dangerous. Fortunately, the young girl seemed to know how to handle injuries.

It turned out that the two warriors accompanying them were not particularly talkative as they spoke only in the harsh accents of the Longobards and knew very little Latin. But the feeling of danger seemed to have evaporated in the bright warm sunshine, amid the comforting sounds of the splashing of the river and the soft bird calls emanating from the lush green surroundings. It was, Fidelma thought, idyllic as they walked their horses along the river bank.

Just after noon Magister Ado called a halt. The two warriors set about catching some fish, which they were soon lifting with dexterous ease from the river. Sister Gisa went to gather some berries and fruits. A fire was lit over which the fish were cooked and they gathered around to eat and drink on the river bank. It seemed, as Fidelma rested in the sunshine, that they were a million miles from any other human being, least of all from any danger. She felt as if she could just drift – drift off into a relaxing sleep . . .

The barking of a dog suddenly caused her to sit upright. A squarely built, wiry-coated animal burst through the trees, paused and looked around. It had an almost comical face, with hairy eyebrows and a moustache that almost hid its powerful jaws. It seemed to glance around and then, tail wagging, it trotted towards Sister Gisa, with a faint friendly yelp. Brother Faro started nervously.

'It is a hunting dog,' he warned.

The young girl reached out and patted the animal's head. It seemed to have a docile temperament.

The two warriors had risen to their feet with their hands on their sword hilts. The little dog allowed Sister Gisa to stroke its head before it gave a final yelp, a sniff, and trotted off.

Fidelma seemed to be the only one who realised what made Brother Faro and the warriors nervous about the appearance of the dog.

'Do you think that there is a hunting party nearby?' she asked Brother Faro.

Even before he could answer her, the sound of horses and

the cries of men came to their ears. A moment more and the first riders emerged through the trees and halted abruptly as they caught sight of the group. One of the riders led a mule and across its back lay the carcass of a red deer which was, apparently, the fruits of the hunt.

Then one of Wulfoald's warriors stepped forward and called out in his own language. Words were quickly exchanged and Fidelma noticed her companions were visibly relaxing. One of the riders, a young man richly attired in embroidered hunting clothes and short cloak, slid from his white stallion. He was handsome, fair-faced with carefully trimmed corn-coloured hair, but cleanshaven. His eyes were a light blue. He came forward with a smile of greeting, his hand held out to Magister Ado.

'You are welcome back from your travels, Magister Ado. It is good to see you back again in our peaceful valley.'

His Latin was colloquial but spoken with the firmness of one educated and used to command.

'You are kind, Lord Radoald,' acknowledged the elderly religieux.

The blue eyes swept over Brother Faro and Sister Gisa.

'Ah, little Sister Gisa . . . and Brother Faro. You are both more than welcome. And . . .' The young man frowned, as he noticed Brother Faro's bandaged arm and shoulder for the first time. 'But something is amiss. What has befallen you, my friend?'

Magister Ado quickly explained and the young lord looked troubled.

'It is rare that bandits haunt this valley,' he replied thoughtfully. 'They usually lie in wait for rich merchants on the old Salt Road and do not enter the Valley of the Trebbia, for such merchants as they seek are few here and they would have to contend with my warriors.'

Brother Faro assured him that he suffered no more than a flesh wound and that he would soon be well. Fidelma wondered whether Magister Ado would make any further explanation or mention the attack in Genua but he seemed content to let the matter rest. 'It was lucky that Wulfoald and his men arrived at the moment the bandits attacked us,' he said. 'He gave us these two warriors to escort us to your fortress, my lord, where we would beg hospitality for tonight.'

'Hospitality? Of course.' The blue eyes alighted on Fidelma. 'And do we have a newcomer to our valley?' he asked.

'This is Sister Fidelma of Hibernia.' Magister Ado performed the introduction. 'Fidelma, this is Radoald, Lord of Trebbia.'

'Fidelma of Hibernia?' The young lord gave her a close scrutiny. 'Indeed, you have the same fiery red hair, fair skin and strange green eyes that I have seen on some of those I have known from Hibernia. Many from your land have come to join the community of the abbey here. Do you mean to stay with us in our little valley?'

'I have come only to visit,' replied Fidelma.

'Fidelma is a princess from Hibernia,' Sister Gisa pressed eagerly. 'Not only that, but she is famous.'

The young lord turned to Sister Gisa with a smile.

'A princess, and famous, indeed? In what manner famous?'

'Sister Gisa exaggerates,' Fidelma said hurriedly.

'No, I do not. Sister Fidelma is a lawyer in her own land and was recently praised by the Holy Father and his *nomenclator*. She solved the mystery of the murder of some foreign archbishop which happened in the Lateran Palace.'

Radoald's eyes widened and then he turned back to Fidelma. 'Is this so? Did you accomplish this?'

Fidelma shrugged, feeling embarrassed by the praise of

the young girl. 'I will not deny that I was able to help in that matter.'

'Well, well.' The young man exchanged a glance with Sister Gisa, who seemed so keen on ensuring that the Lord of Trebbia knew who she was. Fidelma had a feeling that some intimacy passed between them. Then she wondered whether she was being too sensitive. She did not like speaking of her rank or, indeed, her past success as a *dálaigh*, an advocate of the courts of her own land in which she held the degree of *anruth*, the second highest degree that the colleges could bestow. The young lord was laughing with good humour. 'Well, indeed, we have no mysterious deaths here that I could ask your assistance with, lady. But allow me to welcome a Hibernian princess into my poor valley.'

'I am pleased to be here,' Fidelma replied as diplomacy dictated.

Radoald swung round to extend his smile of welcome to all of them.

'My roof is your roof for this night, my friends.' He spread a hand to encircle his hunting party. His companions had already dismounted and were leading their mounts to the edge of the river to slake their thirst. 'We were hunting for some meat for this evening's feasting and, having just brought down a red deer, we came here to the riverside so that we might refresh ourselves before returning home. So now you may join us, and my fortress is yours for this night.'

CHAPTER THREE

'Well, Magister Ado, you must tell us something of your journey to Tolosa,' Radoald invited after he had finished quenching his thirst from a goatskin water bag that one of his warriors had filled from the river.

Fidelma had been standing by him and noticed an oddly suspicious look come into the elderly scholar's eyes.

'How did you know I had been to Tolosa?' His voice was unnaturally sharp.

Radoald did not appear to notice his tone. 'You should know that we are a small community in the valley. News travels quickly.'

Magister Ado was frowning. 'Then you will know that I went to the Abbey of the Blessed Martyr Saturnin to view a manuscript. It was a boring journey but, *Deo gratias*, it was a short one.'

'Ah, I wondered at its shortness. It was surely a long way to go, just to return immediately. You could have barely been there for more than a few days.'

'You are well informed, Lord Radoald.'

'I try to be, my friend, especially in these days. However, did you see anything untoward on your travels?'

Fidelma listened to the exchange with interest, although she tried to keep her features expressionless.

'Untoward?'

'There are constant rumours that the Franks are plotting against us. Even more rumours of their army crossing into our lands in support of Perctarit.'

'I saw nothing.'

'Yet I hear that Tolosa is now a city bathed in darkness, stricken by plague, the flight of its population, and even the great basilica fallen into decay.'

'That is not so, for I stayed several days there and was able to secure the very book I went there to see, the *Life of the Blessed Martyr Saturnin*, and thus was able to bring it back with me for our great library at Bobium.'

'Well, then, that is good news.' Radoald glanced round to check that his men had finished watering their horses, as if his questions had been no more than a passing interest. But Fidelma thought that something lay behind his queries.

'Who is Perctarit?' she decided to inquire.

Radoald turned to answer her. 'He used to be King of the Longobards, a cruel and despotic man who was eventually overthrown and fled for protection to the land of the Franks.' His tone was serious and he seemed to be fighting some angry emotion. Then he relaxed again and said, 'We shall not delay here any longer.'

'Is your fortress far?' she asked.

'We will reach it well before sundown.'

'And is Bobium nearby?'

'Less than half a day's ride further on, not much more. Bobium is a beacon of the true faith in these mountains. I am sure you will have many questions to ask about this land, Fidelma of Hibernia, but let us move on to where we can enjoy the fruits of our hunt, sample our local wine and talk of these matters. And, of course, the sooner we are there, the sooner my physician can attend to Brother Faro, although I think little Gisa's attentions have been enough.'

She followed his nod to where Sister Gisa was sitting next to Brother Faro deep in conversation. From the intimacy of his reference, Fidelma had gathered the impression that Radoald knew Gisa well. How? She supposed that it was a small valley community. Perhaps in that lay the answer.

The young Lord of Trebbia clapped his hands and called for everyone to mount, and it was not long before the party set off. Radoald invited Fidelma to ride alongside him. She soon realised that it was an excuse for him to interrogate her without anyone overhearing.

'Have you known Magister Ado for long?' was his opening question.

'For a few days on this journey, if that is knowing anyone,' she replied. 'We met in Genua.'

She felt rather than saw the young lord glance at her before he said: 'But you knew of him before?'

'I am a stranger here,' she said evenly. 'As Sister Gisa said, I was returning from Rome to my own land when my ship was wrecked. I was some days in Genua looking for a vessel when I met Magister Ado.' Something made her decide not to offer any details of the meeting. 'He told me of the Abbey of Bobium and mentioned that Brother Ruadán was a member of the community there. Brother Ruadán was once my tutor and mentor in my own land. So I accepted an offer to accompany Magister Ado and his companions to Bobium in order that I could see my mentor one last time.'

'Brother Ruadán?' Radoald was interested. 'Were you one of his pupils?'

'I was. I was very young and then went on to study law.'

'Brother Ruadán has been outspoken against some of the bishops who live to the east of this valley.'

'In what context?'

'He criticises their interpretation of the Faith, their support for the profligate nobles there and their way of life, their drinking, wenching . . . all manner of their lives he condemned, and that will not bring him friends.'

'Perhaps he feels that he does not need such friends,' she said dryly.

'Have you been told that Brother Ruadán was attacked and badly beaten?'

'It was that which prompted me to leave Genua and journey here with my new companions from Bobium. Do you have more recent news on his condition?'

'He still lives but his condition is bad.'

'And do you know how this happened?'

'I am told that he used to travel to Placentia, a city to the north of here, and preach in the basilica of Antoninus . . . I am afraid Brother Ruadán created riots by his preaching. He called the Bishop of Placentia, Bishop Britmund, an ass.'

Fidelma raised an eyebrow. 'An ass?'

'He said that an illiterate bishop is only an ass with a mitre. A cleric, he said, is of himself not someone to admire unless he possess virtue and knowledge.'

Fidelma chuckled. 'Poor Ruadán. He is merely stating the old adage that we know so well. There's nothing revolutionary in that view.'

Radoald snorted indignantly. 'Those views have landed him in trouble. To call the Bishop of Placentia illiterate and an ass is flirting with death. Besides which there are other tensions among the religious here.'

'I have been told about the conflict between those who uphold the Nicene Creed and those who support the views of Arius.'

'Then be warned, Fidelma of Hibernia. Brother Ruadán barely escaped with his life from Placentia. Bobium is an island surrounded by powerful nobles who support the teachings of Arius. It is wise not to be so forthright in declaring one's beliefs at this time. Remember that a scholar's ink lasts longer than a martyr's blood.'

Fidelma considered the young man's words seriously. 'I appreciate your advice to a stranger from a strange land, Radoald. Out of interest, as you are lord in this valley, are you one of these nobles that you speak of?'

Radoald chuckled and shook his head. 'I am not that powerful, Fidelma of Hibernia. However, I do try to protect this valley – and that includes Bobium. This is a small valley with few people. The influence of the Abbey at Bobium is strong here and we live in comfort with one another. Beyond the valley, it is different. Have you heard one of the old sayings of this country – *cuius regio eius religio*?'

Fidelma smiled and inclined her head in confirmation. An easy translation, for the saying was – who rules the country, dictates the religion.

'Then let me tell you, outside the protection of the valley you must have circumspection. Brother Ruadán should have learned diplomacy. But, from the few people from Hibernia that I have encountered, I have gathered that you do not treat rank and privilege with the same respect that Longobards are used to.'

'We have a saying,' Fidelma replied. '"No one is better than I am, but I am no better than anyone else." That means everyone should be treated with the same respect.'

Radoald grimaced in amusement. 'Treated with respect according to their station in life – for everyone is allotted his or her place by the Creator and it would be blasphemy to Him should they be dissatisfied with their lot.'

'That is a curious philosophy,' remarked Fidelma.

'Not for us,' replied Radoald. 'Why, think of the chaos if it were otherwise. Wulfoald, who commands my guard, might one day come to believe that he is equal to me. Being dissatisfied, he could attempt to overthrow my rule and take my place. I was born to protect my people, to rule the weak and guide them when they seek my help.'

'In my land we say that the people are stronger than a lord, for it is the people who ordain their chief and not the chief who ordains the people.'

'How can the people be allowed to choose their lord?' The young man sounded astonished by the idea. 'A lord is chosen by the Creator Who ordains him with power to rule.'

'In my land, it is the best among the family, the most intelligent and strongest, who is chosen to rule by his family and his people. I know in this land it is merely the eldest son; whether he be an idiot or a great philosopher makes no matter. So how can you say the Creator has ordained him?'

Radoald smiled quickly. 'If the ruler was an idiot, he would not last long as ruler.'

'So he would be removed?'

'Of course.'

'And often with violence either within the family or by the people?'

Radoald suddenly saw the point she was going to make but shrugged, allowing her to accept it as confirmation.

'Would it not be better to choose him in the way we do,

44

rather than let nature choose the course and then have to correct nature?'

'But to give people choice . . . If they had choice to choose their ruler, why – they would think they had choice in all things.'

'Why not? People live in each other's shelter.'

Radoald took a moment to understand the old proverb. Then he laughed sharply.

'I do not think we shall agree on this, Fidelma of Hibernia. But at least I begin to see why your people have a reputation in my land as stubborn and irreverent towards their superiors. But be careful what you say and to whom, as these are difficult times and I strive hard to keep the peace between this valley and its neighbours.'

Fidelma nodded. 'I shall remember your advice, Radoald of Trebbia. But there is a saying among my people that you cannot have peace longer than your neighbours choose peace.'

'I can see that you are truly a King's daughter, Fidelma of Hibernia,' replied Radoald with grudging admiration. 'But, so far, the neighbouring nobles have not troubled the people of this valley since Grimoald became King.'

'Presumably he was the successor to Perctarit of whom you spoke?'

'He was, and since then there has been peace in this valley.'

'So it is unusual for bandits to make attacks in it?'

He was silent for a few moments as he regarded her thoughtfully. 'Do you imply there was something unusual about the attack?'

'I am unable to imply anything for I am a stranger here. I am merely an observer. Magister Ado at first wanted me to believe we were attacked by bandits, quickly confirmed by Wulfoald, and then you ascribed the attack to bandits.

However, you did point out that it was unusual for bandits
to operate in this valley when the richer merchants do not
pass this way. Those are facts. I would not imply anything
from them.'

'You have a sharp mind, lady.' Then Radoald fell silent for
the rest of their journey as if in brooding thought.

The fortress of Radoald dominated a bend of the river,
strategically placed on the southern bank where it turned
almost at a forty-five-degree angle. From the northern bank
a tributary of a smaller stream joined it. Behind that rose a
great peak among the mountains which bordered the length
of the valley on both banks. It was obvious that no army could
attack in strength over the mountains or along the valley in
either direction without having to reduce the fortress before
they could proceed. It had been built initially, so Fidelma was
to learn later, by the Romans when their legions invaded the
territories of the peoples of Cisalpine Gaul. At first glance,
it seemed dark and ominous, a brooding complex of buildings, its lower walls were covered by creeping moss-like plants
which she could not identify. There were two or three farm
dwellings set outside the walls and the fortress dominated the
area. As they approached, one of Radoald's men placed a
hunting horn to his lips and let forth a series of blasts. Fidelma
saw several warriors patrolling the walls and realised that their
approach had already been observed.

She could not help but ask quietly: 'For a peaceful valley,
your warriors seem well prepared?'

Radoald actually grinned. '*Si vis pacem para bellum*,' he
replied. If you want peace, prepare for war. 'I have found
much wisdom in the *Epitoma Rei Militaris* of Vegetius, an
old Roman military philosopher.'

They entered an inner courtyard where servants came

hurrying forward to take their horses and Sister Gisa's mule to the stables, to remove the carcass of the deer and presumably transport it to the kitchens.

As Radoald dismounted he called to Sister Gisa, 'Take Brother Faro to Suidur's apothecary so that he may be looked after.' It was obvious that she knew the fortress for she took her companion by the arm and assisted him across the stone-flagged courtyard.

Radoald himself conducted Magister Ado and Fidelma to what appeared to be the main building, and led them into a great hall. There were fires alight at both ends of the hall while tapestries hung the full length of the high walls. Several men and women rose respectfully as he entered. An elderly man, who proved to be Radoald's steward, came forward and bowed. The young lord shot a series of instructions at him before turning to them with a smile.

'I have asked for rooms to be made ready for all of you. Baths will be prepared and this evening you will feast and rest with us. And tomorrow you will journey on to Bobium in comfort.' He turned to the rest of the company and said, 'Magister Ado has come back to join us and this is Fidelma of Hibernia, a princess of her country, who travels to Bobium.'

The names of his family and his entourage passed over Fidelma's head. Several of them spoke colloquial Latin but it seemed the main language was the more guttural tongue of the Longobards. As she was passed from one group to another with polite meaningless words, she was suddenly confronted by an ornate, carved wood chair on a dais. She presumed it was Radoald's chair of office. But it was not that which struck her. Above the chair hung a shield. It had a black background with what appeared to be a flaming sword and a laurel wreath painted on it.

A hand jerked on her sleeve and a high-pitched voice asked, 'Do you eat human flesh?'

Shocked, she turned to look down into the ancient face of a woman, bent over, with grey hair and leaning on a stick.

'I do not,' she replied, wondering if she was about to be offered some horrendous dish of the valley.

'But you must,' the old woman insisted sharply. 'People from Hibernia are cannibals. I have read the Blessed Jerome and was he not of the Faith? In *Adversus Jovinianum* he writes that he witnessed, as a young man, the Irish cutting the buttocks off shepherds and their wives and eating them.'

'I have never heard that Jerome was ever in Hibernia,' Fidelma replied, trying not to let her temper rise. 'So no credence can be given to such a ridiculous, malicious and false statement.'

'But he wrote it.'

'People write many things and they are not all true.'

'But he wrote it,' the old woman repeated as if it were a mantra.

Radoald appeared at her side and took Fidelma's arm. He spoke to the old woman roughly in the local language and then guided Fidelma away. 'Let me show you some of the treasures of my fortress,' he smiled. Out of earshot of the old woman, he added, 'She was my mother's nurse. I keep her here as a retainer, for there is nowhere else for her to go.'

Fidelma was about to open her mouth when he shook his head and placed a finger against his lips. 'She reads to occupy her time. Sadly, she believes that if something is written then it must be true. There is no reasoning with her on this matter.'

'Then she must have difficulties when she comes across two accounts that are opposed.' Fidelma smiled thinly.

'An interesting proposition. Sadly, it seems that eventuality has not yet presented itself.'

'I was looking at your chair when she spoke to me. Is it your chair of office?'

Radoald nodded assent.

'I noticed the design on the shield above it. Is that your crest?'

'It is one which serves many of the Longobard nobles, for it is the insignia of the Archangel Michael who has become our patron. It is said that he appeared to our armies at Sipontum three years ago when we drove back the armies of the Byzantines. It is Michael's name which is now our war cry, for he is captain of battle and defender of Heaven.'

'So any one of your people would bear that crest?'

'Only the warriors of our King Grimoald,' confirmed the young noble. 'Indeed, my sword arm is at the disposal of Grimoald. Why do you ask?'

'Tell me something of this Grimoald,' invited Fidelma, ignoring the question. 'When did he become your King?'

'After he seized the throne from King Godepert and married his sister, Theodota. That was four years ago.'

'I thought you said he succeeded Perctarit . . . ?'

'Ah, you have a sharp memory. Perctarit was a joint king with his brother, Godepert. But the two brothers were at war with each other. Both were as bad as one another. Grimoald was then Duke of Benevento. He assassinated Godepert and eventually drove Perctarit into exile. It is Grimoald who hails Michael as the warrior-protector of our nation. We need that protection for we have many enemies. Even now Grimoald is campaigning against the Byzantines in the south. In his absence, Lupus the Wolf, the Duke of Friuli, is Regent. Friuli is a city far to the east of here.'

'You seem to live in turbulent times,' Fidelma observed.

'It is the nature of my people,' Radoald replied grimly. 'Centuries ago we were forced from our homelands far to the north and, each time we tried to settle, we were driven further south and west by those who came behind us. We had to carve new territories, new homelands with the help of our swords.'

'And yet you also fight each other over matters of king-ship?' Her comment was posed as a question.

'Strength must be the catchword of a ruler.'

'Have you no laws of succession? Laws by which your judges can challenge an unjust ruler?'

Radoald stared at her in surprise for a moment and then he smiled, shaking his head in amusement.

'Do not tell me that in your land there are such laws?'

'A king must obey the law as willingly as a cowherd,' pointed out Fidelma.

'We believe a king is the lawgiver. We obey *his* law.'

Radoald then took Fidelma on a tour of his fortress and, she had to confess, she was surprised at the wealth of tapestries and paintings, which she learned were from Byzantium. There were statuettes from Ancient Rome and many other decorative items. Radoald took a pride as he showed her these treasures. It seemed to her that the young man was going out of his way to impress her that he was a man of refinement and appreciative of the arts. Indeed, after a little while, he said, 'When our people, the Longobards, came into this land about a hundred years ago, we were pagans, not having heard the word of Christ. All we knew was conquest and how to govern by the sword. Thankfully, times change.'

The conversation was suddenly interrupted by the entrance

of a tall man of striking appearance. His age was almost impossible to discern, since although his hair was snow-white, his features seemed young. His eyes were dark, almost without pupils; his lips thin and unusually red; his nose prominent and thin. From neck to feet he was clad in robes of black, the sleeves wide and loose so that they hid his hands. There was no jewellery as relief to the blackness of his dress.

'Suidur, this is Fidelma of Hibernia, not only of the Sisterhood but a princess of that land,' introduced Radoald. 'This is Suidur, my physician.'

The dark eyes examined Fidelma without emotion. Then the physician raised his left hand and placed it over his heart, making a short bow.

'Hibernia? You are welcome in our valley, lady. Gisa has told me of your meeting and journey here.' His voice was dry, without feeling. 'She tells me that you were once a pupil of old Ruadán of Bobium?'

'She tells you correctly,' Fidelma confirmed. 'I trust Brother Faro is recovering?'

'Faro is well enough, my lady,' answered the physician. 'Thankfully, the wound is clean and there are no signs of infection. Gisa is a good student. I have also treated the wound with herbs and bound it. Apart from soreness, he has no ill effects. Therefore, he may continue his journey to Bobium tomorrow and make a good recovery. But he must move slowly and easily.'

'Then that is a good outcome.' Radoald spoke with satisfaction.

The physician was looking around at the people in the hall, as if seeking someone. 'I heard that Magister Ado is of your party? I do not see him here.'

Radoald answered: 'Magister Ado begged to be excused for he says he is tired from the journey. He will take some refreshment in his chamber.'

Suidur the Wise turned his dark eyes back to Fidelma. 'Have you known him long then?'

Fidelma wondered why Suidur asked her exactly the same question that Radoald had asked.

'I encountered him in Genua and he told me of Bobium and it was mentioned Brother Ruadán was here. I could not leave your country without seeing my old mentor, especially when I heard he was ailing.'

'You did not know Magister Ado before you met him in Genua?' Suidur continued to gaze at her thoughtfully.

She was about to respond when the young noble interrupted hurriedly. 'Apparently she did not know about the *magister* nor of Bobium until she met Magister Ado by chance at the seaport. She was on her way back to Hibernia from Rome. You will forgive us, lady, but we are always curious about visitors in our small community.' A horn was suddenly blown and Radoald appeared relieved. 'The meal is prepared. Come, sit with us.'

Only Magister Ado was absent from the meal. Sister Gisa with Brother Faro alongside came to take their places. Fidelma was seated between Radoald and Suidur. The conversation veered between questions about Hibernia and information on the Valley of the Trebbia and the Abbey of Bobium. Radoald seemed intent on keeping the topics light, about the different customs of his people to those of Hibernia; about the local food, the wine and other subjects. Fidelma was not sorry when, at long last, she could excuse herself for the night. Radoald ordered one of his servants to conduct her to a guest chamber.

She was led into the main courtyard by the servant holding high an oil lamp. Only one or two people were still about, and they acknowledged her with a look or a few words of greeting as she walked across the cold flagstones. They ascended stairs into a squat building of several storeys high. Her chamber was small, with one window that gave on to a balcony overlooking an inner courtyard lit by the bright light of a waxing moon. The chamber was furnished with a bed and a table with tallow candles in holders, one of which had already been lit. In a corner was another table with a bowl of water to wash in and a linen cloth. There was also a pitcher of fresh water to drink from with a cup. Her escort left and Fidelma yawned with exhaustion and went to the window. The moon cast an eerie twilight over the Trebbia Valley and a chill wind was rustling its way along the valley trees and undergrowth. It was almost with relief that Fidelma climbed on to the bed and closed her eyes.

Fidelma was not asleep. She had not been able to settle at all in spite of her exhaustion. She had started to turn over in her mind the events of the last few days and began to wonder if she had been right in making the decision to accompany Magister Ado and his companions to Bobium. Perhaps she should have remained in the port of Genua, seeking another ship to continue her journey instead of setting off into the alien countryside.

Even when she had been in Rome she had experienced feelings of longing for Cashel, for the rich green plains, the mountains and dense verdant forests of her homeland. Now, she realised, she felt another longing. She felt a sadness when she had parted from the Saxon monk Eadulf who had been her companion and helper in resolving mysteries at the

Abbey of Hilda and later in the Lateran Palace in Rome. She wished he was here now. She wanted someone she could trust, in whom to confide her ideas about the incidents that she had witnessed.

Such were the thoughts that filled her mind as she twisted and turned. It was only the prospect of seeing old Brother Ruadán again that convinced her to go on. How much more isolated must Brother Ruadán feel, being so elderly and so far from home? She felt that she owed a duty to her ageing mentor and teacher. She could bring him some cheer of his native land and friends now that he was nearing the end of his life.

As she lay there, she began to hear the distant sound of people whispering. It encroached on her thoughts. She sat up with a frown of annoyance. It was coming from outside, beyond the open window and balcony that overlooked the small courtyard below. The balcony was only shielded from her room by a thick curtain to keep out the swarming insects, especially the little flies that could bite one during the sultry nights and cause illness.

Fidelma swung off the bed and moved to the curtain, pausing to listen. The sounds made no sense at all and she would have been prepared to ignore things altogether, had she not wondered why people should stand whispering in the middle of the night.

Carefully, she eased the curtain aside and stepped on to the balcony. The night was now dark, for clouds had spread across the sky obscuring the moon. She peered down. The courtyard was in shadows, and it was not until her eyesight grew used to the darkness that she could discern a group of five figures. Three of them were tall, one with white hair, while the other two were short. Of the two shorter figures, one was slight, obviously a woman, and the other, a man, seemed elderly, for he too had white hair, just discernible in the darkness. They were whispering together in a language Fidelma guessed was that of the Longobards. The conversation seemed intense, and as if the man of short stature with white hair was scolding the others. One of the taller men seemed to be protesting.

Well, it was none of her business. She was about to turn back into her chamber and try once more to get some rest before the onward journey when the clouds parted briefly and the bright moon pierced the gloom. It was only for a moment but Fidelma saw the white hair of the tall physician, Suidur. The shorter elderly man and the woman remained in the darkness. She did not see the faces of the others, but their long black robes seemed familiar. Then the woman turned her face so that the moonlight caught it for an instant. Her voice was clear and she suddenly lapsed into Latin.

'The gold must already be here. That means it will happen soon.'

The short, elderly man snapped something at her.

Fidelma gave a gasp and drew back behind the curtain. Whether it was the sound of her withdrawn breath or just a reaction to the sudden moment of moonlight, there was a pause in the conversation. She waited behind the curtain, unable to breathe for a moment, until she heard the talk resume.

Another voice said something sharply and the conversation continued as before in the Longobard language. She waited until the whispering ceased. The voice she had recognised was that of Sister Gisa. She did not know who the short, elderly man was – but was it just her imagination that they, with Suidur, were in conversation with the same two men who had attacked Magister Ado in Genua? Indeed, the same warriors who had attacked them and wounded Brother Faro as they entered the valley?

CHAPTER FOUR

It was well after first light when Fidelma joined her companions in the hall of the fortress at the first meal of the day. She had finally drifted off into an uneasy sleep and awoken feeling tired and irritable. There was no sign of Suidur but Radoald was there presiding over the meal and indulging in a friendly exchange with Magister Ado. Sister Gisa was seated by Brother Faro who still had his arm in a sling but looked none the worse for his experience. Fidelma wondered whether she should relate her experience of the night to Magister Ado as, after all, he had been the subject of the attacks. She decided that she should do so only when a suitable opportunity arose, for if Suidur and Sister Gisa were part of some plot against him, he should be told. Then she began to have doubts. What exactly was the plot against him? Who was involved and why? Surely she should find out more before becoming involved . . . Perhaps Brother Ruadán would be able to enlighten her.

'It seems that we shall have company for the rest of our journey,' Sister Gisa whispered to her as they were finishing their meal.

'Oh?' Fidelma inquired politely.

'Two farmers are taking goods to trade at the abbey.'

'Our local hill farmers often take goods to the abbey,' Radoald intervened, overhearing. 'You arrived here at a convenient moment. The merchants are already outside. But, after what happened to your party yesterday, I'll send two of my own men to accompany you.'

Fidelma's senses were suddenly alert. How convenient for the would-be assassins to travel with them. She could not get the image of the previous night out of her mind. But then she looked at the young, enthusiastic face of Sister Gisa and wondered how the girl could be involved in a conspiracy to murder.

'Are you well enough to undertake this journey, Brother Faro?' she asked. It passed through her mind to use the young religieux as an excuse to delay so that she might find out more about whatever was happening. But the young man nodded vigorously.

'The wound is healing well. I hardly feel it. And the sooner we get to Bobium, the better.'

'I have already given orders for your horses to be ready. Alas, other matters need my attention,' Radoald said, 'otherwise I would gladly offer you my company on the journey.'

Magister Ado seemed content. 'We shall be safe from here on. Bobium is not far now, Fidelma. We should be able to reach it before midday.'

Fidelma followed the others out into the courtyard and carefully scrutinised those who were to be their companions for the rest of the journey. There were two men with pack mules, and the two warriors. To her relief, none of them appeared to have any features in common with the erstwhile attackers. The two with the pack mules were small, rotund men, looking as she imagined typical farmers might look. The two warriors were of average height. She noticed, with interest, that Lord Radoald had provided Sister Gisa with a horse, but she insisted on leading their mule. There was no sign of Suidur when they bade their farewell to the young Lord of Trebbia.

The small caravan set off without fuss. One warrior rode at the head. Magister Ado and Fidelma came next, then Brother Faro and Sister Gisa with their mule. Behind them were the two merchants and their mules. The second warrior brought up the rear.

For a while, Fidelma rode in silence, her eyes watchful on the surrounding countryside.

'You seem pensive, Sister,' Magister Ado finally commented after they had ridden in silence for a while.

'Having been ambushed once, I felt that we should be constantly alert,' she replied apologetically.

Magister Ado grimaced. 'So you think those bandits will try again to waylay us?'

'Why not?' she asked innocently. She did not explain what she had witnessed in the night.

The elderly religieux shook his head. 'I do not think we shall be in any danger in Lord Radoald's territory so near to Bobium.'

'I bow to your knowledge, Magister Ado,' she replied. 'But there is a good saying, however: *semper paratus.*'

Magister Ado was amused. 'Always prepared? It seems a good maxim, lady. But by midday, or soon after, you will see the great walls of the Abbey of Bobium and your fears will then be proved unfounded.'

Fidelma inclined her head as though in acquiescence. 'It is hard to accept that there are those prepared to maim or kill because they disagree with the form of Christian creed another has.'

Fidelma had not meant it to sound so belligerent but Magister Ado only chuckled in good humour.

'You believe that there is something more to it? Some dark secret that I am not telling you? Wait until you have spoken with Brother Ruadán, and you will see that the disagreement runs deep among our people here. Much blood has been scattered in this argument. From what our young friends tell me,' he glanced briefly behind to where Sister Gisa and Brother Faro were following, 'Brother Ruadán has suffered more than I have – suffered for his adherence to the Nicene Creed.'

She did not press the elderly religieux further but rode on in silence. Her anxious eyes wandered constantly over the thickly growing trees that rose up into the mountains on their right. To their left, the turbulent waters of the Trebbia provided a barrier which would have made attack from that quarter difficult. Now and then she glanced back to the plodding farmers behind them.

Then she saw a movement on the hill to their right. It was a man standing on a jutting rock but almost shrouded by the surrounding trees.

'A man is watching us,' she whispered urgently, trying not to show she had noticed. 'To my right by those tall trees on the rock. I can't see a weapon though.'

Magister Ado looked up quickly, suddenly tense. Then he immediately relaxed – and raised his hand as if to wave it in greeting to the figure high above them.

'It's old Aistulf,' he said to her. 'Aistulf the Hermit.'

The figure above them had turned abruptly and went scurrying off among the trees. She caught sight of a bent back and white, long hair.

'He's not a friendly soul,' she commented dryly.

Magister Ado chuckled. 'That is the nature of a hermit.

Old Aistulf lives alone in a cave somewhere up in those hills. He came to our valley only a few years ago, at the end of the wars which brought Grimoald to power. He is a friend of our abbot, Abbot Servillius. I have never seen him up close. No one has, except Abbot Servillius and, I think, Sister Gisa. They sometimes go up into the hills and see him. Aistulf wanders these mountains. I know nothing more about him except that he means no harm.'

'He is elderly,' Fidelma observed. 'He needs more than someone keeping check on him now and again. In Hibernia our laws about the care of the elderly are very strict.'

'Sister Gisa often visits the old man. There is some talk that Aistulf is a member of her family. Gisa was born in this valley.'

Fidelma glanced back towards Sister Gisa. She seemed engrossed with the injured Brother Faro and had obviously not noticed the old man on the hill.

'Tell me about Tolosa. What is it like?' she asked, trying to find a subject to speak of rather than not talk at all.

Not for the first time she became aware of a passing look of suspicion in the elderly man's eyes.

'Why are you interested?' he countered.

'Among my people we have a saying that knowledge comes by asking questions. It is because I have never been to that city that I would know something of it.'

Magister Ado considered for a moment and then said, 'It is a city in ruins, as Radoald observed, though not as desolate as he believed. The great basilica, the abbey, still stands with its library. However, if it were not for the want of our library, I might never have been persuaded to make the journey.'

'I don't understand.'

'Our *scriptor* Brother Eolann heard that the abbey in Tolosa had a copy of the *Life of the Blessed Martyr Saturnin*, who founded the abbey there. He persuaded me to take a copy of the *Life of Columbanus* and exchange it for the book on Saturnin. Bobium has one of the greatest libraries in Christendom, and we are justly proud of it. Our wealth is in our books.'

'Would your enemies know that you had travelled to Tolosa to get this book? Is it as valuable to them as it is to your abbey?'

'I declare, you are a vexatious young lady, to keep dwelling on this question.'

'Questions, as I have said, are a path to knowledge.'

'And sometimes knowledge can be dangerous. Especially when there are people about with evil intent.'

'Better is knowledge of evil than evil without knowledge,' countered Fidelma.

Magister Ado began to frown in annoyance, and then, unexpectedly, threw back his head and burst into laughter.

'Being away from Bobium, I had forgotten the method of argument of my Hibernian brethren. Is this truly the way that you are taught in your land?'

'By question and answer?'

'By taking one answer and forming another question from it?'

'An answer always leads to another question. There is no ultimate answer, for if there was, we would never have progress.'

Magister Ado exhaled with resignation and, somewhat irritably, conceded: 'It seems all those born in Hibernia are philosophers.'

'Not all of us,' Fidelma replied dryly. 'Though all of us think we are.'

They continued on in silence for a while. Behind them, Brother Faro and Sister Gisa sometimes murmured together while the warriors and the two farmers were generally silent, guiding their pack mules. They passed along the river banks, by the swirling waters, under the shade of the tall trees that lined the track. Once or twice they saw men fishing, who raised a hand in greeting as they passed by.

'The local folk have the right to fish the river,' explained Magister Ado. 'There are many good fish to be caught here, especially loach.'

Apart from the few fishermen, they encountered no one else on the track as it followed the bends and flow of the river.

'You can now see the top of Mont Pénas behind those trees there!' Magister Ado exclaimed, pointing. 'It is the tallest mountain in these parts and Bobium is situated on its lower reaches.'

All the mountains seemed to be far taller than those Fidelma had observed before. As they swung around a bend of the river, and emerged through the trees to a section of open stony land, she could see a large watery confluence which seemed to create a broad headland on the far bank. There were many little rivers apparently rising from the mountains which flowed into the main course of the Trebbia. One such large stream joined the Trebbia from the north-east, and on the resulting right-angled headland rose many small buildings, while further up the hillside was a large complex of structures with a tower, contained within high walls.

'Bobium!' The word came from Magister Ado almost as a sigh. He turned to Fidelma and smiled. 'That is Bobium. This is where your countryman, Colmbanus, came with his disciples to settle.'

Fidelma gazed in appreciation at the surrounding countryside; at the rivers, the tall mountains, the lush green forests.
She could see why Columbanus had been enamoured with
the spot. There was something reminiscent about the land of
Éireann . . . something, but it was not quite the same.

'How do we get to the far bank?' she asked. The waters
of the Trebbia that separated them from the abbey were now
broad and quite turbulent, rushing over the stony riverbed.
Magister Ado merely smiled and pointed ahead of them. She
followed his outstretched hand and could make out, not far
ahead, a long stone bridge connecting one bank to the other.
It was the most curious construction that she had ever seen,
since it was built in a series of arches, but the method of
construction had resulted in a series of humpbacks.

'Is it safe?' she found herself wondering aloud.

Magister Ado chuckled. 'It is called the Devil's Bridge,'
he replied. 'There is a story that Columbanus was trying to
construct a stone bridge when the Devil appeared to him. He
offered to build the bridge in a single night, but on one condition: that the first living soul to cross the bridge was to be
his. Columbanus agreed. The bridge was built by morning,
but because of the indiscipline of the imps and goblins that
the Devil employed, each section came out in that series of
humps you see and not one long level stretch.'

'And did the Devil claim his soul?' Fidelma asked
sceptically.

'It is said that Columbanus persuaded a little dog to run
across the bridge and thus the Devil had to be satisfied with
it rather than take a Christian soul which he had desired.'

Fidelma thought for a moment. 'The story is hard to believe.
In the first place, how could such a saintly man as Colm Bán
make a pact with the Devil to achieve such a mundane task

as building a bridge? In the second place, he would not mistreat a poor, innocent animal so callously. And finally, in the third place, why would the Devil take the soul of a dog when the Faith teaches us that only man is possessed of a soul but animals are not?'

Magister Ado was smiling broadly. 'You are truly of a sceptical and practical mind, Fidelma. I perceive that this must not only be because of your land of origin, but also your training in law? Well, perhaps you will be pleased to know that our scholars tell us that the bridge was first built by the Roman legions when they were conquering this land. So, in spite of local tales, the bridge was here *before* Columbanus. Therefore, I think it will be safe enough to cross, Devil or no Devil.'

The stone bridge was narrow, scarcely wide enough for two riding abreast, but the party crossed and found themselves on the lower slopes of the mountain which apparently rose in easy stages. Fidelma could no longer see the peak, which seemed to merge with the surrounding hills. The abbey, with its redbrick tiles and soft ochre stucco walls, dominated the area a little way up the hillside. Near it were various buildings, constituting a small township. Around the settlement were arable lands that had been cultivated for agricultural purposes. As they moved up the track closer to the abbey, Fidelma saw that its main buildings were enclosed by high walls from which some of the stuccowork had fallen, revealing blocks of stone. On the walls, near the gates, rose a bell-tower. Someone had observed their approach, and a slow regular chime of the bell sounded, ceasing after the fourth ring. The gates were tall, fitted in the walls, and seemed of a dark wood. She would have guessed they were made of oak. They were swinging open.

The company had reached a point before the gates where the track divided, and here the warriors turned aside after a brief conversation with Magister Ado and a salute of farewell. They moved off towards the township, where the farmers and their pack mules were already heading. Magister Ado led the way up the short incline through the open gates. As they entered, one of the brethren approached with a look of astonishment on his features as he recognised Magister Ado.

'Magister Ado! Is it truly you?'

'If not I then it is my shadow,' replied the elderly religieux, dismounting from his horse. 'Indeed, Brother Wulfila, I have returned from my journey.'

'The abbot shall be informed of your safe coming at once.' His eyes alighted on Brother Faro, then widened in horror. 'But you are hurt, my—'

'It is nothing,' Brother Faro almost snapped at him. Then, aware of his bad manners towards the steward, he dismounted and turned in more conciliatory manner. 'Forgive me, Brother Wulfila. A slight pain has caused me a distemper. *Mea culpa.*'

Brother Wulfila dismissed the apology quickly. 'You must see the apothecary at once.'

'I can take him there,' offered Sister Gisa. 'We have already dressed and bound the wound, but it needs to be checked.'

Brother Wulfila hesitated. 'You cannot wander the abbey without permission of the abbot. I am told to be strict about the Rule that demands the segregation of the sexes.' He motioned to the man who had opened the gates for them. 'Brother Bladulf, take Brother Faro to the apothecary, for he is in need of attention.' Then he turned anxiously back to Magister Ado. 'A fall from his horse?'

Magister Ado shook his head. 'An arrow from a bandit, I'm afraid.' Brother Wulfila continued to look worried and was about to press for more information when Magister Ado presented Fidelma. 'Sister Fidelma, this is Brother Wulfila, the steward of the abbey. Sister Fidelma's old mentor is Brother Ruadán and it is to see him that she has come especially to our abbey.'

At once, Brother Wulfila's features grew solemn. 'Then I am afraid, Sister Fidelma, that you have arrived only just in time. Poor Brother Ruadán started ailing a week or so ago and now he is not expected to be long in this world. His mind is already wandering.'

'Yet he still lives?' she asked anxiously.

'He was severely beaten and lucky to escape with his life. Age hinders his recovery. Alas, we are told it is merely a matter of time.'

'Then I would see him at once.'

Brother Wulfila looked scandalised. 'This is not a *conhospitae*, Sister. Women are only allowed in here with the abbot's special dispensation. That is why I could not allow Sister Gisa to accompany Brother Faro to the apothecary. The women's house is in the township. Women are only allowed within the abbey walls to attend the chapel and share services and to join us in the main evening meal before prayers.'

Magister Ado patted Brother Wulfila on the arm. 'Then first we must make our presence known to the abbot,' he insisted gently. 'It is etiquette. And Fidelma is not just any visitor, she comes from Rome and is the daughter of a king of Hibernia.'

Fidelma had to contain her impatience at the delay in seeing Brother Ruadán because she knew that Magister Ado was correct. It would be bad manners to go against established convention and disrespect the rules of the abbey.

'I will take you to him,' the steward said, before turning to Sister Gisa and adding brusquely: 'There is no need for you to remain.'

For a moment, Sister Gisa looked unwilling to be thus dismissed. Then she said pointedly to Fidelma, 'I will see you at the evening meal, if not before.' Then, taking the horse that Radoald had given her, she rode back through the abbey gates. Brother Wulfila had signalled to two more of the brethren who came forward, one to take charge of their horses and pack mule while the other brought a bucket, a ladle and a cloth. Fidelma had almost forgotten the ritual of washing newcomers' hands and feet on the entering of an abbey for the first time.

Brother Wulfila then led them across the large stoneflagged courtyard towards the main doors. The news of the arrival of Magister Ado, who apparently had distinction in the abbey, had spread rapidly so that many of the brethren had started to spill into the courtyard to greet him. At the top of a short flight of steps which led to the main doors, stood a tall, swarthy man of the same years as Magister Ado. But he was thin with dark hair and eyes. His jowls showed the blue-black of a beard that would need shaving twice daily, had he allowed it to grow. His features were not unpleasant and he wore the symbols that proclaimed him as Abbot. As Magister Ado approached, with Fidelma at his shoulder, the abbot came down the steps. There was an expression on his face which Fidelma could not quite interpret. Then he symbolically embraced the *magister*.

'Welcome back, old friend,' he greeted. 'I have feared for your safety ever since you set out on your mission on behalf of our *scriptorium*.' The abbot spoke in Latin and Fidelma realised that Latin was the language of choice in the abbey. 'Was your journey blessed with success?'

'It was, indeed. Our *scriptorium* now has a copy of the *Life of the Blessed Martyr Saturnin*.'

The abbot looked quizzically at Fidelma and Magister Ado introduced his companion.

'Abbot Servillius, this is Fidelma of Hibernia. She has been our travelling companion since Genua.'

'Fidelma of Hibernia?' The abbot frowned as if searching his memory. He held out his hand for her to kiss his ring of office as was the custom among the Roman clerics. Fidelma merely took his hand and bowed her head from the neck in accordance with the custom of her own people.

'She is the daughter of a king of her own land,' explained Magister Ado.

'Fidelma?' mused the abbot. 'I have heard this name recently . . . ah! Have you come from Rome?'

'I have,' Fidelma affirmed, knowing what was to follow.

'Ah, I have it now. One of our brethren, coming from Rome, talked of a young religieuse from Hibernia who astonished even the Holy Father by resolving the mystery involving a Saxon archbishop who was murdered in the Lateran Palace itself. Indeed, her name was Fidelma.'

'She is that very person, Father Abbot,' affirmed Magister Ado good-naturedly.

Fidelma gave a quick shrug. 'I played some small part in the resolution of that mystery,' she admitted.

'Then you are most welcome here. It is not often we get such distinguished visitors in our lonely valley, although . . .' he hesitated and glanced at Magister Ado, 'although it seems that this week is one for the distinguished and the noble to grace our community. Come.' The abbot dismissed Brother Wulfila and led them into his study where he indicated that they be seated. It was a small, dark room made darker by oak panels, but there was a small window which cast just enough light for them to see without resorting to lamps.

'You seem to imply that you have another distinguished visitor under the shelter of your roof, my friend Father Abbot,' Magister Ado remarked as he sat down.

'Indeed, we have. Our guest is young Prince Romuald, son of our gracious King Grimoald, who is even now fighting in the south.'

'Prince Romuald?' Magister Ado sounded surprised.

As the question needed no response, the abbot turned to Fidelma. 'And now, Fidelma of Hibernia, you must tell me why you have graced our poor abbey. I presume the obvious answer would be to do with this abbey's connection with your country?'

It was Magister Ado who answered for Fidelma, speaking quickly before she could. 'It is Brother Ruadán who brings her hither. He was her mentor and teacher when she was younger and, on hearing that he was in this abbey, she determined to come here and see him before she continued her journey back to Hibernia.'

Abbot Servillius' pleasant features saddened and he studied Fidelma in sympathy for a moment. 'A former pupil of dear Brother Ruadán? Then it is God's will which has guided your footsteps along our valley to this holy place. You have been told of his infirmity? Of course, you must go and see him but, alas, I must warn you that he has deteriorated in recent days.'

'Can you give any exact details of what happened?' inquired Fidelma.

'Very little. He was found outside the gates of the abbey early one morning with a note proclaiming the word "heretic" pinned to him. We know he tried to preach often to those followers of Arius, trying to persuade them to turn from their foolishness. It is thought that he has suffered the consequence of the anger of some of them. Three weeks ago, he returned from Placentia where he had been preaching. He had been assaulted and barely made it safely back. It did not deter him. He left the abbey again to preach in Travo, down the valley. After that he was found outside the abbey gates and grievously hurt. He took to his bed and has not been able to stir from it since. But perhaps the sight of his young friend,' he motioned towards Fidelma, 'might revive his spirit. A link with his homeland might act as a tonic, a balm to his soul.'

'I presume that he is attended by a good physician?' Fidelma queried.

'Brother Hnikar is one of the best apothecaries in this valley. He attends him daily. But when the flesh is old and weak . . .' The abbot gave a half-shrug, as if to indicate that one could not argue with Fate. 'I have to point out to you that this is not a mixed community and, therefore, your movements are restricted. It would be best to always have a member of the brethren to guide you.' He suddenly reached forward and rang a small handbell. Brother Wulfila immediately appeared at the door.

'This Sister . . .' He stopped, shrugged and began again. 'Take the lady Fidelma of Hibernia to Brother Hnikar. She is to be allowed to see and speak to her compatriot, Brother Ruadán, without restriction.'

The steward hid his obvious surprise by inclining his head to his superior before indicating that Fidelma should precede him through the door.

'Afterwards, return here and we will discuss accommodation and rules for your stay here,' the abbot called after her.

The apothecary, to whom she was introduced, was a short, plump man, whose cheeks shone with a childlike pinkness. His eyes were blue to the point of paleness. Fidelma was not sure whether his central baldness was natural or the result of a tonsure. It was surrounded by long silver hair, raggedly cut. He greeted her with a benign expression.

'You will find poor Brother Ruadán in a sad condition,' he said, when he was told the purpose of her coming. 'As you know, the passing of the years can be unkind, and these last days have enfeebled him beyond measure.'

'His injuries are bad?'

Brother Hnikar's lips compressed. 'It is not so much the hurt that was inflicted on him but, at his age, the shock of the violence. I can heal cuts, bruises and wounds, but when the wounds go deep to the mind and soul . . .' He shrugged. 'Be careful what you say to him, for his mind now wanders and he can imagine all manner of things. Come, I will take you to him.'

The room in which Brother Ruadán lay was small but with a large opening that was so placed to let in the sunshine as it descended towards the western mountain ridge. There was little in the room save a cot on which the elderly religieux lay with a straw mattress and a thin woollen blanket. A simple wooden cross was affixed to one wall. A small table with a jug of water and beaker on it and a wooden chest placed for any personal items or clothing made up the rest of the furniture.

Brother Hnikar ushered her inside and whispered, 'Remember, do not tax the old one. His strength is lessening by the day.'

Fidelma did not reply but moved forward to the bedside.

Brother Ruadán lay as if in complete repose on his back,

his hands folded in front of him. His eyes were shut, his breathing somewhat stertorous.

'Brother Ruadán,' Fidelma said quietly, resorting to her own language. 'Can you hear me?'

The regular breathing seemed to hesitate and then the eyelids flickered and opened. The pale eyes stared upwards as if unable to focus on her.

'Brother Ruadán, can you hear me?' repeated Fidelma.

'Who . . . who speaks?' gasped the old man in the same language.

'It is I, Fidelma of Cashel.'

A faint smile seemed to hover on the lips of the old man.

'Fidelma of Cashel? She is a world away from here.'

Fidelma moved closer and bent over him. 'Try to focus, Brother Ruadán,' she said. 'I am here.'

The eyes seemed to search here and there before they found and focused on her.

'Remember the days we spent on Inis Celtra?' went on Fidelma. 'You once told me that I was your worst pupil, for I asked too many questions about the Faith. You said that I should merely accept it and not question it.'

A look of uncertainty crossed the old man's features.

'I knew a princess of Cashel once,' he muttered. 'She even questioned God's omnipotence.'

'I said, if God was omnipotent and created Adam, then He must have known that Adam would disobey Him.'

'God was omnipotent but gave man free will,' responded the old man from memory.

'But if God was omnipotent, how was Adam's will stronger than that of his Creator?' queried Fidelma.

'God gave Adam his choice.'

'But in our law, a person who knows of a crime before it

73

is committed and could prevent it and does not, is deemed as an accessory before the fact and therefore judged a principal in the crime.'

The head was almost nodding in agreement, The rheumy eyes widened and a clawlike hand sought Fidelma's own.

'Fidelma of Cashel – that was her argument as a young girl. Indeed, she went off to study law under Brehon Morann.'

'Now I am here – here in Bobium, my old mentor. I was journeying back to Cashel from Rome and, by chance, heard that you were here. How could I pass by without coming to see you?'

'Fidelma of Cashel?' The old man gave a long sigh and seemed to sink even deeper back on his pillow. 'Is it truly you?'

'It is I. It is Fidelma of Cashel.'

'Forgive me. I have grown old and my sight grows weaker. I do not think that I have much longer to dwell here.'

'Nonsense,' replied Fidelma fiercely. 'You will outlive us all.'

The old man gave a wheezy smile. 'You were ever the optimist, Fidelma of Cashel. I thought Brehon Morann would caution you on an adherence to optimism. You have been to Rome?'

'I have.'

Suddenly a troubled look crossed the old man's features. His frail hand closed on Fidelma's arm with an unexpected pressure, and he struggled as if he would raise himself up on his bed.

'Calm yourself, Ruadán,' soothed Fidelma anxiously.

'Take care, Fidelma of Cashel. That which was taken from its watery grave must be returned to it. It is cursed!'

The sick man's eyes stared into her face with a strange intensity. His features wore an expression of anguish.

'I do not understand you, Brother Ruadán,' she replied, trying to pacify him.

Both hands now came up, gripping her arms so tightly that the upper half of his body rose from the bed by the strength of his grip.

'There is evil in this place, Fidelma of Cashel! Evil! Leave now – leave at once, for you will not be safe. Leave . . .'

He gave a gasp and fell back exhausted on the bed. Fidelma stared down at him, bemused. She was suddenly aware of Brother Hnikar standing at the door. Now the apothecary hurriedly approached the bed and laid a hand on Brother Ruadán's forehead.

'I told you that his strength was lessening. He has exhausted himself and fallen back into sleep. Leave him now. He needs all the rest he can get.'

Fidelma stood hesitantly for a moment and gave a reluctant glance at the old man. The apothecary was gently pushing her to the door.

'Don't worry,' he reassured her. 'He must rest now. When he is overtired he tends to hallucinate. I will take care of him. Pay no heed to what he says. His mind is disturbed.'

She found herself back in the passage, the door shut firmly behind her. Faintly, from beyond it, she heard the frail voice of Brother Ruadán cry out: 'Tell her to leave . . . leave this abbey now! There is much evil here!'

chapter five

Brother Wulfila was waiting in the passage to guide her back to the abbot's chamber. The steward greeted Fidelma with a sombre expression.

'I heard him cry out,' he said moodily. 'Alas, he tends to think his attackers can still do him harm, even here in the abbey. We are doing our best for him. Brother Ruadán is much respected here. It is very sad.'

'Indeed,' Fidelma replied quietly.

'Was he able to recognise you?'

'He was, but little else.'

The steward was about to say something more but then changed his mind and guided her back to the abbot's study.

Abbot Servillius and Magister Ado were still engaged in conversation. They had been joined by another man who seemed older than either the abbot or the *magister*. He was silver-haired, thin but not gaunt, with tanned features that were quite handsome. He carried himself with the erect posture of a younger man. It was only when one looked care-fully into his face that one realised he was well beyond his allotted three-score and ten years. They all looked up as she entered.

'Ah, Sister Fidelma,' greeted the abbot. 'Allow me to present the Venerable Ionas, our greatest scholar.'

The Venerable Ionas grimaced with an almost embarrassed expression. However, she was aware of a close scrutiny from his dark, penetrating eyes. '*Pax tecum*, Sister. I am merely one of many scholars in this community. Magister Ado here has as great a claim as my own.'

'Abbot Ionas has written the praiseworthy work on the life of our founder,' added Abbot Servillius.

Venerable Ionas seemed to notice that Sister Fidelma was troubled in spite of her best efforts to remain expressionless. 'You are anxious about something?' he asked.

'I have just been to see Brother Ruadán.' She could only explain the obvious. 'He was my teacher when I was little.'

'I did try to prepare you.' The abbot was slightly defensive.

'Poor Brother Ruadán will not be with us long, according to Brother Hnikar,' the Venerable Ionas sighed. 'How bad was he when you saw him?'

'Bad enough,' she replied as she lowered herself into the chair indicated by the abbot.

'I shall call in on him later,' Magister Ado said. 'I would like to see him before it is too late.'

Fidelma felt an annoyance at what appeared to be their casual acceptance of Brother Ruadán's imminent death. 'Perhaps we should not consign him to the grave just yet,' she protested.

'I am sure that is not our intention,' the abbot replied hurriedly. 'But we must face reality.'

'And the reality is . . . ?' queried Fidelma.

'Outside these walls there is a harsh world at the moment,' replied the abbot. 'That is why young Prince Romuald is our guest at the moment.'

Magister Ado looked concerned. 'You were about to tell us the reason for his coming here,' he said.

'He was sent here for protection. The rumours that Perctarit has returned from exile, taking advantage of the King's absence in the south, are growing daily.' Abbot Servillius glanced at Fidelma and smiled apologetically. 'Our King Grimoald sent Perctarit into exile and—'

'I have been told of your change of kingship,' she interrupted.

'Grimoald is in the south. Duke Lupus of Friuli has been left as Regent here in the north during his absence. The King's son, Romuald, was left in the charge of a nurse and the protection of Lupus.'

'So why is he here?' pressed Magister Ado.

'It seemed that the boy's nurse, Lady Gunora, began to entertain suspicions as to where Lupus' loyalties really lay. She took the boy and they left Lupus' fortress in the dead of night to make their journey here, where she knew the brethren would provide Prince Romuald with sanctuary. The boy has a heavy burden on his young shoulders.'

'I presume that the absence of the King in the south of the country is the reason why Perctarit is rumoured to have returned from exile?' mused Magister Ado.

'I would also presume that is so,' agreed Abbot Servillius.

Magister Ado was frowning. 'If this is the case, Father Abbot, do you not think there is a danger to the abbey? If the boy is in danger, then surely the abbey is too?'

The Venerable Ionas leaned forward in his chair. His features were serious as he looked towards the abbot. 'Magister Ado makes a good observation, my old friend. Who knows outside these walls that Prince Romuald is here?'

The abbot took a moment before responding. 'Apart from

Lord Radoald, no one outside the abbey, for he and his escort arrived under cover of darkness only two nights ago. As the Lord of Trebbia is our friend and protector, he had to be informed.'

'It is a secret that can scarcely be kept,' Magister Ado pointed out. 'Have you given any thought to what we should do if Lupus of Friuli makes a descent against the abbey?'

Abbot Servillius shook his head. 'We are a house of God, not a military fortress,' he responded. Suddenly realising that Fidelma had been sitting listening with quiet interest to the conversation, he rose to his feet. 'But where are my manners? I have not afforded our friend, Fidelma of Hibernia, the hospitality that is the custom of our people. I shall instruct Brother Wulfila, our steward, to have a chamber prepared for you in the guest-house and water for washing as is your custom. The guest-house is a separate section of chambers above the apothecary and the *cubicula* for the sick. Indeed, it is situated on the floor above where you went to visit Brother Ruadán. It overlooks our *herbarium*, our herb garden of which we are justly proud and where you may wander freely on your own.

'As you are a special guest, I am making a dispensation of certain of our rules so that you may stay here and not go to the house of the religieuses in the township. The same dispensation I have given to the Lady Gunora, for she must reside close by Prince Romuald. But I must ask you to abide by our rules that segregate the brethren from our guests. Never venture far without permission or the attendance of one of the brethren appointed to guide you. I am sure that you will respect this rule.'

Abbot Servillius reached forward and took up the handbell once again. At its jangle, the door opened and the steward entered. Brother Wulfila listened in silence to the abbot's instructions, trying to hide his disapproval. Then the abbot turned to Fidelma.

'Go, refresh yourself and rest. A bell will be sounded when it is time for the evening meal. Someone will be at the doorway of the guest-house to guide you to the *refectorium.*'

Fidelma had no choice but to accept her dismissal. She could not help the thought that the concern for her rest, after the journey, was merely an excuse to be rid of her presence during the discussion of the political situation.

She followed Brother Wulfila, who now took her on a different route along the darkened corridors before halting before a door. She could smell what was behind the door even before the steward pointed silently to the sign in Latin. It said: *cloaca*. She knew it came from the root *cluo*, 'I cleanse', so she could guess the intention of the room that lay beyond even had she been unable to smell it. Her companion felt he did not have to explain further and turned and led her up a flight of stone steps to an upper level where he halted before another door, which he bent to open. Then he stood aside and motioned her in. She stepped inside.

There was a window which looked out on gardens rising up the hillside. There was a chair, a chest and hooks to hang clothing on. A tub for water – but empty – stood in one corner, with cloths of white linen to use as towels.

'I shall have your baggage sent up immediately and also hot water for your ablutions,' Brother Wulfila announced. Before she had time to reply, the door gave a soft thud as it closed behind him. She stood for a moment examining her surroundings before sitting on the edge of the cot. Brother Ruadán had cried out that there was evil in this abbey. Certainly, she had begun to feel uncomfortable ever since she had entered this Valley of the Trebbia and witnessed the attempt to kill Magister Ado. Religious tensions were not unknown to her. After all, she had attended the great Council of Streonshalh, at the Abbey of Hilda, when the Angles had decided to reject the concepts of the churches of her own land and opt for the new rules from Rome. But this conflict between the philosophy of Arius and the concepts made into dogma at the First Council of Nicaea seemed to be resulting in bloodshed, not merely argument. There seemed a dark cloud in the valley. But was that the evil that Brother Ruadán had warned her against – or was there something else?

It was some time later, refreshed by her wash and with a change of clothing, that Fidelma heard the tolling of a bell which she presumed announced the evening meal. She waited a few moments and decided to follow some members of the brethren who passed her chamber. They, in turn, joined groups of hurrying silent members down a flight of stairs into the main courtyard. Here she found a group of a dozen Sisters of the Faith moving towards the doors of the main building. She saw Sister Gisa among the group and went to greet her.

'Have you see Brother Faro?' was Sister Gisa's first question. 'I hope he is resting his wound.'

Fidelma felt sadness at the girl's obvious feelings for the young man. She knew that the group of ascetics who were trying persuade Rome to issue an edict in favour of celibacy were a vocal minority but growing stronger. They had obviously made an impact with Abbot Servillius. While there was no overall proscription from the Holy Father, it seemed to depend on the individual abbot as to how they viewed the subject. However, Pope Sircius had abandoned his wife and children after he was elected to the throne of Peter in Rome. He tried to insist that priests and other clergy should no longer sleep with their wives. A century before, the same idea was proposed at the Council of Tours which recommended that a rule be made that priests sleeping in the same bed as their wives could not perform religious services. The proposition was never agreed.

'Are you and Brother Faro . . . ?' Fidelma stopped when she saw the blush come to the girl's cheeks.

'We are friends,' Sister Gisa replied, but the blush gave the lie to her statement. 'This is not a mixed house, like those I have heard of elsewhere. Abbot Servillius favours those who argue for celibacy among the religious. However, both sexes gather for meals in the *refectorium* and also for services in the chapel.'

They came to a pair of large double doors made of shiny chestnut wood through which the brethren were hurrying. At one side, the steward, Brother Wulfila, appeared to be waiting for Fidelma with a frown of annoyance.

'I sent someone to your chamber to escort you here,' he greeted her in a tone of rebuke. 'You should not wander the abbey without an escort.' Without waiting for a reply, he requested her to follow him while Sister Gisa disappeared to one side of the hall with the other females, who seemed to share a single table in a corner discreetly sheltered from the brethren. Brother Wulfila led the way through rows of tables and benches. She passed Brother Faro at one table and recognised Brother Hnikar at another. She saw several of the brethren staring at her with varying expressions of surprise or interest. At the far end of the hall, facing these rows was a long table where she recognised Abbot Servillius with Magister Ado seated at his left side and Venerable Ionas on his right. To the left of Magister Ado sat a young boy, perhaps not more than ten or eleven years old, and next to him a woman of matronly appearance.

The abbot rose as Brother Wulfila approached and waved Fidelma forward with a small gesture of his hand.

'I would introduce you to our special guest. This is Prince Romuald of the Longobards, lady.' Then he turned to the boy. 'Highness, I would present Fidelma of Hibernia, who is the daughter of a king of her country.'

The small boy rose and bowed solemnly from his waist. Fidelma found herself hiding a smile at his manner, which seemed so incongruous for his age.

'I welcome you to this land, lady. My people and my own family have long held your countrymen in high esteem for their knowledge and teaching. Do you intend to remain in this abbey?'

'I am here to see my old mentor, who has now made this abbey his home. Soon I must depart back to my own land,' Fidelma replied politely.

The abbot then introduced the woman at the boy's side as the Lady Gunora, companion to the young prince. The woman smiled shyly and bowed her head in acknowledgement.

The introductions being over, they resumed their seats while Brother Wulfila guided Fidelma to a seat on Venerable Ionas' right hand before taking the seat next to her. At the sound of a single bell, the abbot stood up and intoned a prayer of thanks. he sat down and another single chime on a bell allowed the occupants of the *refectorium* to commence the evening meal. Fidelma was surprised as the noise of conversation permeated the great room. During the last weeks in Rome, when she had eaten in the religious refectories, she had noticed that most maintained the custom of consuming the meal in strict silence. In some abbeys, one of the brethren, a *recitator*, read aloud from the scriptures or the Psalms while the others ate.

She turned as Venerable Ionas had been speaking to her. 'I am sorry, you were saying?'

'I was merely asking about Columbanus,' the scholar said apologetically. 'I always ask any newcomer from Hibernia in case they have some knowledge which I could add to my work on the life of our founder.'

'I am afraid I know little. He was from the Kingdom of Laighin and went north to study,' replied Fidelma. 'My own kingdom is Muman which is in the south-west of Hibernia.'

'Hibernia is not one kingdom then?'

'There are five kingdoms but the fifth kingdom is called Midhe – the Middle Kingdom – and it is there that our High King lives. He has nominal jurisdiction over all the king-doms. The High King is chosen from one of the main ruling families. These days it is the Uí Néill of the north who domin-ate the succession.'

Venerable Ionas grimaced. 'I have heard of this from other of your compatriots. I cannot understand it. But tell me, what little is it that you know of Columbanus?'

'In our language his name is Colm Bán and it means "white dove". All I know is that he became Abbot of Beannchar, a famous abbey in the north of Hibernia. It is told that he decided to leave the abbey to journey across the seas in order to set up centres of the Faith among the Franks and Burgundians. That is all. I had no knowledge of this place.'

The Venerable Ionas was nodding slowly, with a faint smile on his lips.

'Indeed, my daughter,' he said. 'He made enemies among the Frankish nobles and there came a time when they ordered Columbanus and all his Hibernian monks to be deported back to their own land. Instead of returning to Hibernia, however, Columbanus came south, crossing the great mountains, and eventually brought his followers to the land of the Longobards. The King at that time, Agilulf, gave Columbanus this land. And here, in Bobium, he set up our community. Soon the religious of many lands joined him. He stuck firm to his old Hibernian ways and even argued with the Holy Father, Gregory the Great, that it was the Hibernians who maintained the true date of the Pascal Festival. He was a great man, a great teacher.'

'Did you know him?'

'I came here as a young man three years after he had died,' replied the old scholar, with a shake of his head. 'But I knew many who had known him and they helped me with my work on his life. When the time came for me to take a religious name, I chose the Greek form of the Hebrew name Jonah, which also means a dove. And you say that was the meaning of Columbanus' own name?'

There was a sudden commotion at the doors of the *refectorium* and they swung open. Heads turned and there came gasps of surprise. One of the brethren came running up the aisle to the table where Abbot Servillius had half-risen, anger on his face. The young red-faced Brother stopped and was gasping for breath.

'Father Abbot . . . Father Abbot, I could not stop them . . .'

'You forget yourself, Brother Bladulf,' thundered the abbot. 'Have you not been gatekeeper long enough to know your proprieties and rules of this abbey? During the evening meal—'

But the young man was glancing over his shoulder. Two men had entered the *refectorium* and were striding almost arrogantly up the aisle between the now astonished and silent brethren towards the top table. Fidelma examined them with curiosity. There was no doubt that the leading figure was a bishop, his robes and crozier proclaimed it.

The man a little behind him was also clad in religious robes, but not of rank.

Abbot Servillius sat back in his chair in shock at the sight of the newcomers.

'*Pax vobiscum*,' said the bishop in greeting, halting before their table with his belligerent gaze sweeping their astonished faces.

Abbot Servillius did not answer the traditional salutation. He simply breathed the name, '*Britmund.*'

There was an uncomfortable silence.

The bishop was short and stocky, florid of feature with greying hair but dark eyebrows, and eyes that seemed like shiny black pebbles. His lips were thin and bloodless, and twisted in a cruel smile. His eyes narrowed as they glanced at Magister Ado at the abbot's side and moved on to the young boy seated next to him.

'So it is true.' He gave a half-bow towards the prince. 'My greetings and blessings on you, Prince Romuald. Your friends at the fortress of Friuli are missing you.'

A soft breath hissed from the mouth of Lady Gunora, who seemed to draw the boy protectively towards her.

'His friends are *here*,' she said defensively.

Bishop Britmund shook his head with an irritating smile on his features.

'I fear that is not the case.' His glance fell on Sister Fidelma. 'It is interesting to see that this abbey of heretics now accepts females dining at the abbot's side,' he sneered. 'Is it not enough you actually allow them to dine in the same hall as the brethren?'

Abbot Servillius now leaned forward, his voice one of scarcely controlled anger.

'Sister Fidelma is our guest, a visitor from Hibernia, and daughter of a king of that country.'

'It is a pity that you do not show respect to all your guests.'
The bishop was sardonic. 'Brother Godomar and I have spent
long days coming to this abbey. Our greeting scarcely merits
the conventions of hospitality.'

'A pity that *you* did not observe the conventions of entry,'
Abbot Servillius replied, 'and allow the gatekeeper to escort
you to my study where I could have greeted you as custom
prescribes. If you prefer to march into this *refectorium* unan-
nounced with belligerence in your voice, then you will find
it takes a while for us to remember our manners.'

'Why should I wait when I knew this was the hour of your
evening meal and when my companion and I are famished?'

'If it is hospitality that you are requesting, Britmund of
Placentia, then we are not heretics enough to deny it to you.
You will find space at that table,' the abbot indicated a table
on the right-hand side of the hall. 'Sit yourselves there and
one of the brethren will provide you and your companion
with food and drink.'

For a moment Bishop Britmund stood defiantly before the
abbot, having expected to be invited to sit at his table by
virtue of his rank. But the abbot had still not risen nor given
the conventional greeting to a cleric of rank; a matter that
intrigued as well as surprised Fidelma. Clearly, no love was
lost between the abbot and the bishop.

'You seek something else, Britmund?' the abbot inquired
mildly. 'Perhaps you came to ask after the health of Brother
Ruadán?'

'That old fool!' replied the bishop harshly. 'Does he still
live?'

For a moment, Fidelma could not believe what the bishop
had said. She found her hands clenching under the table, a
flush coming to her cheeks.

The abbot was speaking before her anger broke out. '*Deo favente,* he lives – no thanks to those whom you stirred up with your fanatical zeal to attack him.' Abbot Servillius' voice was studied and calm, but it was clear that there was hatred behind his words.

'I speak as I find,' replied the bishop indifferently. 'The old man provoked the attack himself by preaching those ideas which we find repugnant in Placentia. He should have kept out of our city.'

'If you find his preaching so repugnant, Britmund, why do you enter here, into this abbey which you call heretical?'

'I am here, reluctantly, at the invitation of the Lord Radoald.'

There was a collective gasp among the brethren in the hall.

'An invitation from Lord Radoald of Trebbia?' asked Magister Ado sharply.

Bishop Britmund smiled thinly at him. 'I know of no other lord of this valley . . . yet.'

'And why would Lord Radoald ask you to come here?' demanded the abbot.

'We left him only this morning, having enjoyed his hospitality last night,' intervened the Magister Ado. 'He made no mention of such a request to me.'

'I am not privy to Lord Radoald's thoughts as to why he should not mention the matter to you, Ado,' replied Bishop Britmund. 'Perhaps he is aware of your facility to use all means in your power to attack those of my faith. However, being lord of this valley, he says he desires peace between those of your creed and those of mine. He asked me to come here so that you, Servillius, and I may discuss a common ground under him as mediator. I am told that he should be at the abbey at first light tomorrow to facilitate these discussions.'

'It would have been better had he informed us of your impending arrival,' muttered Abbot Servillius, 'and the subject of your coming.'

A look of triumph seemed to flit across his features as Bishop Britmund regarded the abbot. 'Perhaps he thought that you might absent yourself from any discussion had you had warning of it?'

Abbot Servillius' jaw tightened. 'I would never absent myself from any debate on the true Faith,' he grunted.

'Then I and my companion shall expect the hospitality of this abbey for as long as these discussions take.'

Abbot Servillius looked towards Brother Wulfila, seated on the other side of Fidelma, before he answered. 'Our evening meal is in progress. You are welcome to join us. Afterwards, we may make the necessary arrangements.'

Bishop Britmund bowed ironically towards the abbot, as if he had enjoyed the verbal duel. Then he moved away with Brother Godomar to the empty seats which had been indicated. It was at this moment that Fidelma became aware that Sister Gisa had risen from her place and was trying to attract the attention of the steward. There were some sharp exchanges and she saw the girl press a paper into Brother Wulfila's hand. The steward examined it and muttered something before rising and going to the abbot's side. Abbot Servillius glanced at the paper and his face grew grim. There was a further exchange and the steward returned and seemed to instruct Sister Gisa to sit back down in her place.

As the abbot was whispering intently to Magister Ado, Fidelma turned to the Venerable Ionas. 'Who is this Bishop Britmund?' She knew she had heard the name before and was trying to recall when.

'He is an Arian, a follower of Arius, and an enemy to our

abbey,' answered the old scholar, who was clearly troubled. 'He is Bishop of Placentia, a town which lies beyond the mouth of the valley by the great River Padus. He and our abbot are almost sworn enemies. Many of our brethren have been attacked when trying to preach in Placentia.'

'Including Brother Ruadán?' she asked.

'Including Brother Ruadán,' he replied quietly.

Abbot Servillius then turned to Venerable Ionas and spoke swiftly to him. The abbot was looking worried. Having ended his conversation with the Venerable Ionas, he rose and went to have a whispered exchange with Lady Gunora. Next he came to Brother Wulfila, who respectfully rose from his seat. Fidelma could hear their whispers behind her.

'You will have to find somewhere for the bishop and his companion to stay. Anywhere but in the guest-house.'

'Not the guest-house?'

'It would be wise to keep the bishop and his companion as far apart from Lady Gunora and her charge as possible.'

'Of course, Father Abbot. I will arrange accommodation in the west tower.' It seemed that the steward was no longer interested in his food because he left the *refectorium* to fulfil his task. Fidelma had observed that these movements were not lost on the dark eyes of Bishop Britmund, who had followed the abbot with an expression almost of derision on his features. Fidelma leaned towards the Venerable Ionas.

'Did this Bishop Britmund have a hand in the injuries suffered by Brother Ruadán?'

'Not personally,' the elderly scholar assured her. 'Britmund is a man who preaches with the violence of words against those who hold to the Nicene Creed. He lights a fire in the mind and lets the people do the rest.'

'The abbot obviously fears he might intend harm to the young prince.'

'It is possible,' admitted the Venerable Ionas reluctantly.

'But the boy is the son of his own king!' She found the idea incredible.

'There is rumour that Bishop Britmund is a supporter of Perctarit, the enemy of Grimoald.'

'Then you believe he is here for a purpose other than discussing matters of Faith?'

The scholar smiled sadly. 'That is exactly what I do believe. I think he came here to learn if the prince had truly been given sanctuary here.'

'The logic would be that Lord Radoald has some hand in this.' Fidelma was recalling the exchange she had witnessed during the night at Radoald's fortress. 'It is strange that the abbot was not informed of this meeting to which Bishop Britmund has been summoned.'

Venerable Ionas nodded. 'We should have been. It seems that Lord Radoald had written him a note which was entrusted to Sister Gisa to deliver. She neglected to do so – until Britmund's arrival reminded her. Doubtless, she will be reprimanded. But Radoald is trustworthy. His family have always been strong supporters of Grimoald and this abbey. Radoald has only been Lord of Trebbia for a few years. He went off to fight with his father, Lord Billo, in Grimoald's wars. The father did not return and thus Radoald became Lord. Billo was a great loss. He was a very cultured man, well read and with a good musical ability. However, Lord Radoald aspires to rule the valley as his father would have done.'

Fidelma reflected for a moment and then said, 'The bishop was curiously satisfied to see Magister Ado in the abbey.'

'Magister Ado is no friend of his,' replied Venerable Ionas.

'Therefore, like others in this abbey, we have to be careful of this wolf in bishop's clothing.'

Abbot Servillius overheard the last part of the conversation and now entered it with a serious smile. 'There are many things that I would not put past Britmund. He is a fanatic. However, it is his words that beget violence – he would not use physical violence himself. At least we are warned and shall keep a close watch on our unwelcome guests.'

Fidelma glanced across to where Bishop Britmund and his companion were eating with apparent unconcern at the furore they had created. There being nothing else to do, Fidelma continued to finish her meal and, as it came to an end, Brother Wulfila reappeared. He approached the abbot and she could hear him say softly, 'It has all been arranged, Father Abbot. A chamber has been prepared for the bishop while his companion may sleep in the main dormitory.'

'And . . . ?' prompted the abbot, glancing up at him.

'I have ensured that the bishop and his companion are placed far away from Lady Gunora and the prince. Brother Bladulf and I will take it in turns to be outside their chamber during the night and keep watch.'

'That is good. A blessing on you,' muttered the abbot.

Fidelma watched Brother Wulfila hurry away. Venerable Ionas saw the frown on her face. 'Brother Wulfila is a good man, even though he has been with us but a short time. He is a former military man who still thinks in such terms, but perhaps that is what is needed in being steward of an abbey.'

'It seems dramatic,' replied Fidelma.

'You are a stranger here, lady,' Venerable Ionas pointed out. 'Abbot Servillius is answerable for the boy's safety to his father, the King.'

'You take this threat that seriously?' she pressed.

'We must be prepared,' the old scholar answered.

Without further ado, the abbot rose and raised his hand. A silence fell among the brethren. Then Abbot Servillius intoned the words of the dismissal and the meal ended with two chimes on the bell.

Fidelma was expected to accompany the brethren to the chapel for the last service of the day. She hesitated at first, wondering whether it might not be the ideal moment to seize the opportunity to speak again to Brother Ruadán without the presence of Brother Hnikar. She was curious to find out what he had meant by his warning of evil and his insistence that she leave the abbey at once. But then she realised that her absence would be immediately noticed and commented on. In fact, Sister Gisa made a point of joining her so that she could accompany her to the section of the chapel set aside for the Sisters of the community. The girl was obviously upset at her lapse of memory.

'I had the note in my *marsupium*,' she confided in Fidelma. 'I meant to hand it over straight way, but Brother Wulfila annoyed me by dismissing me at the gates and I forgot all about the note until this evening.'

Fidelma distracted her by seeking information about the chapel. Once settled in the building, Fidelma realised that Lady Gunora and her charge were not in attendance. She caught sight of Bishop Britmund also peering around as if trying to identify them.

Fidelma found the rituals curious in that she had expected the famous abbey to manifest some of the rules and practices with which she was familiar. After all, Columbanus had established the abbey and she had presumed he had done so on the rules he had brought from the Five Kingdoms. Then she recalled that he seemed to favour the Penitentials. Any resemblances to the rules and laws of her own land were no longer recognisable. She also remembered that Magister Ado had told her that the abbey had adopted the Rule of Benedict.

She noticed other differences too, such as the abbot conducting the service from the front of the altar and not from behind it, and the language of the liturgy being the Latin of the day and not the original Greek of the Gospels. After the service, she found out from Sister Gisa that many years ago, Pope Theodore had recognised the abbots of Bobium as bishops, and made them powerful among the church leaders. It was no wonder that Abbot Servillius scorned the anger of Bishop Britmund. When the abbot came to conduct the service, Fidelma saw that he wore a mitre, a ceremonial headdress named from the Greek word, which was not used in the churches of Hibernia. Abbots and bishops wore crowns instead of mitres, although they did carry a pastoral stick known as the *cambutta*.

In most churches and abbeys of her land, the Mass was not a daily occurrence but usually conducted only on a Sunday, and then at daybreak rather than at any other time. It was as she was considering these matters that Fidelma realised that she truly felt what she was – a stranger in a strange land. She had a sense of not belonging which she had never felt with such depth before, even when she was in the kingdom of the Angles or during the time she had spent in Rome. She knew that it was logical to feel homesick, yet there was something else that made her mood black and created a longing to be elsewhere.

She realised, suddenly and with some surprise, that she was missing the companionship of Brother Eadulf. She felt uncomfortable, for she did not want to admit that she missed the company of the Saxon monk, his sense of humour and

the pertinence of his comments. She smiled as she acknowledged that he would protest that he was an Angle, not a
Saxon, coming from the land of the South Folk at Seaxmund's
Ham. To her eyes, whether people were Angle or Saxon, they
were both Saxon, both *Sasanach*. To Eadulf there was always
a difference and he pointed out that the various kingdoms
carved out on the island of Britain were divided by such
differences, and Angle and Saxon were often at war with one
another.

Fidelma found herself sighing, unable to shake the curious
feeling of isolation. She was roused from her reverie on
hearing the abbot intoning the words: '*Ite, missa est*' which
announced the end of the service.

As she was leaving the chapel with Sister Gisa, they passed
Bishop Britmund and his companion, Brother Godomar. The
bishop's black pebble eyes seemed to fasten on them. Then
she realised that the man's gaze was fixed on her companion
rather than herself. Fidelma felt Sister Gisa shiver slightly at
her side. She said quickly: 'You will forgive me, Sister
Fidelma. I have duties to fulfil. I will bid you a good night.'
So saying, she turned and hurried off across the courtyard
and out of the abbey gates. Puzzled, Fidelma turned back
and saw that the bishop and his companion had waylaid the
Venerable Ionas and their voices were tinged with barely
controlled anger. She presumed it was a continuance of the
argument of their different theologies.

Now she began to realise that ever since she had reached
the abbey, there had been this underlying sense of evil; a
menacing atmosphere which she could not analyse exactly.
She had never known that brooding feeling before, even
though she had come across evil many times in her career
as a *dálaigh*, an advocate in the courts of the Five Kingdoms.

Since she had qualified to the level of *anruth*, one degree below the second highest that the secular and ecclesiastical colleges of Ireland could bestow, she had come across bizarre murders and crimes which she had been able to resolve, sometimes under threat of her own life. It had taken her eight years of study at the school of the Brehon Morann at Tara and she had never felt happier than when faced with a mystery to resolve. But now – now she was unsure what the mystery was. It seemed to simply be the threat of violence between two sects who could not agree whether God existed as one entity or as three.

If she was honest, she was not passionate about the matter; not even passionate about religion. For Fidelma, her passion was law and the principles of justice. Why, then, had she become a religieuse? She might have been the daughter of Failbe Flann, the King of Muman, but her father had died when she was hardly more than a baby, and the kingship had passed to her cousin. Kingship in her land was just as much an electoral system as it was hereditary from the bloodline of the last legal King. That was why her brother, Colgú, was the heir apparent to the kingship and not King. It meant that she had determined to make her own way, using her gifts in law, rather than beg some office from her cousin.

It had been an elderly cousin, Laisran, Abbot of Darú, who had suggested that she join the Abbey of Cill Dara – the Abbey of the Blessed Brigit – as many professionals often did. They had need of someone with legal qualifications. She did so, with almost immediate regret, and soon after left the abbey to accept commissions to represent the prelates of the Five Kingdoms who sought the use of her talents. The last commission had entailed a pilgrimage to Rome to present an abbey Rule for the Holy Father's approval. And thus she had found herself here in Bobium. The only positive development in her journeying had been to attend the Council at Streonshalh, among the Angles, where a debate had taken place between those who favoured the Rule of Rome and those who wanted to maintain the Rule of Colm Cille. That was when she had first met Eadulf.

She compressed her lips for a moment, wondering why she kept thinking about Eadulf. He believed in the Rule of Rome. Not that it bothered her, but it was not what she had been raised to believe. She was confused. She did not really care either way. There were those who believed in one God, Who begat the Son and the Holy Spirit, and those who believed that God was Three in One. Surely, there was no need to kill one another over that?

She suddenly shivered. The hour was growing late and she had been sitting on a stone bench in the courtyard, absorbed in her reflections. She glanced around almost with guilt. A few torches had been lit to illuminate the courtyard but there was no one about. She realised that she had been interrupted in her intention to see Brother Ruadán. Now she tried to remember the way to his sick-chamber, but found that she only knew the way to it from her own chamber.

She went swiftly along the passages and stairs that led to her quarters in the guest-hostel, paused before her door, then took a deep breath and moved on. She was halfway down the dark stone passageway when a door opened right beside her. There was no hiding as the light shone out into the gloom of the passage, directly on to her.

Almost at once, a voice called from further along the passage: 'Who is it? Is aught amiss?'

She recognised Brother Wulfila, as the steward came hurrying forward, holding a lamp in his hand. She had forgotten that he had said that he and the gatekeeper would stand watch outside Lady Gunora's chamber.

'It is all right,' Lady Gunora's voice echoed across her shoulder. Fidelma glanced up. The Lady Gunora was standing in the doorway. The steward had turned and gone back to his position at the end of the passage. Fidelma almost sighed with relief, for had she passed to the end of the corridor it would have been difficult for her to explain herself to Brother Wulfila.

'Sister Fidelma – or should I say Lady Fidelma? I would speak with you.'

Fidelma inclined her head to the Longobard noblewoman. 'I have no preference other than Fidelma,' she smiled.

The woman glanced up and down the corridor and then said, 'Come in for a moment in case we disturb Brother Wulfila again. The abbot recommends him highly. He was a warrior in the war against Perctarit, so takes his job as a guard seriously.'

Fidelma had no option but to step inside the chamber. Young Prince Romuald lay on a bed in a corner, fast asleep. Another bed, presumably for the use of Lady Gunora, stood in the other corner but it showed no sign of having been disturbed.

'How may I help you, lady?' asked Fidelma, keeping her voice low.

Lady Gunora paused for a moment as if trying to think of the correct way of expressing her thoughts. 'I just wanted to warn you, Fidelma. You are the daughter of a king and we of noble blood have a duty to one another.'

Fidelma stared at her in surprise. 'To warn me?' she repeated.

'You do not belong here, lady. It is best that you leave this valley as soon as possible.'

'I do not understand. As for belonging, my countrymen established this abbey. My good friend and mentor, Brother Ruadán, is the reason that I came here in the first place. He is old and, I am told, is not much longer for this world. I intend to leave in my own time.'

Lady Gunora clasped her hands in front of her and looked sad. 'I meant no insult. But I fear the coming storm, lady, which might sweep all things from its path – this abbey, this valley . . . everything.'

'I still don't understand.'

'These years have seen much bloodshed across these mountains and valleys. His father,' she nodded to the sleeping Romuald, 'is not a bad king, but he had to fight his way to power at the cost of much blood. Even at this moment he is in the south of this land keeping our enemies there at bay. Now we hear that the former joint king Perctarit has recrossed the great mountains from Frankia and is coming to seek vengeance.'

'I have heard these stories from Magister Ado and others,' Fidelma confirmed.

Lady Gunora gave a brief smile. 'Magister Ado? Many good things are said of him. But do not trust anyone. Not the abbot, nor Ado, nor Ionas. There is evil here, lady. That is what I wanted to warn you of and to entreat you to leave at once.'

Fidelma was quiet for a moment or so. What the woman was saying was more or less what poor old Brother Ruadán had said. Now she was really intrigued.

'Do you know Brother Ruadán?' she asked suddenly.

Lady Gunora nodded quickly. 'Most people from here to Placentia know of him, for in spite of his age, he has travelled many a road bringing the true Faith.'

'So you are no follower of Arius?'

'You know of this conflict?' Once again she looked to the sleeping boy. 'His father, Grimoald, believes in the teachings of Arius of Alexandria. But he married a woman who upholds the Creed of Nicaea and the authority of the Holy Father in Rome. Grimoald rules with a liberal hand. So far as his rule is concerned, it is left to individuals to follow the Faith in whatever way they wish. But it will be better if the boy does not fall into the hands of Perctarit.'

'And you think that if the followers of Arius get hold of the boy, they will betray him to this Perctarit? That sounds illogical, if his father is of their faith.'

'I know it, lady. Religion has nothing to do with it. Power is everything. Britmund and his lackey Godomar would do anything in the hope they can persuade Perctarit to grant favours. Grimoald has already made clear he will not support one side over another in this theological argument. Beware of Bishop Britmund, lady. He is an ambitious man.'

'Yet he is a man of the Faith, sworn to follow the path of Christ, which is peace.'

Lady Gunora uttered an ugly laugh that surprised Fidelma.

'Peace? I often wonder why we have cast out the old gods and goddesses. Did not the Christ say, according to the words of Matthew, "I am not come to send peace on earth; I come not to send peace but a sword . . . to set man at variance with his father and daughter against mother, and daughter-in-law against her mother-in-law. He that loves his father and mother more than me is not worthy of me, and he that loves his son and daughter more than me is not worthy of me." Peace? Are those the words of a peace-maker? Are those the words that men such as Britmund roar to entice people to take arms against one another?'

Fidelma hesitated; she was astonished by the words and, not having heard them before, decided she must look up this text.

'Do you not feel safe here?' she asked.

'I am afraid for the Prince. He is the responsibility that his mother gave to me before she left to join Grimoald in the south. I fear for his safety, just as I fear there is a storm of blood approaching. I just wanted to warn you, Fidelma of Hibernia, to leave this place as soon as you can.'

Fidelma found herself outside the door in a black mood. It seemed everyone was warning her. But she had a purpose to fulfil and, perhaps, that would provide her with the answer to it. She looked along the corridor. Sitting on a stool at the end of it, with the fluttering lamp at his feet, sat Brother Wulfila. His hands were folded across his stomach and he seemed to be nodding sleepily. Even if he were sound asleep, there was no way of getting past him without disturbance. She stood for a moment, her lips compressed in annoyance. Well, there was no question of pursuing her intention. She would wait until the morning and hope that Brother Wulfila would leave his sentinel's post early.

ChAPTER SIX

Fidelma was up, washed and dressed before first light. She left her room silently, pausing to glance up and down the corridor. She hoped that Brother Wulfila had decided, with dawn approaching, that there was no need to keep guard in the corridor outside Lady Gunora's chamber. There was no sign of anyone. She took her leather-soled sandals from her feet, so that their sound would not alert anyone, shivering for a moment as she felt the cold stone of the flags on her soles. She could hear the faint movements of the abbey stirring to life and moved cautiously forward, still holding her sandals in one hand.

She was passing the chamber where she had spoken with Lady Gunora the night before when she paused with a puzzled frown. The door of the chamber was slightly ajar. All was quiet. She pushed it open and glanced inside. The room was empty and there were signs of a hurried departure. A chair was overturned, and blankets and pillows were still strewn on the floor. But there was no sign of any personal possessions nor bags, which she had seen when Lady Gunora had invited her inside.

Fidelma examined the room closely. Lady Gunora and

the young prince had obviously vacated the chamber in great haste. Then, recalling that she had a more important mission than getting involved in this new mystery, Fidelma drew the door back to its original position and made her way cautiously to the end of the passage. There was no sign of Brother Wulfila. The passages were deserted. She encountered no one on the way to Brother Ruadán's chamber.

Fidelma entered the room quietly. It was now bathed in a soft early-morning light. The frail form of Brother Ruadán lay still on the bed, his breath shallow and asthmatic.

'Brother Ruadán,' she whispered as loudly as she could.

The breath caught for a moment. At least it showed that Brother Ruadán was awake and had heard her. The old face on the pillow turned slowly towards her. She moved to the side of the bed.

'It is I, Fidelma.'

'You came back?' The words emerged in a difficult, wheezy fashion. 'I . . . I thought I had dreamed your being here yesterday.'

She sat down on the edge of the bed and took one of his cold, parchment-textured hands in her own.

'I am here. You seemed agitated when I came before.'

'Is there anyone with you? I cannot see clearly.' The pale eyes darted nervously around the room.

'We are entirely alone,' she assured him. 'What troubles you?'

'What are you doing here – here in Bobium?'

'I was travelling to Massilia but my ship was damaged in a storm. So I was stranded in Genua. I met Magister Ado and was told that you were here in this abbey and so I came to visit you. I am distressed to find you so unwell.'

There was a long, wheezy sigh from the old man.

'I am distressed that you should find me at all. My time is nearly done. There is evil here and, I fear, much danger. Be advised, return to Genua as soon as you can. Continue your journey home and forget this place.'

'And desert you to this evil without help? Come, tell me what this is all about and I will see if I can help you.'

'There is no help for me,' the sick man whispered. 'I shall soon be at rest. I have one thing to ask of you . . .'

'Whatever I can do for my old master, I shall do,' replied Fidelma firmly.

'When you return home, light a candle in the little chapel on Inis Celtra and pray for the repose of my soul.'

'You are not dead yet,' she averred in a strong tone, trying to fight back the tears that were welling in her eyes.

'By the time you reach Genua, I shall be so,' he sighed.

There was a sound from the corridor outside, the slap of leather sandals on stone as one of the brethren passed by. Fidelma felt the old hand gain a sudden strength as it caught on her own.

'You must believe me, Fidelma.' The voice was a hoarse whisper. 'For the love I bore your late father, King Failbe Flann, believe me. I fear you will be in danger. They tried to kill me. They have already killed the boy to maintain his silence. They will not think twice about killing you. They know I have seen the gold. They know I suspect them – that is why I shall soon be dead.'

'The boy?' Fidelma was suddenly aghast. 'Do you mean Prince Romuald?'

The old man shook his head with a vehemence of which Fidelma had not thought him capable.

'No, no, no. I mean the goatherd.'

Fidelma was confused. 'The goatherd? Who are "they" and why should a goatherd be killed? Tell me what you mean.'

The figure again gave a deep wheezy sigh. 'I grow tired and weak. I am confused. The less you know, the better. Just leave this place as soon as you can.'

'Are you saying that you expect to be killed by whoever it is you speak of?' she insisted.

'Killed?' muttered Brother Ruadán in an absent-minded tone. 'The boy . . . poor little Wamba. He did not deserve to die because he had the coins. Dead. Ancient gold – I saw it. What evil can be disguised in a mausoleum.'

'I don't understand.'

There was another noise in the corridor and this time she heard the voice of Brother Hnikar speaking loudly to someone. It was obvious that it would be better if the apothecary did not find her in the *cubiculum* of Brother Ruadán. She leaned over her former tutor.

'I will come back later when there is less likelihood of being interrupted. Then we will talk more of this, Brother Ruadán,' she whispered in his ear. She placed his hand back by his side and moved silently towards the door, pausing and listening at it without opening it.

The voice of Brother Hnikar had grown faint but she could still hear it not far away. She carefully opened the door a fraction and peered through the crack. There was no one in her range of vision so she opened it wider and glanced out. Some short distance along the passage a door was open and it was from there she could hear the voice of the apothecary. She slid into the corridor and gently closed the door behind her and then moved quickly along to where another corridor branched off at a right angle. Only when she turned into it and was thus obscured from the vision of

Brother Hnikar, if he returned to the main corridor, did she relax a little.

She paused for a moment, frowning. Instead of resolving her original questions, she was now filled with many more and she felt frustrated. A bell started to sound and members of the brethren were now moving about. Two of them passed her, glancing down at her feet with some degree of amusement. It was only then that she noticed that she was still holding her sandals in one hand and that her feet were bare. Embarrassed, she slipped the sandals on before realising that the tolling of the bell announced the first meal of the day. She followed the brethren, knowing they would lead her to the *refectorium*.

She saw Brother Bladulf, the gatekeeper, coming towards her. He stopped and bowed his head in salutation.

'I was coming to make sure you knew your way, Sister.' He turned, guiding her to the hall. She was led to the abbot's table. It was deserted apart from the Venerable Ionas. She glanced quickly around the *refectorium*. Sister Gisa was with her fellow Sisters in their corner and Brother Faro was in his place. Of Bishop Britmund and his companion there was no sign. She exchanged a greeting with Venerable Ionas and sat down. The old scholar rose and, in the absence of the abbot, intoned the *gratias* or grace. Then he sat down and there was a single chime of the bell and the meal began.

'Is it unusual that so many senior clerics are missing from the first meal of the day?' she asked.

Venerable Ionas smiled. 'It is unusual,' he agreed. 'A rider has brought word that Lord Radoald is expected soon and Abbot Servillius is making preparations for the meeting. Personally, I do not think there can be any satisfactory outcome.'

Fidelma had heard enough of the problems between the factions and concentrated on her meal. She was leaving the hall when there came the unexpected sound of a trumpet. She had emerged at the top of steps leading to the courtyard just in time to see Brother Wulfila hurrying to the gates of the abbey. As she stood watching, Abbot Servillius with Venerable Ionas beside him appeared on the steps.

Four horsemen entered through the gates and halted in the courtyard. Their leader was immediately recognisable as Radoald, Lord of Trebbia, and behind him, on his pale-grey steed, was the warrior Wulfoald. They all dismounted, and while Lord Radoald and Wulfoald came forward, the others took charge of the horses. The abbot hurried down to greet the newcomers. Fidelma remained at the head of the steps. She observed that Bishop Britmund and his companion had also emerged to greet the Lord of Trebbia and Wulfoald. The abbot was leading the newcomers back and Radoald, catching sight of Fidelma, raised a hand in greeting but passed on without speaking. Wulfoald merely glanced distantly at her. Greetings were being exchanged with Bishop Britmund and Brother Godomar and then they all moved inside.

Fidelma stood uncertainly, wondering what to do next. Brother Faro had been speaking with another of the brethren and, ending his conversation, came towards her. She noticed that he was still wearing his arm in a sling.

'How is your wound today, Brother?' Fidelma smiled in greeting.

'God be praised, Sister, it is much, much better. A little sore but healing exactly as Brother Hnikar foretold.'

'I am pleased to hear it.'

Magister Ado had appeared and, looking about, came directly

towards them. Immediately, Brother Faro said nervously: 'If you will both excuse me, I am reminded that I have to meet with— that I have to see someone.'

Fidelma watched him hurrying away with some surprise but Magister Ado came to a halt beside her and gave a soft chuckle.

'The boy is in love,' he explained softly.

'Sister Gisa?'

'It is obvious,' affirmed the elderly religieux. 'While there is no restriction about consorting, Abbot Servillius, as you know, is of the school that favours the segregation of the sexes in the religious life. Poor Gisa and Faro, they try hard to maintain their secret. Thankfully, Abbot Servillius is not so perceptive in that field.'

'I understand.'

'It is a good day, Sister Fidelma,' Magister Ado said, changing the subject and glancing at the bright blue canopy of the sky. 'I *would* have suggested that you might like to take the opportunity to see the abbey's *herbarium*. We are very proud of our herb garden. It is tended by one of the Hibernian brethren that are still among us – Brother Lonán. Better to be out on a day like this than inside in gloom.'

'This might not be the best time to absent oneself in the gardens,' observed Fidelma. 'However, you used a conditional form. You *would* have suggested it but for what?'

Magister Ado was amused. 'You do have a sharp ear. But I think I shall be called to take part in this meeting, which will be a waste of time.'

'You seem sure of that. I mean, that it will be a waste of time.'

'I am certain of it. Trying to make peace with Britmund is like trying to catch an eel with your bare hands.'

Brother Wulfila emerged from the main door, glanced round and came hurrying towards them, slightly out of breath.

'Magister Ado, the meeting is about to begin and the abbot requests your presence immediately in his chamber.' Then, to her surprise, he turned to Fidelma. 'The abbot especially asks for your presence as well, Sister Fidelma.'

'As I said, a waste of time, but for the sake of Lord Radoald, we must pretend,' muttered Magister Ado as he led the way after the scurrying form of Brother Wulfila.

When the steward showed them into the abbot's chamber they found Radoald and Wulfoald there with Venerable Ionas. Bishop Britmund and his companion Brother Godomar were also present. Abbot Servillius had, surprisingly, vacated his chair to allow Radoald to be centrally seated with Wulfoald, the young warrior, standing behind him. On the left, Bishop Britmund sat, with his companion behind him. Abbot Servillius, with Venerable Ionas, were seated on his right, facing them. As they entered, the abbot signalled to Magister Ado to seat himself to his left. Brother Wulfila guided Fidelma to a seat at the end of the chamber and sat next to her. Bishop Britmund watched her, brows gathered in a frown of disapproval.

Lord Radoald gave a quick glance, encompassing them all. 'As you were informed, Bishop Britmund has come to this place, at my request to see if there are ways, if not of agreeing with the different interpretations of the Faith, then at least finding a consensus by which some of the antagonisms that have prevailed in this valley may be overcome. A *modus vivendi* of obtaining peace. I sit here as your civil lord, sworn to maintain the peace of this valley. It is now up to you, Abbot Servillius, and to you Bishop Britmund, to agree how we may take this forward.'

Bishop Britmund, features set in harsh lines, immediately indicated Fidelma. 'What is that Hibernian woman doing here?' he snapped.

In fact, Fidelma was about to ask the same question.

'The presence of the Lady Fidelma of Hibernia was requested by myself,' replied Lord Radoald in an easy tone. 'In this matter Abbot Servillius agreed.'

Fidelma herself was surprised at the answer.

'Requested? The bishop's tone rose, showing his annoyance. 'Why so? I thought Abbot Servillius disagreed with women taking any degree of office in the churches and, furthermore, believed in the segregation of the sexes. What trickery is this? Does the woman practise witchery over you?'

Fidelma had not liked the bishop previously and now she found a resentment growing within her. She was about to speak when Radoald responded.

'Fidelma of Hibernia is the daughter of a king of her country. We have heard that she now stands in high regard with the Holy Father himself, having recently been in Rome. One of the brethren of this abbey returned from Rome recently and has informed us that she is trained in the law of her land, played a role in the Council at Streonshalh, in the land of the Angles, when a debate of differences in the Faith was held. That experience alone stands her in good stead to sit and consider our discussion and perhaps offer advice. Is that not so, Father Abbot?'

'It is so,' agreed Abbot Servillius. 'But, furthermore, Fidelma of Hibernia is a lawyer of her kingdom's law system and one whose advice is based on logic.'

'She is not a lawyer of our laws,' snapped Bishop Britmund. 'I object!'

'Is that your only reason for objecting?' inquired Radoald.

'I have already conversed with the lady Fidelma and found her to have a most remarkable approach to controversial matters. I am content that she remain and if she can cast light upon our path to resolve these differences, then neither side shall lose.'

Bishop Britmund saw that he was not going to have Fidelma removed and muttered sullenly, 'My objection has been registered.'

'And I have taken it under consideration and find it irrelevant,' smiled Radoald. 'Lady Fidelma, do you have any objection in sitting amongst us and offering opinion based on your experience of previous debates?'

Fidelma considered her involvement for a moment and then said, 'If I can be of any help, I am, of course, willing to be so.'

She settled herself in her chair next to Brother Wulfila to watch the proceedings with interest. Thankfully, all the discussions were to be in Latin.

'It grieves me,' began Radoald, 'as Lord of Trebbia, that there is conflict among the religious of this land. While the religious can resort to words with which to fight, often the people, stirred by those same words, use physical means which inflict pain and injury on others. We come together to see if we might find some resolution of these matters so that my people might live in harmony. That is the purpose of this meeting. Is it so agreed, Abbot Servillius?'

The abbot inclined his head to Radoald. 'It is so agreed.'

'Is it so agreed, Bishop Britmund?'

The stocky bishop emulated the abbot but not in the same words. 'That is why I have agreed to come to this house of heresy,' he replied belligerently.

There was a hiss of outrage from the abbot but Venerable

Ionas caught the abbot's arm, as if to prevent him from rising to respond.

'This discussion must be made in tones of conciliation,' Radoald rebuked the bishop.

'Yet before we can reach that point of discussion, the differences between us must be made clear,' snapped the bishop. It soon became obvious that when Bishop Britmund spoke he had the frustrating habit of not allowing anyone to interrupt him, continuing to talk in deep stentorian tones over them until he had finished whatever point he was making.

'I would have thought the differences are obvious,' replied Abbot Servillius. 'We accept the Holy Trinity, God the Father, God the Son and God the Holy Spirit. The teachings of Arius the Alexandrian have been declared a heresy.'

'He was exonerate at the Council of Tyre,' rejoined the bishop.

'And condemned as a heretic yet again at the Council in Constantinople,' argued the abbot.

Radoald held up a hand. 'My friends, I do not think a history of the decisions of councils in various parts of the world will add to our understanding of the current situation.'

'We must be clear about this,' Bishop Britmund continued. 'There is only one God Who created all things. He was eternal, always existing. But Jesus was the incarnate Son of God, and could not have had existence eternally, not being born before time began and before God created all things. Being the Son of God he, too, must have been created by God. Does not the Blessed Paul say in his letter to the Corinthians that there is one God, the Father, from Whom comes all things? Does Blessed John not point out that Jesus Himself said that His Father was "greater than I"?'

'We are not here to debate these matters of interpretation,' replied the abbot sharply. 'Our Faith was proclaimed at the Council of Nicaea, when the work of Arius was declared heretical. We believe in the divinity of the Holy Trinity. God as Three in One. It is from Nicaea that we take our creed, believing that the Father, Son and Holy Spirit are of the same substance – *homoousios* – that is, of one being.'

'There are enough proofs of our arguments in the Gospels, in the writings of Luke and in the Acts of the Apostles,' replied the bishop with equal firmness. 'We believe in one God. We believe Christ, being the Son of God, is subject and obedient in all things to God His Father. We believe the Holy Spirit is subject and obedient in all things to Jesus and to His Father. The Son and Holy Spirit were created by God. God is eternal and unbegotten, always existing.'

Fidelma was intrigued. As one who prided herself on her logic, she found the argument of Bishop Britmund curiously rational.

Radoald once again held up his hand for silence. 'You have stated the irreconcilable differences of interpretation between you. And we are well aware of them. But the matter at this meeting is how we may come to a practical tolerance in this valley between these two views so that no one walks in fear from those with whom they disagree.'

'We shall not reject our faith and beliefs for they are those approved by the Holy Father in Rome,' declared Abbot Servillius firmly.

'Nor shall we reject the Truth,' replied Bishop Britmund with equal determination.

Radoald sighed impatiently. 'No one is asking you to reject or embrace anything, except that you must find a course in which tolerance binds you and not hatred.'

'Then let the members of this abbey begin,' said Bishop

Britmund. 'Let them cease to preach against us in Placentia. Let them cease travelling to the surrounding towns and churches and denouncing our beliefs as heresy.'

'Then let those prelates and propounders of your heresy cease to tell people that they will receive the blessings of God if they rise up and destroy us and this abbey,' retorted Abbot Servillius.

Bishop Britmund hesitated for a moment before demanding: 'What accusation is this, Servillius?'

'Do you deny the martial cry from your pulpits?' sneered the abbot. 'We hear them even from behind these ancient walls.'

Bishop Britmund turned to Lord Radoald, his face growing red. 'I did not come here to be falsely accused.'

There was a silence and then Radoald looked towards Fidelma. A smile was on his lips.

'And what do you make of this, lady? Were there ever such diametrically opposed opinions at that Council you attended at Streonshalh?'

Fidelma took a moment's thought and then said, 'The opinions were opposed, certainly, but perhaps presented with a little less emphatic resolve. I thought the purpose here was to find a *via media aurea*, the middle way, which is the golden path where both sides may meet.'

'That was my intention,' agreed Radoald solemnly. 'But, so far, that path appears elusive.'

'It seems that we are stuck in the *via militaris*,' Fidelma acknowledged 'Is it not said that in the middle way stands the truth?'

'There is no middle way,' snapped Bishop Britmund. 'There is either truth or untruth. Truth has no compromise.' He rose abruptly and his companion rose with him. 'I came here at the request of the Lord Radoald. I hoped to see in him the great lord that his father was. Instead I find him besotted by this abbey and its heretical philosophies.'

Wulfoald clapped a hand on his sword hilt and made a threatening movement, but Radoald quickly reached up and seized his warrior by the arm, causing him to halt. But Wulfoald was not to be stopped from speaking.

'Have a care, Bishop, when you insult the Lord of Trebbia. Perctarit's warriors have not yet crossed the mighty Padus to protect you.'

Fidelma noticed that Brother Godomar had also reached forward and was tugging at the sleeve of the bishop's robe. Bishop Britmund's eyes blazed. He seemed to consider for a moment the situation and then he shrugged.

'No insult was meant, Lord Radoald. Forgive my clumsy way of expressing my displeasure. I can see no means for an amicable settlement of our differences here. We stand as firm for our faith as do those of this abbey stand for their heresy. We must accept that our middle path is this promise: if we are attacked, we shall retaliate. *Oculum pro oculo, detem pro dente, manum pro manu, pedem pro pede.'*

'I thought,' Fidelma observed softly but clearly, 'that the Faith, by whatever interpretation you give it, was based on the words and teaching of the Christ?'

Bishop Britmund swung round with anger on his features. 'Are you trying to teach me the Faith, woman of Hibernia?'

'I am merely reminding you that Christ taught that it had, indeed, been said, an eye for an eye, a tooth for a tooth, but He told the faithful to ignore that teaching. Furthermore, He taught them that whoever strikes them on the right cheek, they should turn the other cheek to them.'

Abbot Servillius was smiling in approval as he added, 'It is so stated in the Gospel of Matthew. Perhaps Bishop Britmund is not above denying the teaching of Christ as well as the Creed of Nicaea?'

Bishop Britmund did not conceal his anger. He turned to Lord Radoald. 'I need your guarantee of safe passage back to Placentia.'

Radoald lifted an eyebrow. 'Why so? Were you endangered coming here?'

'It is plain that I stand here unharmed, so no danger came to me on my way here.'

'Then you shall return unharmed. No one here wishes to do you or any member of the Faith physical harm, Britmund.'

The bishop hesitated, as if about to say something more, and then swept from the room, followed by his silent companion, Brother Godomar. Brother Wulfila, as steward, went scurrying after them for it was his task to see them safely from the confines of the abbey.

After they had gone, Abbot Servillius slumped back in his chair and gave a long, deep sigh.

'When the Creator handed out charity, He must have missed giving Britmund a share of it.'

Radoald was rueful. 'I am afraid that this is my fault. I tried to play the peacemaker, having been conscious of what happened to poor Brother Ruadán. I want these attacks to cease.'

Fidelma stirred uncomfortably, remembering how she had seen poor Brother Ruadán lying in his bed, an old man attacked and injured because of the arrogance of Bishop Britmund, a so-called man of God.

'What is more worrying, Radoald, is that such prelates as Britmund may well be placed in a position of power if the stories of Perctarit's return are true,' pointed out Abbot Servillius.

'But we have heard nothing more tangible than rumours of his returning. No details, no hard news,' Wulfoald intervened. It seemed the warrior was comfortable speaking his mind before his lord and the prelates of the abbey. 'There is no need to panic until we have news.'

The abbot seemed irritated as he replied, 'We of Bobium are not panicking but we should be prepared for the worst.'

'We do not accuse you of panic, Abbot Servillius,' Radoald calmed him. 'But we can do nothing until we receive definite news.'

'And how can we obtain that?' replied the abbot petulantly. 'By the sight of Perctarit's army marching up the Trebbia Valley?'

Radoald responded with conviction. 'It is my intention to position some of my men strategically to listen to such rumours, to hear the news and to report back to me of any impending dangers. After all, if Perctarit comes here, he will be seeking revenge. I must remind you that it was my father, when he was Lord of Trebbia, who supported Grimoald in the assassination of Godepert and in forcing his brother, Perctarit, to flee into exile. And was I not fighting at my father's side?'

The abbot looked uncomfortable. 'You are right to rebuke me. I was thinking only of the welfare of this abbey and the brethren.'

'And rightly so, Father Abbot,' replied Radoald. 'A father must think of the welfare of his children.'

There was a brief pause and then Magister Ado intervened. 'Lord Radoald is correct. But we are well protected here in this valley by virtue of it not being on any major route which Perctarit must occupy if he does mean to return to overthrow the King. This valley is of no strategic value.'

'I must take up Magister Ado on his observation that this Valley of the Trebbia is a byway which Perctarit would ignore,' corrected Wulfoald. 'As an historian he has forgotten how strategic this valley was in ancient times.'

'I do not pretend to be an historian,' the elderly religieux said immediately. 'I have only written of the lives of the great founders of the Faith, that is all.'

'Then I crave pardon.' Wulfoald smiled. 'But I have read the Greek Polybius and the Latin of Livy, who came from this very territory. They both gave us their descriptions of the Battle of Trebbia.'

Venerable Ionas spoke for the first time in the exchange. 'Most of us know to what you are alluding, my young warrior friend.' He turned to Fidelma. 'This little peaceful valley was once Gaulish territory, and in the distant days of the Roman Republic, the Romans knew that they had to conquer this land to expand their empire. But it was a long and painful business. Many Roman consuls lost their lives here as well as their legions while trying to subdue the Boii, who were the main people that dwelled here. A former consul, Flaminius, managed to reach Genua along the coast and establish a garrison there, which allowed legionaries to march through this valley on their quest to conquer. Later, it was at the mouth of this very valley that the Carthaginians of Hannibal achieved their first major victory against the Romans – it is still called the Battle of Trebbia.'

Venerable Ionas' voice had risen in enthusiasm and suddenly, realising their eyes were upon him, he hesitated and shrugged with a smile. 'Your pardon again. Sometimes I let my fascination for history, especially of this place, carry me away.'

'May I ask a question?'

They turned to look at Fidelma with interest as she spoke.

'Proceed,' invited Abbot Servillius.

'From what I have been told, your King, Grimoald, is a follower of this Arian Creed. This former King, Perctarit, believes in the Nicene Creed. Am I correct in assuming this?'

'You are correct,' agreed Abbot Servillius.

'Then I am confused. How is it that the Arians, such as Bishop Britmund, would support Perctarit, a Nicenine, should he try to wrest back the throne from which he was deposed? It is not logical.'

Abbot Servillius allowed Radoald to respond.

'Religion plays no part in this struggle for kingship. What you say is true, except that Grimoald is a very liberal King and allows people to follow their own faith, whether it be one of the Christian sects or, indeed, whether they want to stick with their old gods and goddesses. Perctarit, on the other hand, will promise and do whatever it takes for him to reassert his power . . . even to permit Britmund to destory all those in his territories who support the Nicene Creed. We hear rumours that Perctarit is negotiating such an aim to secure support.'

Fidelma was sure she saw something in the glance that Wulfoald exchanged with Radoald. Then Wulfoald was speaking. 'Anyway, if Perctarit crossed into the Valley of the Padus, he would have to march east and deal with Grimoald's Regent, Lupus of Friuli, who commands a large army there. Perctarit could not leave that army unchallenged behind him if he intended to march south against Grimoald. He would have to bribe or destroy Lupus before unleashing his followers on Grimoald and the abbeys and churches that still follow the Creed of Nicaea.'

Fidelma remained quiet. The politics did seem entirely

confusing. But it was not her place to intervene in foreign affairs.

Radoald rose abruptly, and they followed suit.

'Well, we can do no more except watch and hope all our fears are in vain.' He turned to Fidelma with an apologetic expression. 'I am sorry that you witnessed this confrontation, lady. I only insisted that you attend in order to draw on your advice from the confrontation you witnessed at the Abbey of Streonshalh.'

Fidelma contrived to shrug. 'I am only sorry that the positions were so entrenched that my advice would have been superfluous.'

'Have you seen Brother Ruadán?' continued the young lord. 'How is he? I was hoping to speak with him myself but Brother Hnikar says he is too frail.'

'I saw him last night,' Fidelma answered truthfully, not mentioning her morning visit. 'He is, indeed very frail.'

'But still lucid?' pressed Radoald, almost eagerly.

'I find him so,' countered Fidelma with a frown. 'But then we spoke in our own language, which may not stress him as much as talking in another tongue. Anyway, I hope to speak with him later.'

'Brother Hnikar, our physician, expects the worst,' intervened Brother Wulfila, who had now returned to attend to the needs of the others, catching the last remark.

Radoald shook his head sadly. 'You must let me know how his condition fares as I would like to speak with him also. A crime was committed and the culprit must be found and punished. Indeed, perhaps I could send my own apothecary Suidur to assist your Brother Hnikar . . . ?'

'That won't be necessary,' Abbot Servillius said, almost sharply. 'We have faith in Brother Hnikar. I suggest we wait for a while to see if there is an improvement. Brother Hnikar could not even sanction more than one fleeting visit from Sister Fidelma because of Brother Ruadán's weakening condition.'

'I did not mean to imply that your apothecary was lacking,' Radoald replied. 'Only that two heads are sometimes better than one. I will, however, abide by Brother Hnikar's ruling.'

'I do not mean to slight Suidur,' the abbot said. 'But from what I hear, Brother Ruadán is beyond the skill of even the best apothecary. All we can do is wait and pray.'

Although she wanted to comment, Fidelma was again silent, feeling that strange alienation from her surroundings, like someone in an unfamiliar bog land who fears that whatever step she might take would be the one that drags her into the mire.

'We shall stay within the vicinity of Bobium today,' Radoald replied. 'If I hear anything definite about the advance of Perctarit, I shall send one of my men to inform you.'

The farewells were taken in the courtyard and Fidelma stood watching Radoald and Wulfoald join their two companions, mount their horses and ride out through the gates. Abbot Servillius had already turned back to his chamber with Magister Ado and Venerable Ionas. Fidelma was surprised to find Brother Faro once again at her side.

'Well,' he grinned, 'I hear that matters almost came to blows in there. You must find all this very curious.'

'I have grown used to prelates arguing semantics,' Fidelma replied, after a moment's reflection. 'Although, I confess, I have not found the intensity of hatred that I witnessed this morning. I begin to understand why Magister Ado thinks the attacks on him were due to the differences in theological opinion.'

Brother Faro grimaced indifferently. 'At least you are among friends here,' he replied. 'But, if you will excuse me, I have to speak with the steward.'

'Magister Ado had intended to show me the herb gardens when we were called to witness Bishop Britmund's display of bad manners.' Fidelma held him back for a moment. She wanted to take a breath of fresh air after the stuffy atmosphere. 'He seems to have forgotten. Perhaps you can show me the way to it?'

'If you proceed through that archway,' he indicated across the courtyard, 'and follow the path, it will bring you into the herb garden. One of your compatriots, Brother Lonán, tends the garden and will doubtless be better able to explain about it.'

Fidelma had almost forgotten that, as an Irish foundation, there would be others from the Five Kingdoms, apart from Brother Ruadán, in the abbey. As Brother Faro hurried off in search of Brother Wulfila, she crossed the courtyard with a feeling of relief at the idea of seeing and speaking to some of her countrymen again. She was so filled with the thought that she had entirely forgotten about the disappearance of Lady Gunora and her charge, Prince Romuald.

CHAPTER SEVEN

Brother Lonán turned out to be a disappointment. He was an excitable little man whose sole interest appeared to be in the herbs that he grew in a walled garden at the back of the abbey complex. With careful questioning, Fidelma managed to extract the fact that he had originally studied at Cluain Eidnech, the Ivy Meadow, a territory whose chiefs gave nominal allegiance to the King of Muman but, because of its position on the eastern borders, next to the Kingdom of Laighin, that allegiance often vacillated depending on what gain was offered.

'How many of the brethren here are from Hibernia?' she asked as he turned his attention to some shrubs she did not recognise.

'At the moment there are twelve of our compatriots among the brethren,' he replied absently. 'I suppose I have been here the longest now. Of course, all of the original founders have passed on.'

'Do many of our people pass through here on their way to Rome or elsewhere in the south? I am told that many of our *peregrinatio pro Christo* have established themselves in this land.'

The question met with a shrug that indicated he was either uninterested or unconcerned. In fact, all of her questions about life at the abbey and personalities were met with similar indifference, while questions about herbs and other plants were greeted with little bursts of enthusiasm, albeit coupled with longwinded responses. Within half an hour, Fidelma had grown bored and decided to end her visit.

It was while she was making up her mind what excuse she could offer to cut the examination of the herb garden short that another member of the brethren passed by and greeted Brother Lonán in his own language. She turned to examine him. He was a young man with thin pale features, light blue eyes and flaming red hair, almost like her own.

'I recognise your accent, Brother,' she greeted him. 'You are from Muman.'

The young man halted and then apparently recognised her.

'I am Brother Eolann, lady,' he replied. 'I am the *scriptor* here. And you are Sister Fidelma. I saw you in the *refectorium*. It is said you are the daughter of the King at Cashel.'

'My father was Failbe Flann who died when I was young. My brother is Colgú who is now the heir apparent to my cousin, Cathal.'

'Do you bring recent news from my native Muman?'

'Alas, I have been away from Muman for many months, Brother Eolann.'

He sighed. 'I have been away from Muman many years and so whatever news you have, even though out of date, will be news to me. Come, join me in my daily walk and tell me what there is to know of home.'

Fidelma was thankful that the *scriptor* of the abbey might be a more interesting conversationalist than Brother Lonán. The gardener had already wandered off with trowel in hand, seemingly intent in the pursuit of his horticultural tasks. Fidelma turned to the young man. 'Where do you come from, Brother Eolann?'

'From Faithleann's Island – do you know it?' he replied as they fell in step.

'But of course. It is a little wooded island in Loch Léin. Is not your chieftain, my own cousin, Congal of the Eóghanacht? You are a long way from home, as am I. How came you here?'

'That is a story simple to tell, lady. I was a scholar in the abbey on Faithleann's Island and was chosen to take some books to the library of the Abbey of the Blessed Gall.'

'Gall?'

'He was one of the disciples of Colm Bán, whom they called Columbanus here. Indeed, Gall is also called Gallen. But instead of accompanying Colm Bán to Bobium, Gall, and some of his comrades, decided to stay at a place further north beyond the great mountains. They established an abbey there by a great lake, the Lacus Brigantius, as Pliny called it.'

'Brigantius?' queried Fidelma. 'That seems to be a name I should be familiar with.'

'It was a Gaulish territory with a city called Brigantium. It is a name familiar in many parts, even in Britain during Roman times. Now it is a territory of the Alemanni, where both Colm Bán and Gall preached for a while. Like Bobium, the community has grown magnificently. I spent a little while there before making my way south, learning the language of the Longobards and eventually arriving in Bobium. That was over two years ago. So instead of returning home, I have remained here as *scriptor*. I have not seen Muman in four years or more.'

'Ah, then you have indeed been away longer than I have,' conceded Fidelma. 'There is little news to give, apart from a list of deaths.'

'The Yellow Plague has been ravaging this country, so doubtless it has also spread to the Five Kingdoms?'

'It has. It has created a long and miserable list of deaths and is still ravaging the land. The plague affected many communities and not even prelates have escaped. Abbot Ségéne, one of the successors of Colm Bán at the Abbey of Beannchar, died of it last year. You might know of Colmán, who was chief professor of Finnbarr's school in Corcaigh? Before I came away, I heard that he had fled with fifty of his pupils to one of the western islands in order to escape the plague.'

Brother Eolann assumed a sad expression. 'I studied under Colmán before I went to Faithleann's Island. Your cousin, Congal, had just become Lord of Locha Léin at that time. But Máenach mac Fingin was still King of Muman.'

'Cathal Cú-cen-maithair succeeded him two years ago, and that was when my brother, Colgú, became his *tánaiste* – his heir apparent,' Fidelma told him.

'Are there any other changes?'

'There is relative peace among the Five Kingdoms under the sons of Aedo Sláine.'

The two sons of Aedo Sláine had succeeded as joint High Kings of Éireann ten years before and had presided over a peaceful decade.

'There are times when I would give up the privilege of my position here to see the still blue waters of the Lake of Léin again,' the young man admitted.

They had already circled the garden.

'Would it impose too much upon you, Eolann of Faithleann's

Island, if I asked you to show me the *scriptorium*?' Fidelma suddenly asked. 'I am more than interested in such matters. I especially want to look at the text of the Gospel of Matthew.'

'You are most welcome there any time, lady,' replied Brother Eolann without hesitation. He continued to use the term of respect for her as the daughter of a king of his land rather than her position as a religieuse. 'Come. We have an excellent copy of the Blessed Eusebius' translation of that Gospel into Latin.' He led the way from the *herbarium* back across the courtyard towards the main abbey buildings.

'I hear there are many good scholars here,' Fidelma continued, 'such as Venerable Ionas and Magister Ado. You must have much talent to be appointed *scriptor*.'

The young man made a gesture of deprecation. 'There is often a difference between the talent of a scholar and a *scriptor*. My talent is in taking care of books, not in the writing of them. I was lucky, for when I arrived here the *scriptor* was ailing and needed an assistant. He died and thus I was made *scriptor*.'

'I am told that you have a fine collection of books here?'

Brother Eolann affirmed the fact with immediate enthusiasm. 'We have one of the largest collections of work of the Faith anywhere in Christendom. Soon after I came here I set up a special group of copyists so that, over the years, copies may be made and sent to the libraries in our other lands.'

Brother Eolann took Fidelma through the main doors, but instead of entering into the *refectorium*, he turned to his left and went along a short, dark passageway and across a smaller open courtyard with a fountain splashing from the mouths of two stone cherubs in its centre. He approached another door which gave access to a spiral stone staircase which rose in the interior of a tower. Halfway up was a stout oak door that gave ingress into a large square room lined with books and manuscripts. On one side were several tall, narrow windows, while at the far end was another large oak door. In spite of the windows, it was dark but, as far as Fidelma could see, the room was empty. With a muttered apology, Brother Eolann spent a little time lighting an oil lamp and then moving to a desk while Fidelma cast her eyes over the books, mentally trying to count them. It was an impressive library but not as impressive as she had thought it would be.

'The copyists work in the next room,' explained the *scriptor*, as if reading her thoughts. 'Most of the main library is in that room. We store many famous and rare books here, from the poems of Colm Bán himself to some of the great histories written by the Romans, the Greeks, Alexandrians . . . it is a great honour for me to work here in peace and security.'

'I am sure it is,' Fidelma replied solemnly. 'Yet you say that there are times when you would give it up to see your homeland again?'

Brother Eolann looked embarrassed. 'I must follow the path God has set for me,' he muttered. 'I would not wish that you thought I was unhappy in my calling.'

'I know that you are not, Brother Eolann. But it is hard not to long for the familiar hills, fields and places of one's childhood.'

'That is true,' replied the *scriptor*. 'Don't we have an old saying – *níl aon tintáin mar do thinteán féin.*'

'No hearth like your own hearth,' repeated Fidelma with a sad smile. 'Indeed, with that I can entirely agree. One has to have great fortitude to settle in a foreign place where there is conflict and tension surrounding one.'

'You mean the conflict between the Arians and those of

the followers of the Nicene Creed? I hear you witnessed the arguments between our abbot and Bishop Britmund.'

'I was thinking more in terms of the Rule that you obey here. It is so unlike the Rule followed in most of our own abbeys and religious houses.'

'It is no hardship for one who is a *peregrinus pro amore Christi*.'

'Alas, I am not,' Fidelma confessed. 'I am just a messenger, an adviser in law, rather than one who sets out to bring the Faith to the heathen and barbarian. But Magister Ado told me that the Rule of Colm Bán was even harsher than the Rule of Benedict. How can that be so? Our own religious houses, mostly mixed houses, do not agree with such penitential methods.'

'You forget, lady, that Colm Bán spent many years among the undisciplined Franks and Burgunds before he came among the Longobards.'

'That is what Sister Gisa said. Then you agree that this shaped his thought?'

'The society is harsh and barbarous. Crime is violent and punishments are severe. Colm Bán might have tried to establish similar religious houses to those in our own land but found that he needed to control and discipline many of those who flocked to join him. I have seen something of the laws of the places in which he dwelled – the *wergelds* – it was not unusual for infractions of the law to result in physical punishments. Half of Colm Bán's Rule was devoted to punishments of the community.'

Fidelma was shaking her head in sad disbelief. 'What sort of punishments?'

'From fasting, confinement in one's *cubiculum* to the saying of additional prayers and . . .' he hesitated '. . . even to physical punishments such as the use of the scourge. He listed two hundred blows, given at twenty-five blows at one time, as the punishment for some infractions. Confessions had to be made in public before the abbot and the entire community.'

'I cannot believe such a Rule would be proclaimed by someone of our land.'

'True, alas. The Rule also declared celibacy was the perfection – a goal one must make every wholehearted effort to attain by making the body a temple of virtue. He had declared a code of behaviour of asceticism and austerity. He claimed that the austere spirit had to be totally obedient and that obedience would win merit in the eyes of God. That was the ultimate aim of the life of the religious.'

'It is amazing. I thought our people were so imbued with the essence of our law that they would never descend to such philosophies. How could Colm Bán believe that he could command the love and allegiance of his followers in this way?'

'He did not. Many left this abbey during the time when his Rule prevailed,' replied Brother Eolann. 'However, his Rule lasted only a decade after his death before the abbey sought the milder form of governance as given by Benedict. I think it is Colm Bán's myth rather than the reality which commands the present love and allegiance.'

Fidelma swallowed as she contemplated the picture that had been painted. Then she shook herself slightly. 'And this Arianism? How does that affect the brethren here?'

'We try to ignore it.'

'But others do not?'

Brother Eolann gave a sad sigh. 'It is good to have someone here from one's own land. There are others of the Five Kingdoms here but not many that one is able to talk with.'

'How do you mean that?'

'Well, I mean to converse with intelligence. I do not wish to denigrate anyone . . . but, well, you have spoken to Brother Lonán? He only comes alive when speaking of herbs and plants. While that is laudable and I do not doubt his knowledge, his conversation on other matters is limited. He would not know the poems of our great poet Dallán Forgaill, nor even the poems of Colm Bán himself, any more than the works of Sophocles or the history of Polybius.'

Fidelma hid a smile. 'Literature is only one form of knowledge,' she rebuked.

'But these books,' Brother Eolann waved a hand towards the ranks of shelves around the room, 'these books open roads to all knowledge.'

'So you would prefer to speak to scholars rather than gardeners?'

'Is that wrong?'

'Much may be learned from both, depending on what you want to know.'

'I am told you spoke with Brother Ruadán last night.'

'He was why I came here – to see him. He was my teacher when I was young,' Fidelma replied, wondering at the sudden change of subject.

'I suppose they would let you see him,' Brother Eolann said reflectively.

'Why would they *not* let me see him?' Fidelma was puzzled.

'Brother Hnikar allows no one to see him. They certainly won't let me near him, and I would claim that I was closer to Brother Ruadán than anyone else in this abbey.'

Fidelma examined him curiously. 'Are you saying that you were expressly forbidden to visit him?'

'I was told that he is too poorly. Sad that, at his age, he should be so violently attacked for preaching the true Faith.'

'Were there any witnesses to this attack?'

'No one saw it. He was found outside the gates of the abbey early one morning. I was told that he had been preaching at Travo, which is further down the valley. I can only repeat the common knowledge which is that he was found at the gates, badly beaten, with a paper on which the word *haereticus* was pinned to his bloodstained robe.'

'Heretic,' nodded Fidelma. 'I have been told.'

'Those of the Arian Creed denounce us as heretics, even as we denounce them. Poor Brother Ruadán, he must have barely made it back to the gates of this abbey before he collapsed. God gave him strength. He is an old man but he survived until he reached here.'

'So no one saw the attack nor can blame anyone in particular for it?'

'With Bishop Britmund absolving any who attacks a heretic, as he calls us, who would bring these attackers to justice?' Brother Eolann's tone was grim. 'The law of the Longobards is not like our own law, lady. The will of their lords and the Arian bishops are all the law that is to be found outside these walls.'

'But on the matter of the conflict in this valley, what is your opinion of Radoald? Is he to be trusted?'

'Lord Radoald of Trebbia? Trust is not something that I am prepared to offer any of these Longobards. Radoald appears to be an affable fellow. He is a supporter of King Grimoald who, as you have heard, is a follower of Arius but liberal in allowing everyone to follow their own path. Radoald vows friendship for the abbey but if the pressures were strong enough, perhaps his ardency would lessen.'

Fidelma was quiet for a moment. Brother Eolann was providing a good source of information. 'You have no reason to suspect any other motive behind the attack on Ruadán than this conflict of religious views?'

'Goodness, no – why?' Brother Eolann was clearly astonished at the question. 'Brother Ruadán had no enemy in the world other than those miserable creatures misled by Bishop Britmund.'

'I just wanted to make sure, that is all,' Fidelma said quickly. 'It is still hard to believe that a different view about whether something is created or begotten could lead men to murder one another.'

'Such is the nature of mankind, lady,' replied the librarian sadly. He rose suddenly and was looking along a line of books. He found the one he wanted and laid it on the desk before her. 'Wasn't it this that you wanted to see, lady? The text of the Matthew Gospel? Read it at your leisure. I have to make sure my copyists are at their work.'

She turned to the papyrus scroll that he had put before her and began to unroll it. The hand was clear and the Latin easy to follow. It took some time, however, before she encountered the passage she was looking for. She had been so shocked at the words which Lady Gunora had quoted the previous night that she was determined to check if they had really existed. She was aghast to find that Gunora had quoted them almost word perfectly.

Nolite arbitrari quia venerim mittere pacem in terram non veni pacem mittere sed gladium . . .

She had always been taught that the message of the Christ was peace, not war. Now she found the Christ Himself admitting that He had come to the world not to speak for peace but war. To bring a sword. What shocked her was the statement that His followers must not love their fathers and mothers, nor daughters or sons, more than Him – for if they did so, they would not be worthy of Him. It was contrary to the laws and philosophies of her people, where love and respect for one's parents and one's children were considered of premier importance. That one had to reject this was tantamount to destroying society, especially the kin-based society of her people. That was why *fingal* – kin-slaying – was considered the worst crime that a person could commit. It struck at the very heart of society. The law of which she was an advocate applied heavy sanctions against the perpetrators of kin-slaying.

She sat back thinking about it for a while and then she remembered the disappearance of Lady Gunora and the young prince. She had almost forgotten about them, apart from the angry quotation that the woman had used.

She heard Brother Eolann re-enter the library room.

'Did you find what you wanted?' he asked.

'I did,' she said, allowing the papyrus scroll to re-roll itself. She pushed it aside and, changing the subject, quickly added: 'You have an excellent library here, Brother Eolann.'

Brother Eolann seemed happy as he glanced with pride along the shelves. 'As I have said, I am proud of the books that we have here. We have been lucky in our collections.' He indicated a shelf. 'One previous *scriptor* was a local man who specialised in collecting ancient works from writers of this area – Paetus the Stoic philosopher of Patavium, poets and essayists like Varus, Catullus, Catius, Pomponius . . . in ancient times, the people of this area were highly literate. And they were not even Romans.'

'You mean that they were Longobards?' queried Fidelma, not particularly interested.

'The Longobards only settled in this territory a century ago. The original inhabitants were Gauls. Then the Roman legions conquered this area and that was a full century before the birth of the Christ. But of the Gauls, you will sometimes see an echo of their language here.'

'So they wrote in their own tongue?'

'They seemed to have a religious prohibition about writing their secrets in their own language. They wrote mostly in Latin and we have learned much from them, but you will see a few original inscriptions and the names of places which show the ghost of their mother tongue.'

Fidelma realised that it was time to leave, since she had other questions to pursue. Her mind turned to the disappearance of Lady Gunora and the young prince. Also, she had meant to visit Brother Ruadán to see if she could obtain more clarity from the frail old man. So she rose and thanked the librarian for his interesting conversation and left him. She remembered the way back through the tower to the small courtyard and along the dark corridor to the main hall. Once or twice, members of the brethren gave her sharp glances, reminding her that this was not a mixed-house and that women were not supposed to wander unaccompanied within its confines. She ignored them and the whispered remarks that followed her.

She found her way back to the guest-house and reached the door of her chamber. She was about to enter when she heard a movement along the corridor. Turning, she saw Brother Wulfila emerging from what had been the quarters of Lady Gunora and her princely charge. Fidelma called to him, deciding innocence might extract more information.

'I have not seen Lady Gunora this morning. I trust she is well?'

There was no mistaking the anxious expression that

crossed the steward's features. 'Well enough, Sister,' he said shortly.

'Ah, is she in her chamber? I will speak with her.'

Brother Wulfila moved slightly as if he would block the door. Then he seemed to make a decision. 'She is not here,' he admitted.

Fidelma waited in silence. It seemed that the steward was trying to think of something to say. 'I believe that she and the young prince have left the abbey.'

Fidelma's eyebrows lifted slightly. 'Left the abbey? I thought there was some danger for them outside these walls?'

'I am sure that the Father Abbot knows what he is doing,' the man muttered.

'Ah! Then they left with the approval of Abbot Servillius?'

'I am not at liberty to say.' Brother Wulfila was agitated. He turned and scurried off along the corridor.

Fidelma stared after him a moment or two. If anyone knew why and how Lady Gunora and the boy had left the abbey, it was surely the steward, who had been in the corridor during the night.

Fidelma entered her own chamber and took a moment to tidy herself and wash her hands. A bell began to ring, but she knew it was not to summon the brethren for a meal. She left her room to find one of the Brothers hurrying by. When she asked him what the bell signified, he answered it was for the midday prayers. She let him hurry on. The abbey was quiet now and she realised it was the ideal time to see if Brother Ruadán was able to talk further with her. She made her way down towards his chamber and had just rounded the corner into the passage when she came face to face with the apothecary.

'Ah, Sister Fidelma.' The portly man greeted her with disapproval, almost barring her way.

'Brother Hnikar. I was just on my way to see Brother Ruadán. I trust he is well enough to see me today?' She hoped that he would not suspect that she had visited her old mentor earlier that morning.

A shadow crossed the features of the apothecary. He paused a moment and then cleared his throat, his lower lip jutting out like a child about to burst into tears.

'That will not be possible.'

'Not possible?' Fidelma tried to control her irritation. 'Why not?'

Of all the answers she was expecting, she did not expect his next sentence.

'I am afraid Brother Ruadán is dead. He died in his sleep during the night.'

chapter eight

Fidelma paused but a second before she dodged nimbly round the portly apothecary and thrust open the door of Brother Ruadán's chamber. She could hear Brother Hnikar's outraged protests behind her. She hesitated briefly on the threshold. Brother Ruadán lay on his bed. Then she strode to the bedside and stood looking down at the body.

The elderly Brother looked peaceful now. It was clear that his body had already been washed and prepared ready for the services that would precede the burial. Then her eye fell on his hands, carefully folded on his breast. Some of the fingernails were torn – split, as if ill-kept – with dried blood visible beneath them. They were not the nails of the hand she had held that morning. One of the things that people of her country prided themselves on were their hands and finger-nails. Among the aristocracy and the professional classes, the fingernails had to be kept carefully cut and rounded as a sign of breeding. To be insulting, one of the worst terms one could use against another person was to call them *crécht-ingnech* or 'ragged nails'. Between the time that she had seen the old man earlier that morning to the time of his death, Brother Ruadán must have fought with his hands against something, against someone, breaking his nails and causing blood from his assailant to be caught under them.

Her expression was stony as she gazed down at her old tutor. Ill as Brother Ruadán had been, someone had determined to end his life. He had been murdered.

She re-examined his face, the slightly blue texture of the skin and the lips stretched over the yellowing teeth and the eyes that had not been completely closed after death. She noticed little spots of dried blood around the nostrils. In a flash she realised that the killer had probably held a pillow over the old man's face, holding him down while he made a desperate attempt to push them off, scratching and clawing at the powerful arms of his assailant. That was how he had damaged his hands.

Fidelma glanced up at the apothecary who had followed her into the chamber, still protesting at her behaviour.

'When did this happen?' she interrupted him.

'I told you, it was reported to me that he had died in the night. Really, Sister, you presume too much to enter without approval—'

'He has already been washed and prepared for burial. Why was I not informed when this happened?'

Brother Hnikar blinked at the sharp tone of her voice.

'I have known poor Ruadán since I was a little girl,' she went on. 'I have a right to know.'

'You have no right to be here without permission of the abbot.'

'Then I shall address my questions to the abbot,' replied Fidelma coldly.

An uneasy look entered Brother Hnikar's eyes. 'What questions?' he asked.

Fidelma did not respond but gave one last took at the corpse, turned and left the room.

Fidelma entered the abbot's study before he had finished his invitation to enter. He was speaking with Magister Ado and Brother Faro.

'Have you been informed of Brother Ruadán's death?' she demanded without preamble.

Abbot Servillius seemed surprised at her belligerent tone.

'We have, my child, and allow me to express my condolences to you on the passing of your old friend and tutor. This abbey has lost a good man in his passing.'

'His body has already been washed and prepared for burial. Why was I not told of his death earlier?'

The abbot's frown deepened. 'Earlier than what, my daughter?' he asked softly. 'As soon as Brother Hnikar told me the news, I sent Brother Faro to look for you.'

'I thought you were in the *herbarium*,' confirmed Brother Faro. 'But you were not there and Brother Lonán did not know where you had gone.'

Fidelma swallowed sharply. It was true that she had spent a long time in the library and no one had known that she was there apart from Brother Eolann. It seemed, perhaps, that it might be her own fault that she had not been informed earlier.

'When did it happen?' she went on. 'When was his death known?'

'Brother Hnikar was informed that something was amiss and went to attend him.'

'Who informed him?'

'Probably the steward, as it is his task to make a daily check on all matters. The apothecary came to find me immediately but, of course, we were locked in debate with Britmund. He felt he should not interrupt. So he waited until he heard that we had finished, by which time you were reported to have gone to the herb garden. So we sent Brother

Faro to find you. I appreciate that this is upsetting for you. Such a long journey to see your old mentor and now to find him dead.' He paused, cleared his throat, and then dismissed Brother Faro.

When he had departed, Abbot Servillius indicated that Fidelma should be seated while Magister Ado said: 'We must also remember that Sister Fidelma is a lawyer in her own land. As such, perhaps she is used to deaths being reported immediately to her. So we can forgive her agitation at being the last to find out.'

The abbot took a jug from his table, pouring its contents into three beakers.

'As the Blessed Timothy advised, *Noli adhuc aquam bibere, sed vino modico utere propter stomachum tuum.*'

Fidelma had heard the saying mentioned before: drink no longer water but use a little wine for your stomach's sake. She realised that wine would be welcome, for it was hard to take the shock of Brother Ruadán's murder. And now she did not know whom to trust with her thoughts.

'Brother Ruadán was fond of our local red wine,' the abbot said as he handed her the beaker. 'His body will be taken for burial at midnight in our necropolis. It lies on the hillside behind the abbey buildings. I believe the ceremony is not dissimilar to the one you practise in Hibernia.'

Fidelma sighed deeply as she sipped the wine and tried to gather her thoughts in some order. 'If there is something, some relic of his, that I could take back to his abbey on Inis Celtra . . . ? That was where he came from and studied, and where I first knew him.'

'Of course,' agreed the abbot at once. 'I also believe it is your custom to have someone who knew the deceased to speak some words about him at the graveside?'

'That is so.'

'I shall say a few words of his labours here in the abbey, but we know nothing of his life before he left his own land. I believe God has guided your footsteps here so that you may speak the praises of this worthy servant of His. Will you speak those words?'

Fidelma had no hesitation in agreeing.

'Death always comes as a shock,' went on the abbot, 'even when one is entirely prepared. If Brother Ruadán had a fault it was in his zeal to bring the truth of the Faith to those who had been led astray into heresy. They had no respect for his frail body but they feared the strength of his voice and the truth of his words.'

'Are you satisfied that your abbey contains no followers of Arius?' she asked, her mind still thinking over who might have murdered her mentor as he lay helpless in his bed.

The question seemed to startle both the abbot and the Magister Ado.

'We are a refuge from such heresies,' said the abbot. 'What makes you ask such a thing? We are an island of the true Faith. Why would heretics need to send one of their number among us?'

'Oh, just something he said.' She made the prevarication without a blush. 'We lawyers are inquisitive people and so the slightest remark that we do not understand tends to irritate and worry us.'

Magister Ado examined her suspiciously. 'Something Brother Ruadán said? But I thought you had not spoken to him apart from when you first arrived, when his mind was wandering.'

Fidelma realised that she ought to be more careful when trying to gather information. But she was sure now that

Brother Ruadán had not been calling out in fever when he warned her that there was evil in this abbey. He had been murdered. She was sure of it. Now she had to find out who had smothered him on his sickbed – and why.

She rose and placed the empty beaker of wine on the table. 'It was just that I was thinking about those who had beaten him because he was preaching against the Creed of Arius. You'll forgive me. I shall return to the guest-house and lie down.'

She was almost at the door when Abbot Servillius said, 'I understand from my steward, Brother Wulfila, that you were concerned that Lady Gunora and Prince Romuald had left the abbey. Lady Gunora was apprehensive for the boy's safety and came to me last night. She announced her intention of leaving the abbey before first light and making her way to the fortress of Lord Radoald where she believed that she would have more protection.'

'That does not seem a wise plan, judging from what I have been told,' Fidelma replied. 'If the country here is in such a state of alarm, she would have been better within the walls of this abbey.'

The abbot grimaced without humour. 'I think Lady Gunora and yourself have much in common,' he observed. 'You share a determination that will accept no counter-argument. When I put it to her that her proposal lacked wisdom, even as you put it, she told me that I was an aged fool and she would leave the abbey whether she was wise to do so or not.'

Fidelma flushed. 'I can only point out where logic does not prevail,' she told him.

'In Lady Gunora's case, that is accepted,' replied the abbot. 'Rest well, Fidelma. Brother Ruadán's body will be removed to the chapel soon where the community can take their turn in praying over it until midnight, which is our traditional hour of interment.'

'I shall attend,' Fidelma said, with a glance of acknowledgement to both men before leaving.

A long, lonely afternoon stretched out before her. Curiously, she did not feel enthusiastic about sitting in the chapel and watching over the corpse of her old teacher. Outside, it was hot, the sky blue and the sun still strong. It was a time to be out in the fresh air, outside with the living. Death should only come at night, Fidelma thought. Night and death went hand in hand. It did not suit blue skies and warm sunshine. She would go and wake the dead at nightfall but not during such a day given over to life.

Brother Ruadán was dead – but *why*? Everyone was saying he had been set upon and beaten because of his vehement denunciation of the Arian Creed and his support of the Nicene Creed. And yet he had been killed by someone who had access to the abbey. So was there a different motive? Had he been murdered because someone was afraid of what he would say? What *had* he said? Something to do with coins, gold coins . . . She tried hard to remember exactly.

With these thoughts running in her mind, Fidelma walked slowly through the abbey and her footsteps initially took her back into the *herbarium*. Her head bowed, she traversed the paths among the beds of plants. Now and then she passed by figures, who stood aside and muttered acknowledgement with, '*Laus Deo,*' '*Deus misereatur,*' and so on. It seemed inevitable that her footsteps would eventually lead her back to one person with whom she felt at ease, and so she climbed the tower to the *scriptorium* of Brother Eolann. He rose, somewhat confused, from his desk as she entered.

'I am sorry, lady. I heard that poor Brother Ruadán has passed on. I knew him well during my days here and I am saddened by that loss. He was a great teacher and a scholar, as well as being one of our own. He will be missed among our brethren.'

'Thank you, Brother Eolann. He was, indeed, a fine teacher,' she replied gravely.

'He had a sharp mind.'

'A sharp mind,' Fidelma echoed as she seated herself by his desk. 'Did he ever talk to you about coins? Gold coins?'

Brother Eolann regarded her in silence for a moment. 'Coins? In what way?'

'Maybe not coins but missing treasure?'

The *scriptor* shook his head firmly. 'I have to say that he did not. Brother Ruadán was interested in many things, as you know, but I never heard him express any inclination to know about coins. Why do you ask?'

'So he never came here to inquire about such a subject?' Fidelma ignored his last question by inserting one of her own. 'He never expressed interest in coins or treasure?'

'Never.'

'Could he have come here and found a book on the subject without you knowing?'

Brother Eolann replied with an almost painful smile. 'There is always that possibility. We try to ensure that anyone who uses the *scriptorium* is known. Even in such a place as this, we find that not everyone places the same value on books as should be given to them. Sometimes people abuse the books, may they be forgiven. I consider such abuse a crime.'

'People abuse the books?' She was distracted by the thought.

'We had good copies of the histories of Polybius and of

Livinius and I recently found that both these works were damaged.'

'I don't understand.'

'Some time ago I was checking a reference in Polybius and found that someone had cut some pages out of the book.'

'It is a sacrilege to treat a book so,' Fidelma agreed.

'What is worse, the same thing happened with the history of Livinius – pages cut out with a sharp knife. It took my copyists several days of checking through all our books to ensure that nothing else had been damaged.'

He went to a shelf and took down a book. She noticed that it was entitled *Ab Urbae Conditae Libri*. It was Livy's history of Rome from the birth of the city. He turned to a page and pointed.

'See, this page has been cut out.'

'I wonder why.' She glanced at the preceeding one and saw that it was about someone called Marcus entering the Senate in triumphal dress. 'You say it was recent? What do you intend to do?'

'I shall report the matter to the abbot. I suspect there is little he can do except preach a sermon to the community and pronounce God's punishment on those who do not confess this crime.'

'Can the books be restored?'

'Only if we find an original copy. I have sent a messenger to the community of the Blessed Fridian at Lucca. They have copies of these books. I hope we can copy or purchase them. It is a stain on my reputation as *scriptor* that such a thing could happen in my *scriptorium*.'

'It is hard to believe that someone could treat books in such a fashion. Perhaps it was someone not of the community?'

'It had crossed my mind, lady, but who, apart from members of the community, would be able to access such works? Surely it indicates that whoever removed the pages wanted those particular books or those particular pages. If it was just for the sake of any pieces of parchment, why not take them from the nearest books? Look!' He pointed. 'Other books were more easy to access than those two, which were placed on different shelves.'

'Then, if one knew what the passages on the missing pages were, what they related to, it might give a clue as to the interest of the person who cut them out. With such a clue one might be able to track down the culprit.'

Brother Eolann considered this and grew excited at the prospect. 'You are right, lady. Ah, hopefully, we may secure copies before long. I am already intrigued.'

'You have no idea of what they might be about?'

'Alas, I do not.'

'Well, I am sorry to bother you on the matter of coins. It was of minor interest.'

The abbey bell began to ring to call the brethren to the evening meal, and with a sigh she thanked him and went to join the others in the *refectorium*. It had been good to have her mind distracted by the problems of the library rather than dwell on the death of Brother Ruadán. But dwell on it, she must. There was a mystery to be solved. A murderer to be caught.

In Fidelma's culture it was the custom to watch the corpse for a night and a day. She found the custom here slightly different, but it carried the same intent. The body had been watched in the abbey chapel all afternoon and evening. After the evening meal, Fidelma joined the brethren and some of the Sisters in prayers in the chapel, seated before the bier. All the senior clerics were in attendance now, from the abbot to Brother Lonán, the gardener. After a while, Lord Radoald, accompanied by the warrior, Wulfoald, entered the chapel and came straight to her side to sit down.

'Brother Ruadán was a good man and well respected in this valley,' whispered the young Lord of Trebbia. 'I am truly sorry, especially for you, having travelled to this place to see him and then to find him dead.'

'I saw him . . .' Fidelma began, then saw that Brother Hnikar, seated just in front of her, was leaning backwards in an attitude of apparent unconcern, in order to eavesdrop. 'I saw him when I arrived,' she said, 'but his mind was wandering for he made no sense.'

'Sad, indeed. I presume this means you will shortly start on your journey back to your own land?'

Fidelma frowned, wondering if there was a hidden eagerness in his voice. Was he anxious to get rid of her?

'I shall commence my journey back to Genua soon.'

'Then when you are ready, it would be my pleasure to send an escort with you as far as Genua, for we would not like a repeat of the unpleasantness that attended your journey hither.'

'You may rest assured that I would not like it either,' Fidelma replied solemnly. 'I will inform you when I am ready.'

The young Lord of Trebbia rose, with Wulfoald at his side, then went to make his obeisance before the altar and the bier of Brother Ruadán.

In a custom that she was familiar with in her own land, at midnight the corpse of Brother Ruadán was carried on its bier from the chapel and out of the abbey. The necropolis was not far away. It was an area on the slope of the hill behind the abbey, surrounded by a small wall and entered by a stone arched gateway.

In front of the bier strode one of the brethren bearing a cross on a pole, flanked by two others bearing brand torches. Behind the bier, which was carried by six brothers, came Abbot Servillius, Venerable Ionas and Magister Ado. After them, came Fidelma side by side with Brother Eolann. Others of the brethren, like Brother Lonán, Brother Faro and Brother Wulfila, followed, along with several women of the sisterhood, including Sister Gisa. Others had joined the torchlit procession outside the gates of the abbey. With them came the Lord Radoald and Wulfoald and some of the local townsfolk. It seemed that Ruadán had been well respected. The column of mourners moved under the archway into the necropolis, progressing slowly up the hill towards a spot where Fidelma could see several other torches burning.

There were an assortment of grave markers on either side which she could just make out in the flickering light of the torches. Yet, at the top of the rise, which marked the back of the necropolis, stood three small houses, though they were not houses that she had ever seen before. It was hard to make them out in the darkness.

As the brethren had entered the necropolis, they had begun a chant in Latin which Fidelma had not heard before.

'*Dominus pascit me, nihil mihi deerit . . .*' The Lord rules me and I shall want nothing.

They moved in file behind the bier as it was carried by torchlight to the place where the grave had been dug.

'*Sed et si ambulavero in valle mortis non timebo malum quoniam tu mecum es virga tua et baculus tuus ipsa consolabuntur me . . .*' For though I should be in the midst of the shadow of death, I will fear no evil, for You are with me. Your rod and Your staff, they have comforted me . . .

They moved through the gates and Fidelma saw several of the brethren already awaiting them. They stood by a hole freshly dug in the dark earth.

The body was lowered into it, prayers were said and then Abbot Servillius motioned Fidelma to step forward.

She suddenly found that she wanted to turn on them and accuse one of them for the murder of her mentor. She wanted to cry out that he had not died of injuries received from a week or two ago but that he had been murdered that very morning after he had spoken to her. That he had tried to issue her with some warning and had told her to leave this evil place. But she gathered her racing thoughts and calmed herself.

'Brother Ruadán was from the Kingdom of Muman, one of the Five Kingdoms that you call the land of Hibernia. He was named after a holy man who is regarded in my land as one of the Twelve Apostles of Hibernia. This Blessed Ruadán became the first Abbot of Lothra, which was near the home of the young Brother Ruadán, who grew up with a thirst for learning and piety. He entered the Abbey of Inis Celtra, a small island in a great lake, where he devoted himself to his books and the pursuit of knowledge. I, among many others, studied under him and grew rich in knowledge from his instruction and profound in wisdom from his guidance. His life was one of the few beacons of light in this dark world.'

Fidelma then took up a handful of earth and threw it down into the grave.

Abbot Servillius gave her a glance of approval and stepped forward in turn.

'Hibernia's loss was the gain of this abbey. It was a sad

day for Hibernia when Brother Ruadán left its shores and became a *peregrinus pro amore Christi*. But it was a great joy to us when he entered the gates of this community. He became one of our greatest preachers, going out among the heathen and trying to bring them to the path of truth. He suffered for the truth, and we may say he was a true martyr – for he died of the beating inflicted upon him by those whom prefer heresy to obedience to the Faith. His soul will be gathered to God and there will be joy in the heavens.'

He, too, bent and picked up a handful of earth. Then, one by one, those gathered there did likewise. Each stood a moment with their thoughts of the old man before turning away.

As Fidelma and the others moved away from the grave, an eerie wailing sound pierced the night air. It had a ghostly, musical quality and Fidelma recognised it as the sound of bagpipes. It was almost like the instruments used in her own lands, but more thin and reed-like than the pipes she had grown up with. It seemed to echo round the mountains with a lamenting cry, like a soul in torment. She turned with a startled look to the Venerable Ionas, whom she found next to her.

'Have no fear, daughter,' the elderly scholar said with a smile. 'It is only old Aistulf playing the *muse* – a lament for the departed.'

'Aistulf the hermit? What is the *muse*?'

'It is the bagpipes played by the folk of the mountains here. Sometimes, at night, when sound carries across the valley, you may hear old Aistulf playing the pipes. Do not let it concern you.'

The mourners were leaving the necropolis. One of the torch-bearers waited to accompany Fidelma and others. As they walked down the path between the gravestones and wooden crosses, she caught sight of a rough wooden cross with a name on it. It was unlike the well-crafted memorial stones around it, and in the flickering light she noticed that the name was not so much engraved as burned into the wood by means of a hot iron. They had passed on before the name had completely registered in her mind. *Wamba*. Where had she heard that word before? Then she almost stopped dead in her tracks. The name had been spoken by Brother Ruadán!

'The boy . . . poor little Wamba. He did not deserve to die because he had the coins.'

Those were the very words that he had said that morning. What coins? Why *the* coins? How did Wamba die? Whom could she ask? Whom could she trust?

By the time she had returned to her chamber in the guest-house, her mind was swimming with so many questions that she knew she would be unable to sleep. But exhaustion caught up with her and suddenly she was waking to the early-morning light.

ChAPTER NINE

A t the first meal of the day, Abbot Servillius greeted her
with a sad smile. 'Have you rested well, Sister?' He
seemed unusually concerned.

'I have,' she replied.

'Excellent. A good sleep can be a great healing of
emotions.'

The prayers and the single bell proclaimed the ritual of
the meal which was eaten this time in a self-imposed silence.
Even Magister Ado and the Venerable Ionas seemed engrossed
in their own thoughts. It was not until the end of the meal
that Abbot Servillius approached her again. He reached into
his *marsupium*, drew out something wrapped in a piece of
cloth and handed it to her.

'As I promised, here is the item that you may take back to
Brother Ruadán's abbey, where he started out on his journey,
as a token of the love we bore him.'

Fidelma unwrapped it. It was a silver cross that Brother
Ruadán had worn on a small chain around his neck. She remembered it well from the time she was a child when he had been
teaching her. Solemnly, she re-wrapped it and put it in her
own *marsupium*.

'The brethren of Inis Celtra will appreciate this, Abbot Servillius. Thank you for this gesture.'

The abbot waved her thanks aside. 'I suppose you will be thinking of making your plans to travel back to your own country now?' he said. 'The autumn will soon be approaching. I would not delay any longer, for the road between here and Genua becomes very bad. The Trebbia is inclined to flood and make it impassable.'

Fidelma was about to reply when the abbot apparently seemed to catch sight of someone across the *refectorium*, asked her pardon and hurried off. Then she was aware of Magister Ado at her side, speaking to her.

'It was my fault, encouraging you to make a journey all this way for nothing,' he was saying. 'You could have been halfway across the ocean by now.'

'I came to see Brother Ruadán,' she replied reprovingly. 'At least I was able to do that before his death and am now able to tell his brethren at Inis Celtra how he was gathered to God after serving this abbey. The abbot was kind enough to give me a relic to take to them in remembrance.'

Magister Ado appeared embarrassed. 'I chose my words in a clumsy manner, for which I sincerely apologise. I am glad to offer you any assistance you require to help you back to Genua. Have you made any plans as to when you will leave?'

It seemed to Fidelma that there were many people suddenly willing to help her leave the abbey and return to Genua: Radoald, Abbot Servillius and now Magister Ado. She wondered why.

'I have made no plans yet,' she told him. 'I am hoping I will have time to study the abbey and the surrounding countryside a little before doing so.'

Magister Ado looked astonished. 'Why?' It was almost a demand.

'So that I am able to report to the scholars of Hibernia how the Blessed Colm Bán chose this place to end his days,' she replied easily. 'I have barely seen anything yet. I shall depart when I have gathered sufficient information to satisfy the scholars of Hibernia, and you, as a scholar, should appreciate that above all people.'

She left the *refectorium* and made her way to the gates of the abbey. Her intention was to examine the gravestone that had caught her eye the previous night. At the gate was Sister Gisa, waiting.

'How are you this morning, Sister Fidelma?' the young girl greeted her with apparent concern.

'Well enough,' replied Fidelma. It seemed everyone was also solicitous about her welfare.

'A sad thing it is, to have come all this way to witness the death of your old master.'

'At least it can be said that I saw him before he died,' Fidelma replied before changing the subject. 'Are you waiting for Brother Faro?' she asked. The girl actually flushed.

'Why would I be?' she countered almost aggressively.

'You and he are greatly attached to one another,' Fidelma observed gently. 'That much is obvious.'

'Oh, I . . .' The girl was startled.

'Do not worry. There is surely nothing wrong in that?'

There was scarlet on the girl's cheeks. 'I have not broken the rules of the abbey.'

'Of course not.' Fidelma smiled reassuringly. 'Forgive me if it is something that you do not wish to speak of.'

'Please,' the girl was clearly worried, 'please say nothing. Abbot Servillius is very strict on the rule of segregation and on celibacy.'

'Then why do you and Brother Faro not move to a mixed-house where married religious are allowed? If you are serious about your feelings for one another, then there is no problem in finding such a sanctuary. Those who advocate celibacy among the religious are still a minority – the ascetics who think denial of life is a way to fulfil life.'

Sister Gisa actually smiled, albeit anxiously.

'You are discerning, Sister. I hope that there are none here who are as discerning as you.'

'I believe Magister Ado knows how you feel.'

At once a look of alarm came back to the girl's features. 'He knows?'

'I am sure that he would not betray you but would bless your resolve if you went to find a place that is more congenial to your thoughts.'

'But Faro is his disciple – he educated him in the Faith. And Faro does not want to leave Bobium.'

'So you have spoken to him about it?'

Sister Gisa sighed. 'I have. He wants to finish his studies here before he thinks of moving on. He joined the abbey only two years ago and feels he must study further before he seeks another place.' Then she changed the subject. 'Where are you going now?'

'I am just on my way to the necropolis to lay a flower on Ruadán's grave as is our custom in my country,' Fidelma answered.

Sister Gisa fell in step with her. 'I shall accompany you then,' she announced. The girl was silent for a moment and then asked: 'When will you be starting back for Genua to find a ship for your homeland?'

Fidelma suppressed a sigh. She wondered how many more would ask the same question. 'Within a few days. Perhaps a week. But I would like to see more of the abbey and its surroundings first.'

This time the girl did not ask why but suddenly pointed to a group of bushes not far away. 'There are some flowers, white ones. They would be suitable, would they not?'

Fidelma followed the girl to the bushes and gathered some of the white lily-looking flowers. There was no one about in the abbey's necropolis as they climbed the hillside and entered. Once again her attention was drawn to the three curious constructions at the top end of the necropolis. Now, in the daylight, she realised they were sepulchres, burial chambers built in the fashion of tiny palaces that she had seen in Rome. Ornate structures of white stone that resembled the Ancient Roman buildings.

'To whom are those dedicated?' she asked.

'They are the burial chambers of the abbots.'

'But there are only three.'

'That is because the community has only started to erect them. The grave of the founder of the abbey, Columbanus, is under the High Altar in the abbey chapel. But the other abbots are placed out here. That one on the end is where Attala rests. He succeeded Columbanus. That next one is the tomb of Bertulf. He went to Rome and accepted the authority of the Pope over the abbey. And the third one, that is where Abbot Bobolen lays. He was the one who accepted the Rule of Benedict and the mitre of a bishop from Pope Theodore just twenty years or so ago.'

'I see that they are still working on the sepulchre of Bobolen.'

Sister Gisa shook her head. 'It is only some minor paint-work. The shrine was finished and sealed before Faro and I set out for Genua to meet Magister Ado. You see, Faro has to oversee the workmen and report their progress to Abbot

Servillius. It is the intention to build a mausoleum for every abbot.'

'The tombs are very impressive,' admitted Fidelma. 'Was Faro a builder or architect then?'

'No, but he is a good organiser. He designed Bobolen's tomb himself and persuaded workmen from Placentia to come and build it for charity's sake. It involved much work. I lost count of the wagons of stone brought along the valley.'

'Stone?'

'A special stone – a marble. It is not available in the valley.'

They had arrived at the newly filled-in grave of Brother Ruadán and halted. Fidelma placed her flowers on the freshly packed earth and stood with head bowed for a few moments.

Sister Gisa was staring out across the hillside. 'Were you scared last night when you heard the *muse*?' she suddenly asked.

'The *muse*? Oh, you mean the bagpipes. No, I was not scared but surprised. We have such instruments in Hibernia and, for a moment, I thought it might have been one of the Hibernian brethren playing. But there was something that did not sound right about it – I mean that they did not sound quite like the Hibernian pipes.'

'Ah, yes. Some of your compatriots have remarked on it. They are similar but I think slightly different.'

'How so?'

'They have the mouthpiece, a drone and a chanter and the air is held in a goatskin bag. They sometimes call them the Apennine pipes after the mountain range here.'

'I was told that they were being played by an old hermit.'

'Aistulf? He is a master of the pipes.'

'You know him?'

'Oh yes. He is a kindly man. I often go to see him to make sure he is well.'

'He certainly plays well, but he must be a solitary person to dwell in these mountains alone.'

'Oh, he is not denied of company that much.' She sighed. 'Although he is lonelier now than he used to be.' When she saw from Fidelma's features that she had not understood, she added: 'He is a master of his instrument and now and then has taught others so that the art may be passed on.' To Fidelma's astonishment, Sister Gisa turned and pointed to the very wooden cross that had brought her to the necropolis. 'He was teaching poor Wamba the pipes before he died.'

'Wamba?' she said, feigning puzzlement as she pretended to notice the headstone for the first time. 'That is odd.'

Sister Gisa frowned. 'Odd? Why so?'

'Well, all the other grave inscriptions have *Frater*, Brother, prefixing the name. But this gives just his name.'

'That is because he was not a member of the brethren.'

'What work did he do at the abbey then?'

'Wamba? He did not work at the abbey. He was just a goatherd. He lived up the mountain here with his mother. He used to sell goat's milk to the abbey. But he also played a small pipe as most of the boys do who tend the flocks of sheep or the goats' herds on the mountains. He was so good that Aistulf asked him to come to learn the pipes with him.'

'You give me the impression that he was very young when he died.'

'God be merciful to him, he was barely eleven years old.'

'And he died recently?'

'Just before Faro and I set out for Genua. It was the day after poor Brother Ruadán was found outside the abbey gates.'

'Do you know how the boy died?'

'We were told that his body was found, having fallen from some rocks. The poor boy broke his neck. He was discovered and his body taken to the abbey.'

'Isn't it unusual for a goatherd to be buried in the abbey's necropolis?'

'The abbot gave special permission that he be commemorated here in view of his service to the abbey. You seem very interested in him, Sister Fidelma.'

'Call it my natural curiosity.'

'Well, Brother Waldipert had far more to do with him than most of us. He is in charge of the abbey kitchens and used to buy the goats' milk from Wamba.'

'Surely the abbey has its own goats and cows to supply it?' Fidelma asked. Self-sufficiency was usually a key element in any of the abbeys she had known.

'Of course,' agreed Sister Gisa. 'But it was a custom from the days of Columbanus to help the local people. From each according to their ability, to each according to their needs. It is a good system of community living.'

Fidelma realised she could not press further without being forced to compromise herself or trying to invent reasons for her questions. Moving away from the headstone, she said, 'It is sad that this Wamba died so young when he was so talented.'

Already her mind was turning over those last words of Brother Ruadán. The boy had been killed for coins. But Sister Gisa said that he had fallen from some rocks and broke his neck. That was surely an unusual end for a goatherd on a mountain? Now she had to be rid of the company of Sister Gisa and try to find Brother Waldipert. The answer to the first problem came almost immediately. They had emerged from the gates of the graveyard when Brother Faro came into sight. At once Sister Gisa's face lit up, causing Fidelma to suppress a smile. How could the abbot be so blind as not to notice the intimacy between them?

'How is your wound progressing, Brother Faro?' she greeted him.

The young man glanced at Sister Gisa with a quick nervous smile before turning back to Fidelma.

'It is almost normal, thanks be to God. I feel no discomfort and I can use the arm freely.'

'Well, I am sure the administrations of Sister Gisa had much to do with it,' Fidelma said gravely. 'I shall remember the garlic compress that you used,' she added to the girl.

'I was taught by my father,' Gisa said. 'He is . . . *was* a good physician.'

'Anyway,' interrupted Brother Faro, 'this is nothing, compared to some wounds.' He stopped, a slight flush on his face.

'You have been hurt before?'

'But not by an arrow. It was before I came here.'

'At another abbey?'

'I was not a religieux then.'

'I thought you looked more like a warrior than a religieux,' replied Fidelma.

There was a slight uncomfortable pause before Brother Faro said, 'I was, but I saw the futility of the wars and came here looking for peace and seclusion.'

Fidelma glanced around the calm scenery of the valley and mountains and nodded slowly. 'I can see why,' she said. Then she excused herself and went back to the abbey. As she left, Sister Gisa and Brother Faro were already deep in conversation.

The door to the abbey kitchens actually led on to the *herbarium*, Fidelma discovered, and that made it easier for her to find them without anyone wondering why she needed to be in the kitchens. She entered the herb garden and uttered a prayer of thanks that Brother Lonán was not about. Then she made for the doorway whence the pleasant odours of cooking emanated.

Someone shouted a question at her in a harsh voice as she entered. A large man with an apron covering his robes was bent over a table gutting a fish, which he then threw into a simmering cauldron. He had glanced up as she entered and repeated his question in Latin when she did not answer.

'What are you doing here?'

'I am Fidelma of Hibernia,' she replied. 'I am looking for Brother Waldipert.'

The man sniffed and bent back to his task. 'Then you have found him. You are the guest of the abbot who came to see Brother Ruadán, aren't you? Sorry to hear that he died. He was a good man.'

'Actually, I came to ask you about another death. The death of the boy, Wamba.'

Brother Waldipert stopped and gazed at her in surprise. 'Wamba the goatherd? Why do you ask about him?'

'I was interested by the name on the memorial stone, the fact that someone who was not a member of the brethren was buried there.'

The fat face of Brother Waldipert was sad. 'He was one of the community to all intents and purposes. Poor little devil. He came every day to sell us fresh milk. He was good on the pipes, too.'

'When I asked Sister Gisa how one so young was buried in the necropolis of the abbey, she told me a few details as far as she knew them. That was not much. Can you tell me about him?'

Brother Waldipert sighed. 'Indeed, he was eleven years of age or thereabouts. A happy-go-lucky lad who, as I say, came daily to the abbey to give us milk from his goats in return for vegetables and herbs that we grow here.'

'He was surely very young to have his own herd of goats.'

'Oh, goodness me, no – he did not own the goats. It was his mother, Hawisa, who owned them. He herded them for her on the upper slopes of the Pénas, that is the mountain behind us.' He waved his hand towards the window, where the slopes of the hill rose up behind the abbey.

'I am told that he fell from some rocks on the mountain and killed himself.'

'That is true. He was found lying beneath them,' confirmed the cook.

'Is it known how the boy came to fall and break his neck?' Fidelma asked. 'It seems an unusual occurrence for a moun-tain goatherd to fall in such a manner.'

Brother Waldipert stared at her suspiciously for a moment before responding. 'Alas, he was alone on the mountain. Who knows how it happened? Accidents can and do happen. Why are you so interested?'

'It is just that in my experience, goatherds are usually as sure-footed as their goats.'

The cook shrugged. 'Wamba was certainly raised on the upper slopes. Perhaps he was just too sure of himself. When I last saw him, and that was a few days before he was found, he was very confident. He came here so happy, not just with the milk for sale but saying that he had found some old coin that he thought would bring his mother great fortune.'

Fidelma tried to control her interest. 'He found *a* coin? One coin?'

'Yes. He gave it to me,' confirmed the cook. 'He was pleased with his find and very boastful. He said that if he found more he would be rich enough to rule the valley. I nearly boxed his ears. *Vanitas vanitatum, omnia vanitas!*' the cook intoned. Then he added: 'Imagine the vanity of a goatherd saying he could rule in the place of the Lord of Trebbia!'

'Even a goatherd can dream,' Fidelma replied solemnly. 'Did he say where he had found the coin?'

'I think he just said that he had found it,' Brother Waldipert said reflectively. 'He asked me if I would exchange goods for it as I had for the milk.'

'And did you?'

The fat man's jowls shook as he gave a negative gesture. 'No. I knew the coin was worth a lot for its gold weight alone. I do not even know what coin it was. An ancient one, that is all. So I told him that I would take it to the abbot and see what could be arranged. The boy trusted me and was happy to part with the coin. He went off, quite satisfied that some agreement would be reached. Then, a few days later, I was told he had been found dead.'

'Who told you?' Fidelma asked sharply.

'It was the warrior who found him, Wulfoald. Do you know him? He had been coming across the mountain when he found the body of the boy at the foot of some rocks. In fact, I believe he brought the body straight here with the abbot, who announced his intention to bury him in the necropolis.'

'That was unusual.'

'The abbot felt it appropriate.'

'And did you give the coin that Wamba found to the abbot?'

'I promised the boy and so I kept that promise.'

'And what did the abbot do with it?'

'He gave Hawisa some goods in exchange. It was an old coin but not that valuable. Anyway, Hawisa was pleased to have something, for she had lost her only son. I think that Hawisa gave her goats to a nephew, another goatherd, and he now supplies us as Wamba once did. A sad story. But I can't understand why you are asking all these question about the boy.'

Fidelma forced a smile of assurance. 'Call it idle curiosity. I was merely interested.'

Once again the words of Brother Ruadán echoed in her mind. 'He did not deserve to die because he found the coins.' *The* coins? Why not 'a coin'? Suddenly she was confused. She was sure Brother Ruadán had said 'had the coins' not 'found the coins'. Perhaps, after all, Brother Ruadán was not thinking clearly. There was a difference there, but did it mean something? Or was she reading too much into simple words?

She thanked Brother Waldipert and went out into the *herbarium*. There was still no sign of Brother Lonán so she sat down on a wooden seat in a corner to consider what she knew of the facts.

She had no doubt that Brother Ruadán had been deliberately killed – suffocated, most probably to prevent him saying anything further to her. But no one had known about her visit early on the morning he was killed. No one knew that he had mentioned the coins or the boy, Wamba. According to Sister Gisa, the boy was killed about the same time that Brother Ruadán was severely beaten. What was the link? There must be one. But if the boy had been killed for the value of the coin, it was the abbot himself who had been its ultimate recipient. He had compensated the boy's mother for it. If the abbot had been part of this affair, would he have done so? Fidelma did not even know what affair she was talking about, except that Brother Ruadán called it 'evil'. She could hardly go to the abbot for information. What could she say? What excuse could she give without revealing what Brother Ruadán had said?

There was a mystery here which centred around the death of the boy Wamba and an ancient coin. But how could she set about resolving it without bringing attention upon herself?

CHAPTER TEN

What would Brehon Morann, in whose famous college Fidelma had studied law, have advised her to do? *Consult all the witnesses.* But who were the witnesses? Wulfoald had found the boy's body. The coin had been given to Abbot Servillius. Who else? What was the name of the boy's mother? Hawisa. She might be worth speaking with. But Fidelma was faced with two problems. The first was finding out where the woman lived. The second was that, even if she did find her, Fidelma did not have any knowledge of the language of the Longobards. She doubted that a goatherd's mother could speak Latin. She was going to be restricted in what she did unless she could trust someone to be her interpreter.

She considered all her limited choices. Brother Eolann was one of the few in the abbey with whom she had been able to establish an immediate rapport. Moreover, he was of Muman. Belonging to the same country was a bond. If the ascent of the mountain proved difficult, at least he was young and physically fit. With her mind made up, she left the *herbarium* and made her way back to the *scriptorium*. She encountered no one before she reached the oak door in the tower. Brother Eolann was once more at his desk.

'Do you know Hawisa, the mother of the goatherd Wamba who was found dead a week or so ago?' she asked without preamble.

'I know *of* her,' he said guardedly. 'But I would think that Brother Waldipert would be able to help you more than I can. Wamba used to supply the abbey with goat's milk. All I know is that Hawisa lives on the middle reaches of the mountain behind us.'

'I have spoken with Brother Waldipert, but I need someone to help me. I would rather that no one knew the extent of my interest in this matter.' Fidelma spoke softly, confidentially. 'I want to find Hawisa and have a word with her about her son. Presuming that she would speak only the local language, I need someone to act as my interpreter.'

Brother Eolann was astonished. 'Are you suggesting that I take you to her cabin and translate for you?'

'That is precisely what I am asking.'

'There are difficulties.'

'Which are?' demanded Fidelma.

'Getting permission for me to leave the abbey. Aside from the Rule of the community, the abbot would be more strict after what happened to Brother Ruadán and with the stories of rebellion in the land.'

Fidelma thought carefully. 'You think that he would refuse?'

Brother Eolann chuckled sourly. 'I am sure he would.'

'If his permission could be obtained, would you be willing to accompany me?'

'I think, with all due respect, that I would need to know more. What is the purpose behind this? What is your interest in Hawisa? And why do you approach me, of all the brethren here?'

'I ask you because you are from Muman. You know the

function of a *dálaigh* and the rules connected to that function. And, while I shall tell you that which you ask, before I share that knowledge with you, I must place you under a *géis* that you must take oath on.'

The young *scriptor*'s expression was one of surprise. 'A *géis*?' he echoed in astonishment.

Anyone from Hibernia knew the importance of the oath well. It was an ancient sacred bond which, when placed on someone, compelled them to obey the instruction. Any person transgressing or ignoring the *géis* was exposed to the rejection of society and brought to shame and outlawry.

'I do not ask this lightly,' Fidelma assured him.

Brother Eolann was quiet for a while and then slowly nodded his agreement. The words of the ritual were spoken softly and with solemn intent. Afterwards, Fidelma sat back on a stool opposite the *scriptor*.

'I will tell you now why I am interested in Wamba's death, Eolann of Faithleann's Island, and then you will understand. You see, I believe that Brother Ruadán was murdered . . .'

Ignoring his shocked expression, Fidelma told Brother Eolann what had transpired when she had seen Brother Ruadán and the nature of the observation which caused her to believe that his death had not been natural.

'In telling you this, and not keeping my own counsel, I open myself to your trust, for you might argue that the *géis* has no validity in this land of the Longobards where I am just a stranger.'

Brother Eolann considered what she had said in silence. Then he shrugged in acceptance. 'I accept the *géis* in honour and sincerity. If there is murder abroad in this abbey, then it must be stopped.'

'I need to find this woman, Hawisa, and ask her some questions. You can help me by being my mouth and my ears as to my questions and her responses.'

The door suddenly opened and Brother Wulfila entered, paused and began to back out with an embarrassed look at Fidelma.

'I am sorry,' the steward mumbled. 'I came to collect a book for the abbot and—'

Brother Eolann rose hurriedly. 'I have it in the copying room, Brother Wulfila,' he said, in annoyance. 'Excuse me, Sister, while I deal with this.'

He went through the side door, followed by the steward. Eventually they returned with Brother Wulfila carrying a book, the steward giving a slight bow of acknowledgement to Fidelma as he left.

'Now.' Brother Eolann settled himself back on his stool. 'We would still need an excuse to go up into the mountains and Abbot Servillius' permission to leave the abbey.' He contemplated the matter for a few moments. Then a broad smile spread across his features. 'An excuse is more easy than at first I thought.'

'How so?' asked Fidelma.

'You may tell the abbot that you have been told of the sanctuary which Colm Bán built on top of this mountain. You express a desire to visit it so that you can tell the people at home all about it. You may say that I have offered to guide you there. On our way up the mountain, we shall pass by Hawisa's cabin.'

Fidelma went to the window behind Brother Eolann and peered up the steep slopes of the mountain. 'Is it high?' she asked.

'It is, but not a difficult climb.'

'And what is this sanctuary?'

'Well, it was originally a pagan temple built by the Gauls, a people called the Boii, who once dwelled in this area. Colm Bán had promised the Longobard, Queen Theodolinda, that he would build a sanctuary dedicated to Our Lady where she would be venerated for all the ages to come. So when he settled here and began to build the abbey, he took some of his followers to the top of the mountain – Mount Pénas, it is called – and they reconsecrated the temple on the top into a chapel of the Faith and dedicated it to Mary the Mother of Christ.'

'Who was this Queen Theodolinda?'

'She was wife to Agilulfo who gave Colm Bán this land to build his abbey on.'

'The sanctuary would certainly be worth seeing for its own sake. An excellent excuse to ask for permission to leave the abbey to see it. How long would we need to be away?'

Brother Eolann glanced at the position of the sun through the window. 'If it were just to see Hawisa, we could reach her cabin and be back within the day. But to go on to the sanctuary, we would have to stay overnight on the mountain. If we left immediately we could be back by tomorrow afternoon. If the abbot gives permission, we have a reasonable excuse for being away overnight.'

'I shall speak with Abbot Servillius immediately. If I get his blessing, can we set off straight away?'

Brother Eolann seemed amused at her eagerness. 'If there are no objections from the abbot. Stout shoes are necessary, for there are some places where the ascent is steep and rocky. A bag and a blanket are also advisable, for it can be cold on the summit.'

'But we will definitely have time to speak with Hawisa and get to the sanctuary?'

'Of course. I have climbed the mountain before.'

Abbot Servillius looked up from his desk in mild surprise when Fidelma had told him her intention.

'I did tell you that I wanted to see one or two places in this vicinity associated with Colm Bán that I might take news of this abbey back to the land of his birth,' she reminded him. 'Having come all this way, I could not return to Hibernia without seeing this sanctuary.'

The abbot was less than enthusiastic. 'Of course, I understand that you would want to see the sites connected with our blessed founder, your illustrious countryman,' he said. 'But this might not be the best of times to wander the mountains.'

'But I *have* no other time, Father Abbot.' She gave an impression of a tearful pout. 'I shall be leaving soon, and not to have seen this little sanctuary that Brother Eolann told me so much about . . . that would be shameful. Perhaps you should have told me about it sooner.' She thought an implied criticism might help strengthen her argument.

Abbot Servillius blinked. 'I should have mentioned it,' he admitted, on reflection. 'A group of us from the abbey ascend the mountain to the sanctuary every year in order to celebrate the Pascal festival and the martyrdom of the Christ. It was at the sanctuary that Columbanus died during one of his retreats.'

She felt him weakening so she pressed again. 'I learned of its existence from your *scriptor*, Brother Eolann, who has offered to show me the sanctuary if we can obtain your permission. He comes from my father's kingdom and wants me to take good stories of this place back to his brethren.'

'I knew that the *scriptor* came from Hibernia,' agreed Abbot Servillius. He had conceded defeat. 'I suppose that he would be best qualified to show you the sanctuary. Very well, Sister Fidelma. You have my permission. At least the days are still warm, but you had best take ample clothing, for the weather can change rapidly in the high places. Be warned of any bands of armed strangers. We must all be vigilant if the rumours are true that Perctarit has returned.' He shrugged. 'Send Brother Eolann to me and I will give him instructions.'

It seemed that it was only a short time later that Fidelma and Brother Eolann were looking down on the abbey below them and climbing upwards on an easy track in the midday sunshine. Brother Eolann had suggested that they make the journey on foot as, although he believed they could reach Hawisa's cabin on horseback, they would not be able to continue on to the sanctuary by those means. As the *scriptor* had advised, Fidelma wore her strongest leather sandals while slung on her back was a sack in which she had a blanket and her toiletries, together with some basic items to eat.

The ascending slopes were covered with thick woods and rocky outcrops, and even naturally hollowed-out areas where water was trapped on the mountainside, forming little pools. Now and then they encountered a local shepherd or goat-herd and exchanged greetings. Hawisa's home turned out not to be very far at all. They eventually found a small cabin built under the shelter of some trees by the side of a stream that tumbled down the hillside. As they approached, a dog started to bark a warning. A heavily built woman with coarse black hair and weatherbeaten skin, tanned a rich chestnut-brown, came forward to greet them.

Her words were spoken in the gutturals of the Longobards,

which Fidelma was beginning to generally identify, although still unable to understand it. Brother Eolann replied and Fidelma heard the name 'Hawisa', at which the woman frowned and nodded.

Fidelma turned and, using Brother Eolann as her interpreter, said: 'Tell her that I would like to ask a few questions about her son, Wamba.'

The woman's eyes narrowed at once. 'He's dead,' she said flatly.

Fidelma continued speaking through the *scriptor*.

'We know, and we are so sorry for your loss. I am told that he fell from some rocks while tending his goats.'

The woman made a sound like a snort. 'Wamba was not the sort of clumsy boy who would fall. Ask Wulfoald for the truth.'

'The warrior? I thought he was the one who found Wamba and took his body to the abbey.'

Brother Eolann seemed to be searching for the right words.

'And why did not Wulfoald bring the body home to me?' the woman demanded.

'Did he know where Wamba lived?'

'Ha!' It was almost a bark of laughter. 'And when word was finally brought to me that my son was dead, and I went down to the abbey, my boy had been buried, so that I could not see him. How do I know now what injuries he had, or even the cause of them?'

'Have you reason to suspect that things did not transpire as you were told?'

'Speak to your abbot and leave me in peace with my suspicions.'

Fidelma pursed her lips for a moment. 'What are your suspicions, then, Hawisa?'

'I say nothing but there are questions to be answered. They must be answered by Abbot Servillius and Wulfoald. He knew well enough where my cabin is. Why did he proceed to the abbey?'

'But what purpose would he have for conspiring to keep news of your son's death from you until he was buried?'

The woman stood with arms folded and lips compressed. It was clear that she had had her say and was not going to release any more. Fidelma suppressed a sigh.

'I wanted to ask you whether Wamba ever spoke of a Brother Ruadán, an old Hibernian Brother in the abbey.'

The woman slowly shook her head. 'Wamba used to sell our milk to Brother Waldipert at the abbey's kitchens,' she told Fidelma through Brother Eolann. 'My nephew, Odo, has now taken over my herd of goats and continues to sell milk to the abbey. Apart from Brother Waldipert, I do not think my lad knew anyone else among the brethren.'

Fidelma felt disappointed at not being able to form an immediate link between Brother Ruadán and Wamba. 'I am told that Wamba found something on the mountain a few days before he died.'

The woman blinked. A suspicious expression crossed her features and she said defensively, 'There is a saying that what is found on the mountain and not claimed immediately belongs to the finder and cannot be reclaimed later.'

'Do not worry,' Fidelma assured her. 'I am not here to claim anything. I just want to know the circumstances of that find and what happened to it.'

The woman looked from her to Brother Eolann, who had been translating this, and back again to Fidelma.

'Sit you down,' she said heavily, indicating a wooden bench by the trees. 'I will fetch cider for you. The day is hot, and though I am not enamoured of your abbot, there is no need for you to suffer in his stead.'

Fidelma had noticed some long pauses in between the translations and so took the opportunity to ask Brother Eolann if he found the task difficult.

'The woman speaks with an accent of the peasantry. Sometimes it is hard to understand.'

A few moments passed before Hawisa returned with an earthenware jug, which had been standing in the stream, and some mugs. She poured a rich, dark golden liquid into them, and they sipped gratefully at the chilled liquid. Hawisa now seated herself nearby and stared into her own drink for a moment or two and then spoke with sad reflection, pausing every so often for the Brother to translate for the lady.

'Wamba came back from herding the goats one day and told me that we would soon be rich.' She grimaced fleetingly at the memory. 'He told me that he had found a little gold coin. Alas, he did not know the value for it did not make us rich, but the abbot gave me sufficient goods in exchange that lasted for a while.'

'I am sorry, but I do not understand.' Fidelma glanced at Brother Eolann, wondering if he had misinterpreted what she was saying. 'I understood the boy took the coin to Brother Waldipert and *he* promised the boy a valuation of the coin. Wamba died before he could go back to the abbey to conclude the deal.'

Brother Eolann had a hesitant exchange with the woman.

'She confirms what you said,' the young man responded at last. 'She saw Abbot Servillius, who told her that the coin was old but not valuable. He arranged for her to be provided with some produce in compensation for the coin. She says that it was a pity. Wamba had hoped to increase their little herd by purchasing another goat or two.'

Fidelma turned back to Hawisa.

'So it was not worth very much. What sort of coin was it?'

The woman shrugged. 'Coins are rare in this part of the world. Yet I have seen gold before.'

'So the abbot kept this coin?'

'He did.'

'And you are sure that it was an old coin?'

The woman nodded and set down her empty earthenware mug beside her.

'I have been robbed of those I loved. First my fine husband was taken to serve in Grimoald's army three years ago. He never returned and others told me he had been slain. Now my only child is dead. I have nothing to lose now so I care not what you report to your abbot. Wamba was killed because he found a piece of gold. That was why he was buried hurriedly, so that I should not see the wounds.'

She leaned forward suddenly and, using two forefingers, sharply tapped Fidelma's chest. She repeated a short sentence three times, but the only word Fidelma could make out was *Odo*. She glanced at Brother Eolann. 'What does she say about Odo – that's the nephew, isn't it?'

'She says Odo will confirm her story,' replied Brother Eolann. 'I don't think there is a need for that. I have translated all she has said.'

'We can accept her account of what happened,' agreed Fidelma. Yet there is something illogical here,' she went on. 'Even if the coin *was* gold, it could not be so valuable that it would need several to be involved in the conspiracy to kill the boy. There wouldn't be enough for anyone to take a profit from the deed.'

Brother Eolann regarded her uncertainly. 'What do you mean?'

'First, we must include Brother Waldipert in this affair. Then we must include Abbot Servillius himself, as he valued the coin. Then we must include the warrior Wulfoald. The implication is that he might have killed the boy. He certainly found the body and took it to the abbey. We might even add Brother Hnikar who, as apothecary, would have washed and laid out the body for burial. He would have noticed if the body carried any marks to indicate an unnatural death – for I think Hawisa is arguing that the boy was buried *before* she could see the body and be aware that her son had been murdered.'

Brother Eolann shrugged. 'I have not your clever tongue nor way of thought.'

Hawisa had been watching them very carefully during this exchange and suddenly spoke vehemently.

'She says that all she knows is that she saw the gold coin. Wamba took it to the abbey and he was dead the next day. And now he lies in the graveyard of the abbey where she cannot pray daily, for the journey is too much. She contents herself by praying at the spot where he was found.'

The woman suddenly snapped out something in a harsh voice.

'Report me to your abbot. I have no fear,' translated Brother Eolann.

'Neither do you need to fear,' Fidelma assured her. 'We are not here to report to Abbot Servillius. He does not know that we are here anyway, and we would prefer it that you did not tell anyone of our visit.'

Hawisa looked puzzled.

'Tell her that I am just a visitor from Hibernia. I came

here because I am cursed with a curiosity about all things. And I heard about the story of her son, Wamba.'

Hawisa was still puzzled but seemed to accept that this was some sort of explanation. Once more Brother Eolann began to translate as she spoke. 'The founder of the abbey was from Hibernia. I am told several of your countrymen come to visit the abbey in his memory.'

'Exactly so.' There was a silence and then Fidelma added: 'Before we leave, we would say a prayer at the spot where Wamba fell, where you now go to say your daily prayer. Would you tell us the way there?'

Once again Hawisa was regarding Fidelma suspiciously. 'Why would you want to see where my son fell to his death?'

'It is not to see where but merely to say a prayer for his soul.' Fidelma knew she was lying and hoped that Brother Eolann could translate her words with more sincerity. Hopefully, she would be forgiven for the lie as it was in the cause of seeking the truth.

Hawisa did not answer at once. She seemed to think carefully before telling them, 'If you follow that path,' she indicated a track through the trees just beyond the cabin, 'follow it to the north-east, you'll eventually come to two large rocks that divide the pathway. Do not take the descending path but follow on and you'll emerge along a series of high rock formations. There is a small cairn which I raised to mark the spot. It was said that is the point from where he fell.'

Fidelma reached forward and placed a hand on the woman's arm.

'We are most grateful for your help, Hawisa.'

'I ask you not to damage the little cairn. Someone did so between yesterday and this morning when I went to pray.'

'We will not damage it,' Fidelma promised, then she frowned. 'What sort of damage?' she asked.

'The stones were knocked aside,' replied Hawisa.

'Oh. Perhaps it was some animal then?'

'Not so. I built the cairn around a small wooden box in which poor Wamba used to keep a few things he prized. Coloured beads, stones and his favourite pipe.'

'Pipe?' queried Fidelma.

'Most lads play pipes on the mountain. Simple things. It was only a rough box that he had made himself. Someone has taken it, and a curse on their soul for doing so. They are a disgrace to their cloth.'

Fidelma stared at the woman. 'Their cloth? What makes you say that?'

Brother Eolann seemed to have some difficulty with translating. 'A neighbour saw a man in religious robes taking the box and climbing down to his horse.'

'It was taken by a religieux?'

'Someone looking like a religieux,' added Brother Eolann hurriedly.

'Did this neighbour describe him or his horse?' Fidelma waited impatiently for Brother Eolann to pose the question.

'The neighbour could see no more,' said Eolann, after a further exchange. 'I asked where this neighbour was and she says that he has gone to the market of Travo and will be gone for some days.'

Fidelma thought for a moment and then rose slowly. 'We will not damage the cairn. Be assured.'

'Then I would be grateful for your blessing and your prayers before you leave. Forgive a grieving mother for my sharpness.'

It was Brother Eolann who intoned the prayers in the local

language before they bade farewell to the woman and followed the path indicated by her.

Although they were high on the mountain, they were still within the treeline, where tall beech trees interspersed with rowan were still dominant. Here and there were other trees which reminded Fidelma of oak, but were different. She had noticed these curious oaks before. She took the opportunity to ask Brother Eolann if he knew what they were. He told her that they were called turkey-oak and were native to the area. Here and there, birds flitted from branch to branch and she caught sight of white and yellow wagtails and sparrow-hawks.

Brother Eolann cast a glance at the sky, saying, 'We mustn't delay in reaching the sanctuary at the top. It will not be very long before twilight is upon us.'

'Are there dangerous animals on the mountain if we do not make it and have to encamp for the night?'

'In terms of big animals, I have seen foxes and wolves. But the one thing I hate is something that is not seen in our land.'

'Which is?' asked Fidelma curiously.

'There is a snake called a *vipera*; its bite can be dangerous, for it injects a poison.'

Fidelma shivered a moment and glanced around her feet. 'I have heard of the like but never encountered one.'

'I have only once seen one,' confided Brother Eolann. 'Brother Lonán found it in the *herbarium* last autumn. It was curled up basking in the sun. He tried to pick it up, thinking it was a slow-worm, and it bit him and he was in pain for several days. Thankfully, Brother Hnikar had some potion and told Lonán to go and lie down and not to exert himself, for the action would carry the venom through his body. He recovered but it took many days.'

'Then you must warn me if you see such a creature in my path,' Fidelma said fervently. 'Wolves and foxes do not worry me, but the idea of such creatures as snakes . . .' She shuddered again.

They moved out of the shaded pathway on to an open rocky path on the mountainside. To their left the hillside rose steeply and was studded with boulders and dark grey rocks. To their right, the hillside fell equally steeply.

'Ah!' Fidelma exclaimed and pointed to a small pile of stones that lay a little way ahead of them. 'That must be Hawisa's cairn.'

There was nothing remarkable about the cairn, which Hawisa had raised in memory of her son.

Fidelma looked about with a critical eye. Then she moved to the edge of the path, to where the hillside fell away steeply. Some twenty metres or so below them was a broad track which was obviously used frequently.

'What track is that?' she asked.

'It is a track that leads across the mountains from the north and, if one continues down into the valley, it comes to the abbey,' confirmed Brother Eolann.

Fidelma peered over the edge. 'It's quite a fall, but easy to climb down. That is doubtless where this person who took the box left his horse, climbed up and then returned with the box.'

'It is also where the boy must have fallen, to be found by Wulfoald as he rode by.'

'How would a sure-footed lad who had tended goats on these mountain slopes all his life manage to fall from this place? The edge is so clear and the dangers obvious.'

'Maybe one of the goats had wandered too near the edge and in trying to rescue it, he slipped?' suggested Brother Eolann. 'I think we should consider that.'

'Perhaps,' Fidelma admitted, albeit with reluctance. 'However, speculation is not going to reveal any secrets to us. I shall climb down.'

Brother Eolann protested at once but she waved his concerns aside. 'There are more difficult descents among the high peaks in Muman,' she said.

'But what are you seeking?'

'I won't know until I see it,' she replied, and then she walked to the edge, examining the rockface carefully.

'Careful!' called Brother Eolann nervously.

'If you are going to shout like that,' admonished Fidelma, 'you will cause me to start and fall. Ah, I see a way . . .' She climbed over the edge and began to move down the rockface. As a child, she and her brother, Colgú, had scrambled over the hills of Cnoc an Stanna and Sliabh Eibhlinne. Such climbs held no fears for her. Her descent was as nimble as one of Wampa's goats, and in a short time, she stood on the rocky path below.

'Stay there,' she called up. 'If there is anything to be seen, I shall see it.'

She walked along the base of the rockface, her eyes searching the ground but unable to see anything that seemed out of place. Not that she really expected to see anything. If the boy had been killed or, if he had fallen, there would be no traces left, so long after his death. As she walked up and down the stony area below the rocks, the only thing that caught her eye was what appeared to be a small piece of smashed twig among some pieces of coloured pottery and glass beads. There was something odd about the twig. She picked it up and turned it over in her hands before suddenly realising what it was. It was less than a finger-length and about as thick. It had been smashed at both ends but was hollow, like a piece of cane. Halfway along were two neatly cut holes. At one end were markings which showed something had been attached there. A mouthpiece?

'Are you all right?' came Brother Eolann's anxious voice from above.

She glanced up and realised that he could not see her because of the overhang.

'All is well,' she called up. Standing away from the cliff face so that she could see Brother Eolann, she added, 'I won't be long.'

'Have you found something?'

'Nothing yet,' she replied. She moved back to where she had found the items and peered around before gazing up the rockface. There was a shelf of rock a little way above the spot where she stood. It was just above the level of her head, but she was able to find some holds so that she could scramble to head height.

A crude box lay on its side on the shelf, its lid open. It was made of rough wood and no more than twenty centimetres in length and ten in width, and not very deep. Fidelma lifted it carefully so that the few things still in it did not spill out as she climbed down again. The box was of very unskilled workmanship indeed. The two hinges were of metal but it was obvious that the hand that had made them had not made the box. Letters had been burned on the underside of the lid. They were badly formed and probably made with the point of a hot poker. WAMBA.

It was obviously the box stolen from the cairn. But the thief must have dropped it as he scrambled down to his horse. It must have caught on the rock shelf when the thief had dropped it, having taken flight when he saw himself observed. The observer had not seen where the box had fallen, however, since it had not been recovered. Inside were some curious little knick-knacks of no particular value, the mouth-piece that went with the pipes and some cheap ceramic jewellery and clay items.

Why would a thief desecrate a memorial? She began exam-ining the items in the box – then she noticed something. Emptying out the contents, she shook the box. It rattled as if something was still loose. She began to run her fingers over the bottom of the inside. It did not fit tightly and she was able, with care, to prise it free. Underneath it lay a small object. She lifted it out between thumb and forefinger. It was a gold coin.

She replaced the false bottom and the other items, but put the coin into her *marsupium*.

'What's happening?' called Brother Eolann from above.

'I've found Wamba's box,' she replied. 'I'm coming up. Can you let me have your cincture?'

'What?' Brother Eolann sounded puzzled. The word she used in their own language was *crios*, for the cincture was a ropelike cord encircling the waist which most religious wore.

'Throw it down, so that I can carry the box up with me.'

The task to secure it did not take long. 'I'm coming up,' she called.

She began to climb carefully up again, refusing Brother Eolann's offer of a helping hand as she scrambled over the edge back to the path they had come by.

'You had me concerned, lady. Imagine if you had fallen. How would I have been able to report such a matter to the abbot?'

Fidelma pouted. 'I would have been in no position to have imagined that,' she replied dryly. 'And I could not have advised you anyway.' She gazed around before letting her eyes settle back on the cairn. Then she untied the box and returned the cincture to her companion.

'Well, at least we can replace the box in the cairn. The thief must have dropped it.'

'Was there anything in it?' queried Brother Eolann.

She reached into her *marsupium* and showed him the coin.

'But Wamba gave the gold piece to Brother Waldipert,' pointed out Brother Eolann, perplexed. 'And didn't Waldipert give it to Abbot Servillius?'

'This is certainly a very old gold coin, the like of which I have not seen before,' Fidelma said, while turning it over in her hands. She paused, remembering the words of Brother Ruadán. He had used 'coins' in the plural. 'I wonder . . .'

'You wonder?' prompted Brother Eolann expectantly.

'Perhaps young Wamba found two coins and decided to keep one hidden until he found out the value of the other. He may have thought they would be taken away from him if he offered both. His mother could not have known of its existence otherwise she would have removed it before she placed the box in the cairn.'

'That seems logical,' Brother Eolann agreed.

'But did the would-be thief know it was there?'

Fidelma examined the gold coin again. It was small, definitely of gold and not a mixture made with any baser metal. It carried the image of a chariot drawn by two horses with a charioteer guiding it, while the small symbols around it seemed to represent stars in the sky.

'I believe I have seen similar coins before,' she commented thoughtfully.

'Venerable Ionas has knowledge about such coins.'

'I wonder if Abbot Servillius consulted him about the coin

Wamba brought to the abbey? This is a mystery that I must resolve,' Fidelma said firmly, trying to recall the last gasping words of Brother Ruadán.

'Should we not return this to Hawisa?' protested the *scriptor*.

'Eventually. If Brother Ruadán was right, that the boy was killed for the first gold coin, the warrior Wulfoald and Abbot Servillius have some questions to answer.'

She realised, as she said it, that she was in no position to pose those questions. She might be an advocate of the law in her own land, and she might have been invited by King Oswiu of Northumbria to solve the murders at Streonshalh and by Venerable Gelasius to solve the crime in the Lateran Palace, but here – who was she? Just a passing stranger of no local rank. A foreigner without standing. Lord Radoald was the only power in the land and he was hardly likely to grant her any authority to investigate this matter.

She placed the gold coin carefully in her *marsupium* again.

'This is turning out to be frustrating. Perhaps I was expecting too much.'

'How could Brother Ruadán know about the coin?' demanded Brother Eolann. 'I do not understand this matter at all.'

'Those are the questions that I came here seeking the answers to. But it looks as though I will not find them. It is always irritating when one encounters a blank wall.' She glanced up at the sky. They would not have a great deal of time until the darkening eastern skies were upon them. 'Perhaps we should continue our climb to this sanctuary?'

'If we go back to Hawisa's cabin and continue up the track from there, it will put extra time on the journey, although that is easier and safer,' mused the *scriptor*.

'What do you suggest?'

Brother Eolann thought for a moment. 'If you don't mind heights, lady, there is a small footpath along here, where people may pass only in single file. It becomes very steep in places. But after passing a rocky outcrop, it joins the main path, and it is an easy journey to the summit. It would save us considerable time in reaching the sanctuary. Having witnessed your abilities just now, I think you should be able to make the passage with ease.'

'In that case, let us try this quicker path.'

He led the way, turning up what appeared to be a goat's track that Fidelma would have missed altogether. Inconspicuous and overgrown, it inclined rapidly, scarcely the width of a foot wide.

'You seem to know these mountain tracks very well, for a stranger and a *scriptor*,' Fidelma said. She had made the remark automatically, but when she began to think about it, it *was* curious. The suspicious thought had barely crossed her mind when Brother Eolann paused and turned back to her.

'As you said to Hawisa, I am cursed with a curiosity,' he said seriously. 'Confined to a library, one is likely to be without exercise, to grow weak and idle. Now and then I seek permission from the abbot to climb the hills here in order to maintain myself in fitness. Juvenal, in his *Satires*, exhorted one to maintain *mens sana in corpore sano* – a sound mind in a sound body. I believe that to keep the mind sound you also need to keep the body sound. Hence, in the two years I have been here, I have come to know many byways and tracks.'

'Then your knowledge is lucky for me,' Fidelma replied.

They continued to climb upwards and, at times, Fidelma

had to pause and close her eyes to stop herself becoming dizzy on the often precipitous slopes. But finally, as Brother Eolann had forewarned, they came to a rocky outcrop which seemed to block their path. Next to it was a sheer drop. Brother Eolann turned with an encouraging smile.

'This is the difficult part,' he said. 'There are handholds on the rock and you have to lean almost backwards and rely on the handholds to keep you balanced. Are you happy about this?'

Fidelma glanced down at the fall, shivered slightly as she realised the dangers of the height, and nodded swiftly. 'Let's get on with it,' she muttered. It was better to do this quickly than to stand talking about it.

'I'll go first and show the way. Make sure your bag is firmly fixed to your back and that you are balanced.'

He adjusted his own bag on his back and waited while she did the same. Then he set off crawling under the overhang where she could not see a path and yet somehow there must have been. He seemed to be finding handholds to steady him and then . . . then he had vanished on the other side of the rock.

'Can you hear me?' she called anxiously.

A moment passed. Then: 'Sorry, I was just catching my breath.' His voice came from a short distance away. 'Now, can you remember how I crawled under the overhang?'

'I think so.'

'You'll see some places where your hands can take a good hold. You'll find yourself leaning backwards as if you are going to fall. Keep a good hold with one hand before you move to the next hold.'

Fidelma took a deep breath and began to move slowly forward, almost crouching at first as she came under the overhang. She saw what he meant almost immediately and found she was in a position to move forward. There were little ledges where she could secure a grasp. Slowly, hand by hand she moved forward. She tried not to think what was behind her, the emptiness and the fall to the rocks below. The worst moment was when she found herself leaning backwards into that frightening space with only her hands clasping at the rocks to prevent her falling.

'You are nearly there,' cried Brother Eolann's voice in encouragement.

She reached forward to grasp the next handhold, missed it and felt herself swinging out. The full weight of her body was hanging on one hand while her other hand was grasping at nothing.

'Help me!' she cried in panic.

It seemed an eternity before a strong hand seized her wrist and pulled. For a moment she was suspended in space – one hand clinging desperately to the rock and the other caught by the wrist in the hand of Brother Eolann. For a curious moment, their faces were separated by inches, her fiery green eyes staring into his light blue ones. It seemed as if time had stood still and all she was aware of was the void below her. Then she was lying on a sloping bank, gasping for breath. She realised she was on the other side of the overhang. Brother Eolann was still clutching her wrist.

'Are you hurt?' he asked anxiously.

Fidelma shuddered and shook her head. She felt the pressure on her wrist relax as he released it and automatically she reached with her other hand to massage it. 'You caught hold of me in time.' She knew she was stating the obvious.

Brother Eolann was still anxious. 'I trust I did not hurt you.'

'You saved my life,' she said solemnly. 'I can stand a bruise or two for that.'

'I warned you that it was a difficult point to cross. But see along there . . . we are a short way from joining the main track to the top and,' he glanced again at the sky, 'we would not have made it before dark had we gone any other way.'

'Then let us move on. The sooner we are away from this place, the more I shall like it.'

He stood up and led the way forward again. The rest of the journey was simple and without incident. Even so, dusk had already spread over the mountain-top when they reached a hut, built in a little hollow. She could make out no details in the gloom. It was a cloudy night and there was no moon-light to assist them. Nevertheless, Brother Eolann seemed to know his way about and, after a while, with flint and tinder, he had lit a brand torch and then proceeded to get a fire alight outside the small hut. To Fidelma's amusement he built a large fire that she was sure would be seen on the moun-tain-top for quite a distance around. He did not smile when she commented that she only wanted to keep warm and not roast to death.

'It is very cold up here, lady. The temperatures during the night, even in late summer, can be freezing. Besides which . . . well, there are many animals which wander the slopes at night. The fire will keep them at bay.'

Inside the hut was an oil lamp which he lit. There was, apparently, a water supply nearby and he filled a jug with fresh water. Soon they were sitting eating a frugal meal in silence and watching the dark clouds sweeping low across the mountain-tops, creating a damp, chilling mist in the moments before darkness descended. There were no stars, for the clouds obliterated them. Fidelma felt exhausted at the unexpected exercise. She only vaguely remembered crawling into the hut.

It was bright sunlight when she awoke to the hunting cry of buzzards. The fire was still sending a plume of smoke upwards and Brother Eolann was already building it up again. He had food ready and directed her to the source of water behind the hut where she could wash in private.

She was impressed by the breathtaking view of hilltops that surrounded her.

'This is one of the highest peaks in these hills,' Brother Eolann offered, seeing the rapt look on her face as she gazed around the vista. The day was warm and pleasant and the clouds that had obscured the moon on the previous night had dispersed and given way to brilliant sunshine.

They were in a sheltered dip on the peak and she could well understand why it had been chosen by Colm Bán for his sanctuary. A little way off, on the highest part of the bald, rounded hilltop, stood the half-completed building which was clearly dedicated to the Faith and marked by a large cross outside. Brother Eolann accompanied Fidelma to it and they spent a few moments in contemplation inside the darkness of the little chapel.

'I will be reluctant to leave this spot,' Fidelma remarked as they came out into the sunshine again. 'Are those caves I see down there, behind the hut?'

'They are,' Brother Eolann confirmed. 'They are not big ones but it is said that it was one of those that Colm Bán used as his retreat and, sadly, where that great man passed on, into the arms of Christ.'

'Yet he is buried in the abbey.'

'The brethren removed his body to the abbey and built a crypt for him under the chapel's High Altar.'

'I should pay my respects at the cave before I depart.'

The caves were not big. In fact, in the larger one there was scarcely room enough for two people to crawl in. This one showed signs of having been used recently, while the other held little of note. Fidelma left the caves and returned to examining the countryside around them. A short distance below them, the thick under-bush of ferns and bracken began, and beyond that, looking down the southern slopes, conifers and beeches marked the beginning of the dense forests that spread among these hills. Fidelma gazed once more across the impressive vista unfolding before her. As she was turning back to the hut, something caught her eye amidst the under-growth.

'Look!' She pointed to a splash of colour that was out of keeping with its surroundings. It appeared to be a piece of richly coloured fabric.

She moved quickly down the hill, followed more slowly by Brother Eolann. She was plunging into the undergrowth when the *scriptor* called out a warning.

'Be careful, lady. This is the sort of growth that the *vipera*, the venomous snake, is found in. Let me go first.'

She halted while he picked up a stout stick and began to move forward, hitting the ground and making much noise.

'The *vipera* will not attack unless it thinks it is attacked,' explained the *scriptor*. 'If it hears you approaching, it will slither away for shelter. It is only if you approach in stealth and come upon it unexpectedly that it will strike.'

Fidelma was content to let him beat the path to what they thought was the fluttering fabric. But it was not just fabric. It was a body – the body of a woman. She had been dead for some time, judging from the sickly stench of decomposition that was drawing the attention of several flying insects. The clothing now seemed familiar to Fidelma. Placing a hand across her mouth and nostrils, she crouched down to examine the features. She recognised the corpse at once.

'It's the Lady Gunora,' she gasped.

CHAPTER ELEVEN

The head of the woman had been almost severed from her body by several blows to the neck from a sharp-edged implement such as a sword.

Fidelma almost retched at the mangled form and she fought for a moment to control herself. At her side Brother Eolann was offering up a prayer in a horrified voice.

Once Fidelma recovered her equilibrium, she glanced intently at the area surrounding the remains.

'What is it?' Brother Eolann asked. 'Do you think that her killers are hiding nearby?'

'She has been dead for over a day,' Fidelma replied quietly. 'They would not delay here so long. But she left the abbey yesterday with the boy, the young Prince Romuald. Do you see any sign of . . . of his body?'

Brother Eolann, still pale, joined Fidelma in searching the surrounding shrubland. There were no obvious signs of another body nearby, so she returned her attention to the corpse; wrinkling her nose in distaste, she bent down and checked through the clothing, searching for any personal items. Surprisingly, there were none. It seemed that the Lady Gunora had not even been carrying the customary bag for toilet articles, which most women of her rank carried tied at her waist. Or had she already been searched and the items taken?

'Do you think this might be the work of Perctarit and his men?' the *scriptor* asked, glancing at the corpse. 'They might have seized the prince when they killed Lady Gunora.'

'At the moment, Brother Eolann, we do not have sufficient knowledge to think anything. However, we shall learn nothing more here. Is there a spare blanket in the hut here?'

'I think so,' Brother Eolann replied, puzzled.

'Since we cannot do anything here, I suggest that we get a blanket and use it to carry the corpse to the chapel where it will be safe from those,' she indicated the circling buzzards, 'or any other wild beast.'

The *scriptor* did not look happy but he made no demur. It took them quite a while to transport the body to the chapel and place it inside, covered by the blanket.

It had been such a warm, pleasant day when Fidelma had awoken with the vast panorama of the hills. Now the day seemed to have turned cold and unpleasant.

'Is it time that we started back down?' she suggested.

'We have time enough,' returned Brother Eolann. 'I'd rather let the fire die down a bit so that it will be safe to leave it.'

'I thought you had stacked it rather high this morning,' Fidelma replied and went into the hut to brush herself down. She finished packing her bag, which she slung on her back, and re-emerged into the sunlight.

Facing her were three warriors with swords drawn and glistening threateningly in the sunlight. A fourth man stood by Brother Eolann. His sword was resting lightly with its point against the *scriptor*'s chest.

No one spoke or moved for a moment until Fidelma recovered from her surprise and demanded: 'Who are these men?'

Brother Eolann cleared his throat and spoke in the local language to them. One of the men laughed gruffly before responding.

'He says that we will soon find out. Meanwhile, we are his prisoners and will accompany him.'

'Can't you tell him that we are poor religious from the Abbey of Bobium?' queried Fidelma.

Brother Eolann grimaced. 'I fear that he knows that already, lady.'

'You mean these are—'

The warrior who had responded suddenly shouted at her. She did not need Brother Eolann's translation to interpret what he said. She thought of the corpse of the slain Lady Gunora and was silent.

The leading warrior said no more but turned and led the way. His men fell in around them, using the tips of their swords as prods, and began to push them along. Fidelma saw that the path they were taking led down the opposite side of the mountain from the route back to Bobium. She glanced at her companion but Brother Eolann gave a slight shake of his head, as if trying to warn her not to speak again. These warriors, whoever they were, could not be trifled with.

The country on the north-east side of the mountain seemed just as spectacular as it had been in the Trebbia Valley. Perhaps more so. She could see blue strips of rivers in valleys, surrounded by numerous peaks stretching away in all directions. In the distance were slabs of bare grey rock, which had been worn away by water erosion. Even with her concern that they were prisoners of men who cared little for their lives, Fidelma studied her surroundings carefully in case a

PETER TREMAYNE

chance offered itself for escape. She registered that this side
of the mountains was the weather side, where there seemed
little protection against hill erosion. The usually hard rock
and brittle surface often gave way to soft clay and limestone.

They marched on in silence until they descended well
below the treeline and began to walk through a thick, noise-
filled forest. A myriad species of bird calls rose in cacophony,
while the bark of foxes and the solitary howl of a wolf came
to Fidelma's ears. They seemed to be trudging along for an
eternity. The incline eventually began to grow more gentle,
and here and there they passed boys and old men with herds
of goats or flocks of sheep. Still no one spoke. Finally,
unable to bear it any longer, Fidelma said to Brother Eolann:
'Please ask him how much longer he intends to keep this
pace up.'

Immediately she felt the pressure of the point of one of
the men's swords between her shoulderblades. Brother Eolann
was clearly too nervous to obey her.

Ignoring the guard, Fidelma repeated her question, calling
out to the leader in her book Latin.

The man halted and turned back with a scowl. He snapped
a question at Brother Eolann, who answered hesitantly. The
warrior suddenly chuckled; it was not a pleasant sound. Then
he said something to Brother Eolann. The *scriptor* shrugged
and muttered, 'He says that you are impertinent for a woman,
lady. You will know soon enough . . .' Then he added anxiously,
'Best not to mention your rank, lady. People around here are
not above holding those of rank to ransom.'

There was a sharp command from the leader. She interpreted
it as another command for silence.

They moved on again. This time it was a shorter trek until
they came to a clearing in the forest where there were half

198

a dozen horses tethered, with two other warriors apparently looking after them. They called out excitedly to one another and some conversation was exchanged in which the other two examined the captives with curiosity.

Fidelma and Brother Eolann found themselves pushed forward to the horses. Two of the warriors sheathed their swords and leaped nimbly up into the saddles. Then, before she realised what was happening, strong hands seized Fidelma and almost threw her on the horse behind one of the warriors. She did not need to know the man's rough words to understand the exhortation to hang on. He began to move off at once and she looked to one side to see that Brother Eolann had been similarly treated.

They rode on until Fidelma lost all track of time and place. She only knew that it was late in the afternoon and the band of horsemen were now trotting along a fairly easy path across the side of a hill. Below them was a valley with a broad river flowing through it. After a further descent they came to a small settlement under a precipitous rocky hill. Now she could see, balanced on the very top, overlooking the small settlement, a stone fortress with an imposing square tower. At first, she thought there was no way up, but then they were ascending a winding path towards the summit. Whatever the building was, it was clearly the place that their captors were making for.

Indeed, eventually they came to high walls in which were set two large dark oak gates, with sufficient space to admit men on horseback. Warriors looked down on them from the walls. One of the men accompanying them produced a hunting horn and let forth two short blasts, ending with one long wailing sound. The gates swung open and they rode through and halted in a small courtyard.

Fidelma was aware of hands pulling her from the horse and a host of rough faces surrounded her. Some were grinning and some shouted at her, words that she did not understand. Then someone called a command and brutal hands removed the bag she was carrying on her back but did not take the *marsupium* at her waist. One of her captors came forward, grasped her by the arm and pushed through the curious crowd towards the buildings that ran the length of the inside walls. As she was propelled forwards, Fidelma glanced up to where a balcony jutted over the courtyard. Two men were standing looking down on the proceedings. Two tall men, clad in long black cloaks. They appeared to be warriors. One of them had the left side of his cloak flung back over his shoulder and she caught sight of a badge on his shoulder. Although he stood at some distance and above her, she was sure it was the flaming sword and laurel wreath emblem. She almost tripped and fell as it came to her that these looked like the same men who had attacked the Magister Ado in Genua; the same who had ambushed them as they entered the Valley of Trebbia. The same men who, she believed, she had seen in the darkness at the fortress of Radoald.

Recovering her balance, she managed to glance behind and saw Brother Eolann being manhandled in a similar fashion. At least it seemed that they were being kept together. Indeed, a door was opened and she was pushed, with scant ceremony, inside a room. Brother Eolann was propelled after her, bumping into her. The door was slammed shut and they heard a wooden bar crash into place to secure it.

The room was lit by a single window situated well above head height. There were no bars on it. Apart from two rough beds, a chair and a table, there was little else in the room. Brother Eolann sat down on one of the beds, seemingly exhausted by the ordeal. Fidelma seized a chair and went to the window, placed it underneath and then balanced herself on it to peer out. At times, the fact that she was above the average height for her sex proved helpful. She quickly found the reason why the window was unbarred. It presented no other exit than a sheer drop into the valley below. She climbed down and sat with a sigh. There was nothing else in the room, not even an oil lamp.

'Well,' she said at last, 'any ideas who our captors are?'

Brother Eolann shrugged. 'That they have no respect for the religious, is certain,' he replied. 'I know little of these valleys on this side of the mountains, but I think this is the territory of the Lord of Vars.'

'Does he hold allegiance to this King Grimoald?' Fidelma was thinking of the two men bearing the symbol of the Archangel Michael on their clothing. It was no use trying to explain this story to Brother Eolann.

'I am sure he does not,' the *scriptor* said immediately. 'I have heard that there is enmity between Trebbia and Vars.'

'But I thought you said that you had climbed these mountains regularly and that was why you knew the paths on – what was it called – Mount Pénas? How do you not know this place?'

'It is true that I have climbed the mountains, but I always kept to the side overlooking the Valley of the Trebbia. I was always warned to be careful, for we were told that to the north and east are the lands that once held allegiance to Perctarit. If they do not hate Grimoald, then they are followers of Arius and have cause to hate the brethren of Bobium.'

'And who are these?'

'Either or both. It makes no difference.'

'You have no idea where we are?'

'I should think that the river is called the Staffel in the Longobard language; it is called the Iria in Latin. We must be overlooking the old Salt Road to Genua.'

'Well, we can do little until we find out who these people are and what they want. There is certainly no way out of this room except through the door.'

Brother Eolann sighed. 'I hope they bring us food and drink soon. We have had nothing since dawn and must have been travelling a good part of the day.'

Fidelma remembered that the food they had taken for their journey on the mountain had been in their bags. 'Did they take your bag as well?' she asked.

'They did. There was dry biscuit, cheese and fruit in it. Now we have nothing.'

Fidelma smiled wanly. They had forgotten to take her *marsupium*, but there was no food in it. It was where she carried her *ciorr bholg* or 'comb bag'. It was a small handbag which all the women of rank in Hibernia carried. It usually contained a *scathán*, a small mirror, *deimess*, scissors, a bar of *sléic* or soap and, in Fidelma's case, a *phal* of honeysuckle fragrance. Unlike many women she did not carry a *phal* of berry juice with which to redden her lips or blacken her eyebrows, which was often the custom among Hibernian women.

Fidelma was not thinking of her toiletries but of the gold coin that she had, thankfully, placed in it. A thought struck her. 'If these are the people who killed poor Lady Gunora, then they may have brought Prince Romuald here as a prisoner.'

'Do you think these men are truly the killers of Lady Gunora?' Brother Eolann's nervousness was evident.

'Why else would they have been lurking around that particular area?'

Brother Eolann looked uncomfortable. 'It is a situation that is new to me. I am not able to guess who they are or their motivations. This must be the fortress of a local war lord. That is all I know. As I said, I am not familiar with this part of the country. What can we do?'

'Do? I don't think there is anything we can do until our captors make the next move.'

'We can't just wait, hoping they will bring us food.' Brother Eolann's voice rose in protest.

Fidelma gave him a look of pity. 'Were you never taught the *dercad*?'

The *dercad* was an ancient form of meditation which some church leaders disapproved of as it was practised in the time before the Faith of Christ came to the shores of the Five Kingdoms of Éireann. It was a way of making the mind as still as water in a dark mountain pool, ridding oneself of the chaos of emotions and fear, the worst of all the emotions.

'Of course I was,' protested the *scriptor*. 'But how does that help us now?'

'I suggest we can occupy the time in no other constructive manner than by ridding our minds of expectation and fear.'

Fidelma took a seat on the other bed, sitting cross-legged with her hands folded in her lap. Then she closed her eyes and began to breathe slowly and deeply.

Brother Eolann pursed his lips for a moment or two, then shrugged and copied her.

How much time passed was difficult to say. But the day had grown dark. They could hear faint sounds, laughter, shouting and conversation from around them. Suddenly the stillness was broken by the scraping of the wooden bar being raised and the door was pushed open. Fidelma's eyes opened immediately and she rose from her position. Brother Eolann stirred and looked about sleepily, showing that instead of being in a true state of the *dercad*, he had actually fallen asleep.

A man entered carrying a lighted oil lamp which he set on the table; he then withdrew without a word. But even as he left, another man came in bearing a pitcher and clay beakers. These were placed on the table in silence, and then the first man reappeared with wooden platters on which was bread, cold meats, cheese and fruit. He turned and left just as Fidelma found her voice.

'Wait! Who are you? What do you want with us?'

Her words were spoken in Latin and she was going to tell Brother Eolann to translate them when a deep voice answered her.

'Peace, little sister. All will be answered in good time.'

In the door stood a big man, so large that his shoulders seemed to brush either side of the frame. He looked fat but on closer inspection he was built of solid muscle. He had a mass of black curling hair and dark eyes that blazed curiously as they reflected the lamplight.

'Who are you?' demanded Fidelma again.

'I am Kakko, little sister.'

'And is this your fortress?'

The big man threw back his head and roared with laughter, as if she had said something exceptionally funny. She waited patiently until his mirth subsided. She was aware that Brother Eolann was staring longingly at the food and drink that had been placed on the table, trying to restrain himself. However, this was an opportunity not to be missed.

'Have I said something to amuse you?' she asked coldly.

'I am only the steward here, little sister.'

'Then whose fortress is it?'

'This fortress and the lands along this valley belong to my lord.'

Fidelma suppressed a sigh of impatience. 'And who is your lord?'

'My lord is Grasulf son of Gisulf.'

She looked across at Brother Eolann but he shook his head, indicating that the name meant nothing to him.

'And who is Grasulf exactly?'

Kakko's dark eyes widened almost in horror. 'You do not know of the Lord of Vars?'

'We are strangers here.'

'Strangers?'

'We are of Hibernia. I had been in this land but a few days when your warriors abducted me and my companion.'

The big man stared thoughtfully from Fidelma to Eolann. 'Who are you?' he demanded of Fidelma.

'I am Fidelma and he is Brother Eolann, the *scriptor* at Bobium.'

Kakko was staring at Brother Eolann. 'Hibernians, eh? There are many in this land. Perhaps too many. They are the ones who set up Bobium in the first place.'

'As I have said,' Fidelma added firmly, 'I have been in your country but a few days and plan to stay little longer. I do not know why you have taken me captive but I demand my release.'

The steward's eyes widened again and then a big smile spread over his features. Humour seemed to come easily to him.

'You demand?' he grinned. 'I will tell that to my lord Grasulf when he returns.'

'When he returns?' snapped Fidelma. 'Returns from where?'

'My lord is on a boar hunt and is not expected back until tomorrow.'

'So who gave instruction for our abduction?'

'It has become a standing practice that any stranger in his territory should be detained and questioned,' Kakko told her.

Finally, Brother Eolann was stung into speaking. 'When has the Valley of Trebbia been in your lord's domains? It is Lord Radoald of Trebbia who governs there.'

'You were on Mount Pénas,' pointed out the steward.

'On the Trebbia side of the mountain. We were at the sanctuary of Colm Bán when your men captured us,' he protested.

The steward was unmoved. 'You may present your complaint to Lord Grasulf on his return.'

'What is this Lord Grasulf afraid of?' Fidelma suddenly said.

This drew a frown from Kakko. 'Who says my lord is afraid of anything?' he hissed.

'He is afraid of something, otherwise why would he give orders that strangers be seized and brought here for questioning, even when they are not found in his domain?'

'You are a stubborn person, little sister,' Kakko mused, still retaining his good humour. He gestured to the food on the table. 'You have not eaten. You are the guests of my lord Grasulf, and he would be displeased if you were not treated well.'

'Then your lord will be disappointed, for we have not been treated well at all, starting with our abduction,' Fidelma replied coldly. 'Then we have had our bags taken from us. If we are kept prisoners overnight, I demand the return of them.'

Kakko spread his hands in a gesture almost of resignation.

'I will ensure that they are returned. We needed to be certain that you carried no weapons or secret messages.' Fidelma's look was enough to quell him.

'As soon as this Grasulf returns, I demand to see him at once – do you understand?'

Kakko turned, shaking his head. 'You are more than a mere religieuse, Sister,' he said quietly. 'Your manner betrays you.' Then he was gone, shutting the door. They heard the wooden bar being set in place.

'I don't think you were wise, lady,' Brother Eolann muttered through a mouthful of bread and cheese. 'I told you not to reveal your rank.'

'I did not,' replied Fidelma.

'As the man said, your manner did. An ordinary Sister of the Faith would not be asserting herself in such a fashion.'

'Did you say that you had never heard of this person Grasulf?'

'I hadn't, but I *have* heard of the Lord of Vars. I said that I thought we might be in his territory.'

'Do you have any idea of the manner of man he is?'

'I know only that there is much enmity between him and Trebbia.'

'Do you think that this story of watching out for spies and informers is true then?'

'I can only repeat that there is much tension in this land. Isn't that why the Lady Gunora fled to the abbey with the little prince, because she did not believe that Grimoald's Regent, Lupus of Friuli, was to be trusted? Everything fits into a pattern. There is much fear in the land.'

'Indeed. And what if these people are the ones who killed Lady Gunora? If so, what have they done with the boy?'

'Let us pray that we will be enlightened tomorrow,' replied Brother Eolann.

'Tomorrow?'

'When you see Grasulf. That is,' Brother Eolann said with a thin smile, 'if the Lord of Vars accedes to your demand to see him on his return from his boar hunt.'

CHAPTER TWELVE

It was nearly midday before they heard the wooden bar being lifted once more from its position securing the door. Kakko, the steward, stood framed against the sunlit courtyard beyond.

'You will come with me, little brother,' he boomed. Then, glancing at Fidelma, he added: 'You will stay.'

Hesitantly, Brother Eolann rose and moved to the door.

'Why him,' Fidelma demanded, 'and not me?'

Kakko's permanent smile seemed to broaden. 'Again, a question? Always questions,' he said. Then: 'My lord Grasulf might spare you the time to meet with him later. At the moment, he only wants this one.' He jerked his head to Brother Eolann.

Fidelma would have preferred that they kept together, but there was no alternative. As time passed, she began to pace the chamber in frustration. Eventually, the big steward returned. The *scriptor* was not with him.

'And now, little sister, you will come and meet Grasulf,' he announced.

'Where is Brother Eolann?' she asked.

'He is happy enough, little sister. This way.'

She was clearly not going to get any further information from the steward and so she suppressed her feelings of apprehension and followed Kakko. She felt the immediate heat of the day as she moved from the cool of her prison into the small courtyard. The open space with the sun shining directly overhead was hot. Kakko led the way across the paved yard at a surprising pace for one so large. Once again Fidelma observed that the big man was not fat but well-muscled.

A door on the far side led into another courtyard, at one end of which were two large doors, half-open, with warriors lounging outside. They stared curiously at Fidelma as she and Kakko passed them and went into a small chamber. This, however, proved to be an antechamber, leading into a large hall. Fidelma had seen such halls before and always associated them with the traditional feasting places of chiefs and princes. She was right, for at one end, on a slightly raised dais, stood an ornately carved chair. On the back of the chair, on either side, were carved two birds of prey: she saw that they were ravens. In her own land, ravens were birds of ill-omen, symbolic of the goddess of death and battles. Smaller chairs and a table stood nearby. Colourful tapestries showing scenes of warfare and various weapons hung from the brick walls of the hall. Fidelma had noticed that most of the buildings in this land were constructed of red baked bricks which seemed to be a favourite material of Roman buildings. It was so unlike the stone blocks and the wood of her own land. The hall was well lit through a series of tall windows but it was cool after the blast of hot air she had been met with on her brief walk here.

At first glance it seemed the hall was empty. Then she heard a soft growling and became aware of two hunting dogs lying at either side of the ornate chair. They lay upright, forepaws stretched before them; heads up, alert with eyes watching them as they entered. Kakko took a pace forward and halted.

From an open doorway a man emerged, walked to the ornate chair and slumped into it. He was thickly built. Like the steward Kakko, he was muscled, showing he was more a warrior than one used to an easy life. He was not tall, more of average height, and certainly not handsome or, at least, not so far as Fidelma was concerned. He wore his fair hair long and with a full beard. So far as she could see, his eyes were pale and his features ruddy. She estimated that he was in his middle years. His expression was unfriendly. He waved a beckoning hand – a curt, impatient gesture.

Kakko strode forward until he was near the dais and then he halted and bowed, glancing at Fidelma to ensure she followed his example. She did not. She merely halted at Kakko's side and stared defiantly at the man.

'This is the one called Fidelma, my lord,' Kakko announced.

The pale eyes studied Fidelma.

'I am told that you are a religieuse from Hibernia,' the man said in Latin, speaking as if it was his first language.

'And you are . . . ?' countered Fidelma. She was angered by the arrogant manner of her captor.

Kakko gasped at what he saw as her lack of humility in front of his lord. The man's eyes widened slightly and then he held up a languid hand to his steward as if instructing him to respond.

'You stand in the presence of Grasulf son of Gisulf, Lord of Vars,' Kakko announced. 'It is an insult not to bow before him, even if you are a foreigner.'

'Lord of Vars?' Fidelma echoed Kakko as if considering the title. Then she spoke coldly and deliberately. 'Then, Grasulf son of Gisulf, know that I am Fidelma of Cashel, in the land of Hibernia, daughter of King Failbe Flann of Muman.'

Kakko stared at her for a moment and then smiled grimly. 'I thought she was more than a mere religieuse by her manners,' he said with some self-satisfaction.

'Is a daughter of a king prohibited from being a member of the religious?' she snapped. Then she tried to translate her title of *dálaigh*. 'I am also a *procurator* in my own land.'

Grasulf leaned forward, his brows drawn together as he examined her with interest. 'A princess, a religieuse and a lawyer, all these in one? Is that possible?' His voice was filled with irony.

'Indeed, all these in one,' she responded coldly.

'Bring a chair for Fidelma of Hibernia,' the Lord of Vars addressed his steward. 'Then fetch wine.'

Kakko hurried to one side of the hall to fetch the chair.

'My steward was right to suspect you were of noble rank,' Grasulf said. 'Why did you not tell him?'

'I told him only what he needed to know: that I am a visitor in your land, spending a few days here to see an old mentor of mine at the Abbey of Bobium.'

'You mean the man whom you travel with, the *scriptor* of Bobium?'

'Not Brother Eolann, who was simply showing me the sanctuary of Colm Bán on the top of Mount Pénas when we were kidnapped by your men.'

Kakko had placed the chair by her and Fidelma sat down at her ease. The big steward then went to a side table and took up two earthenware goblets and a large glazed pitcher which appeared to be full of red wine.

'Colm Bán?' Grasulf was asking, puzzled.

'You call him Columbanus. He that founded the Abbey at Bobium.'

'Ah, so,' sighed the Lord of Vars. 'I have heard of him and he is long dead. So who were you visiting at Bobium if not this *scriptor*?'

'Brother Ruadán, who died recently.'

Kakko stirred slightly. 'I met this Brother Ruadán once, my lord,' he said. 'He was very elderly. He used to wander the territory up to Placentia preaching against the Christian belief of the Arians.'

Lord Grasulf took a goblet of wine from Kakko and swallowed eagerly before speaking.

'You say that he is now dead?'

'He is,' confirmed Fidelma. 'Now I demand to be released with my comrade, Brother Eolann, and to be allowed to return to Bobium so that I may continue my journey back to my own land.'

'Released?' Grasulf sat back in his chair and stared moodily at her for a moment. 'Life is not as simple as that, lady. These are troubled times and people do not always tell the truth. Who knows why you and your companion were really on the summit of the Pénas overlooking this valley. Perhaps you were spying?'

Fidelma thrust out her chin. 'The truth is as I have told you. There is nothing else.'

'We will see.'

'I protest—'

'To whom, lady? I am Lord of Vars and any authority you have does not exist here either by birth, by law or by your religion.'

'Not by religion? Then I perceive you are all followers of Arius here?'

For the first time Grasulf's features broadened into a smile while Kakko gave one of his great guffaws of laughter. Grasulf took another large swallow of his wine before responding. Fidelma deduced that he was a man fond of his drink.

'Lady, we are true Longobards,' replied Grasulf. 'We hold to our own beliefs. We worship only Godan, Father of the Gods, King of Asgard, ruler of the Aesir. Lord of War, Death and Knowledge. He is our true god and protector.'

Fidelma gasped involuntarily. 'Then you are pagans?'

'We are only those who follow a different god to you.'

'How long do you propose to keep us prisoner?' she demanded, having absorbed this information. 'And where is Brother Eolann? Has he been harmed?'

'Do not distress yourself, lady,' boomed Kakko humorously. 'My lord has a small *scriptorium* to which your companion has been taken. My lord's *scriptor* died several moons ago, since when the books have been abandoned.'

Grasulf added: 'I have decided that while you and Brother Eolann are here you may make yourselves useful in sorting out my books.'

'So,' she said finally, 'you propose to keep us here indefinitely?'

'Until I ascertain that you are no threat.'

'Threat to whom?'

'Threat to the peace and well-being of my people.'

'Who do you fear, Grasulf, apart from a wandering woman of Hibernia and a *scriptor*?' she sneered. 'Maybe it is this Perctarit or maybe Grimoald, who are fighting over this kingdom.'

'Why should I fear either?' replied the Lord of Vars indifferently. 'Who pays me well, has my allegiance.' He was helping himself to more wine when he realised that Fidelma had scarcely touched her goblet. 'You do not drink your wine, lady. Can it be that you have no love for the juice of the grape?'

'I love freedom even more,' she replied. 'If my companion and I are to be kept as prisoners here, I would make a plea to your chivalry that we are not continually confined to the same stuffy cell.'

Grasulf almost chuckled. 'What do you suggest? That I let you wander freely outside the walls of my fortress?'

'We will respect the confines of your fortress. But there must be a place where we may rest our minds and bodies – an *herbarium*, a place of greenery, a place where we could relax yet keep our minds active. Let us have some freedom from the confines of cells and libraries. I ask this as the daughter of a king in my own land, for does not the saying exist in your land that a king may grant respect to others if he is strong and secure in his own kingdom? You tell me that you are strong and secure in your territory: you may now prove it to me.'

'The saying is that an excess of caution does no harm for it is better to have eggs today than only the promise of chickens tomorrow,' replied Grasulf. Then he turned to Kakko and spoke rapidly in the language of the Longobards, before he gestured a dismissal with his hand and turned to refill his goblet from the pitcher.

Fidelma wondered if it would be politic to ask whether his men had killed Lady Gunora and if the young prince was a prisoner in the fortress. Then she decided she must find out more first. If the Lord of Vars *had* killed Lady Gunora and kidnapped the boy, then he would have no compunction in killing her and Brother Eolann. And the thought also struck her that if the two men she had seen the previous day with the flaming sword and laurel wreath emblem, were the same ones who had attacked Magister Ado – what were they doing in a fortress of pagans? Many thoughts ran through her mind.

Kakko did not lead her back to the chamber where she had been a prisoner but took her on a different route. As they crossed the smaller courtyard he was still chuckling.

'You have impressed my lord Grasulf, little sister. You will be released from your chamber in the mornings and returned to it at night. During daylight you will be taken to the library. Next to that you will also find a small open area where you may take exercise. There is a door on the far side which gives access to the *necessarium*.' He glanced at her and added, 'Do not have any false hopes, little sister. The area is enclosed on three sides by the fortress walls and on the fourth . . . well, if you had wings to fly, like Huginn and Muninn, you might fly away.'

'Like who?'

'You saw the ravens carved on my lord's chair? They are Huginn and Muninn, the ravens who guard our great god, Godan.'

Fidelma did not bother to reply. Her mind was busy thinking that if they were not confined to the claustrophobic chamber in which they had been held, there might be a better chance of escape. They were crossing the main courtyard again, though not in the same direction. A thought suddenly struck her.

'You promised to return our travelling bags. There are personal items in them that we might use to make ourselves comfortable during our stay here – for however long that may be.'

Kakko grinned. 'No harm in that. They will be returned to you.'

He opened a door at the base of a tower in a corner of the

courtyard. Once through the tower door they turned immediately to the left, where dark wooden doors gave access into
a large chamber with a long central table. All around the
walls was shelving, with books piled everywhere. Fidelma
gazed round the library. She had certainly seen larger ones
in her own land, where the books were usually hung on pegs
in book-satchels rather than stacked on shelves. Brother
Eolann was there with his head already buried in one of the
scroll books. He looked up, his face smiling and eager.

'This is truly amazing, lady,' he greeted her. He remained
seated at the table and was tapping a thick scroll before him.

'I would not call it amazing,' she replied, her eyes travelling to the high windows which let in a certain amount of
light but not sufficient to read by. There were candles and
an oil lamp and disused writing materials scattered about.
Apart from the door which she had come in by, there was
another one at the far end of the room.

'Through that door you will find a large space which is
often used for exercise,' Kakko said, pointing. 'I should warn
you not to go too near the edge as it is a long way down into
the valley below.' He grinned at them and left, and she heard
a key turn in the lock.

'By amazing, I meant this, lady.' Ignoring the interruption,
Brother Eolann was again tapping the book before him.

'Why, what is it?' Fidelma was not particularly interested
as she surveyed the confines of the library.

'*Origio Gentis Longobardotum.*'

'The Origin of the Longobards?' translated Fidelma.

'Exactly so, lady. I have heard of this book but never seen
it before. It tells how their gods Godan and Frea set the
Longobards free from their unjust rulers to move south to take
over these lands.'

'It's an old book then?' she asked absently.

'I doubt more than twenty years old. It is said to have been drawn up by King Rothari, who was grandfather of Godepert and Perctarit.'

'Perctarit again?'

'The same Perctarit who is trying to regain his throne here. Rothari died twelve years ago and he ordered this book to be written and also the *Edictum Rothari* which is the first codification of the laws of the Longobards.'

Fidelma sighed impatiently. 'In truth, Brother Eolann, my head is swimming with all these strange, unpronounceable names. I am longing to return to the sweet sounds of our own language in Muman. Now, first things first. How did they treat you? You weren't hurt during your questioning?'

'Hurt? Oh, you mean by Grasulf. No, he did not hurt me. He just asked me questions about what we were doing, and then told me to come here.' He glanced at the scroll and confided, 'This was the first book I saw. I have to say, my first thought was whether our abbey library had a copy.'

Fidelma was still walking about the room. 'Let us take a look at the extent of our prison,' she said, turning to the door that Kakko had indicated. 'Have you examined the outside yet?'

Brother Eolann looked embarrassed and shook his head. So she opened it and stepped through. Beyond was a terrace; on three sides, the walls of the fortress towered above it, while the fourth side was opened to a distant vista of mountains and skies beyond. A small protective wall ran along this side as a barrier from the sheer drop. Tubs of earth with plants were placed here and there to relieve the grey paved surface of the terrace.

There was only one other door giving access to the area

apart from the one from the *scriptorium*. There were no handles on the outside of this door. Fidelma strode across to it and gave it a push. It was as solid as the wall around it, bolted or barred from the inside. Fidelma gazed up. There were a few high windows but it was clear that the area was enclosed and hardly overlooked at all – if anyone could, in fact, peer down from above.

Fidelma then walked across to the small parapet with Brother Eolann following. She halted and gazed down. At first glance it appeared to be a sheer drop down a rockface to the valley below. She was used to mountains and heights but this view made her dizzy. She took a deep breath and stood back.

'It is estimated to be one hundred and fifty metres to the valley floor,' came a familiar voice, speaking Latin.

She swung round to see that Grasulf, Lord of Vars, had stepped out through the mysterious door in the central wall.

'An impressive view,' conceded Fidelma.

Grasulf's features were solemn. 'It is not the recommended path out of this fortress. At least, not for our guests. It has other usages. Those we find attempting to betray us, or those who commit crimes against us, thieves and murderers, come to know it as a ready means of crossing the Ormet into the arms of our goddess Hel.'

Fidelma was puzzled. 'It is used as a method of execution,' explained Brother Eolann. 'Hel is the goddess who presides over their underworld, Helheim.'

'I am impressed with your knowledge, Brother Eolann,' the Lord of Vars said with a smile. 'That is precisely what I mean. Ormet is the river that separates life from death. And now, how do you like my little library? I have been looking for someone who would appreciate the books here ever since my own *scriptor* died. Perhaps it was the Fates who brought you hither?'

'Yes – if the Fates are what you call the warriors who abducted us,' replied Fidelma dryly. 'But I doubt we shall be here long enough to appreciate your books, Grasulf.'

The Lord of Vars nodded in appreciation. 'It is a long while since I have met with a person of wit. You shall feast with me this evening. Yes, Brother Eolann as well. You will tell me about your world beyond these valleys. I will send Kakko to escort you. In the meantime, continue to enjoy the *scriptorium.*'

He turned and exited as he had come. They heard the door being secured on the inside.

Fidelma walked back to the parapet.

'What are you doing?' asked Brother Eolann nervously.

'Just checking to see what the way to the infernal regions looks like,' she replied without humour.

She spent a few minutes gazing down at the dizzy descent to the valley floor. Then she turned back into the library where Brother Eolann was once again examining the scroll book that he had found so amazing. Fidelma, whose thoughts were on escape, regarded him with disapproval. Then she turned to the shelves and a new thought struck her as she recalled the mystery of the library at Bobium.

'Do you recall telling me that some of the books in your library had been vandalised?'

'I do.' The *scriptor* looked up with sudden interest. 'Why?'

'Do you recall the titles?'

'Yes, for as I told you, I had to send to other libraries seeking copies to replace the ones whose pages were cut out.'

Fidelma was blessed with a good memory. It was part of

a *dálaigh's* training. 'One of them was Livy's history, *Ab Urbe Condita Libri*, as I recall.'

'It was. Why?'

'Because I see a copy of it.' Fidelma pointed to the book. 'It occurs to me that you might wish to know what was on the pages that were cut out.'

Brother Eolann took the book from the shelf and placed it on the table. 'This volume appears to be an exact copy. I recall how the next page started after the deleted one.'

'I don't suppose you can recall the pages that had been cut out?'

'I have a pride in my task in life, lady,' he protested. 'I would be a poor librarian if I did not know what had been damaged in my own library.' Brother Eolann began to turn the thick vellum pages. Then he paused and looked carefully at one particular page before reading, '*Marcus triumphali veste in senatum venit . . .* That is on the page after the one cut out.'

Fidelma translated. 'Marcus entered the senate in triumphal dress. So what is on the page that was cut out?'

He turned back to the page: 'Ah, it starts: *Caepionis cuis tementate clades accepta erat damnnati bona publicata sunt.* Caepio, who had caused the defeat by his rashness, was convicted and his possessions confiscated.'

'It sounds as if it is an account of some battle, and someone called Caepio's role in it.' Fidelma was curious. 'Why would anyone want to deface a book for that extract?'

Brother Eolann shrugged. 'Ancient battles are not a particular interest of mine, lady.'

She took the book from him and scanned the text. It was of little interest so far as she was concerned. 'This seems to recount that a Roman Proconsul called Caepio commanded part of an army at a battle that took place at Aurasio. The senior General, Gnaeus Mallius Maximus, commanded the major part of the army. It seems Caepio was a patrician. Because his superior, Mallius Maximus, was not an aristocrat, he refused to cooperate with him or obey his commands. He thought it beneath his dignity.

'The passage goes on to say that when the General succeeded in brokering a peace with the enemy's army, Caepio attacked on his own. The result was that his army was wiped out before the enemy turned on Mallius' army and wiped that out as well. Some one hundred and twenty thousand were slaughtered. Caepio managed to escape back to Rome but Rome was in an uproar at the news. They tried Caepio and found him guilty of misconduct. He was saved from death only by his aristocratic position, but was sent into exile, while all his wealth, goods and property were confiscated.' She glanced at the *scriptor*. 'I wonder when this happened. Can you tell from the text?'

Brother Eolann leaned over her shoulder and pointed to some tiny figures in the margin: 'According to the dates,' he replied, peering at the text, '*Anno Urbis Conditae* six hundred and forty-eight . . . that means what we calculated as roughly a hundred years before the birth of Christ.'

'Well, it teaches us nothing as to the reason why the passage should be cut from the book.' Fidelma grimaced in resignation. 'Maybe we should search for the Polybius and see if that is related to the same battle and this man Caepio. But it doesn't seem significant. Maybe it was just wilful vandalism.'

The key in the door suddenly scraped and Kakko appeared.

'My lord Grasulf has told me that he has invited you to feast with him. I have taken the liberty to prepare baths and changes of clothing for you, as I have heard of the daily bathing customs of the Hibernians.'

Fidelma had been feeling sticky and awkward in the heat. Now that it was mentioned, she realised she had not bathed properly since they had left Bobium.

'That is good,' she commented.

Kakko merely grinned. 'The Lord of Vars is very sensitive about who joins him at his table and their state of cleanliness.'

'Our state of uncleanliness was thanks to his warriors who abducted us and brought us hither against our will,' snapped Fidelma in answer to his jibe. 'And further to your imprisoning us in a chamber without—'

'Your bags have been placed in the chamber,' interrupted Kakko, realising that he was unable to assert verbal domination over her. 'Perhaps that will make it seem more tolerable. I shall return shortly and conduct you to where you may bathe and change.'

'It would be even more tolerable if you provided us with separate cells for decency's sake,' she asserted. 'We are not man and wife to be closeted together. There are times when separation is needed. Or do your worries on cleanliness not go as far as that?'

The big man glowered at her for a moment, then decided to say nothing and left, locking the door noisily behind him.

Brother Eolann shook his head. 'I am sorry about this, lady.'

'Sorry? For what?'

'I should not have suggested staying at the sanctuary and delaying there.'

'As I recall, I insisted on seeing it. Anyway, our delay was due to the finding of Lady Gunora. We must keep silent about that. This Lord of Vars may be the killer. The less he thinks we know, the better.'

223

She stood up abruptly as another thought came into her mind and she went to the door leading on to the terrace.

'Where are you going?' demanded Brother Eolann.

'Don't worry, I am just going to have another look at the rockface. See if you can find that volume of Polybius. You might be able to check whether that passage related to – what was his name? Oh yes. Caepio.'

The *scriptor* began to explore the library half-heartedly, turning over the books stacked around.

When Fidelma returned she had a brightness in her eyes. 'Any luck?' she asked.

'Luck?' He seemed preoccupied.

'With finding Polybius?'

'Oh, no luck.' He frowned at the suppressed excitement in her features. 'What is it?'

'I have an idea . . .' she began.

Then the key turned in the lock again and Kakko reappeared. 'Your baths are ready,' he announced.

A sullen-looking woman waited to guide Fidelma to the room where she was to bathe. She was relieved when Kakko took Brother Eolann to another room. It was good to slip into the warm waters of the wood tub and relax with perfumes and oils. She took her time while the dour-looking servant, who alas spoke no other language than the Longobard dialect, waited impatiently for her to finish. Finally, feeling refreshed and relaxed and clad in the fresh clothing which had been provided for her, Fidelma followed the woman back across the main courtyard.

As she was proceeding across the flagstones, there was a sudden shouting and the gates were pulled open. A horseman galloped into the courtyard and reined in his steed so abruptly that it reared up, its forelegs kicking viciously at the air.

Jumping from the saddle, the rider flung his reins at a nearby attendant and almost ran in the direction of the main hall.

Fidelma's guide prodded her forward as she looked after him.

Brother Eolann was already in the chamber that had become their prison.

'I have been told that they will give us separate cells for tonight,' he said, somewhat embarrassed. 'It is being arranged now.'

'That is some progress then,' Fidelma said absently.

It was not long before Kakko opened the door and indicated that Fidelma and Brother Eolann should follow him back to the great hall. A table had been laid and the steward now assumed the role of organising the servants as they carried in the dishes from the kitchen and prepared wine for the table.

'It is not often I receive travellers from Hibernia in this valley,' Grasulf said, as he gestured for them to be seated. It seemed that there were only the three of them at the meal.

'How often do you abduct travellers?' Fidelma replied dryly.

Grasulf seemed amused at her retort. 'I think, in your case, my men did well – for they have provided me with a good foil for my intellect,' he replied gravely. 'I find your responses most stimulating. By the way, the boar,' he pointed to the meat dish that had been set on the table, 'I killed yesterday.'

There were various dishes brought in while Grasulf made commentaries about them and the wine that was served. Brother Eolann was content to let the conversation flow between Grasulf and Fidelma, concentrating on emptying his plate as each dish appeared. It seemed that the part of the meal preferred by the Lord of Vars came in a pitcher that Kakko kept filled at his side. He did not sip his wine but devoured it in large swallows like a man whose thirst was unquenchable.

'Time was that preachers from your abbey came into this valley to convert my people,' he said reflectively. 'However, there are still many true Longobards left, though we are a dwindling number. We place our faith in Godan and the power of our swords. We stand above the squabbles between you Christians. Nicene Creed and Arian Creed – what difference? What is the choice between dying by the sword and dying by the dagger?'

'You see the Faith as a means of death?' inquired Fidelma with interest.

'However you perceive your Christ, He is your god, not mine.' Grasulf dismissed the subject. 'And how have you passed the time in my little *scriptorium*? Did you find it interesting?'

'All knowledge is interesting,' conceded Fidelma.

'So, what in particular?'

'The history of Rome.' It came automatically to her, although she had little interest in the subject.

'Ah, Livy?'

'You have read his history?' Fidelma was surprised but then realised that there was no reason to be so.

'Of course,' replied Grasulf. 'Livinius was from Patavium so he took an interest in this area. What period did you find interesting?'

'It was just a passage about someone called Caepio that caught my attention.'

She was not prepared for the effect of the name. A suspicious look came into his eyes and then Grasulf threw back his head and uttered a false-sounding chuckle.

'Caepio?' he said. 'You surely don't give credence to that

silly tale! What stories have you been filling your compatriot's head with, Brother Eolann?'

Fidelma turned quickly to find that Brother Eolann had coloured in embarrassment.

'What stories would you have been filling my head with?' she asked quietly in their own language.

The *scriptor* replied almost violently. 'I have no idea, lady. Truly, I don't know what he is talking about.'

Fidelma turned back to Grasulf. 'I alighted on the page by chance,' she said cautiously. 'What story should I have been aware of?'

'By chance? Why, it has even become part of the Latin language.'

'I still don't follow your meaning.'

'What does one say when one has achieved some ill-gotten wealth – wealth that brings a curse with it?'

Fidelma had not learned a colloquial form of Latin and looked to Brother Eolann for some guidance. The *scriptor* still seemed embarrassed and shook his head. So she turned back to Grasulf.

'It is said that the person has the gold of Tolosa – *Aurum Tolosa habet*,' explained the Lord of Vars.

'And how does that relate to this man Caepio?'

'He was the governor of this very territory in ancient times and marched his army into Gaul. The story is that he seized a fabulous treasure in the town of Tolosa. He sent this wealth of gold back here to his villa in Placentia meaning to keep it, but it disappeared. Some will even tell you that he hid the gold in these very mountains. Every now and then, some fool claims they have found Caepio's gold.'

'But the passage in Livinius merely says that his stupidity caused several Roman legions to be annihilated.'

'The story also says that before that battle, his legions had sacked Tolosa and carried away forty-six wagons of gold and treasure and sent them here.'

'And these wagons disappeared?'

'They vanished,' agreed Grasulf. 'Anyway, it is not mythical gold we want, eh, Brother Eolann? Many lords in these valleys would bring their men rushing like wolves from the hills down on Grimoald and his supporters for a bag of Frankish gold.'

Brother Eolann was looking uncomfortable. 'I would not know,' he muttered.

'The story of the gold is local gossip,' said Grasulf, picking up his goblet of wine again. It was clear that he had dismissed the topic.

Fidelma waited a few moments and then raised another topic that had crossed her mind.

'I saw a rider come into the fortress not so long ago. He had clearly arrived here after a hard and hasty ride. I presume he brings important news about the dangers that beset this country?'

The Lord of Vars looked at her speculatively over the rim of his goblet. 'You have a sharp eye, lady.' Was there a dangerous tone in his voice?

'It is my training to observe.'

'Well, the news is interesting. Lupus of Friuli, Grimoald's Regent in these northern lands, and his army have been defeated.'

'I heard that this Lupus had turned against Grimoald.'

'That is true. You have a good memory as well as a sharp ear, eh?'

'I repeat, it is my training to observe and remember.'

'How was he defeated?' intervened Brother Eolann. He sounded concerned.

'Lupus, as you know, had decided to stand against Grimoald. He declared for Perctarit. Grimoald signed a treaty with the Khagan, the Khan Kubrat . . .'

'These names mean nothing to me,' Fidelma pointed out irritably.

'The Khagan rules the Avars who dwell to the north and east of our lands, in what used to be called Illyria. They attacked into our lands to overthrow Lupus. The rider you saw brought the news that Lupus and his army held out in Friuli for four days against the Avars. Lupus is now dead, his army slaughtered or scattered.'

'Surely that is good for Grimoald?' Fidelma commented.

'Only if the Khan respects the treaty. At the moment the entire Valley of the Padus is open to invasion by the Avars. In that, Grimoald might have made a mistake. Grimoald had marched to the Meridies, south of this land, to fight the Byzantines. So he is still marching back northwards. The other news is that Perctarit and his Frankish allies are already in the lands just north of Mailand not far from here. Blood, fire and pillage sweep across the land. We must be vigilant. That is why strangers are stopped and questioned.'

'But this has nothing to do with me, nor does it present any reason for holding me or my compatriot as prisoners in your fortress. You should allow us to return in peace and safety to Bobium.'

'You are persistent in that matter, lady. But I have not yet satisfied myself that you do not present a threat to me or to my people.'

Kakko reappeared with two servants who began to clear away the plates under his supervision.

Grasulf rose to his feet, smiling thinly. 'It is my hope that we will have many more of these stimulating exchanges.'

'But it is *my* hope that this will be the only such exchange,' replied Fidelma, also rising.

The Lord of Vars chuckled sardonically. 'I fear your hope will be a vain one. You have a refreshing boldness, lady. We say that there is no sharper blade than the tongue of a woman. But I think you will find that I am a match for you.'

'We also have a saying among my people. "A cur is bold in the place where he is well known".'

His face darkened and he turned to Kakko. 'Our guests may return to their quarters.'

The big steward came forward, led the way to the doors and swung them open.

A tall man, clad in a long black robe, stood outside, about to enter. His hair was snow-white. He had a nose that was prominent and thin bloodless lips, and his eyes were dark, almost without pupils.

He started as he caught sight of Fidelma and stepped back in surprise.

The recognition was mutual.

Kakko was unaware of the recognition that passed between them as he turned to give a gentle shove to Brother Eolann. Fidelma and the *scriptor* followed him through the door, neither of them speaking to the newcomer; nor did he speak to them.

They passed Suidur the Wise, physician to Radoald, Lord of Trebbia, without a word.

CHAPTER THIRTEEN

Outside the hall, as Kakko signalled to a bored-looking warrior to escort them back to their prison chamber, Fidelma took the opportunity to ask Eolann in their own language: 'Did you see who that was?'

'I did not recognise the man, why?'

'That was the physician of Radoald, Lord of Trebbia.'

'I didn't notice. I have never met him but only seen him once from a distance.' Brother Eolann sounded surprised. 'What is *he* doing here? I would not have thought that Radoald had much in common with this Grasulf.'

Fidelma was thinking of the group that she had seen in the courtyard at Radoald's fortress and of Suidur talking with the two tall men in black cloaks who might have been the attackers of Magister Ado. Now Suidur had appeared in the fortress of the Lord of Vars. What could be the connection?

'I have an idea,' she began, but they were already at the chamber door. However, instead of allowing them both to enter, the guard pointed to Fidelma to go through and then shut the door behind her. She found a lamp had been lit already for her. She then heard the guard say something roughly to Brother Eolann and a door banged nearby. She stood inside the room for a moment. Now the matter would have to wait until the next day when she and Brother Eolann would be allowed back to Grasulf's *scriptorium* where they could talk freely.

She was turning towards the bed when Eolann's voice came clearly from somewhere nearby: 'Can you hear me, lady?'

She swung round. She could see nothing.

'I hear you,' she replied. 'Where are you?'

'There is a grille in this wall. I think it connects with your chamber. I am in the next chamber to yours.'

The voice did seem to come from a wall. She caught sight of a small grille in it just above head-level.

'I see the grille.'

'Good. They have separated us but we can still talk.'

'That we can,' she agreed.

'You mentioned that you had an idea,' prompted Brother Eolann.

'My idea?' Fidelma went to the wall and leaned against it, just under the grille. 'Why to escape, of course.'

There was a silence from Brother Eolann before he spoke again. 'You'll forgive me, lady, but I had that idea the moment we were taken prisoner on Mount Pénas. However, there is no escape from here and if you are thinking of escape from the *scriptorium*, well, as the steward said, it seems that the only way to achieve that is if we could fly.'

'Or if we could climb,' replied Fidelma pointedly.

She heard Brother Eolann gasp. 'How do you mean? Climb where?'

'You believe yourself to be a good climber, don't you? I saw so myself when we climbed under the difficult overhang on Mount Pénas.'

'A slope is different from a vertical cliff face. Climbing down there is impossible.'

'Why so?'

'Firstly, we are locked in here. It is only during daylight hours that we will be allowed into the library, so someone would see us even if we were crazy enough to begin the descent. To escape we need to take a little more than we stand up in, especially once we have succeeded in the miracle of getting down into the valley. So how do you convince Kakko to allow us to take our bags to the library? And what if we did reach the valley floor? There is a small township down there and if no warriors are waiting for us at the bottom, then there will be people.'

Fidelma considered the matter for a moment. 'You have raised some good objections, Brother Eolann. But it is better to take the opportunity than do nothing. I say that it *could* be done. It looks impossible from the centre of the terrace where you have a sheer drop. That is where they throw their condemned prisoners from. But I also looked at the corners, especially where part of the wall of the library seems to over-hang. It doesn't. It balances on a thrust of rock – and from what I saw, one could scramble with ease to the underside of that stonework. The rockface has more handholds and has a more gradual slope.'

There was quiet from the grille. Then Brother Eolann whispered, 'One thing I will grant you, lady; you do have the blood of the Eóghanacht in you. A fighting race. But that is about all. I think such a plan is ridiculous. You cannot see the rock-face all the way down from the terrace. You may easily get stuck halfway down.'

'I shall try to investigate it more closely tomorrow. If it looks as though it can be done, then I am determined to do it, ridiculous or not,' she said decisively.

'And what about the other problems, such as transporting

our bags to the library, getting food for the journey, planning a route which will bring us unobserved to Mount Pénas, let alone over it and back to Bobium – what of those little problems? There is no way of escaping. We have to resign ourselves to it.'

'Pity the man drowned in the tempest, for after the rain comes the sunshine,' snapped Fidelma, using an ancient saying of her people to chide those who advocated inaction. 'I am determined on my course. The sea does not wait for the ship to load its cargo. The ship must be ready to catch the tide.'

Brother Eolann did not respond.

It was some time before Fidelma closed her eyes and fell asleep.

She came awake with the sound of the wooden bar being removed at the chamber door. She swung swiftly from the bed. The room was curiously bright as the moon was full and shining directly into it.

A tall figure stood in the doorway with a lamp whose flame was partially concealed by his hand.

'Suidur!' she gasped, recognising the figure. 'What do you want?'

'Silently does it, lady,' came his sibilant tone. 'What I want is for you to get dressed and fetch your belongings. Quickly now.'

'Do you mean me harm? If so, I shall not stir.'

'No harm is meant to you, lady. At the moment, I am the only means you have of escape from the Lord of Vars's fortress, so hurry. Every moment's delay means discovery.'

Fidelma blinked in surprise. 'Where . . . ?' she began.

'Grasulf and Kakko are in a drunken stupor,' he whispered. 'Of course, that being thanks to the help of a little potion of mine as well as their propensity for strong drink. But we do not have long. Have you something to cover your head?'

She hesitated a moment, wondering whether she should trust him. What did old Brehon Morann once tell her? *Catch the pig by the leg when you can.*

'Very well,' she said decisively. 'Is Brother Eolann coming?'

'Of course, lady. He is already here and waiting.'

'Then I shall do what you say.'

Suidur stood just inside the door as if keeping sentinel over the courtyard. Within moments, Fidelma had joined Brother Eolann who was already dressed and had his bag slung on his back. Suidur, still holding a lamp, whispered: 'Keep close.' Then he raised a forefinger to his lips.

Although filled with numerous questions and anxiety, Fidelma uttered no word but followed the white-haired physician across the courtyard, conscious of Brother Eolann at her shoulder. The gates were shut. However, with an attitude of assurance, Suidur went to where one of the guards was sitting on the ground, nodding sleepily. The man suddenly became aware of Suidur standing over him and scrambled to his feet.

'A bad thing if Grasulf caught you asleep at his door,' Suidur told him sternly.

The guard looked around fearfully as if expecting the Lord of Vars to appear.

'I was not really asleep, master. You would not tell . . . ?'

'Only if you move quickly and open the gate for my companions and me. We are late already and must hasten on an errand for the Lord of Vars.'

The gatekeeper, to Fidelma's amazement, hurried to the task, almost bowing as they passed silently through.

Outside, as she remembered it, the track began to wind steeply down the curiously shaped thrust of rock on which the fortress of the Lord of Vars balanced. Suidur, who had extinguished his lamp for the full moon was adequate light for them, walked swiftly down the track without speaking. They hurried behind him.

They finally came to the lower reaches where woodland started. From this dark band of trees, the figure of a warrior suddenly appeared on the path before them. Suidur did not pause but called out something softly, to which the man seemed to assent and waved. A second man emerged from the woods, leading three horses. Suidur turned to Fidelma and Brother Eolann. 'I am afraid that you must ride double behind my men,' he said. 'I cannot get extra horses and we must be well away from here before first light.'

'Can I ask why you are doing this?' Fidelma inquired.

It was hard to see Suidur's features in the shadows but it seemed that he spoke with irony. 'Did you like being a guest of the Lord of Vars so much that you wanted to stay?'

'Of course not, but—'

'Then postpone your questions until we have put some distance between ourselves and this place. I want to get into the shelter of the mountains.'

The two warriors mounted their horses and then Fidelma and Brother Eolann were helped to swing up behind them. Suidur was already in the saddle and the three horses moved off quietly through the woods, skirting round the few lights that showed the extent of the settlement that spread under the fortress of the Lord of Vars. For a physician Suidur showed a surprising knowledge of how to trek quietly through the woods. The thought crossed Fidelma's mind that perhaps the man had been a soldier before he became a physician.

She clung on to the rider before her, trying to make sense of the events that had transpired. Could these be the same men she had seen speaking with Suidur in the fortress of Radoald? The same men who had witnessed Brother Eolann and herself being brought as prisoners to the fortress of the Lord of Vars? Suidur had appeared at Grasulf's fortress and apparently been welcomed there. Why had he rescued her and Brother Eolann? It made no sense at all.

With the questions swimming in her mind they rode on, moving without speed, until the township was well behind them. They reached an open track which ran alongside a noisy gushing river. Fidelma noticed from the white frothy movement of the current that they were heading upstream into the mountains. By her reckoning, the mountain that they had come over, Mount Pénas, lay behind her left shoulder. But it was still a long way from first light and although the sky was cloudless and the moon high and bright, she could not be sure.

It was now that Suidur raised his hand and gestured in a forward motion. The pace of the horses began to increase to a trot and then a canter. Fidelma had ridden almost before she had begun to walk and considered herself a capable horsewoman. The horse beneath her had certainly not been bred for the fields or for hauling carts. She felt the strong muscles as the beast stretched its powerful limbs beneath her. She knew instinctively that the rider was keeping it in check otherwise it would break into a full-scale gallop. This was a horse bred for warriors, a warhorse. She could not see in the darkness but she suspected it was of the singular breed that she had seen in the valley before.

There came a point when they began to climb so steeply that eventually the canter was slowed and fell back to a walking pace. By this time, a light glimmered in the eastern sky, indicating the coming dawn. Fidelma knew that they had crossed several streams. Perhaps they were crossing and re-crossing the same watercourse? An attempt to throw off any trackers with hunting dogs?

It was not until the sun was pushing above the far eastern hills that she realised they had climbed a fair way into the mountains. It was then that Suidur pointed to a distant herder's hut. At least, she assumed it was, because she could not think of anyone else who would dwell this high up in the mountains. Suidur did not make any explanation as they continued slowly towards the hut. Only when they reached it did he halt and announce: 'Here we will rest.'

Fidelma slid from her perch, feeling remarkably alert for someone who had had so little sleep. Brother Eolann was stretching himself after the lengthy ride while the two warriors, for the dawn had revealed the two silent men to be such, had taken the horses to a small paddock behind the hut to rub them down and fodder them. Fidelma peered at the peaks that arose all about them before she said to Suidur: 'We are nowhere near Mount Pénas.'

The physician smiled. 'You are observant, lady. True, we have come further south. We have followed the Staffel River, and that high peak before us is the mountain on which it rises. It is said that the Carthaginian Hannibal climbed up it when he was resting his army in the Trebbia Valley on the far side.'

'So we are not far from Bobium?'

'No, not far. We will eventually cross the mountains almost opposite Radoald's fortress, a little to the south. This way we may fool Grasulf, who may think you will head directly to Bobium and therefore send his men to stop you crossing Mount Pénas. I suggest that you and your companion get some sleep. We have only done a third of our journey, for both the climb on this side and the descent into the Trebbia Valley are difficult. That mountain is the highest in this range and we will skirt it, going over via a lesser height and come on a trackway that will wind down to the Trebbia.'

Brother Eolann came forward, looking sleepy. '*Gratias tibi ago*,' he said. 'I do not know you although I have seen you from a distance. But Brother Hnikar speaks highly of your skills. I thank you for your timely intervention.'

'*Non est tanti*,' replied Suidur, dismissing his thanks with the traditional saying that it was nothing.

Fidelma, however, knew that there were questions to be asked, and the sooner the better. At least, with daylight, she could see that the two warriors who accompanied them were *not* the same men who had twice attacked Magister Ado – although they wore the same manner of clothing and emblem.

'Why?' she suddenly asked.

'Why?' repeated Suidur.

'I do not understand why you put yourself into such danger to rescue us. You went to the Lord of Vars and seemed to be welcomed as a friend. You say that you drank with him and his steward and even placed some sleep-inducing potion in their drinks and then helped us escape from our prison. It occurs to me that I should ask the question – *why*?'

Suidur gazed thoughtfully at her. 'Would it not be easier to have some rest first and then discuss this question at more leisure when we have eaten?'

Fidelma shook her head firmly. 'I cannot rest with such questions swimming in my mind,' she said simply.

'Very well.' Suidur went into the hut and motioned them inside. Fidelma was surprised to see ashes still glowing in a central hearth and within a few moments the physician had added more fuel and stirred it into a blaze. 'This is one of the places Lord Radoald maintains to keep watch on his western borders.'

He motioned them to be seated. There were rugs and blankets which they arranged around the fire.

'And now,' Suidur said with a smile, 'how did I come to the fortress of Grasulf? Last night I was visiting . . .' he hesitated '. . . shall we say a loyal servant of Lord Radoald. Oh yes, we have spies here. You may have deduced that Grasulf is a man of certain beliefs. One is a belief in gold. We have learned that Perctarit, the deposed King, has offered Grasulf gold for his allegiance. Once Grasulf has that gold, he will raise his people to attack his neighbours.'

'It does not explain what you were doing in the fortress,' pointed out Fidelma.

'All in good time, lady. My men,' he indicated the two warriors outside, 'often go there, pretending to be in sympathy. You might have seen them before, because they were in the fortress when you arrived as prisoners. They alerted me when I came to make contact with my . . . my spy.'

'I saw them,' Fidelma agreed.

'They recognised Brother Eolann and described you. I knew Lord Radoald would not want you to remain in the hands of Grasulf, who has been known to sell women to slavers. Leaving my men, with the horses, at the bottom of the hill, I went up to the fortress and sought entrance. It is not the first time that I had been an envoy between Radoald and Grasulf, therefore I was known at the fortress.

'As you saw, Grasulf welcomed me, thinking I had arrived in this role and, naturally, I pretended that I had come with counter-proposals to pay for his allegiance. However, it was decided that we needed to prepare our negotiation in liquid form. Grasulf was most willing to do so; he had already drunk much wine and it was easy to pour my potion into his drink. I also did the same with Kakko. My men had told me which chambers you had been placed in, and the rest was simple.'

It sounded simple. Perhaps too simple, Fidelma thought. Her mind was spinning with questions again.

'And now,' Suidur was saying, 'since you have asked me for my story, lady, may I ask how you came to be prisoners in Grasulf's fortress?'

She glanced quickly at Brother Eolann, hoping to warn him not to mention the finding of Lady Gunora's body. No need to part with all the information until she knew how, or if, these matters related. However, Brother Eolann had sunk back and was breathing deeply. Suidur followed her glance, saying, 'Our friend is asleep, as you should be.'

'Then my story first, Suidur. Brother Eolann offered to take me to the sanctuary of Colm Bán on the peak of Mount Pénas – with the approval of Abbot Servillius, of course. When I return to Hibernia, my people will want to know all about the abbey. So, we climbed up the mountain and stayed the night at the sanctuary. Just when we were about to return to the abbey the next morning, Grasulf's men appeared and took us captive to his fortress.'

'You are a stranger in this land, Fidelma of Hibernia,' Suidur said solemnly. 'There are many things that are going to be unusual and even curious to a stranger's perception. If I might offer some advice, I would return to your own land as soon as you can. There is an evil spreading through these mountains.' Suddenly he stood up. 'Now once more, I plead with you to rest. We shall move off at midday. We will not reach Radoald's fortress until tomorrow, so we will have to spend tonight on the mountain.'

It was midday when Fidelma awoke. The sun stood high in a cloudless sky. Brother Eolann was also stirring but there was no sign of Suidur, although she could hear movement outside the hut. She rose quickly and looked out. Suidur was talking to the two warriors in the swift, guttural tones of the local language. Fidelma glanced back to the *scriptor* who was sitting up and blinking.

'Brother Eolann,' she whispered urgently, 'a word of warning. Do not mention finding the body of Lady Gunora, nor anything about the coins or Wamba.'

Brother Eolann frowned. 'Or anything about the missing prince?'

'Exactly. Let us be circumspect.'

'Ah, you are both awake.' The shadow of Suidur had fallen across the doorway. 'That is good. We must be on our way soon.'

'A wash and some food would be appreciated before we set off again, if that is possible,' Fidelma said.

'There is a stream and a little waterfall behind this hut, lady,' Suidur replied. 'And there is something to eat before we set off.'

Fidelma took her *ciorr bholg*, her comb bag with her toiletries, and made her way to a sheltered spot at the back of the hut. The cold water was refreshing, splashing down the mountain to form both a pool and a shower. She hurried over her toilet so that Brother Eolann could follow her example. She presumed that Suidur and his men had already washed for they looked refreshed as if they had not ridden through the night. The meal was of goat's cheese and fruit, washed down by the crystal waters of the mountain stream.

It turned out that the two warriors spoke no Latin and so

the conversation was limited to Suidur. Brother Eolann exchanged a few words with them but they gave the impression of preferring not to engage in conversation.

'I think Radoald mentioned that his family would suffer if Perctarit returned as King,' Fidelma commented, as they began to eat. 'Is that why he is anxious about Grasulf?'

Suidur nodded. 'Radoald's father helped Grimoald to overthrow Perctarit, driving him into exile in the lands of the Franks. Radoald fought alongside his father, Lord Billo. His father did not return to Trebbia and Radoald became Lord. I doubt whether Perctarit will feel kindly towards Radoald if he returns to power in this land.'

'When we were in Grasulf's fortress a messenger rode in to say that Lupus had turned against Grimoald but had been destroyed with his army after four days of fighting somewhere. Is that bad?'

The physician studied her with keen interest.

'For a stranger, lady, you have picked up much. We heard about this story too. The answer is that it might be bad for us, for it depends on what the Khagan will do next.'

'The one who defeated Lupus?'

'The same. It seems that Grimoald, unable to march north quickly enough to face Lupus, offered an alliance with the leader of the Avars. The Avars threw themselves against Lupus and defeated him. But what will the Khagan demand of Grimoald in return? Will the Avars flood into this land? If so, then God help every one of us. To the Avars we are all sheep ready to be shorn.'

'I presume the Avars are not followers of the Faith?'

'So far as I know they will follow any faith they believe helps them – from their chief god, Ts'ob, to various forms of our own Christ. But they are hungry for land and power and, frankly, the news that Grimoald had formed an alliance with them is not pleasing to our people.'

'You think these lands are in immediate danger?' interposed Brother Eolann.

'What is happening is setting brother against brother and neighbour against neighbour. The Pale Horse will be sweeping through these valleys soon and none will be spared.'

'Pale Horse?' queried Fidelma.

'The rider is Death himself,' replied Suidur. 'That is why I offered my advice – leave this land while you can.'

Fidelma turned her gaze across the mountains to the north and the east and sighed. 'It seems so peaceful and beautiful.'

'Even from ancient times these valleys have been drenched in blood. The Ligurians, the Gauls, the Romans, the Carthaginians, then the Romans again and then my own people, the Longobards – they have all fertilised these beautiful valleys with their blood. It will be so again.' Suidur stood up and appeared to be contemplating the prediction for a moment before turning to his men and snapping an order. They began to pack up and prepare the horses.

Seeing Suidur's mount in daylight, Fidelma realised that her thoughts in the darkness had been right. It was of the same breed and colouring, the same pale grey, that she had seen several times in the valley. She had seen Wulfoald and Brother Faro mounted on this same short-backed animal with the narrow croup and long tail. It had certainly displayed a hardiness and stamina and galloped like a sprinter for all its fiery temperament. It was truly a warrior's horse.

'Is that Wulfoald's horse?' she asked Suidur, for the beast was so alike.

'What makes you think that?' the physician demanded, puzzled. Then he smiled. 'Oh, I see. This is of the same breed.

They were introduced in the valley only a decade ago and have flourished.'

'I have never seen the breed before. They are light, sturdy animals.'

'I see that you are a judge of horses, lady. Lord Billo, when he was Lord of Trebbia, bought half a dozen of them from a Byzantine merchant in Genua and bred them. We are not sure where they came from, although it was said that the merchant brought them from the east.' Suidur paused abruptly and gazed intently towards the north.

'You see something?' asked Fidelma, aware of the slight tension in his body.

'I do,' replied the physician. 'If seems that Grasulf was not long in recovering before raising the alarm.'

Fidelma stood and tried to follow his gaze across the valley. 'What is it?'

'About twenty-five horsemen following us. Don't be alarmed, we are in no immediate danger.'

Brother Eolann was straining in the same direction now. 'How far away?' he demanded.

'Oh, it will take them some time before they manage to climb up here,' Suidur assured him.

Fidelma could now just make out a series of tiny dots at the far end of the valley. They were moving in line like a string of ants.

'You have good vision, Suidur,' she said. 'I can barely see them. Is it Grasulf?'

'No one else would be riding so hard. You might not be able to discern them well, but I think that is as it should be. We would not wish to see them any closer to us.'

He checked with his warriors that all was ready. Once more Fidelma and Brother Eolann took their bags and hoisted them on their backs, before mounting behind the warriors. They set off at a walking pace, continuing along the track which wound at a steep incline up through the hills.

'Don't worry,' Suidur called back. 'I think even Grasulf will turn back once we are well inside the territory of Radoald.'

Fidelma realised that, although they continued to move steadily up sharp gradients, they were not actually climbing over the mountains but rather weaving their way through them. The tracks were often wide enough only for one horse to proceed at a time. And now and then the way was so steep that they had to dismount and lead the horses. It was, for her, an extraordinary experience. Once more the conditions meant there was little exchange of conversation. They moved on through the hot afternoon with Fidelma now and then casting an apprehensive glance behind. But they had circled through the mountains so much there was little prospect of seeing any pursuers. They stopped only once at a mountain spring to allow the horses to drink and to refresh themselves. It was not until nearly sunset that they came to a strange little dell, an area that seemed to be carved unnaturally into the hillside. Yet, as she inspected it closer, she saw that it was in fact a natural shelter with overhanging bushes.

'This will be our last halt,' Suidur explained. 'We start down into the Trebbia Valley tomorrow.'

'Will it be safe to halt here?' asked a nervous Brother Eolann.

'Grasulf for all his pagan beliefs does not have wings like his ravens,' replied Suidur with a smile. 'I am sure he will have given up the chase a long time ago.'

Before long, a fire was lit and food distributed and they curled themselves up with their blankets. The shelter was not as convenient as the previous one and there was no gushing spring with shower or pool. But a small trickling spring provided water for drinking and enough to splash the face and hands.

That night Fidelma didn't bother pursuing any conversation but was asleep almost immediately.

At first she thought it just part of a dream. She became aware of whispering. She lay for a moment trying to struggle into full consciousness without opening her eyes or moving. To her amazement the voices were speaking in Latin, and while one of them was Suidur, she could not identify the other one.

'. . . dripping moisture hollows out a stone,' Suidur was saying. 'Grimoald acts far too quickly and as a result makes rash decisions. He should have waited.'

'Now the magister is alert and we will never find it.'

'There is still a chance, my lord. Grasulf will not move before he has the gold in his hand, that is for sure. My men and I went to his fortress pretending to make a counter-offer. He has certainly not been paid yet.'

'And the foreigner and the *scriptor*? How do they stand in this matter?'

'They are not involved. They had to be rescued. A pity, I might have found out more if I had stayed, but you know what Grasulf is like. He has no morals and would have used the girl as he thought fit or sold her to slavers. No, she had to be rescued from Vars.'

'And you are sure that Lady Gunora was not a prisoner there?'

'If the boy is right, Lady Gunora must be dead.'

Fidelma felt herself go cold listening to the exchange.

'If Perctarit and his main force are at Mailand, then his

247

men would have to move quickly now,' said the strange voice. 'Once Grasulf is paid for his services, he can turn on Radoald, and once Radoald is destroyed, then the routes to Genua are wide open. While Perctarit occupies the entire plain of the Padus, his Frankish allies can land by ship at Genua and march with their supplies and reinforcements all the way to him.'

'I agree that if anything is to happen, it must happen during the next day or so. We are still no nearer to knowing where the gold is or who will supply it. It may be that we were entirely wrong about the *magister*.'

'You will be in the mountains?'

'I will go to see my son first and inform him.'

Hearing receding footsteps, Fidelma allowed her eyes to flick open, but from where she lay she could see nothing. She heard a rustle nearby and closed her eyes again. Her thoughts were confused but while she tried to sort them out, sleep overcame her once again.

She awoke to a glorious dawn. The sky held a brilliant light which spread across the mountain-tops all around them. The air was still and fresh. The men removed themselves a little distance so that she could carry out her toilette, and food was ready when she returned.

'Well, it will not be long before we reach the Trebbia, just below us,' Suidur greeted her. 'It's a steep descent on this side of the mountains but better than a steep ascent.'

'And no sign of Grasulf pursuing us?'

'No sign at all. Didn't I say that he would give up?'

'Let us hope you are right.'

'Are you still worried then?'

'The Lord of Vars told me that an excess of caution does no harm. In fact, would it not be foolish to refuse caution?

I am thinking that Grasulf would reason that we would eventually be heading to Bobium. Surely he could cross the mountains to the north of here and lie in wait for us in the valley somewhere between Radoald's fortress and Bobium?'

'I see you have a mind attuned to strategy, lady.'

'The daughter of a king in Hibernia is taught many things and can even lead her people in war.'

Suidur nodded as if this did not surprise him. 'Well, if he did backtrack from where we spotted him and his men, he would have to go a considerable distance through the mountains to reach a suitable place to intersect our journey. I swear, lady, you need not worry. We will protect you.'

It was not long before they started down the mountain track on a zigzag path that seemed steeper than those they had ascended by. She could see the blue ribbon of the river she presumed was the Trebbia, snaking its way through the rocky valley below. Here and there were farmsteads and cultivated areas of trees, which she was told were olive trees, while others she knew to be vines. She wished that she could assimilate these new sights, sounds and smells, but her mind was filled with the curious mysteries that beset this valley, its abbey and its people.

The journey today was done more leisurely and as they came to the lower reaches, into the treeline and then through the great forests that edged the river – which they could now hear as a soft roar against the other noises such as the rustling of the leaves, the occasional bark of a fox and the cry of birds – Fidelma began to feel more relaxed than she had been for the last few days.

They emerged into a broad clearing by the river. There was a large farmstead and outbuildings, and beyond, a small group of olive trees and vines. A dog started barking, and a man appeared from the building. Fidelma recognised him at once. It was Radoald's warrior, Wulfoald, who greeted Suidur with a friendly wave. A rapid-fire conversation was exchanged, in which the name of Grasulf was frequently mentioned. Finally, Wulfoald turned to Fidelma as she slid off the horse and stretched her limbs.

'Well, lady, it seems that we have much to apologise for.'

'Apologise?'

'As I recall, some days back you had no sooner entered this valley than you and your companions were attacked. And now I hear that you were abducted by Grasulf, an evil man if ever there was one.' He turned and greeted Brother Eolann before saying to Fidelma: 'We must make up for our inhospitable neighbours.'

Wulfoald's manner was warm and friendly. Fidelma, however, was thinking about his finding of young Wamba and Hawisa's accusation against him and her own suspicions. She wished the questions did not continually buzz around in her head like swarming bees. She must stop thinking awhile.

'I was just about to depart with my men for Bobium. We have spare horses so we could escort you to the gates of the abbey and make sure you reach there in safety. That is, unless you want to remain here and refresh yourselves? There is no need to break the journey at Radoald's fortress. We could have you at Bobium by mid-afternoon.'

Fidelma considered. In fact, it suited her to return to Bobium as soon as possible, and when the matter was put to Brother Eolann, he agreed at once. Wulfoald gave instructions to his men who brought forward two spare horses.

Fidelma felt awkward when it came to taking a farewell of Suidur and his silent companions. It was true that he had rescued her and Brother Eolann but, once more, her mind was awash with unanswered questions. Perhaps it was because she disliked mysteries that she had become a *dálaigh*. When she could not resolve a problem it gnawed at her like a toothache. Yet she realised that there was nothing else she could do but pretend that she felt all was well, hiding her suspicions and doubts. She therefore thanked Suidur as warmly as she could for his intervention, and told him to translate her thanks to his companions. Brother Eolann responded more emotionally and profusely with his thanks. Finally they mounted up and joined Wulfoald and two warriors as they moved off alongside the track by the river which would lead them back to Bobium.

ChAPTER FOURTEEN

The Abbey of Bobium was a-throng with excitement even before Fidelma and Brother Eolann reached the main gates. Brother Bladulf, the gatekeeper, stood by them almost hopping from one foot to another in his apparent exhilaration. Wulfoald and his companions had left them within sight of the gates. He and his men were apparently staying the night in the township. They agreed to collect the horses when they returned to Lord Radoald's fortress. Fidelma had considered it inappropriate to raise the matter of Wamba with Wulfoald. It was a subject that would have to be treated carefully.

Brother Wulfila, the steward, came hurrying through the crowd of curious brethren who had assembled to greet them. Willing hands were already helping them down from their horses. The pair ignored the numerous questions shouted at them and asked the steward to take them directly to Abbot Servillius.

The abbot met them in his chamber. Venerable Ionas was at his side but there was no sign of Magister Ado. Brother Wulfila remained in the chamber, shutting the door behind him.

'My first question must be to ask whether you are in good health. Do you need any attention from Brother Hnikar?' the abbot greeted them.

'We are both well, *Deo gratias*,' Brother Eolann answered for the two of them.

'*Deo optimo maximo*,' intoned Venerable Ionas gravely.

'And now,' invited the abbot, 'keep us in suspense no longer. Tell us of your adventure which has so worried our brethren.'

Fidelma and Brother Eolann had already held a quick exchange in their own language as they had ridden back down the valley as to the extent of what they should reveal. It had been agreed that while they must report the death of Lady Gunora and the disappearance of Prince Romuald, they should say nothing about the boy Wamba, the gold coins nor his mother Hawisa. Omission was not the same as telling a lie, Fidelma reasoned, remembering a teaching of the Brehon Morann. When one is faced with such a dilemma one should always choose the path of the greater good even though you must do the lesser evil. Fidelma felt guilty nonetheless. Apart from that, they decided to stick to the truth.

It was Brother Eolann who announced the brief facts of their abduction and short imprisonment, and the details of their rescue. It was Fidelma who then described the finding of the body of Lady Gunora.

The abbot's face was white with shock. 'It cannot be true,' he whispered.

Venerable Ionas laid a hand on the abbot's arm. 'If this is true, my friend, we had best resolve this mystery and quickly.'

Abbot Servillius became agitated as he shot a series of questions at Fidelma until Venerable Ionas intervened to advise him to allow Fidelma to complete her story before leaping to conclusions. It was clear that the abbot blamed the Lord of Vars for the death and believed the young prince, Romuald, was a prisoner at Vars.

'Grasulf,' Venerable Ionas explained quietly, when Fidelma had ended her story, 'has long been an enemy of this abbey and, as you have discovered, he is an enemy of the Faith. He adheres to the ways of the old gods of the Longobards.'

'We saw no sign of the boy in his fortress,' Fidelma pointed out.

Abbot Servillius began to reassert his belief but was politely interrupted by Venerable Ionas. 'Although Grasulf is certainly the sort of man who would have abducted Lady Gunora and the prince, as he abducted Sister Fidelma and Brother Eolann, he would not have them murdered. They were too valuable alive. He would have sold them to the highest bidder. He is a man without morals. If Perctarit paid the price, he would have handed the prince and Lady Gunora to him. Or if Grimoald wanted his son back and paid the price, then he would have sold them to him. A dead body is worth no ransom at all.'

'It could be that the boy is still his captive at Vars and that Lady Gunora was killed in her attempt to stop the abduction,' insisted the abbot.

'But what was Lady Gunora doing on the mountain with the boy in the first place?' Fidelma demanded. 'You said that she had left the abbey to find a place of greater security for herself and the boy at the fortress of Lord Radoald. Why would she go in the opposite direction up that mountain?'

The abbot and Venerable Ionas exchanged a nervous glance. Then Abbot Servillius spoke. 'It was as I said. Lady Gunora was worried when Bishop Britmund arrived here and witnessed her presence with the young prince. She said she did not feel safe and preferred to move on. She wanted no one told so left the abbey with the prince before first light.'

Brother Wulfila coughed to attract attention. 'Even I, as steward of the abbey, was not informed, lady. I would most certainly have advised against it. It was a foolhardy thing, to leave here in darkness.'

'I remember that you were looking for her,' agreed Fidelma. 'And she told no one else that she was leaving?'

'She told me,' answered the abbot. 'I shared that information with the Venerable Ionas here and with Brother Bladulf, the gatekeeper, since he had to get her horse and open the gate. I swore him to secrecy and placed him under total absolution for any untruth he had to commit to maintain that secret. So there were only the three of us who knew that Lady Gunora and the boy were leaving.'

'You said that Brother Bladulf had to get her horse. Are you saying that Lady Gunora and the boy left on one horse?'

'One horse,' confirmed the abbot. 'The boy rode behind her.'

Fidelma considered the matter. 'The fact remains that her body was found in entirely the opposite direction. If she and the boy were heading across Mount Pénas, in contradiction to her intended refuge with Lord Radoald, is there anywhere in particular that she might be making for?'

Abbot Servillius shrugged eloquently. 'I cannot conceive of anywhere.'

'There are practicalities to be considered,' Venerable Ionas interrupted. 'You have told us that you placed her body in one of the caves behind the sanctuary of Colmbanus. Then we must organise a party to retrieve the body. It is not fit that Lady Gunora lies unburied on the mountain. We should also inform Lord Radoald.'

'Wulfoald and his men escorted us here,' Fidelma pointed out. 'He is staying overnight in the settlement. He could provide some protection if the brethren set out to retrieve the body of Lady Gunora.'

'Protection?' The abbot seemed shocked. 'You think that Grasulf will attack the brethren sent to retrieve her body?'

'It is possible,' replied Fidelma.

'There is little to be done today,' Venerable Ionas decided. 'If I may make some suggestions, Father Abbot? Let us allow Sister Fidelma and our good *scriptor* the opportunity to refresh themselves and have their evening bathe as is the custom of the Hibernians. Then let them rest and partake of the evening meal.' He paused and glanced quickly at Fidelma. 'We will ask Wulfoald to join us and present our request that he accompany Brother Bladulf and some members of the brethren to retrieve the body.'

Fidelma was hesitant. 'Wulfoald has not been informed of our finding the body.'

'Why ever not?' demanded Venerable Ionas in surprise.

Fidelma thought rapidly as she did not want her suspicions of Wulfoald made obvious yet.

'With our adventures, escaping from the fortress of Grasulf, it did not arise,' she answered blandly. 'My thoughts were concerned with returning safely to the abbey.'

'Of course,' the abbot seemed to agree. 'But Wulfoald and Lord Radoald must be informed now. Brother Wulfila will go to the settlement and invite Wulfoald to attend our evening meal. Then we can inform him in detail of this tragic event.'

As Fidelma prepared to leave, she hesitated. 'Where is Magister Ado? I do not see him. I trust he is also well?'

'Magister Ado?' replied the abbot. 'He has gone to Travo.

He left the morning after you began your journey to the sanctuary on Mount Pénas.'

'Where is Travo?' she asked. She seemed to recall the name.

'It is further down the valley, towards Placentia. It is the site of the martyrdom of the Blessed Antonino, who suffered death under Diocletian. Magister Ado wished to make an offering at the church there which is one of the earliest dedicated to the Faith in this land. He should be back within a day or so and will be delighted to hear of your safe return.'

It was some time later after Fidelma had bathed and changed, and feeling unusually alert after her adventures, that she entered the *refectorium*. She found herself dismissing the expressions of concern from the brethren with a smile. There was also the small gathering of religieuses who shared the hall at mealtimes but she saw no sign of Sister Gisa. Nor could she see Brother Faro. She made her way to where Wulfoald stood with the abbot and Venerable Ionas.

It was clear that Wulfoald was not pleased. 'I should have been informed immediately about your discovery of Lady Gunora's body! Lord Radoald has been searching the valley for her,' he greeted Fidelma curtly.

Fidelma was about to respond when Abbot Servillius interrupted to point out that it was better to continue the conversation after the meal. Once they were in their seats, he then decided it was appropriate to intone a lengthy homily in praise of God for guiding the footsteps of Fidelma and Brother Eolann out of danger and back to safety. He then added a brief attack on the pagan idolatry of Grasulf of Vars.

After the meal Abbot Servillius invited Wulfoald, Fidelma,

Venerable Ionas and Brother Eolann back to his chamber. Fidelma explained to Wulfoald where the body of Lady Gunora had been found and where they had placed it.

'Had we known this sooner, Radoald could have stopped wasting the time of his sentinels,' grunted the warrior. 'But I think we may assume that all immediate danger will come from Vars.' He turned to Fidelma. 'You saw no sign of any other prisoners during your incarceration in Vars?'

'No. We saw no other prisoners.'

'It does not mean to say that Prince Romuald was not there,' pointed out Abbot Servillius.

'That is true,' agreed Fidelma. 'So you believe that Grasulf would be the most likely person responsible for the death of the Lady Gunora and the disappearance of Prince Romuald?'

'The only person, without doubt. He is a danger to the security of these valleys.' Wulfoald was emphatic.

'What intrigues me is this: how is it that, if Lady Gunora set off to seek refuge at Lord Radoald's fortress, her body was found on the upper reaches of Mount Pénas, which is in the opposite direction?' Fidelma had posed the question before without receiving an answer.

Wulfoald raised a shoulder a fraction and let it fall. 'There might be several reasons for that. Perhaps she was captured and transported there before she was killed.'

Fidelma accepted that it was a logical explanation but she was not impressed by it.

'I will send one of my men this very night to inform Lord Radoald about these matters,' Wulfoald went on. 'The rumours are increasing and ominous. If Perctarit has reached north of Mailand with a Frankish army, then we must be extremely vigilant. He is very near.'

Abbot Servillius was still showing apprehension in his drawn features. 'And what of the body of the Lady Gunora?'

'As you have already suggested, let Brother Bladulf take some of the brethren up to the sanctuary early in the morning to retrieve it. I will send two of my warriors to provide them with an escort. I shall also send a messenger back to Lord Radoald to inform him of the situation.'

'The track we followed up towards the sanctuary led past a goatherd's cabin where an old woman named Hawisa dwells,' Fidelma said.

'I know Hawisa's cabin,' Wulfoald assured her easily. He did not notice Fidelma's quick look of surprise.

Abbot Servillius glanced around at them. 'I think we are all aware of the dangers. So we should let our guest, Fidelma, rest after such a terrifying adventure. You as well, Brother Eolann. Wulfoald will organise that which he needs to organise.'

Fidelma was the last to leave the abbot's chamber but, at the door, she paused and turned back.

'I nearly forgot,' she told him. 'I was speaking to Brother Waldipert before we left the other day.'

Abbot Servillius looked up absently. 'Brother Waldipert the cook?'

'This is something not pertinent to the grave matters in hand. I have just remembered it – forgive me if I raise it now. I once mentioned in passing that I had an interest in ancient coins. Brother Waldipert said that he had recently come by one such coin and that he had given it to you. He found the coin strange and could not assess its value.'

'He did? I can't think . . . oh yes, that was some weeks ago.'

'He seemed to think it was found locally and was of a great age. I was wondering if I could see it? As I say, I am fascinated by such matters.'

The abbot stared at her blankly for a moment and then gave an off-handed gesture. 'That is not possible, Sister Fidelma.'

'Oh?'

'It disappeared from my study within a day or so of it being given to my safekeeping. We hunted high and low for it, but it was never found. It is terrible to think ill of one's brethren but, alas, I can think of no other reason other than it was taken deliberately. However, it was only a small coin of no great value, even though it was of gold. The loss was negligible.'

There was a note of dismissal in his tone and Fidelma inclined her head and left.

Outside the door, she hurried through the now-deserted hallway into the courtyard. It was dark and only a few brand torches were blazing outside, casting shadowy, flickering lights across the almost empty area. Thankfully, Wulfoald had stopped to talk awhile with the Venerable Ionas, for they were just parting and Wulfoald was moving towards the gates.

'Wulfoald, stay a moment!'

He turned at her breathless call.

'Sister Fidelma. How can I help you?'

She came up to him in the light of a nearby torch. 'I realised that I needed to ask you some questions.'

'Questions, lady? About what?'

'You found the body of the boy, Wamba, did you not?'

His eyes narrowed slightly. She could see the action clearly, even in the half-light.

'Wamba?' he repeated. 'What have you heard of Wamba?'

'I know he was a young goatherd who now lies buried in the abbey necropolis.'

'He was buried there a week or so before you came to Bobium. How does he concern you, lady?'

'It would be easier if you answered my questions first,' insisted Fidelma, 'and then I will see if things make sense or whether I am chasing shadows.'

Wulfoald shrugged indifferently. 'So what is it you want to know?'

'You confirm that you found his body?'

'I did. You want the details? Then know that I was riding back over the hills, on the road to this abbey across Mount Pénas. I happened on the boy's body lying alongside the track underneath a cliff face. It seemed that he had fallen and broken his neck.'

'After you found the body, what then?'

'I knew the boy. He was a goatherd and lived with his mother, Hawisa, not far from the place where I found him. You said that you passed her cabin on the way to the sanctuary.'

Fidelma controlled her surprise. 'You say you know her?'

'Of course. Most people know each other throughout this valley.'

'So what did you do? With the body of Wamba, that is.'

'I took him home.'

'You took him home?' Fidelma blinked.

'To his mother Hawisa.'

'You took his body to her cabin?' pressed Fidelma.

'Where else would I take it?' the warrior replied in irritation.

Fidelma made a decision that she must now confront Wulfoald with the facts as Hawisa had told them.

'What if I told you that Hawisa says that you took the body straight to the abbey, and by the time she came here, the body of her son was already buried?'

Wulfoald's face wore a look of amazement. Then he said, slowly, 'I would say, lady, that one of us was not telling you the truth.'

'Why would the old woman lie?'

'Why would *I* lie?' the warrior retorted.

'There might be many reasons.'

'Then ask Abbot Servillius, if you doubt my word.'

Fidelma frowned uncertainly. 'Abbot Servillius? What has he to do with it?'

'He was at Hawisa's cabin when I brought the boy's body there.'

It was Fidelma's turn to stare at him in amazement. 'What was *he* doing there?'

'He had gone to see Wamba or Hawisa about giving them the value of a coin that the boy had found and brought to the abbey. Apparently it was only a small coin and not worth much, but the boy had thought it valuable. We agreed with Hawisa that the boy's body would be taken to the abbey graveyard as a tribute. We all came down to the abbey for the burial that night. Hawisa stayed with a relative in the settlement.'

Fidelma stood unable to move, totally bewildered at the man's confidence. 'I say again,' she finally said, 'why would the old woman lie?'

Wulfoald's tone was belligerent. 'I can offer no explanation, lady. But there is one way to answer the question.'

'Which is?'

'To put it to the person who can answer it.'

'Hawisa?'

'Exactly so. Tomorrow, when my men go to the sanctuary, I shall accompany them as far as Hawisa's cabin. They can go on but I shall put the question to her.'

BEHOLD A PALE HORSE

'Then you will have no objection if I accompany you?' she said coldly.

'I would expect no less. However, having been once abducted on that mountain, are you sure that you are willing to ride up there again? Is that wise?'

'Wise or not, I think we should both hear the answer that Hawisa gives us as to what are two diametrically opposed accounts over the death of her son.'

'Agreed, lady. You are right. Let us meet here at first light.'

'Very well. One more thing,' she said as Wulfoald started to turn away.

'Only one?' He turned back with a thin smile.

'When you came across the body of Wamba, was there anything suspicious about it?'

'Suspicious?' She had his full attention now. He took a small step towards her, staring down into her face as if trying to read her mind. 'What do you mean?'

'Everything appeared as if he had missed his footing at that point, fallen down the cliffs and broken his neck?'

'What else could have happened?'

'What else?' echoed Fidelma softly, but did not answer the question.

'I don't know what is in your mind, lady, but I have told you what I know. Now, tomorrow we will attempt to discover why you have been told one story which I know is contrary to what happened.'

He turned on his heel and strode rapidly for the gates of the abbey. A shadow emerged – she realised it was Brother Bladulf – and a gate swung open to allow him to leave. Fidelma stood for a while gazing thoughtfully after him. Then, making up her mind, she returned to the abbot's chambers. The steward, Brother Wulfila, was outside.

'I wish to see the abbot,' she told him.

'He has retired for the night with strict instructions not to be disturbed. I am surprised that you are still up, lady, after our exhausting adventures.'

'I presume the abbot rises early?'

'He does.'

'Then it will have to wait until the morning.'

The steward inclined his head. *'Vade in pace.'*

Outside, Fidelma glanced quickly up towards the windows of the *scriptorium*. A flickering light was showing in the window above. She strode purposefully through the hall, turned to the left, through the small cloistered area, and then ran up the stairs into the tower.

The door to the *scriptorium* was not locked. She entered and found Brother Eolann seated at his desk before a tall tallow candle. He looked up with a tired smile.

'You are working late, Brother Eolann,' she said. 'And at a time when you should be resting after the adventures we have had.'

'I have much work to catch up on, lady.'

'We both should be resting,' she said.

Brother Eolann looked at her expectantly as she paused. 'But there is something on your mind, lady?'

'You remember our conversation with Hawisa, the mother of the boy Wamba?'

The *scriptor* looked puzzled. 'I do.'

'Are you satisfied that she was telling us the truth?'

'I thought so. Why do you ask?'

'I wanted to know why Wulfoald had taken the boy's body directly here to the abbey for burial and not to her cabin. That is what she told us, was it not?'

The look of bewilderment increased. 'I remember what she said clearly.'

'I do not wish to cast aspersions on your knowledge of this Longobard language, nor on your interpretation, but are you satisfied that she was telling us the truth?'

'As I said, I thought she was.'

'When I asked Wulfoald just now, he said that this was not so. He claims that he took her son's body to her cabin and, moreover, Abbot Servillius was there with Hawisa at the time.'

'Abbot Servillius was . . . ? I was not told that. I mean, she did not tell me that.' Even in the candlelight it seemed that Brother Eolann's features had paled. Then he shook his head in denial. 'That cannot be, lady. Someone is lying and I would say it is Wulfoald. The woman Hawisa was clear in her statement. I cannot see where there is any misunderstanding.'

'I thought so,' sighed Fidelma.

'Anyway, there is one way to discover the truth,' Brother Eolann went on. 'Ask Abbot Servillius if he was there.'

'He has retired for the night. I shall question him in the morning. But I want to find out why Hawisa lied to us.'

'Then I am not sure what you—'

'I have agreed with Wulfoald that we shall ride to Hawisa's cabin at first light and speak with her again,' she interrupted.

'Is that a good idea?' he protested. 'If it is not Hawisa who is lying then it must be Wulfoald, and why would he lie unless there were some good reason – one that he does not want you to discover.'

'I thought of that, which is why you must come with us. Once more I would have to rely on your ears and tongue as my interpreter so that I know what Hawisa is saying to Wulfoald.'

Brother Eolann was hesitant. 'Is it necessary?'

'It is.'

'Then, of course, I shall come with you.'

'Excellent. We shall meet in the courtyard at first light.'

As she reached the arch that led into the courtyard, Fidelma heard the sound of horses leaving the abbey. She paused in the shadow of the cloisters and saw two riders moving through the gates. Although they had their backs to Fidelma and only the torch-light to illuminate them, she could make out that one was male and one female. They disappeared into the darkness outside. Curious, she made her way to where Brother Bladulf was closing the gates after them.

'Who was that leaving the abbey?' she asked.

Brother Bladulf turned, surprised. 'Oh, it is you, Sister . . . er, lady,' he said, recovering. 'That was the abbot.'

Fidelma stared at him in astonishment. 'But the abbot had retired for the night and left instructions not to be disturbed. Who was the woman with him?'

'Sister Gisa, lady. She came to get the abbot. An emergency, she said.'

'An emergency?' she echoed.

'Old Aistulf. He is unwell and Sister Gisa came to fetch the abbot.'

'Aistulf?'

'So you have heard of Aistulf? Apparently, he was an old friend of Abbot Servillius but he only appeared in this valley two years ago. He is a hermit, who plays the pipes yet shuns regular intercourse with his fellow beings. He prefers to sleep in a cave and wander the woods at will.'

'So there is an emergency with Aistulf. Does the abbot usually rise from his bed in the middle of the night to respond so promptly to his call?'

Brother Bladulf pulled a sad face. 'Not often, although sometimes he has sent word and the abbot has responded.

This time Sister Gisa was in a panic so perhaps it is some medical matter.'

'Then why not send for Brother Hnikar?'

'Brother Hnikar?' The gatekeeper's expression was dour. 'He is a good physician, do not mistake me. But Brother Hnikar is the last person I would send for if I was dying and needed comfort rather than a lecture on how I should have led my life before I reached the point of death.'

'He is as bad as that?' Fidelma tried to keep a straight face.

'If I were a hermit, in love with nature, I would not send for him. Anyway, I do not think that enters into it. Aistulf only trusts Abbot Servillius and Sister Gisa. I am told that Sister Gisa has a good knowledge of the apothecary's art.'

'Do they have far to go?'

'A good question, lady, but one without an answer. Somewhere up into the hills across the river,' he pointed in the opposite direction to the slopes of Mount Pénas. 'No one but the abbot and Sister Gisa are allowed to know where he bides. And now, lady, the hour grows later . . . I have to be up early to lead the brethren up to the sanctuary to recover the body of Lady Gunora.'

Fidelma took the hint and turned back towards the guesthostel. Suddenly realising just how exhausted she was, she collapsed straight onto her bed and was asleep before she could put the cavalcade of thoughts into some order.

Someone was shaking her by the shoulder. She blinked and tried to focus. Then she started nervously.

Brother Wulfila, the steward, was standing by her bed with a candle.

'Venus, the morning star, is already clear in the eastern sky. It will soon be dawn, lady. I was told to wake you. Brother Bladulf and some of the brethren have already left on foot for the sanctuary.'

She struggled up in the bed. 'Dawn already?' She tried to think.

'Wulfoald is in the courtyard and has given orders that a horse be saddled ready for you.'

'Wulfoald?' She paused for a moment and then groaned as memory came flooding back. 'I am sorry, Brother Wulfila. Last evening saw me exhausted and my mind is still confused. My apologies. Tell Wulfoald I will join him shortly.'

As he set down the candle for her and turned for the door, she called, 'Is Brother Eolann already in the courtyard as well?

Brother Wulfila turned back with a frown. 'Brother Eolann, the *scriptor*, Sister?'

'Yes.'

'No, he is not there.'

'He might have overslept as I did,' Fidelma said. 'Could you make sure he is roused? He is joining Wulfoald and me, so he must be quick.'

The steward looked astonished. 'You are free to come and go as you will, lady, but the *scriptor* must have permission from the abbot.'

Fidelma sighed impatiently. 'Has Abbot Servillius returned then? He rode out last night in answer to a plea from Aistulf the hermit.'

Brother Wulfila was shaking his head. 'He has not returned, lady.'

'Very well. If he must secure permission, then seek it from Venerable Ionas but go and make sure Brother Eolann is ready to join us. It is necessary.'

'Very well, Sister. There are not too many people stirring in the abbey at the moment, for many were up to see the fire earlier.'

Fidelma kept her irritation under control. 'The fire? What fire?'

'Oh, there appeared to be a great fire high up on the mountain, on Mount Pénas. It blazed brightly in the darkness. Several of our brethren were roused and went out to stand watching it. It blazed a long time. Sometimes, when the weather is hot, fires start among the trees up there.'

ChapTER FIFTEEN

When Fidelma entered the courtyard, she saw Wulfoald waiting patiently by his pale grey horse. He was holding a second horse, presumably meant for herself. First light was creeping in, but it was still too dark to see clearly up the mountain and there was no sign of the conflagration that Brother Wulfila had mentioned. Fidelma glanced round. There was no sign either of Brother Eolann.

'Brother Eolann is coming with us,' she asserted, 'so we had best get another horse.'

Wulfoald looked surprised. 'Why is the *scriptor* coming with us?'

'Because he is my witness to what the old woman said and which is so contrary to what you told me.'

The warrior's mouth tightened. 'This is delaying us, lady. Brother Bladulf and his companions have already left to ascend to the sanctuary with two of my men.'

Before she had time to reply, Brother Wulfila came hurrying across the courtyard. He seemed agitated.

'Where is Brother Eolann?' demanded Fidelma before he had time to recover his breath.

'Sister . . . er, lady, you had best come with me. He's in the *scriptorium.*'

'What is it?' she pressed.

However, the steward simply shook his head and waved her to follow him.

With a muttered apology to Wulfoald, she turned and went after him through the small cloisters to the stairs ascending in the tower to the *scriptorium*. Brother Eolann was seated in a chair, with Brother Hnikar bending over him and dabbing at a wound in his forehead with a wet cloth. Blood had stained his robe and he looked very pale.

'What happened?' Fidelma gasped.

Brother Hnikar answered first. 'I think he fell down the steps and knocked himself out.'

'Is that so? she demanded of the *scriptor*, who nodded and then winced at the movement.

'Truthfully, I do not know, lady,' he said, resorting to their own language. 'I was working late here, as you know. Then, when I had finished, I extinguished the lamp, for I am used to finding my way in the twilight. I was crossing the *scriptorium* when I think I tripped and hit my fore-head.' He raised a hand to show her: there was bruising and signs of a lump.

Fidelma examined the wound closely, much to Brother Hnikar's annoyance. 'You *think* you tripped?' she repeated.

'I am sure I did. But I am confused. I can't recall much.'

Then the steward, Brother Wulfila, was speaking. 'When you asked me to find the *scriptor* I looked for him in his chamber and then came to the *scriptorium* and found him semi-conscious on the floor in a pool of blood. I sent for our physician and came to find you.'

'I knew nothing until Brother Wulfila was dabbing water on my head,' confirmed Brother Eolann. 'He placed me in this chair and went for the physician.'

Brother Hnikar turned, regarding Fidelma with disapproval.

'I can allow no more questions until I have administered balms for the wound and allowed the *scriptor* to rest.'

Brother Eolann glanced up with an unhappy expression. 'I am sorry, lady. Brother Hnikar will not allow me to join you to see Hawisa this morning.'

Fidelma grimaced sourly. 'That much is obvious.' Without someone she could trust to translate Hawisa's words, the whole exercise of going to see the old woman again was pointless.

'Be careful, Brother Eolann,' she said in her own language. 'I'll find an alternative translator.'

Brother Hnikar's features were even more disapproving now.

'The Rule in this abbey, Sister Fidelma, is that all conversations are carried on in the common language of the abbey – that is, Latin. We, who are one under God, have no secrets from Him, and therefore should have no secrets from one another.'

Fidelma lowered her head, more to hide her irritation than in a sign of submission.

'Sister Fidelma was merely wishing me a speedy recovery,' Brother Eolann said hastily in Latin.

'Indeed, a speedy recovery,' she added in Latin.

Brother Eolann hesitated and then said: 'I am truly sorry, Sister Fidelma. I am sorry for *everything*.'

She left the *scriptorium* with a slightly puzzled frown at the inflection on his last word. Brother Wulfila came hurrying after her.

'Has Abbot Servillius returned yet?' she asked as they came down the tower stairs.

'Neither he nor Sister Gisa have returned,' replied the steward.

'And Brother Faro?'

'Brother Faro left yesterday to take alms to the poor of a settlement down the valley, and has not returned to the abbey.

Fidelma's mind was working furiously as she emerged into the courtyard. It was now bright daylight. Wulfoald was still waiting, albeit impatiently, with the horses. The courtyard was unusually crowded: everyone seemed to be staring upwards, looking towards the mountain. Fidelma too glanced up. A long pall of grey-black smoke was trailing into the sky at some point on the mountain slopes. A feeling of apprehension came over her.

'What is that smoke?' she asked Brother Wulfila, who had followed her out and was also gazing upwards.

'I told you,' the steward reproved. 'During the night there was a blaze on the mountainside that lasted quite a time.'

'Where would you say it was located?'

'It is difficult to say exactly. Somewhere along the trail leading to the sanctuary on the mountain-top but, *Deo favente*, it does not seem to be anywhere near the sanctuary of the Blessed Columbanus.'

Wulfoald overheard the exchange and said, 'If you are worried about the journey, you have only to look there. See, there are the remains of rainclouds sweeping across the peaks. It must have been raining heavily up there. That will have dampened the fire, so there is no danger. Now, where is Brother Eolann?'

'He will not be coming,' she replied shortly. 'He had an accident.'

Wulfoald's eyes widened. 'That is unfortunate. Is he badly hurt?'

'Not badly, but enough to prevent him journeying up the mountain.'

'Then how . . .' began Wulfoald.

'. . . will I know what Hawisa is saying unless I rely on you to translate? In the circumstances . . .' She smiled tightly.

'This is a bad business.' They turned to find that the Venerable Ionas had joined them. For a moment Fidelma was uncertain about what he was referring to. Then she realised that he was staring at the black pall of smoke on the mountain. The elderly scholar suddenly observed Wulfoald waiting with the horses. 'Where are you off to?'

Wulfoald indicated the mountain. 'I was heading up there with Sister Fidelma. However, I think she might have changed her mind.'

The Venerable Ionas seemed puzzled. 'I thought you were sending your warriors with Brother Bladulf to the sanctuary? Is there need for Sister Fidelma to show you the way?'

'Bladulf and my warriors have already gone but Sister Fidelma and I are on another errand. We were going to Hawisa's cabin with Brother Eolann, since she needed someone to interpret our language for her. Brother Eolann has had an accident and cannot go.'

'I need someone who knows your Longobard language as well as Latin,' she began to explain, and then cursed herself for a fool as the reply was obvious.

'But Wulfoald speaks—'

'Alas, I would not be suitable for Sister Fidelma.' Wulfoald smiled tightly. 'She needed another voice.'

Venerable Ionas regarded him with incomprehension. Then he shrugged and waved to a rotund little man, unshaven and with bad teeth. The man was strapping a bag to a mule in a corner of the courtyard. He had a mass of black hair flecked with silver and a shaggy beard.

'Ratchis,' Venerable Ionas called, turning to Fidelma as the man came waddling over, slightly out of breath. 'Sister, if you are certain you need another translator, then here is the very man. It is a happy coincidence that he is starting over the mountain this very morning.'

The man halted before them with a lopsided smile and greeted them all in Latin.

'Ratchis,' Venerable Ionas said, 'are you good as a translator? Can you construe our good tongue of the Longobards into Latin?'

The fat merchant looked surprised at the question.

'I have been trading in these mountains all my life, Venerable Ionas. You know I can.'

'Then will you accompany Sister Fidelma here up the mountain and translate as she requests?'

The merchant looked doubtful. 'I am on my way to Ticinum Papia. I cannot delay long.'

'This will be on the way there,' intervened Wulfoald, adding in a sour tone, 'It will not take long. A brief halt and you will be on your way with the blessing of this abbey.'

The merchant glanced at Wulfoald in surprise. 'Are you coming as well? But you speak both—'

'Let us delay no longer with questions,' snapped the warrior in irritation. 'The sooner we leave, the sooner you will be on your way to Ticinum Papia.'

Fidelma turned to thank the bemused merchant for his services before mounting the horse that Wulfoald held ready. The warrior swung easily into the saddle while the merchant scrambled on to his mule.

'We could not take the horses all the way up to the sanctuary,' Wulfoald volunteered, 'but they can reach just below Hawisa's cabin. The track across the mountains to Ticinum Papia leads off there: that is the track our merchant friend will take to his destination. That is also the track on which I found Wamba. Let us try to make up now for the lost time.'

Fidelma did not respond. She was still brooding about the fact that Wulfoald seemed so confident that he was in the right.

Brother Wulfila opened the gates, in the absence of Brother Bladulf, and the three riders trotted out and alongside the walls of the abbey to join the track that wound up the mountain towards the distant peak. They had ridden in silence for a while when the merchant Ratchis spoke. His mule was making good time behind them; in fact, the animal was obviously used to climbing the hilly terrain.

'Did I hear we are going to Hawisa's cabin?' he called.

Wulfoald glanced across his shoulder. 'You know her, merchant?'

'I know many in these mountains, warrior,' the small man asserted. 'I even recognise you as one of Lord Radoald's men. Why are we going to see the old woman?'

'To ask a few questions about the death of her son, Wamba,' Fidelma replied.

'But Wamba fell from some rocks and killed himself. I remember the gossip well. That was a few weeks ago. I thought he was buried at the abbey.'

'Were you at the abbey when it happened?' inquired Fidelma.

'I arrived in time for the burial that night. I had been at Travo that day. You were there as well, Wulfoald.'

'Where do you come from, Ratchis?' Fidelma asked.

'From Genua.'

'It's just that you do not travel with a large caravan of goods.'

Ratchis uttered a hollow laugh. 'That is because I travel seeking custom at first and, when I have sufficient orders, I return to organise men and mules to deliver the goods. Alas, it seems there is little business to be done in your Valley of Trebbia these days. There is too much tension in the air. That is why I head for Ticinum Papia and will return along the old Salt Road by Vars.'

'I doubt whether you will find the tension any different there,' muttered Wulfoald.

'Why would that be?' asked the merchant with an air of innocence.

'Come, Ratchis, you must know as well as I do,' Wulfoald returned sternly. 'At the moment Grasulf, the Lord of Vars, controls the old Salt Road from Genua all the way to Ticinum Papia and so all the way on to Mailand. And Mailand has always been loyal to Perctarit. If Grasulf gained control of the Trebbia, then he would control both routes from Genua, the Trebbia to Placentia as well as the old Salt Road to Mailand. Through either route troops and equipment landing at Genua by sea could strike inland in support of Perctarit, if he is at Mailand.'

'Spoken like a warrior.' The merchant smiled. 'Strategy? Alas, you see everything only in terms of strategy.'

'In these times there is no other way to see things,' replied Wulfoald, unperturbed.

'I am a merchant and I see things only in terms of trade and profits. If one has to pay the warlords, such as Grasulf or Radoald, then one merely has to add that cost into the price.'

'Are you not fearful these same warlords would kill you?'
Wulfoald asked.

Ratchis chuckled. 'Then where would they get their
supplies afterwards?'

Fidelma was silent, listening to the exchange. They had
come a fair way up the mountain and, finally, Wulfoald
suggested halting their ascent for they had gone beyond the
spot where the main track turned off to start its winding
climb. Fidelma recalled that it was not far up to Hawisa's
cabin. It was at this point that the low whinny of a horse
came to their ears. At once Wulfoald's sword was in his hand.
He slid from his horse, glanced towards the others with a
finger raised to his lips, and cautiously moved up the path
before them. They sat and waited. Wulfoald was not gone
long but soon re-emerged, his sword sheathed.

'It is the horses and mule of Brother Bladulf and his party,'
he explained. 'They have tethered them in a little clearing yonder
and continued up to the sanctuary on foot to recover the body.
We'll leave our mounts at the same place as it will become too
difficult for the animals to attempt to ascend further.'

The horses and mule were tethered among the trees well
below the area blackened by fire. There was a natural shelter
and a gushing stream among the grassy slopes for the comfort
of the horses.

'If I remember correctly, Hawisa's cabin is just over that
rise in the track.' Fidelma pointed.

'Your memory is correct, lady,' Wulfoald replied with a
tight expression on his features.

Even from this distance, Fidelma could smell the acrid
stench of newly burned wood. The soft wind had begun to
blow a fine ash on its gusting breath. Wulfoald had noticed
it too and set off determinedly up the track.

'Let us see how far this fire has eaten into the forest,' he called back over his shoulder.

By now Fidelma was experiencing the same apprehension she had felt when standing in the courtyard and seeing the smoke on the mountain. She was wondering if it had been a natural fire. If it was not, if it had been set by Grasulf and his men, then they might still be waiting in ambush.

'We must be careful from here on,' she advised.

'Why so?' The voice of Ratchis, the merchant, was high-pitched with nervousness. Neither of the others bothered to reply.

As they approached the blackened section of forest, Fidelma began to feel really uneasy. If her accusation was correct – that Hawisa had told the truth and Wulfoald was lying about taking Wamba to the abbey – then Wulfoald had a reason to mean her harm. She was glad that the Venerable Ionas had asked the merchant to accompany them. He would be better than no help at all. But it was very confusing. Wulfoald was obviously confident in his statement. Maybe she was wrong. If so, why had Hawisa lied? Was it something about payment for the coin, about the gold?

The area seemed familiar to Fidelma as they left the main path and headed into the forest, and now the foreboding she had felt when they set out came back with a vengeance. The sudden heavy showers seemed to have dampened every-thing apart from the all-pervasive smell of smoke and burned tinder and . . . was there something else in the air? There was a peculiar odour, which reminded Fidelma of roasting pig. Then she saw the ruins of a cabin. She recognised it at once because of its position and the still-gushing mountain stream which provided the only unchanged items in the blackened landscape. Before what might have been the doorway of the cabin near where she had sat only a few days before, were the remains of a body, too charred and distorted to be identified.

Fidelma stood still, her face grim.

Without any warning at all there was a cry, a shrill animal-like shriek. A figure was suddenly charging towards her, one hand holding high a flashing knife-blade. Fidelma froze with shock at the sudden appearance of the figure out of the black gloom of the burned forest. Then she was aware of Wulfoald, stepping before her and knocking aside the attacker, who dropped his knife and went sprawling in the ash-strewn floor of the clearing. Wulfoald stood over the man, his sword at the ready for a further attack. But the figure lay there, shoulders rising and falling strangely. It took a moment or so to realise he was sobbing uncontrollably.

Fidelma became aware that the merchant, Ratchis, had given a cry of terror and was running back down the hill to the spot where they had left their mounts. She called after him but knew it was in vain and went to stand by Wulfoald.

The warrior bent forward and seized the assailant by the back of his neck and hauled him to his feet. It was a young man scarcely in his twenties. He was tousle-haired, his face smudged with soot, the tears creating stains across his cheeks. His dress was typical of the goatherders of the area.

Wulfoald shook the unhappy creature as she had seen a wolf shaking its prey. Questions shot out fiercely. Then Wulfoald turned to Fidelma to interpret.

'The youth thought we were the ones who did this.' He jerked his head at the burned-out ruins. 'Hawisa is dead and some of her livestock as well. That's why he attacked us.' He turned back to the youth, then peered closer at him. 'This is the nephew of Hawisa. His name is Odo. I recognise him now under the soot and grime.'

Fidelma was surprised when the youth suddenly said in very poor but understandable Latin: 'Yes, Hawisa was my aunt. I do not know you.'

'I am in Lord Radoald's service,' replied the warrior. 'This is Fidelma of Hibernia.'

'So your name is Odo?' asked Fidelma. 'And you are the goatherd that took over the goats when your cousin Wamba died?'

'You are a stranger here,' replied the youth with caution in his tone. 'How did you know this?'

'Your aunt told me of you. I talked with her several days ago.'

'She did not speak Latin.'

'I know. But I had an interpreter with me. How is it that *you* speak Latin?'

The youth drew himself up. 'I was taught by the brethren and still speak with Aistulf when I can.'

'Aistulf the hermit?' Fidelma was surprised. 'This Aistulf does not appear to be such a hermit, after all. I gather he also taught your cousin Wamba the bagpipes. What is it you call them locally – the *muse*?'

'I suppose Hawisa told you that? Wamba was clever. He would have been a very good piper . . .'

'. . . had he lived.' Wulfoald finished the sentence for him.

'It was about Wamba that I came to speak to your aunt some days ago,' Fidelma ignored his interruption, 'and I wanted to clarify things with her today. But this is how we found her cabin, and . . .' She did not finish the sentence but merely nodded at the charred remains. Then she said: 'Let us remove ourselves to a more pleasant area where we may talk.'

They walked downhill a short distance. Odo had placed a blanket on some rocks and went to pick it up. When he saw them looking, he explained, 'I brought it to cover my aunt with and perhaps get her body away so that she might be given a decent burial.' They waited while he placed it over the charred corpse before they walked down to the place where they had left their horses, the little clearing that had escaped the flames. Through it a stream still gushed and sparkled with the green vegetation around it. Although their horses grazed peacefully, there was no sign of Ratchis' mule.

Wulfoald peered about in resignation. 'I think our merchant friend has deserted us. Did you still want him?'

Fidelma shook her head and seated herself on the trunk of a fallen tree, indicating that Odo should do likewise. 'Now, Odo, let us talk. You believe that this was no natural fire?'

'Yes – what do you know of this fire, lad?' put in Wulfoald, who was leaning against the trunk of a tree. 'By attacking us, you made it plain that you knew that it had been deliberately set.'

Odo looked up at him, an expression of anguish on his features as he tried to gather his thoughts.

'Something awoke me in the night. The alarm of animals and birds, I suppose – the fire must have frightened them. I live not far down the mountain, just over the shoulder of that hill. I could not see what was causing the animals to flee that area of the woods at first. I heard the sound of the fire before I saw the flames and the direction of it. What could I do? I knew from its ferocity that I could not reach my aunt's cabin. I had the animals and myself to protect as well. Across the hill is a rocky ground with a pool, almost as big as a lake. I took the herd and went there, knowing the stony land and water would create a break for the fire.'

282

He paused and swallowed hard before resuming. 'The fire burned long and fiercely. I was there until morning before I dared believe that the heavy rains had dampened it out and there was no chance of it starting again. Then I felt safe to return. By the time I reached the area of the fire, it was too late. My aunt . . .' The youth suddenly began to sob again and Fidelma reached forward and laid a hand on his shoulder.

'The fire seemed confined to your aunt's cabin and the immediate area,' Wulfoald observed. 'It could be that she had an accident. Perhaps a cooking fire became out of control.'

'But you felt it was deliberate,' interrupted Fidelma. 'Who did you think had set the fire? In other words, *why* did you think this was arson?'

'Just before I started moving the herd to safety, I glanced up towards my aunt's cabin,' Odo told her. 'I couldn't see much with the flames and smoke, but I saw a man on horseback leaving the area.'

'I thought your aunt's cabin is impossible to reach on horse-back,' Fidelma said.

'A trained rider on a good horse could make it,' corrected Wulfoald.

'I saw him,' affirmed Odo. 'He was riding down the mountain but I lost sight of him in the smoke. He was the man who did this, there is no doubt.'

'Can you describe him?' Fidelma leaned forward eagerly.

Odo shook his head. 'He was just a figure in the darkness. All I remember was that the horse was pale. It could have been white or grey.' He suddenly peered at Wulfoald's horse and frowned. 'It was much like that one.'

'Set deliberately . . .' Wulfoald was thoughtful. 'It is lucky that the fire did not spread further.'

'There was a heavy rain that swept the area, and other mountain people came to make sure there were fire-breaks in case it restarted. They have all returned to their homes to ensure their herds are well. I was about to leave when I saw people passing up the road to the sanctuary . . .'

'That would have been Brother Bladulf and his brethren,' Wulfoald observed.

'They passed by on foot along the main track up towards the sanctuary. I waited in case they returned and then I saw you coming directly to Hawisa's cabin and thought you must have been responsible.'

'If someone was responsible for the fire, and therefore the death of the old woman, then there are many questions to be answered. By the way,' Fidelma had a sudden thought, 'did your aunt tell you about the day Wamba was found?'

'She had spoken of nothing else since the burial,' confirmed the goatherd. 'My cousin was her only child. Why do you ask?'

'And what did she say? Explain the circumstances.'

'That day she came to my cabin, which, as I say, is not far away down the mountain. She told me that a warrior had found Wamba where he had apparently fallen from a rockface. He was dead. She asked me to tend to the goats while she went to the abbey where the body was being taken for burial.'

'Did she say how she knew the warrior had found her boy?'

Odo stared at her in puzzlement. 'Because the warrior told her so.'

'She had not gone to the abbey when you saw her. When had the warrior told her about finding the body?'

The young man looked bewildered. 'I do not understand. He told her when he brought the body to her cabin.'

Fidelma heard Wulfoald's suppressed exclamation of satisfaction but ignored it.

'Did she tell you who this warrior was? His name?'

'Only that he was one of Lord Radoald's men, that's all I know. Strangely enough, Abbot Servillius was with her at the time. He had come to give Wamba payment for some old coin that Wamba had been given. Apparently he had taken the money to the abbey.'

'You did not go to Wamba's funeral?'

'I could not. Hawisa asked me to look after the goats. She went.'

Fidelma was sitting back, her mind racing. The story was totally contrary to what Hawisa had told them on their visit to her. This account entirely supported Wulfoald's version of events. How could such a thing be?

'Well.' Wulfoald smiled almost triumphantly. 'Now you know my story is correct.'

'So one other thing, Odo. Did you know that your aunt had placed a box belonging to Wamba in the cairn that she had erected?'

The youth nodded sadly. 'It was stolen almost immediately,' he replied. 'One of the goatherds even saw it being taken. He actually saw a man in the robes of a religieux climbing down from where the cairn was, with the box in his hand. He scrambled up to the path to intercept him, but by the time he reached the spot, the thief had escaped on a horse. Curiously enough, yesterday morning my aunt found the box, slightly damaged, but placed back in the cairn.'

Fidelma did not bother to explain but asked, 'Was the colour of this horse mentioned?'

Odo thought a moment and then he realised the implication. 'It was pale grey too.'

'Where would this witness be now?'

'Gone, lady. He went to Travo soon after the cairn was desecrated and has not returned.'

Fidelma sat back, gazing moodily at the gushing waters of the stream. Not for the first time, questions cascaded in her mind. Why had Hawisa told her and Brother Eolann such a different tale? Why would she lie so blatantly? Then she realised she was asking the wrong question. She had not thought of it before – indeed, had never contemplated it. How did she know what Hawisa had told her? Her story had been relayed through interpretation only. Fidelma had totally relied on her interpreter and that was Brother Eolann. But why should Brother Eolann have misinterpreted what the old woman had said? If Hawisa was not lying at the time, why would the *scriptor* purposely distort her words? There were other questions. Why did Abbot Servillius climb all the way to Hawisa's cabin to compensate her for a coin that was not worth much? And why had Brother Ruadán claimed that Wamba had been killed because he found the coins?

Fidelma rose to her feet, turning over the answers she had received and coming up with more questions. Another thought struck her. She turned quickly back to Odo.

'You said that Abbot Servillius had come to Hawisa's cabin that day to recompense Wamba for some coins that he had been given and taken to the abbey.'

'That's right.'

'Do you mean Wamba had found the coins or been given these coins by someone else?'

'Wamba told me that he had been given two coins, not that he found them. He believed they were gold and ancient, but he never showed them to me. He only mentioned one to his mother.'

'But let me make this absolutely clear. Wamba was given the coins?'

'That's what he told me and what he told his mother.'

'Who gave him the coins?'

'Some old religieux, one of the Hibernians at the abbey.'

'Can you remember the name?' pressed Fidelma.

'Not really. A name that sounded like strong rope.'

The Latin word he used was *rudens*. Fidelma gave a quick smile of satisfaction.

'Brother Ruadán?' she asked.

Odo had no hesitation. 'That was the name.'

Fidelma heaved a deep sigh. So it had been Brother Ruadán who had given Wamba the coins, coins that the old man considered had brought about the death of the boy.

'I would be careful, Odo,' she advised him. 'There are strange things happening on this mountain. After we leave here, I would take your goats to some new pasture where you might protect yourself for a while.'

Wulfoald was on his feet looking moodily at the horses. 'I was hoping we could use the merchant's mule to help carry the old woman's body back to the abbey. It would be appropriate if she could be buried with her son.'

Fidelma glanced at him in appreciation. 'You can put it on my horse,' she offered. 'I can ride double behind you.'

'Thank you, lady. I can help you move the body,' Odo said. 'It would be the right thing to do.'

It did not take long to carry out the gruesome task, arranging Odo's blanket to wrap the body in. The youth agreed to come to the abbey before midnight when such burials were carried out, to pay his last respects to his aunt.

'Nothing further we can do here,' Wulfoald said, as he stood with the horses. 'I don't understand it. If the fire was deliberately set, and it seems it was, then are we saying that this was an act of Grasulf and his men?'

'I am as perplexed as you are, Wulfoald, by what we have seen and heard,' Fidelma replied quietly.

Wulfoald grimaced almost humorously. 'I am sure that this has not turned out satisfactory to whatever ideas you had, lady,' he said to Fidelma. 'However, I would urge that we return to the abbey as quickly as possible. We ought to have a word with the *scriptor*, Brother Eolann, to see if he can cast any light on what Hawisa originally said to you and, perhaps, why.'

'You are right, Wulfoald,' Fidelma acknowledged. 'I am sorry. I should have realised long before this that you were telling the truth.'

Wulfoald looked amused but said, 'Why is that, lady?'

'When Brother Waldipert, the cook, told me that you had brought Wamba's body to the abbey, he said quite clearly that you brought the body *with* the abbot and not *to* the abbot. That meant that you and the abbot had both escorted the body to the abbey. It was stupid of me to have overlooked it.'

Wulfoald pursed his lips for a moment and then shrugged. 'A small word, a tiny inflection. Easily missed. *Grammatici certant et adhuc sub judice lis est?*'

Fidelma smiled wanly. 'Grammarians discuss, and the case is still before the courts,' she repeated. 'But remember, wars hang on such linguistic misunderstandings.'

'Let us hope no war hangs on this mystery,' Wulfoald replied as he untethered his horse and mounted, holding out an arm to help Fidelma swing up behind him. Then he bent and took the reins of the beast that carried the corpse of the old woman and began to lead it carefully behind them down the mountain track towards the abbey.

Fidelma felt bewildered as she held on to the back of the warrior. There was something not quite right here, something that made her believe that the answers to all these mysteries still lay in the abbey itself.

ChAPTER SIXTEEN

Fidelma and Wulfoald left their grisly burden at the gates of the necropolis with one of the brethren, to await instructions on the burial, before continuing into the abbey itself. When Brother Wulfila swung back the gates to allow them to enter the courtyard, he looked nervous, and Fidelma immediately became aware of a tension in the air as they dismounted. One of the brethren took the horses to the stables.

'Did all go well?' demanded the steward. 'Did you find out the cause of the fire?'

'It seems that the fire was deliberately set,' Wulfoald replied. 'It destroyed the cabin of Hawisa and she perished in the flames.'

'Deliberately set?' gasped the steward.

'I have to inform you, as steward, that we brought the body of Hawisa down and left it at the necropolis. We considered it appropriate that the old woman should be buried with her son.'

'Perhaps it is best, then, if the body is taken to the chapel overnight.'

'We thought it would be more expedient to leave it at the necropolis,' Sister Fidelma said. 'I am afraid the odours would be offensive to the brethren if it was brought into the abbey.'

Brother Wulfila looked undecided. 'But the body should be given a blessing before burial. It ought to be brought to the chapel for services . . .'

'I suggest that the blessing be done at the graveside,' Wulfoald replied dryly. 'Death, in such circumstance, does not smell sweet.'

It took the steward a few moments before he understood. 'Of course, of course,' he muttered, anxiously peering around as if looking for someone.

'Is something wrong?' Fidelma asked. 'You appear preoccupied, Brother Wulfila.'

'I am sorry, lady. I have a matter to attend to,' he said, and then he left them to hurry away.

Wulfoald glanced at Fidelma with a shrug and hailed Brother Hnikar who was passing by.

'Is Abbot Servillius in his chamber?'

The apothecary halted. 'He has come back but is not to be disturbed.'

'Not to be disturbed?' queried Wulfoald, amazed.

The other man explained: 'Abbot Servillius returned a short while ago. He has retired immediately to his chamber for he is exhausted. I have never seen him look so worried. He told the steward specifically that he is not to be disturbed until the bell for the evening meal.'

'And Sister Gisa – where is she?' Fidelma asked, recalling that they had ridden out together on the previous night.

'Abbot Servillius says Sister Gisa has remained with Aistulf. It is very curious.'

Wulfoald gave him an encouraging smile. 'Then I am sure the abbot will explain when he emerges from his rest. Doubtless he is exhausted, having been away all night. If Sister Gisa is with Aistulf, then she will be all right.

Meanwhile, Sister Fidelma, we must go in search of Brother Eolann.'

Fidelma agreed. 'Has he recovered from his er . . . fall?' she asked Brother Hnikar.

'Yes, yes. He is fine and he claims no pain at all from his injury, even though he has a bruise and a bump on his head. I saw him a short time ago, heading for the *scriptorium*.'

Fidelma led the way to the entrance to the *scriptorium* through the smaller courtyard and up the tower. The chamber in which Brother Eolann was usually to be found, however, was empty and in gloom. Although it lacked a long time until dusk, every time she had been in the room there was a lamp or tallow candle spluttering with light. There was none now. With a puzzled grimace to Wulfoald, she turned and opened the door into the copyists' room. Here the lamps blazed as a dozen or so of the brethren were seated at their desks with maulsticks to rest their wrists on as they used their quills to copy texts on to vellum from the skins of goats or sheep. There was an industrious scratching as they painstakingly bent to their various tasks.

One of them looked up and caught sight of Fidelma and Wulfoald. He rose from his stool and came forward with an inquiring glance.

'I am looking for the *scriptor*, Brother Eolann,' she told him.

'We have not seen him for a while, Sister,' the scribe replied. 'We thought he might have left the abbey again.'

'Left the abbey *again*?'

'He was away nearly four nights with you, Sister,' replied the scribe solemnly but without guile.

She flushed in annoyance. 'He was here this morning and had an – an accident. A fall. He has not been seen by you today?'

BEHOLD A PALE HORSE

'He was here some time today,' offered another of the copyists, glancing up.

'He may be with Venerable Ionas, Sister,' said another. 'He is often in conference with him. Venerable Ionas works in his own chamber through there.' He pointed to another door.

Fidelma thanked them and, with Wulfoald behind her, followed the direction that the copyist had indicated through a door into a small passage. Even before they began to search for Venerable Ionas' chamber, they saw the elderly scholar himself walking along the passage as if on his way to the copyists' room. His expression grew concerned when they told him who they were looking for.

'I have also been in search of Brother Eolann. I saw him briefly after Abbot Servillius returned. In fact, he said he was going to make confession to the abbot but he has not been seen in the *scriptorium* since then. I was told that he had a bad fall this morning and perhaps he is still suffering from the shock of it.'

Venerable Ionas told them the location of Brother Eolann's chamber but they had no luck there. The *scriptor* believed in living frugally for there was hardly anything that could be described as personal belongings in the room, only a spare set of sandals, some clothing and personal toilet articles. There was not even a book nor a set of scribal implements to mark his profession.

Fidelma turned to Wulfoald with a look of resignation.

'There is little more that we can do until we find Brother Eolann's whereabouts.'

'I agree. This matter is becoming curious, lady. Unfortunately, I have the security of the valley to occupy me and so must return to Radoald's fortress to discuss these matters with him.'

'You believe warfare is imminent?'

'That is one thing that is sure. And another thing that is also sure is the fact that Grasulf of Vars will be part of it. But he will go with the side that pays him the most. That's why Suidur went to see him, to find out what Perctarit was offering him.'

They had made their way back down to the courtyard and Wulfoald called for his horse to be brought out.

Fidelma waited a moment before making up her mind to bathe after her journey. Later, she lay down in her chamber and dozed for a while. It was growing late when she opened her eyes. Time had passed quickly. Her feelings of unease began to increase. She must not delay in questioning Abbot Servillius about his visit to Hawisa. When she went down to the main hall and found Brother Wulfila, she was informed that the abbot had not yet emerged. His strict instruction was that he should not be disturbed before the bell for the evening meal.

In response to her question, the steward declared that he had not seen Brother Eolann since midday. There was no further news of Sister Gisa, but Brother Faro had returned – although on being told of Sister Gisa's absence, he insisted on leaving the abbey again to see if he could find his companion. The steward seemed distressed that no one appeared to be obeying the rules of the abbey any more.

Annoyed at what she saw as timewasting, Fidelma decided to seek out Venerable Ionas again to see if his scholarship could shed light on those matters that were worrying her. She retraced her steps to the *scriptorium* and then found his chamber. A few seconds after tapping on the door, the elderly scholar's voice invited her to enter. He was sitting at his desk with some manuscript books laid out in front of him and a quill in his hand.

'Venerable Ionas, may I bother you for a moment?'

The old man sat back from his desk with a frown and laid down the quill. 'If you are still looking for Brother Eolann, he has not been seen yet. It is very vexatious.'

'I have heard as much from Brother Wulfila,' she replied, entering and shutting the door behind her. 'But it is about another matter I have come to seek your advice.'

'Then how can I be of help, Sister Fidelma?' he asked with interest.

'I hear that you know something about ancient coins.'

'I know a little, for in the study of history, coins can sometimes be useful.'

'Can you tell me what this is?' She had taken the gold coin from her *ciorr bholg*, or comb bag, and placed it in his hand, before sitting by his desk on a small stool.

Venerable Ionas peered at it shortsightedly, turning it over in his frail hands. Then he nodded slowly. 'A gold piece from ancient Gaul. It looks quite old. Where did you find it?'

'Oh, it was given to me.' Fidelma glossed over its provenance. 'But are you sure it is from Gaul, not a local coin?'

'See the charioteer on it, the horses with stars above them?' Venerable Ionas held up the coin to the light of his lamp. 'And see those letters on the obverse? That is a gold coin of the Tectosages of Gaul. Their capital was the city of Tolosa.'

Fidelma tried not to reveal that Tolosa meant anything to her. She was about to thank the old scholar when a thought struck her.

'You have been here many years, Venerable Ionas?' It was a question rather than a comment.

'I came here a few years after the death of our dearly beloved Columbanus, and met and spoke with those who had known him in life,' he replied. 'That was when I began writing my life of our founder. After that I wandered in several parts of Christendom, even among the Franks and then to Rome. That is where I picked up my knowledge of Gaulish coins, so I can identify the one you hold.'

'Brother Eolann mentioned you had such knowledge.'

'He is a good *scriptor*.'

'Do you know much about him?'

The old man was surprised. 'I thought that he came from the same part of the world as you do?'

'He does,' agreed Fidelma quickly. 'I meant, since he came to this abbey.'

'Oh, he has only been here two or three years. I am told that he first went to the Abbey of Gallen, an Hibernian whom you called Gall. Then he crossed the high peaks and spent some time in Mailand. That was about the time when Perctarit still ruled from there, before he was driven into exile. Brother Eolann then came here, seeking peace and solitude. He had talent and soon rose to become *scriptor* of the abbey.'

'But he was sad at being criticised when some of his books were needlessly ruined. Some of their pages were cut off and disappeared.'

'I do not remember mention of that,' said the old scholar. 'I was not told and I use the library every day.'

'I see,' she said thoughtfully.

'It is a great crime to destroy books,' he went on.

'Brother Eolann and I managed to ascertain that the pages had been cut from books by Livy and Pliny. We identified the pages from Livy. They had been removed from one of the books containing a passage about a Roman Proconsul named Caepio. His legions were destroyed in Gaul.'

Venerable Ionas looked at her with quick interest.

'Caepio? Yes, he was the Proconsul and Governor of this

very territory in the days of the old Empire. He was the great-grandfather of Marcus Brutus, one of the assassins of the General Julius Caesar.'

'I have heard of Julius Caesar,' Fidelma admitted. 'But that must have been in very ancient times then? I had a feeling that Caepio had some more immediate connection with this area – some legacy.'

'Caepio?' Venerable Ionas shook his head. 'No, he lived a long time before Julius Caesar – many years, in fact, before the Coming of the Christ. Caepio's legacy was reviled throughout the Empire. There is a good reason why his life was not considered worthy. His arrogance destroyed two Roman armies, tens of thousands of men, but he escaped with his life. He was taken before the Roman Senate, tried and found guilty of the destruction of his army and of embezzlement of money. Being a patrician he was stripped of his citizenship and ordered into exile. No one was allowed to provide him with fire or water within eight hundred Roman miles of the Senate House, and he was fined fifteen thousand gold talents. He was not allowed to speak to friends or family from the moment of his sentence. The story is that he managed to reach a Greek city in the east and died there in exile.'

Fidelma was quiet. Venerable Ionas' account more or less confirmed and expanded the few words that she had seen in the book in the library at Vars.

'Why would pages relating to Caepio be cut out of the books in the abbey library?' asked Venerable Ionas.

'I was told there was some legend connected with gold from Tolosa,' she said.

The elderly scholar looked at the coin and grimaced. 'The same old dream. *Aurum Tolosa*, eh?'

'Then you know of it?' Fidelma asked quickly.

'The people of these valleys often talk about it. It is more or less the gold of fools. A myth. It doesn't exist.'

'But tell me about it.'

'Before the battle in which the Roman armies were annihilated, Caepio and his legions attacked and sacked the town of Tolosa and carried off a vast amount of gold and silver. Some stories even say that the people had hidden the gold in a great, dark lake, but Caepio managed to recover it . . .'

'That which was taken from a watery grave must be returned to it,' muttered Fidelma.

'What?' frowned the old scholar.

'Forgive me, I was just remembering something that someone said. Go on.'

'Well, the figures vary, but it is said that the legionnaires filled forty-six wagons with gold and silver. Caepio then sent them back to his villa in Placentia. When the Senate asked him where the gold was, he claimed it had never reached Placentia – that the wagons had been attacked by bandits and looted on the way. The Senate didn't believe him. They believed that he had appropriated the gold for himself and had buried it somewhere in these very mountains – hence the severity of his sentence. The fact was that it disappeared and over the many centuries since, it has become a myth. So why are you interested in this?' He held up the coin and examined it. 'A gold coin of Tolosa . . . a coin of the Tectosages.' He began to smile. 'Ah, don't tell me that someone is trying to persuade you that this coin is part of the lost gold of Tolosa?'

Fidelma flushed slightly. 'Not at all,' she asserted. 'I was mainly concerned why the pages about Caepio should be removed from the books in the library. Brother Eolann was most upset about this.'

'Well, I can understand that the destruction of a book would be a great affront. He should have reported the matter. I would not believe that the contents of the pages would be important in themselves. We have far more detailed accounts about Caepio in another book, which I have used recently. There is a little book in the *scriptorium* on the life of the Proconsul. Brother Eolann was especially proud of it as it was a very rare copy. Apparently it was banned by the *curule aediles* in Rome.'

'The what?' Fidelma asked, puzzled.

'*Curule aediles*? Ancient Roman magistrates. For some reason we had one of the copies that escaped destruction. I believe it might have survived because it was written by a Gaul from Narbona – Trogus Pompeius.'

'Why would the life of Caepio be banned? Because of the subject or the writer?'

'I would think that Proconsul Caepio was not the most worthy of the Servillius clan.'

Fidelma was about to turn away when the name registered with her. 'Did you say the Servillius clan?' she asked.

'Servillius was a patronymic name. The Proconsul's full name was Quintus Servillius Caepio. *Vitae Quintus Servillius Caepeio* is the volume that you are looking for. The Servillius family were an ancient patrician family in the days of the Republic and Empire, and often obtained the consulship. They survived many, many centuries.'

Fidelma was thoughtful. She picked up the coin and went to the door, pausing to say, 'Thank you for your wisdom, Venerable Ionas. It is of much help to me.'

'As I recall, you will find the story told by Trogus more in keeping with mythology,' called Venerable Ionas. 'He claims that the gold of Tolosa was initially looted from the sacred

Greek temples of Delphi. The Tectosages were one of the Gaulish tribes who invaded Greece just after the death of the Great Alexander and sacked the gold and wealth of the temple of the Oracle. Each time the story is told, it becomes more fabulous in the telling. Trogus was a Gaul and a good storyteller. He knew many of the local legends associated with the campaign against the Gauls. So his account might give you further information.'

Fidelma left as the Venerable Ionas bent over his work again. Outside his study, she replaced the gold coin safely back in her comb bag. Her mind turned over the patronymic of Caepio in her mind. An ancient patrician family that had survived many centuries . . . She made her way into the *scriptorium*. Now she felt that she was getting nearer to that elusive connection. Brother Eolann was still not there, yet now there was a lamp lit on the table. Beside the lamp was a book opened at the first page. She caught sight of the title.

It was Trogus Pompeius' *Vitae Quintus Servillius Caepeio*.

She swung round quickly, glancing into the darkened corners of the library. Was she being set up for some purpose? The book did not get there on its own just when she needed it. With tightened jaw she leaned towards the book. She began to turn the pages – and then stopped with a gasp.

The book was a thin volume – but when opened, it was obvious why. Several of the pages had been cut from it.

Now she knew whom she had to confront, but she also knew that she could not do it alone. She retraced her steps to Venerable Ionas' study. He looked up in surprise as she entered, without knocking this time, and sat down. She held out the copy of the book to him. He saw the section where the pages had been cut and turned a frowning glance to Fidelma.

'I think it is time I had a word with Abbot Servillius.' She laid a heavy stress on the last name.

'Abbot Servillius?' asked Venerable Ionas. 'Why?'

'You told me that Servillius was a *nomen*, a patronymic name. Quintus *Servillius* Caepio.' She laid stress on the middle name.

Abbot Ionas regarded her with some amusement. 'I cannot quite see how your mind is working, my child. You comment on the similarity of the name.'

'I seem to have stumbled on a series of matters that relate to this fabled gold hoard of Quintus Servillius Caepio. I believe a boy was killed because he stumbled on the hoard or the route to it. The killer wanted it kept secret. But it became known that the boy had spoken to someone in this abbey who might be able to work out what it was all about. Therefore the killer decided to eliminate all the clues that he could. Cutting pages from the books in the *scriptorium* which linked to the story of this fabulous treasure was one way.'

'You mean the references to what Caepio did? His sack of Tolosa, his appropriation of the gold and silver; the story that he brought the treasure back to this land, where he was Proconsul and Governor; that he hid it, before his final disgrace in Rome.' Venerable Ionas was still smiling. 'That seems somewhat far-fetched.'

'The killer tried to expunge any route that might have led to Caepio's gold – *Servillius*' gold.'

Venerable Ionas sat back, chuckling softly. 'You are arguing that our abbot is a descendant of the Servillius family. That may well be. Servillius has always been proud that he is descended from an old and local patrician family. But are you arguing that he also holds the secret of Caepio's gold – that he has tried to prevent others from finding it?'

'Or indeed that he or some other discovered the hiding place and then the boy Wamba stumbled on it and . . .'

Now the old scholar's eyes widened. 'You seriously contend that Abbot Servillius had the boy Wamba killed to keep the secret of where the fabled *Aurum Tolosa* might be found? Impossible! Even if it did exist, to suggest that my old friend Servillius . . .'

'. . . had him killed or killed the boy himself,' Fidelma said steadily.

Venerable Ionas sat for a while in silence, his bright eyes keenly searching her face.

'I have perceived you to be an intelligent person, Sister,' he finally said, like a father sadly chastising an erring child. 'I know that you have trained in the law of your land. I know, too, that Venerable Gelasius of the Lateran Palace holds you in high esteem, as does the Holy Father himself, because you tracked down the killer of the Archbishop Wighard. But this is an incredible accusation that you lay at the door of poor Servillius. Why, I have known him since the day he came to this abbey.'

'I do not make my accusations lightly,' Fidelma replied.

'Then I suggest that you tell me your story and your evidence before you go any further.'

'It is a long one and starts with the murder of Brother Ruadán.'

The eyes of Venerable Ionas widened again. 'Murder?' His tone was incredulous.

Fidelma began the story, slowly and carefully, and gradually the disbelief of the old scholar's expression began to change into one of serious attention. He did not interrupt her once. When she had finished he sat with head bowed, saying nothing. Then he exhaled deeply.

'And such things have happened to you, my child, since you came to our peaceful Abbey of Bobium? You should have come to me sooner.'

'How could I trust you?' demanded Fidelma. 'I do not know if I can trust you now, only that I desperately need to trust someone.'

The elderly man smiled softly. 'You may trust me, my child. We will go together and put these matters directly to Abbot Servillius.'

'He could simply deny them,' pointed out Fidelma.

'Perhaps he will. But in his explanation of certain aspects of this story we may be led to uncovering the truth.'

'I have no authority here to question an abbot.'

'That I know. From writing the life of Columbanus and mixing with many of your compatriots of Hibernia, I have learned about the role of the Brehons of your land. The Venerable Gelasius, *nomenclator* to the Holy Father, asked you to investigate the death of Archbishop Wighard of Canterbury. He did this, I am informed, over the heads of the law officers of the Lateran Palace, even over the head of the *Superista* of the Lateran Guard.'

'That was due to politics,' Fidelma explained, 'because of the nationality of the archbishop and the nationality of the one accused of his murder, one of the Hibernian brethren. And it was done with the knowledge and approval of the *Superista*, Marinus, the Military Governor of the Lateran Palace, rather than over his head, as you express it.'

'You are precise as befits your profession, Fidelma,' noted Venerable Ionas. 'Precision is what is needed here. But the point I am making is that what is good for the Venerable Gelasius and the Holy Father should be good enough for us in this abbey.'

'You are kind. But the only authority in the abbey is Abbot Servillius himself. His authority cannot be questioned, especially since you have adopted the Rule of Benedict here. So are you saying that you might work a miracle to persuade him to give me permission to question him, having accused him of being central to crimes of murder? To question him about a crime in which he is the only suspect?'

Venerable Ionas sat back and chuckled deeply. 'That is not what I am suggesting, Fidelma.'

'What then?' she demanded. 'The Rule of Benedict demands the renunciation of one's own will and calls upon every member of the brethren to have prompt, ungrudging and absolute obedience to their superiors, in this case, to the abbot, for unhesitating obedience is called the first step to humility.'

Venerable Ionas was shaking his head good-naturedly. 'I know what the Hibernian brethren think of unquestioned obedience but, as your brethren say, do not break your shinbone on a stool that is not in the way.'

'I don't understand.'

'It is simple enough. The Blessed Columbanus used to say that there are two kinds of fool. Those who will not obey and those who obey without question. He therefore thought the time might come when the abbey abandoned his Rule, so he left instructions for a separate governance here which our abbots have never altered. That is, the two senior clerics can call the abbot to account if there is a decision to be questioned.'

'You mean yourself and Magister Ado?'

'We are currently the two senior clerics here.'

'Therefore you and Magister Ado could force the abbot to answer my questions?'

'We can. So now we shall talk with Abbot Servillius. I shall designate you to act in the role of my interlocutor. If he does not agree to answer the questions we will await Magister Ado's return – but answer them he must.'

'Will it work?'

'Are you sure that you have clear questions to put?' He ignored her question and posed his own.

'I am sure enough.'

They walked from Venerable Ionas' study, passing the *scriptorium* door, down the stairs to the main hallway and across to the abbot's chamber. They had not reached it when they realised someone was standing in the doorway, which was open. The figure turned. It was the rotund cook Brother Waldipert. He stood staring at them with wide terrified eyes; his skin had a sickly pale tinge. He took a step forward. For a moment they thought he was going to collapse. He swayed, his mouth open, lips moving but making no sound at all.

'What is it, Brother Waldipert?' demanded Venerable Ionas.

Still the man could not speak but just stared as if he was not focusing on either of them.

With an exhalation of exasperation, the Venerable Ionas moved past him and halted on the threshold of the abbot's chamber. He moved no further, frozen for the moment. Then slowly he turned back to the fat cook. The man still stood shaking. Some brethren were passing through the hall. Venerable Ionas called to one of them. 'Ask Brother Hnikar to come to the abbot's study immediately. He – there has . . . has been an accident.'

One of them scurried off on his errand.

'What is it?' asked Fidelma.

'Abbot Servillius is dead,' intoned Venerable Ionas.

Fidelma pushed by him, even though he tried to hold her

back. But she, too, halted on the threshold. It was obvious why Venerable Ionas had no need to enter further.

Abbot Servillius lay sprawled on the floor just inside the door. His skull was a bloody mess, beaten to a pulp by some heavy object. Only his robes and crucifix on its silver chain provided a means of identification. Near the body she saw a large brass candlestick. It did not need any clever deduction to see the bloodstains on it and realise that this was the murder weapon. This was no accident but murder, plain and simple.

ChAPTER SEVENTEEN

Fidelma stepped back into the hall. 'What happened?' she asked the cook.

The man had still not recovered, was still staring and trying to utter words. To Fidelma's surprise, Venerable Ionas stepped forward and struck the cook sharply across the cheek. The man staggered back, blinking; a hand went to his reddening cheek.

'*Ignosce mihi* – forgive me, Brother Waldipert,' the elderly religieux said. 'There was no time to bring you from your shock in any other way, and each moment is precious.'

Brother Waldipert stood rubbing his cheek and gazing dumbly at Venerable Ionas.

'How came you here?' continued the elderly cleric.

'I . . . I came with some accounts for the Father Abbot to approve.' The words emerged slowly.

'How long ago?'

'A moment or two only. I knocked on the door and then opened it and saw . . . saw . . . I don't know what happened. You hit me. You hit me on the cheek.'

'Brother Waldipert,' Fidelma intervened. 'You opened the door and saw the abbot on the floor. Did you see anyone else

in the room, someone leaving the room by other means –
the window, for example?'

The cook shook his head. 'There are no other means. The
window is too small for anyone to leave by.'

There was a noise across the hall and Brother Hnikar
appeared. He glanced at them as he hurried into the abbot's
chamber. They saw him go down on his knees beside the body.
It was a cursory examination.

'Dead,' he said. 'He has had his skull smashed in.'

Fidelma had the urge to say they did not need his opinion
to tell them the obvious, but restrained herself.

'I presume that brass candle-holder would be the weapon.'
She pointed to it.

Brother Hnikar followed the direction of her hand. 'I would
imagine it was.'

'How long ago did this happen?'

'It is hard to say,' replied the physician. 'The blood has
dried and the body has stiffened. Perhaps half a day has
gone by.'

'Half a day?' Fidelma was surprised. 'Are you sure?'

The man did not deign to answer her but merely responded,
'Who found him? You?'

'It was Brother Waldipert who discovered the body.'

Brother Hnikar rose to his feet and regarded the cook for
a moment.

'This is a bad business,' he said, now speaking directly to
Venerable Ionas.

'Indeed, it is,' agreed the elderly scholar. 'I shall take
charge.'

'But we must await the return of Magister Ado before we
can appoint a new abbot,' Brother Hnikar protested.

'I did not say I would take charge as abbot,' Venerable

Ionas replied grimly. 'I will take charge until Magister Ado returns and then we shall discuss the matter.'

'We need to establish when the abbot was last seen alive,' Fidelma told them.

Brother Hnikar regarded her with disapproval. 'I have to remind you that you are a visitor in this abbey. Distinguished, so I am told. But nevertheless a visitor.'

Venerable Ionas cleared his throat. 'Dear Brother Hnikar, our distinguished visitor does have a point. These things need to be done. And, as custom dictates, this night we must lay to rest the remains of our great friend and former abbot. To him we owe a duty to find his murderer.'

'I stand corrected, Venerable Ionas,' sniffed the apothecary. 'It was probably some barbarian intent on robbery. Although I would say that the person who has committed this crime will have escaped to the forests long ago. Therefore we need to find Wulfoald and ask that he send his warriors out to track the culprit down.'

'I don't think it was some robber,' Fidelma was prompted into saying and then shut her mouth firmly as Brother Hnikar's lips visibly thinned. However, Venerable Ionas distracted him quickly.

'Time irretrievably passes, my brother. We must seize it if we are to get anywhere. As you have said, Sister Fidelma is a distinguished visitor. She is a lawyer and judge in her own land, and as such she was entrusted by the Holy Father and his adviser and military governor to solve the mystery of the murder of an archbishop at the Lateran Palace.'

Brother Hnikar made a dismissive motion with his hand. 'I have already heard about that.'

'Then, as the senior cleric in this community, I tell you this – I am appointing her to make inquiries about the matter.

She has my full authority to come and go as she likes and to inquire of whomever she likes.'

Brother Hnikar was looking shocked. 'But the Rule . . .'

'The Rule continues but in no way blocks her authority nor the authority that she holds from me.'

The apothecary was going to open his mouth again, hesitated and then bowed towards Fidelma.

'Will there be any objection, Sister Fidelma, to my removing the body to prepare it for burial, now we know how he met his death?' His voice held a thinly veiled sarcasm.

'You may remove the body as you will, but only after I have made an examination of the room. We may know how the abbot met his death but we must also learn why and by whom.' She turned to Venerable Ionas with a nod of thanks. 'It seems that Brother Hnikar cannot help us for the moment and we will have a further word with Brother Waldipert later.'

It was a clear dismissal of both men who then departed, one with a scowl and the other in bemusement, leaving Venerable Ionas and Fidelma alone.

'You will not have long,' the elderly cleric said with a sigh. 'Brother Hnikar does not like what I have done and he will be off, even now, to find Brother Wulfila to support him. And when Magister Ado returns . . .' He ended with a shrug. 'Perhaps we had best do what Brother Hnikar suggested and alert some of Wulfoald's warriors to search the surrounding countryside. The murderer cannot have gone far on foot, and he would be recognised if he left on horseback.'

'That is true enough, if the murderer has even left the abbey. Anyway, Wulfoald is no longer here. And it would be a waste of time searching outside the abbey walls.'

Venerable Ionas' eyes widened. 'Am I to take it that you mean the murderer is still hiding in the abbey?'

'Not hiding,' replied Fidelma grimly. 'I think he is known to the community. I believe that I have been led on a false trail. A trail deliberately laid to confuse me.'

'How?'

'The death of Abbot Servillius.'

'I am sorry, I do not follow you.'

'I was so keen on following clues that led me to the abbot. Whoever laid the trail knew that sooner or later I would connect the name Quintus Servillius Caepio with Abbot Servillius. One and one can make two, but sometimes you have to ensure that the two numbers you are given in the first place are accurate.'

Venerable Ionas looked perplexed. 'I am still not following your logic, Sister Fidelma, but I will trust you for the time being. You mean that all you told me in my study just now was wrong?'

'Not necessarily wrong,' she explained quickly. 'It was the information that I was being carefully fed. Information that someone had painstakingly laid as a trail in such a clever way that I would think I was uncovering it myself. It was laid so as to ensure my curiosity would be roused. Someone removed pages from the books in the library, not because they did not want me to see what was on the pages, but precisely because they knew my curiosity would lead me to find out what was on them.'

'But there was little on those pages apart from the story of Caepio's lost gold.'

'The gold of Quintus *Servillius* Caepio,' corrected Fidelma. '*Aurum Tolosa*.'

'And?'

'You provided the last clue – you told me Servillius was a patronymic. You admitted that the abbot was proud of his ancient patrician roots in this area.'

Venerable Ionas was frowning thoughtfully. 'So I gave you this last clue? Yes, I remember telling you about the name . . .' A suspicous look suddenly crossed his face. 'Are you suggesting that *I* led you on a false trail?'

'It is more complicated than that,' replied Fidelma. 'The person behind this would make a great *fidchell* player.'

'A what?'

'It is a board game played in my country, and its name means "wooden wisdom". In many ways it is like *ludus latrunculorum*, the board game of military tactics that is played here in this country.'

'I still find it hard to follow your reasoning.'

'There is a master player, a strategist involved in this matter; he or she has laid out all the pieces so that I have been led into a blind alley. He or she thought that it would take me longer to work things out, but realising that I was shortly to confront the abbot, they also realised it was too soon for their purpose. That is why, I'm afraid, Abbot Servillius had to die. I think he was killed soon after he arrived back in the abbey yesterday.'

'It sounds as though you know the identity of this strategist, as you call him.'

'In my country,' replied Fidelma, 'we have a saying: "woe to him whose betrayer sits at his table".'

There was the sound of raised voices at the main door and a moment later Magister Ado came hurrying into the hall; behind him was Brother Faro.

'Is it true?' he demanded, looking at Venerable Ionas. 'I have just returned from Travo to be greeted by the news that Abbot Servillius is dead – that he has been murdered.'

'News seems to travel quickly,' Fidelma muttered.

'As far as the abbey gates,' Magister Ado replied with

uncharacteristic sharpness. 'Brother Wulfila just told me. I met with Brother Faro on the way back. We heard nothing until we arrived here. So it is true?'

'I am afraid it is true, Brother,' admitted Venerable Ionas. 'The abbot was beaten to death, his skull crushed.'

Magister Ado crossed himself swiftly. '*Deus adjuvat nos,*' he muttered piously. 'Has the culprit been caught?'

'Alas, no.'

'Is it known who did this?'

'I think so,' Fidelma replied. 'And we might lay many deaths at his door.'

'Many deaths?' queried Magister Ado.

'I think our Hibernian sister means the death of Lady Gunora and others.'

Magister Ado's expression was grim. 'We live in evil times, Fidelma. We are pawns between the ambitions of Grimoald and Perctarit. Abbot Servillius gave sanctuary to Prince Romuald, and once it was known to people like Bishop Britmund, it would have become known to those who hoped to use the prince to attack the father. I suggest Abbot Servillius was murdered in retaliation for giving shelter to the young boy.'

'I do not think so,' contradicted Fidelma in a quiet voice.

Venerable Ionas and Magister Ado were both looking at her expectantly.

'You said that you think you know who did this and that he is still in the abbey,' Venerable Ionas said. 'Then speak—'

Outside in the courtyard they heard a wailing sound. It started faintly and became louder, and then it was taken up with other cries, creating a human chorus of fear and anxiety. They were moving to the door when one of the brethren, dishevelled and grubby, burst into the hall.

'The Evil One is at large in the abbey,' he shouted. 'Save us! Save us from him!'

The cries were in Fidelma's own language. She realised that it was Brother Lonán, the herbalist and gardener, who had come running towards them. She grasped the hysterical man by the collar and almost shook him.

'Control yourself, Brother! There is no evil in this place other than that which is made by men. What ails you? Speak! Speak in the language of the Faith so that these others may understand.'

The man blinked at the harshness of the words in his own language. Then he stared at her. 'Death stalks the abbey, Sister. Evil stalks the abbey. We must flee from this accursed place.' He fell to shivering and weeping, the hysteria unabated.

'What is it?' demanded Venerable Ionas, before he turned to Brother Wulfila, who had followed the herbalist in, and said sharply: 'Get outside into the courtyard and stop our brethren from making that awful wailing noise.'

Fidelma stared at the sobbing man with distaste and then said, still in her own language: 'You have one more chance to control yourself. If you do not speak, I am told the Rule of Benedict provides punishments for those who refuse to obey.'

Brother Lonán started back, a look of shock on his face.

'Now,' she said firmly, 'know who you are and where you are. Speak in the language of the brethren and tell us what is the matter.'

The herbalist swallowed nervously. 'I . . . I was in the *herbarium*,' he began.

'It is dark,' snapped Magister Ado. 'What were you doing there at this time?'

'I always go for a walk around the garden during the warm

summer evenings. The smell of the herbs and flowers, the scent of the evening garden . . . well, it is my pleasure.'

Magister Ado sniffed in disapproval. 'We are not here for individual pleasures, Brother Lonán, but—'

'Better to hear what has caused him to be in this state, than to lecture him on what is correct behaviour,' Venerable Ionas intervened reproachfully.

'The moon is already bright and full, as you can see,' the herbalist went on after some encouragement. 'I was walking along the path by the olive trees when I heard a growling sound – the sound of a wolf.'

'Wolves often come down into the valley in their hunt for food,' observed Magister Ado. 'What was unusual about this? Was this a reason to be afraid and cry like some whimpering child?'

'I am used to wolves prowling at night, Venerable Ado,' Brother Lonán replied defensively. 'I know what to do when I encounter them. I threw stones at it and was surprised when it did not run off with the same alacrity that its kind usually display. It seemed that it would dispute with me. Then I threw some heavier stones and shouted and it moved away.'

'And so?' prompted Fidelma, after he had paused.

'It had been digging by the trees. I moved forward. It was dark and shaded. And then the moon suddenly came out and shone between the branches down on the spot where the animal had been digging. Something pale and white was peering up at me from the soil . . . God help me!'

Magister Ado gave a sharp intake of breath in his exasperation.

'Tell us what it was,' Fidelma said quickly.

'It was the face of Brother Eolann.'

* * *

It was a short time later when Brother Lonán guided the party into the herb garden. Venerable Ionas and Magister Ado walked behind him with Fidelma. Brother Hnikar and Brother Wulfila and Brother Faro, armed with lamps and spades, came next. They were led towards a group of olive trees at the far end of the garden. The herbalist stood back while they edged forward to the spot at which he pointed. There was no doubt that the body had been partially uncovered by the digging of the wolves. The lamps of the party played on the deathly white features of the *scriptor* Brother Eolann.

Brother Hnikar bent down and examined the head.

'He can't have been buried that long. The burial seems shallow, which is a sign of a hurried disposal of the body. No wonder the wolf was able to uncover it. However, the state of the body makes me believe that he, too, like the abbot, has been dead for some time.'

'Any idea how he came by his death?' asked Fidelma.

Brother Hnikar stood up and she thought she saw him sneer in the flickering lamplight.

'Not from the blow on the head that he received this morning,' he replied. 'I will need to examine the body more carefully. Brother Wulfila and Brother Lonán, dig the body up and bring it to my apothecary.' He turned to Venerable Ionas and Magister Ado. 'There is no need for us to remain here. Let us proceed to the apothecary and await the body, and then I shall be able to see if an Evil One is stalking the abbey and what manner of death he is inflicting.'

The last remark was aimed in a cutting tone at the still shivering Brother Lonán.

They did not have to wait long in the odour-filled apothecary. Brother Hnikar was not a likeable person but he was certainly a professional as he bent over the body. Almost at once he observed: 'He was killed by that wound under the hair. It was inflicted by a broad-bladed weapon. If I were given to guessing, it was probably a sword like a *gladius*.'

'A *gladius*?' Fidelma repeated.

'A short, stabbing sword used by the Roman Legions,' he explained. 'It is still favoured by some of our warriors these days. I have seen Wulfoald use one.'

Fidelma frowned. 'So is it a commonly used weapon?'

'Not that common these days.' It was Magister Ado who answered her this time. 'I think warriors on horseback like to use long, slashing swords. It depends on who one is fighting. These short swords are efficient at close quarters, but faced with a charging warrior with a lance or a full-length sword, their use is limited.'

'You cannot tell if he was killed this morning or this evening?' Fidelma pressed.

Brother Hnikar actually chuckled. 'If the day comes when a physician can tell the exact time a body has died, that will be when we shall be able to solve all killings. All we would need is the time when the person died and seize whoever was next to them then. That is a fantasy.'

'I saw him not long before you returned to the abbey, Sister,' offered Brother Hnikar. 'I told you so.'

'So he was killed sometime after that.'

Brother Hnikar shrugged. 'He was buried after dark, that is all I can say, for the earth has not had any pronounced marking on his clothing or body.'

'Then he must have been in the abbey when I was looking for him,' Venerable Ionas said. 'But where was he hiding?'

'Or being hidden,' added Fidelma. She had been quiet for some time as she pursued a vagrant train of thought. Then she turned suddenly to Magister Ado. 'Was it Brother Eolann's idea that you make the journey to Tolosa to negotiate for that book . . . what was it? *The Life of the Blessed Saturnin.*'

Magister Ado was surprised at her memory. 'It was. Why?'

'Would you have gone otherwise?'

'I would not. The *scriptor* was quite insistent that that volume must be added to our library, as it would enhance the reputation of our abbey as a great centre of learning. As I had been to Tolosa before, it was felt that I was the best person to negotiate the matter. But how does this connect with the murder of the abbot? How do the two deaths come together?'

'Six deaths,' Fidelma corrected softly.

'What?' Magister Ado was shocked.

'Six deaths,' she repeated, 'plus an attempt on your life and the wounding of Brother Faro. All these are mixed together. Let us hope there are no other deaths.'

Brother Wulfila interrupted sharply. 'I must remind you that it is the custom of the abbey to bury the dead at midnight. Now we have the bodies of Abbot Servillius, Hawisa and Brother Eolann to consign to the earth.'

'Then I suggest we put an end to these speculations and prepare ourselves for the burial of these bodies, unless there are any strong objections?' The Venerable Ionas glanced toward Magister Ado.

Magister Ado inclined his head. 'I concur, Venerable Ionas. Since you are senior here and we will be asked by the brethren to make a choice of a new abbot and bishop, as is custom, let me make clear now, that I intend to nominate you.'

Venerable Ionas was uncomfortable. 'While I thank you for your confidence in me, *magister*, the choice may be left to the wishes of the brethren. But for now we have these bodies to take to the necropolis. It is, indeed, a dreadful day for the abbey.'

They were moving back across the courtyard, lit by brand torches, and it was clear to Fidelma there was much on the mind of the Venerable Ionas. It was as if he were trying to ask her a question. The others had dispersed and she waited expectantly. He halted and turned to her.

'You said there have been six murders. I count three. Those are bad enough but who else?'

'I count Wamba.'

'Because of the coin? Who else?'

'His mother, Hawisa. The fire was purposely set.'

'And the third? Ah, Brother Ruadán. But Brother Ruadán died from the injuries inflicted on him by a mob of Arians. He died over a week later in his bed – you saw him.'

Fidelma shook her head slowly. 'He was smothered in his bed by the same hand that is responsible for all these killings.'

'But why?'

She smiled uneasily. '*Cui bono*?'

'I do not understand.'

'Did not Cicero attribute those words to a Roman judge: *who benefits*? When we find out who stands to gain from the deaths, then we will know the identity of the killer.'

Fidelma sat alone in her chamber deep in thought. She had been a fool. Perhaps she was still a fool. Why didn't she simply head back to Genua and find a ship to Massilia before this valley erupted into the war that was threatening? She had nothing to do with the ambitions of the exiled King Perctarit nor those of Grimoald. She cared nothing about them. She longed to be back in her own land, among her own people. She had only come here to see her old master, Brother Ruadán and, in remembering him, she understood why she was staying. She owed it to him to discover his killer.

And Brother Eolann? What was the proverb? *Superbum sequitur humilitas*: arrogance will bring your downfall. It was her arrogance and pride that had allowed her to be led along the false trail of the *Aurum Tolosa* – a fool's treasure, indeed! She heaved a sigh and once more began to think that she was stupid to stay here and be arrogant enough to believe that she could solve this puzzle. It had been Paul, in his advice to the Philippians, who exhorted them to do nothing from selfish ambition or conceit but to always act with humility.

Humility. What did she know when it came to simple facts? Brother Ruadán had given the young boy Wamba two ancient gold coins. Why? The boy had brought one to the abbey and the next day he was dead, said to have fallen from some rocks. Shortly afterwards, Brother Ruadán was found beaten almost to death outside the gates of the abbey. Brother Ruadán, on his deathbed, believed Wamba had been killed because of the coins. Her old mentor would have eventually died from his injuries, but someone had to make sure that he did not talk to her first. Had it not been for her determination, going in stealth to his chamber before anyone was stirring, she would not have heard of the coins or the boy, Wamba. Then she had shared that knowledge with Brother Eolann.

As soon as she had mentioned the coins and Wamba to Brother Eolann, she found that she was being led into a fantasy about an ancient treasure. *Aurum Tolosa*. Or was it a fantasy? She had been misdirected about the name Servillius. Now Brother Eolann was dead. She had thought that he was the culprit. She realised that she was overlooking something, but she could not remember what it was. She was too tired. It had been a long day and there were still the obsequies for the dead to go through.

Finally she gave up trying to find a coherent train of thought about the matter and decided to prepare herself for the midnight ceremony. Down in the chapel, the brethren had already gathered to pay their respects to the abbot and the *scriptor*.

As she entered, Brother Faro seemed to be waiting for her.

'I have not been able to find Sister Gisa,' he opened immediately. 'I suppose you have no idea where she might be?'

'None at all,' replied Fidelma, surprised at his question and the agitation in his voice. 'I am told that you went out to look for her.'

'I thought I had a vague idea of the whereabouts of the caves used by the hermit Aistulf.'

'But you found no sign?'

'Not of her, nor of the hermit. I was returning when I met Magister Ado on the way. And now there are more deaths to contend with. I heard that Venerable Ionas believes that you are capable of solving these murders. But you do not even speak the language of the Longobards. With respect, for I know both Venerable Ionas and my own master, Magister Ado, have much respect for you, I would advise you to start back to Genua tomorrow. There is much danger here.'

Fidelma gazed at the intense young man thoughtfully.

'How do you interpret this danger then, Brother Faro? Why are you afraid of my staying here?'

'I do not understand.'

'I am a stranger here, true. But you are scarcely more. You told me so. You said you came here two years ago looking for a peaceful sanctuary. Why do you urge me to leave but stay yourself?'

Brother Faro seemed embarrassed. 'I think you know why else I stay.'

'Then you will continue your search for Sister Gisa tomorrow?'

He nodded quickly. 'As soon as it is light. But if it happens that you see her before I do, I would advise you both to leave this valley, for I believe there is a storm coming.'

'Tell me about Gisa,' Fidelma said. 'Does she know this area well? Would it be easy for her to get lost in this valley?'

'She was raised in this valley. Many people here seem to know her well.'

'Do you know any of her family?'

'She has never told me about them. There are rumours that the hermit Aistulf is related. She has a good knowledge of healing plants and herbs. She has said her father was a physician. But that is all I know.'

'Well, I will bear in mind your advice, Brother Faro. Tomorrow, perhaps, there will be others who will help in your search.'

He stared thoughtfully at her. 'You are staying?'

'I am staying,' confirmed Fidelma. 'It would be an insult to the memory of my old master, Brother Ruadán, if not to the others, for me to flee from this valley without resolving this situation.'

'I trust you will not regret that decision. I am sure that the storm is upon us.'

It was approaching midnight when the torchlit procession wound from the abbey gates up the hill to the necropolis. It was very different to the procession that had accompanied the body of Brother Ruadán only a few days before. The fear and tension of the brethren was almost a tangible reality. Only a few had obeyed the Venerable Ionas' call to attend and these were mainly the pallbearers. The only outsider that Fidelma recognised was the youth, Odo. Hawisa had already been

covered in winding sheets and laid by the now open grave of
Wamba, which had been dug by the stronger members of the
brethren. There was an air of dread, of horror combined with
a nervousness which caused people to start at the smallest and
most insignificant sounds.

Venerable Ionas and Magister Ado led the procession
behind the biers of the abbot and *scriptor*, followed by the
steward, the apothecary, and then Fidelma with Brother Faro.
Firstly the body of Hawisa was lowered into the same grave
as her son, Wamba, with a simple blessing. Then the body
of Brother Eolann was buried and Fidelma was asked to come
forward to say a few words about her compatriot. She found
it difficult, knowing that he must have been central in the
conspiracy to lay a false trail. She managed only a few words.

'Brother Eolann came from my father's Kingdom of
Muman,' she began. Although her father had died when she
was a child, it was easier to phrase it in this way than to
explain that, as there was no hereditary kingship in her land,
kings were elected albeit from the same bloodline. It was
true that her brother, Colgú, was now heir-apparent to their
cousin Cathal, the current King of Muman. 'He came from
a place called Inis Faithlean, the island of the blessed
Faithlean, who was one of the great teachers of the Faith in
our land.

'It was a place much like this, although it was on an island
in a lake, surrounded by mountains covered in luxuriant
growths of plants and trees, of evergreens like holly, mountain ash and arbutus. It seemed a curious fate that while he
was sent on a mission to St Gallen, his footsteps eventually
led him . . .' She paused with a frown, distracted by the
thought of something she had been overlooking. Then she
quickly continued: 'His footsteps led him to Mailand and

thence here to the Valley of the Trebbia and your abbey, which Colm Bán founded many years ago. I am told he was a good *scriptor*, but he made a mistake. He took an oath, what my people call a *géis* – and he should have known that no one breaks it with impunity. The evil rebounds on the person who breaks it. And so, his life was taken . . .'

She came to a faltering end for there was little else she could positively say, but Venerable Ionas stepped forward and added: 'But there is one person who knows, who sees the perpetrator, and even if we poor mortals fail to discover him in this life, he will be found and punished in the next.'

When it came to lowering the remains of Abbot Servillius into the ground it was the Venerable Ionas who led the tributes. In Fidelma's culture this would have been called the *écnaire*, the intercession for the repose of the soul, followed by the blessing.

'Servillius was of a Roman patrician family of Placentia. His ancestors had a long and noble tradition of service in this land. He served this abbey not only as abbot but as bishop. I was here when Servillius first came through the gates of this abbey. That was two score years ago, when there were some here who had known our blessed founder Columbanus. I knew them well and was inspired by them to write a life of that blessed man.

'Servillius was also blessed in different ways. When he became abbot he inherited our founder's desire to make this abbey not only a centre of piety but of learning, of knowledge and of progress. He tried to stop the abbey from falling into the hands of the followers of Arius, and it was through my offices I went to Rome and secured a recognition of our allegiance to the Holy Father and the granting of the mitre for our abbot as bishop. I secured the same distinction for

Abbot Bobolen before him. Together we fought off the evil intentions of the followers of the Arian Creed . . .'

He suddenly paused and glanced at Magister Ado. Fidelma noticed the glance as it had registered in her mind that the Venerable Ionas was being a little too egocentric in his observations, which were supposed to be in praise of Abbot Servillius.

'In that great cause of true Faith we were supported by the Magister Ado who had later joined this abbey and became one of our most renowned scholars. I – we – shall not allow our abbot to die in vain but will continue to ensure that this abbey becomes that centre respected throughout Christendom for its piety and learning.'

It was as the abbot's body was being lowered into the grave that they all heard it, echoing across the valley. It was the high-pitched echoing drone of the pipes, the lamenting cry of a soul in torment.

Consternation broke out among the brethren. Some fled back down the track towards the abbey. Even in the glow of the flickering lamplight, Fidelma saw the pale, ghastly look on the faces of Brother Hnikar and Brother Wulfila. Even Brother Faro swung round to stare at the dark shapes of the rising mountains. The only person who stood, a faint smile discernible on his lips in the candlelight, was Odo.

It was Magister Ado who turned to those brethren who remained hesitating by the graveside. 'Have you never heard the *muse* before?' he remonstrated. 'Have you never heard the pipes played whenever there is a burial here?'

Fidelma turned to Brother Faro, who was standing at her side, head to one side, listening to the mournful dirge. There was a strange, almost worried look on his face.

'It seems that Brother Wulfila was wrong when he thought

Abbot Servillius and Sister Gisa had gone to see the old hermit because he was ill,' she commented. She then turned to Odo, who still stood nearby. 'I am no expert in your local pipes, but who would you say is playing that lament?'

The youth replied immediately. 'It is the favourite lament of the hermit. Only Aistulf plays the *muse* in that fashion.'

ChAPTER EIGHTEEN

For the first time in her life, that night as she retired to bed, Fidelma pulled some heavier items of furniture as quietly as she could across her door before lying down and falling into a fitful, dream-ridden sleep. It was halfway through the night that she suddenly sat up in the darkness, a sweat on her forehead and a coldness on the back of her neck. 'Of course,' she muttered as her thoughts cleared. 'Of course! How stupid of me. How very stupid!' She managed to doze again but felt exhausted on waking the next morning.

She rose, washed and, in spite of her exhaustion, there was something coursing through her that excited her into activity. She went to join the brethren for the first meal of the day but found she was unable to concentrate on it. Venerable Ionas led the prayers while Magister Ado sat brooding and picking at his meal. Fidelma glanced around the *refectorium*. She could see no sign of Brother Faro and when the meal was finished, she asked Brother Wulfila where he was.

'He has already left the abbey again in search of Sister Gisa,' the steward responded disapprovingly.

The bell had rung and everyone was dispersing to their daily tasks. Fidelma went hurrying after the Venerable Ionas.

'I need to speak to you,' she began without preamble. 'It is a matter that, for the moment, needs to be kept strictly between us.'

'It is not our custom to keep secrets from one another, Sister Fidelma,' reproved the old scholar.

'Certain members of this community have already broken that custom. When I say that the abbey is in imminent danger, then I think secrecy is expedient.'

The Venerable Ionas regarded her with a troubled expression. 'With the deaths that have recently occurred, Fidelma of Hibernia, I think I might have arrived at that decision myself. Last night I supported you in the proposition that you should investigate these deaths. Are you now saying that you have come to some conclusion?'

'Not a complete one,' she admitted, 'although by the time this day is over, I think I will have most, if not all, of the answers.'

'So what is this secret that you must share with me?'

They were standing on the steps of the hall overlooking the courtyard. Fidelma glanced round. 'Is there a way that we might proceed to the necropolis without being seen?'

Venerable Ionas frowned. 'And what would be found there?'

'I hope to show you. But we must not be observed.'

'You cannot tell me more?'

'Only that before he died, Brother Ruadán asked me a question. I thought his mind was wandering. I now realise he was speaking rhetorically. He said: "What evil can be disguised in a mausoleum." It has taken me a long time to realise what he meant, because I had been following a false trail.'

Venerable Ionas motioned her to follow him. They went back into the hall and through a passage that led beyond the kitchens. They did not go through them or into the *herbarium* but along another passage and into what looked like a disused storeroom. Venerable Ionas set about removing some boxes in one corner, to reveal the iron handle of a trap door.

The old scholar smiled wryly at Fidelma. 'When I was young and first came to the abbey, I was shown this way out should we younger religious want to escape the attentions of the gatekeeper. He was a tougher man than Brother Bladulf, and the rules were far stricter in those days. Sometimes it was just necessary to get away to the mountains and walk in the silence, soft winds and sunshine.'

He opened the trap door and descended some stone steps into a short passage, not more than three strides in length, that seemed to be cast in a shadowy green light caused by the light infiltrating through creepers that hung over the entrance. Fidelma followed him.

They were suddenly outside the abbey in a wooded area, and Venerable Ionas led the way, surefooted through the trees, upwards and then along a level area until, to Fidelma's surprise, they came out at the top end of the necropolis, at the back of the curious mausoleum buildings.

'So, what now?' Venerable Ionas asked.

'I think we shall find what I am looking for in the third mausoleum.'

'Abbot Bobolen's mausoleum? You don't mean that we should open it? That is sacrilege. It has only recently been finished and sealed.'

'Sacrilege has already been committed, if my suspicion is correct, and to prove it we must examine the interior.'

Venerable Ionas was unhappy as they moved cautiously towards the marble edifice. There seemed no one in the necropolis nor on the surrounding hillside; they were unobserved.

Fidelma halted at the doorway of the tomb. The doors were extremely wide, as befitted the massive building, and they were made of iron. Venerable Ionas was frowning at the locking device.

'That is curious. It does not seem very secure – more of a temporary fixing. This lock should have been made stronger.'

'I assure you, therefore, that it is important to look inside,' insisted Fidelma. 'We must do it and do it now.'

'But why?'

'The answer to all the deaths that have happened and may happen will be found in this mausoleum. I ask you to trust me.'

Venerable Ionas stared at her in amazement, but he could feel her sincerity. He hesitated a moment more and finally agreed. 'Very well. Thankfully, it is easy enough to replace such fittings as these.' He bent down, picked up a piece of rock and banged it against the iron lock. It fell away with only three sharp blows. Together, they drew back one of the doors. Whatever Venerable Ionas was expecting to see inside, it was not a wagon piled with leather sacks. This occupied most of the interior and there was no sign of any sarcophagus.

Fidelma's expression did not change as she stepped forward and began to tug open one of the sacks. She held it for Venerable Ionas to see. Inside it was stuffed with golden coins.

'Is this the *Aurum Tolosa*?' breathed the old scholar, staring at it. 'Does it truly exist?'

Fidelma gave a shake of her head, saying, 'It might well be from Tolosa, but it is not the fabled gold of Caepio.'

'Then what . . . ?'

'It is meant as payment to the Lord of Vars for his services, and I think he will be coming for it soon. We had best try to fix the lock and return to your chamber to discuss this matter.'

When they were back in his chamber, they sat for a while in silence.

'How long have you known?' Venerable Ionas finally asked.

'Only since last night,' Fidelma replied. 'I was too busy chasing the mythological gold to come to a solution earlier.'

'The *Aurum Tolosa*?' asked Venerable Ionas, bewildered. 'But where does *this* gold come from? You say it is payment for the Lord of Vars – but for what, and why?'

'From Perctarit to Grasulf to persuade him to join him in an uprising against Grimoald. One thing I learned at Vars was that Grasulf was expecting such payment. When Perctarit was ready, he would tell Grasulf where it had been placed by his agent.'

'His agent? Who placed it there, in the mausoleum of Bobolen?'

'I think I know, but I need to confirm things. I am sure the wagon has been hidden there for some time. I don't know how, but I believe poor Brother Ruadán discovered the secret. He found some coins and, presumably out of charity, gave two of them to Wamba.'

Venerable Ionas was shaking his head in bewilderment.

'I still cannot understand. Was it something to do with Brother Eolann?'

'He had a hand in it yet he was not the central person involved.'

'There are many questions to be answered, Fidelma.'

'I know,' she agreed grimly. 'That is why I cannot reveal who I think is the instigator of this plot.' She rose and added: 'Matters will soon come to fruition. I leave you for a while.'

'Where do you intend to go?'

'To seek out Lord Radoald. I believe that he can supply some answers to this mystery.'

'You must be careful,' insisted Venerable Ionas. 'If it is known that you have discovered this gold, even the fact that you are a woman – indeed, a princess from Hibernia – will not protect you.'

Fidelma smiled thinly. 'I never thought it would,' she replied. Then she asked: 'Are there any men of strength in the abbey? A blacksmith and his assistant?'

Venerable Ionas pursed his lips for a moment in thought. 'We have three or four such men.'

'Then they must be men that you totally trust. Only you are to communicate with them and let them take an oath of silence about what you will ask them to do. No word of what I want you to ask them must be revealed to anyone else in the abbey. Nor must you mention it to anyone yourself, not even to those whom you trust, like Magister Ado, Brother Bladulf or Brother Wulfila or even Brother Lonán.'

'I do not understand but I shall trust *you*, Fidelma. I will make the men take such an oath and bind them to silence.'

She outlined her instructions. 'This must be done in secret. If I am right, it should buy some time, at least. I hope to return to the abbey well before the end of the day, and by that time all will be clear.'

'I pray that it is, for you are saying that I cannot trust some who are my closest associates . . . even friends.'

'I would also ask you to request the brethren to stay close to the abbey today,' she added.

'Are you some soothsayer that you are sure of this impending danger?' queried the elderly scholar in resignation.

'Ah, had I eyes that foresee the future, I would never have left the port of Genua.'

'Well, there are no footsteps backwards in life, my child. Once the die is thrown, we must accept the outcome and make of it what we will.'

Fidelma paused at the door. 'You are right, Venerable Ionas. Sometimes I give way to a selfishness of spirit, of which I should be ashamed. I have learned much from the mistake of putting trust in Brother Eolann.'

'God made you as you are, Fidelma, and for that this abbey is grateful. Stay safe and hurry back to us.'

She left the abbey soon afterwards and only the Venerable Ionas saw her leading a horse out of the stables. He had contrived to send those brethren in the courtyard on some errands and he, himself, opened the gates for her. He followed her with a worried eye as she mounted the animal and trotted it down towards the river.

The way to Radoald's fortress was easy as Fidelma was beginning to know it well. She crossed the hump-back bridge and turned to follow the turbulent waters of the Trebbia upstream beside the thick woods that spread along its banks. It was still early and the day tranquil with sunny blue skies. The various forest noises were so soporific that Fidelma had difficulty in accepting the grim reality of the deaths that had taken place in this pleasant countryside; in accepting the threat of warfare that would tear this peaceful valley apart.

She was concentrating so hard that a sudden shout caused her to look up in dismay. Two warriors had emerged from the trees, long black cloaks streaming, but without weapons in their hands. They were upon her before she could react. One of them grabbed at her horse's bridle and, without slowing, began to canter along the side of the river. The other rider followed behind.

She could do nothing but feel anger with herself that she had been daydreaming, unaware of them lying in wait. The anger was enhanced by the fact that she now recognised the men. She did not need to examine the flaming sword and laurel wreath emblem on their jerkins nor look closely at the manner of their dress. They were the same men who had attacked Venerable Ado in Genua, the same men who, she believed, had shot an arrow at Magister Ado and hit Brother Faro by mistake when they had first arrived in the Valley of Trebbia.

They said nothing to her. One was leaning slightly forward, still holding her horse's reins so that she had no control over the animal; the other man rode behind. She had no choice but to hang on, for the momentum of the horses made it difficult to do anything else.

She knew that they were heading upstream still, the Trebbia gushing along by the track, and she was not entirely surprised when they turned off and headed up the slope towards the fortress of Radoald, which had been her very destination.

The gates of the fortress swung open and her escorts cantered into the courtyard. Her jaw tightened. Fidelma realised that there were still several questions to be answered, but she felt confident that she had the outline, if not the detail, of the mystery.

No one said anything, no one made any move, as the dust settled around them. Then, from the main door to the great hall, a figure with white hair emerged – a tall, smiling figure. It was that of the physician, Suidur the Wise.

'Well, Sister Fidelma – or should I call you Lady Fidelma? I am never quite sure of the correct usage for a princess who has become a religieuse.' He bowed with a touch of irony. 'You are most welcome here. Get you down and come inside and take some refreshment. The dust of travel causes the throat to dry.'

Chapter Nineteen

'Welcome?' parried Fidelma, sliding from her horse. 'A strange welcome, to be sure.'

'These are warriors from Grimoald,' Suidur explained when he saw her glance towards her captors. 'I am afraid they can become a little too enthusiastic, for which I apologise.'

'I have observed their enthusiasm before; first in Genua and then again when I entered this valley,' she responded.

Suidur regarded her with a smile. He turned to the warriors and spoke rapidly in their own language. They saluted him and took the horses away. He gestured to her to follow him, saying, 'I have always thought that you had a sharp eye, lady.'

Inside the great hall, she found Lord Radoald in the company of an older man clad in rough homespun, with long grey hair and a bent figure. They both rose to their feet as Suidur led her in. As the elderly man rose, Fidelma's quick eye saw that the stoop of his back had been feigned. She studied his features and a smile of satisfaction formed on her lips.

'Well, Fidelma,' greeted the young Lord of Trebbia. 'We have been expecting you.'

'Expecting me? Oh, I suppose your spies saw me leaving

the abbey and coming this way. Is that why the warriors ambushed me?'

It was the man in rough homespun who replied. 'We are engaged in a conflict of shadows, lady. We cannot afford to take chances.'

Radoald turned to the man and said, 'This is—'

'Aistulf.' Fidelma smiled. 'There is no need for you to play the bent, elderly hermit before me. You are a strange hermit, Aistulf. A player of the pipes, but one who speaks Latin and commands warriors. Why is it that you hide in the mountains and let your son rule in your place as Lord of Trebbia?'

It was Aistulf who finally broke the surprised silence that followed her question.

'I think we have underestimated you, Fidelma of Hibernia,' he said softly. 'How did you know? You, a stranger? I have let no one, apart from Servillius and Gisa, see me close enough to identify me as the former Lord of Trebbia. My household has been sworn to secrecy. How have I been betrayed?'

'You have not been betrayed, Lord Billo. At least, not so far as I am concerned,' replied Fidelma. 'It was a matter of logic, confirmed by the fact that I overheard you on the mountain when Suidur was bringing us back into the Trebbia Valley. You thought me asleep. When you said that you would speak to your son, it was obvious. It is known that Lord Billo and his son Radoald went to fight for Grimoald. Radoald came back from the wars and was proclaimed Lord of Trebbia. At the same time, a new person came to the valley, a recluse, Aistulf. It was easy to draw the conclusion.'

'I came back after the wars against Perctarit seeking peace but knowing there were many things which might prevent it. I gave up my domain to my son, Radoald, changed my name and set out to live in the peace of this valley. I wanted to end my days without seeing another man, woman or child stained with blood, and hearing the cries of the wounded and dying. That is why I lived as I did. My son is now Lord of Trebbia. But unfortunately, death has followed me into this valley and now I must help to repel it. My son remains Lord of Trebbia, and if we bring this matter to a successful conclusion I will go back to being Aistulf the hermit, for that is all I want.'

Radoald signalled a servant to come forward with a flagon and goblets. 'Be seated and refresh yourself,' he invited Fidelma.

Fidelma had long practised the philosophy that when one was faced with no alternative it was better to appear to accept the inevitable. She sat down and accepted the goblet but asked for nothing more potent than the rich, cold water from a mountain spring.

'So why were you expecting me?' she asked, turning to Aistulf.

'We were expecting you because my dear friend, Servillius, said he would send you here,' Aistulf said. 'Did he not explain that he thought you could be of service?'

'Abbot Servillius was murdered last night,' she announced flatly.

The brief silence that followed her statement was ended by a sharp intake of breath. Standing at the doorway was Sister Gisa. Fidelma felt a momentary satisfaction. At least she had not been wrong in her suspicion that she would find the girl at Radoald's fortress. Sister Gisa had run to Suidur, who was comforting her.

'I also heard that you found Lady Gunora's body,' Aistulf said quietly. 'I had not realised, when I played the lament, that it was also for my poor friend. I thought it was for Gunora.'

'Brother Bladulf had not returned from the mountain with her body. You played the lament not only for Servillius but also for Hawisa and Brother Eolann.'

Aistulf's eyes widened in horror. 'So many deaths?'

'We heard of Hawisa's death from Wulfoald, but—' began Radoald.

'You had better tell us how this came about, lady,' intervened Aistulf.

Fidelma told them what she knew.

'Let me get this correct,' Aistulf said at the end of her recital. 'Wulfoald left you at the abbey, having learned that Servillius had arrived back but had retired with orders not to be disturbed. You say that Venerable Ionas and you went to see Servillius but found him dead?'

'Essentially correct.'

'So you never saw Servillius and he never explained why you should come here?'

'What was he supposed to tell me?' she countered.

'Among other things, he was supposed to tell you that we were expecting you and Wulfoald to return here. Wulfoald told us that he had not seen Servillius and received no such message.'

Fidelma compressed her lips. 'He had no opportunity to see him. I was too concerned in following a wrong trail laid by Brother Eolann, and so when I went back to the abbey, I went to talk with Venerable Ionas and told him what I thought was happening. I was foolishly misled. When Venerable Ionas and I went to see the abbot, having wasted time, we found he had been killed almost as soon as he returned to the abbey.'

'So, if it was not the message we sent you with Servillius, what led you here this morning?' Suidur asked sharply.

Fidelma ignored the question. Instead she asked: 'I presume that Prince Romuald is safe here?'

Radoald leaned forward in surprise. 'How could you possibly know that he is here?'

'That's simple. Abbot Servillius said that Lady Gunora and the prince left the abbey before first light to reach this fortress. I found Lady Gunora's body, as you know. The boy was missing. However, Wulfoald, when I told him that Lady Gunora's body had been found, was not concerned about the prince. He simply rebuked me for not informing him sooner.'

'What did that tell you?' Aistulf was interested.

'That it was only Lady Gunora who had been missing. It meant Prince Romuald was safe here. That was confirmed by you, Aistulf.'

'By me?' he asked wonderingly.

'When I overheard you on the mountain, saying, "If the boy is right, Lady Gunora must be dead." So what did the boy tell you?'

'What do you think happened?' countered Radoald.

'That Lady Gunora and the boy did not leave the abbey unobserved. I believe they were followed. They had one horse. Lady Gunora may have noticed and told the boy to dismount and hide while she tried to draw off the pursuit. She succeeded so far as the boy was concerned. But she was overtaken and slain.'

A silence followed and then Aistulf nodded slowly. 'You are right, lady, so far as the boy is concerned. Wulfoald found him wandering along the river early that morning. The prince told him that Lady Gunora had turned back towards the abbey, having instructed him to hide. She told him that, if she did not return, to go to the fortress of my son, Radoald, and on no account return to the abbey.'

'So Lady Gunora tried to draw off the pursuers across Mount Pénas?' mused Fidelma. 'Poor lady. She sacrificed herself. But the boy is safe?'

'Even as you said,' agreed Suidur.

'There is one thing that might interest you, lady,' Aistulf added. 'The prince, while hiding, caught sight of their pursuer. There was, in fact, only one. My son gave us the same description which Odo gave to Wulfoald and yourself. It was the same as that of the person seen leaving the vicinity of Hawisa's cabin at the time of the fire.'

'A man on a pale horse?'

'And the prince also insists that the rider of the pale horse was a warrior.'

Fidelma was quiet for a while. 'Now tell me why you wanted me to be here?'

Aistulf said, 'My friend, Servillius, thought you could be trusted.' Then he looked around at the others. 'It will come as no surprise to you that we are supporters of King Grimoald.' When Fidelma did not respond, he went on: 'It would seem that you have little interest in the war that is erupting now. It is that war which is our concern – the attempt of Perctarit, with those who remain loyal to him and his Frankish allies, to return to the throne of the Longobards.'

'As you say, the politics of the matter should be of little concern to me, for this is not my country,' replied Fidelma.

'True enough. That being so, why did you leap to defend Magister Ado in Genua when the warriors of King Grimoald tried to capture him?' Aistulf observed.

'Merely chance. I saw two men assaulting an elderly cleric in a back street. When we entered this valley, these same men tried to assassinate him from behind the shelter of trees and bushes.'

'If it had not been for your shout of warning,' intervened Sister Gisa resentfully, 'they would not have missed their target and hit Brother Faro.'

'It is one of the matters I need clarification on. The would-be assassins were dressed as your King's men and therefore your allies. Can it be that you would applaud the assassination of an elderly cleric of such outstanding scholarship as Magister Ado – simply as part of your cause?'

'He was considered an agent of Perctarit,' Sister Gisa declared, thrusting her chin out aggressively. 'An enemy to King Grimoald. You saved him from being captured by the two men that Grimoald sent to question him.'

Aistulf pulled a face. 'Unfortunately, they were not the brightest of minds, as you have discovered. Having failed to take him prisoner, they took it on themselves that if they could not capture him, then the next best thing was to kill him.'

'They wounded Brother Faro instead,' repeated Sister Gisa.

'So, after the failed assassination,' Fidelma said thoughtfully, 'these two warriors came here to this fortress to report. I saw you, Suidur, with Gisa rebuking them.'

'How . . . ?' began Radoald.

'Courtyards are not the best place to discuss matters even in the dark of the night, especially when there is a moon.'

'But you do not speak the language of the Longobards,' Suidir pointed out. 'How do you know what went on?'

'Perhaps you will recall rebuking Sister Gisa for her lapse into Latin?'

There was a silence and Suidur finally said, 'I did so. Grimoald's men were told that no more attacks should be made on the person of Magister Ado. He should be allowed freedom to see if he could lead us to the gold,' continued Aistulf. 'Give him enough rope to hang himself, as the saying goes.'

'And if he were not Perctarit's agent?' Fidelma sighed. 'I am surprised, Suidur, that you have not taught your daughter the importance of evidence *coram judice.*'

Sister Gisa stared in astonishment but the physician actually smiled. 'You do have a sharp mind, lady,' he acknowledged.

'I presumed that she is your daughter from the fact of her knowledge of the healing arts, that she was raised in this valley and it was said her father was a physician.'

'Servillius himself said just before he left here that we should leave you alone and you would guide us to the conspirators,' Radoald commented dryly. 'Wasn't that what he said, Father?'

The erstwhile hermit chuckled. 'Indeed. He said *alis volat propris*: she flies on her own wings.' Fidelma knew the phrase well. It indicated that she was independent of spirit and had her own way of doing things.

Radoald leaned towards her. 'Then let me tell you why we were concerned about Magister Ado. The man has a reputation as a good scholar at Bobium. He is known for his allegiance to the Nicene Creed . . .'

'As is the allegiance of Bobium,' pointed out Fidelma.

'But Bobium is content under the kingship of Grimoald who, although a follower of Arius, pursues a liberal policy, allowing his people to choose which path to the Christ they want to tread.'

'I know.' Fidelma sighed irritably. 'And Perctarit follows the Nicene Creed. I have heard all this.'

'So when Magister Ado went on a journey to Tolosa, we

suspected that he was Perctarit's agent and had gone to raise the shipment of gold to pay Grasulf.'

'Had you spoken with Magister Ado, you would have found that he went to Tolosa at the insistence of Brother Eolann, who was one of the real conspirators. Appealing to Magister Ado's scholarship and his knowledge of Tolosa, they enticed him into going to the abbey there to bring back a book for the library. I suspect that Brother Eolann, or someone else, might have made a point of twisting the facts of this trip so that it seemed the *magister* had instigated it.'

Sister Gisa had paled and was holding a hand to her cheek.

'Perhaps she was told that Perctarit was in Tolosa?' went on Fidelma, ignoring her reaction for the moment. 'It was another false trail to lead people away from the culprits. There were three conspirators at Bobium but Magister Ado was not one of them. While you were looking to Magister Ado at the seaport of Genua, the gold had already arrived in this valley. It was at the abbey before Brother Faro and Sister Gisa set out to meet Magister Ado on his return.'

'But . . . how?' demanded Radoald in astonishment.

'Let me ask a question before I continue. Why is it important to thwart Grasulf, the Lord of Vars, from raising his warriors to take control of this valley? The gold is meant for him, and I have learned that he is of a mercenary nature and will not fight until he is paid. But why here? I think I know the answer but I ask you to confirm the matter for me.'

Radoald said, 'The answer is simple. You will have heard already just how strategic are the roads that lead from Genua through these mountains. There is the old Salt Road from Genua to Ticinum Pavia, which passes through the Valley of the Tidone and is dominated by the Lord of Vars. Then there is the way through this valley leading to Placentia. This route is dominated by this very fortress.'

'That I have already been told,' Fidelma acknowledged.

'Excellent. We shall proceed. These roads are vital for Perctarit, if he is to launch his main army from Mailand. Ticinum Pavia is a short march from Mailand and from Placentia. If he launches his army against Grimoald, then he not only has to seal this flank from attack but use the same passes to supply and reinforce his army through the port of Genua. It is through these same passes that the Romans marched their legions and reinforced their troops in ancient times when they brushed aside the Ligurians, defeated the Boii and headed across the great River Padus to destroy the Taurini, the Insubre and Cenomani. These lands they once called Cisalpine Gaul and they became part of Rome. Placentia itself was the first Roman colony in the area. Now just consider . . . what would happen if Perctarit won control of those passes?'

'I would say that the outcome would be fairly obvious,' admitted Fidelma.

It was Aistulf who posed the next unexpected question. 'Did you know that this place was said to be where the Carthaginian Hannibal came with his elephants, and that he was supposed to quarter his men here while he climbed the mountain on the other side of the Trebbia to view the territory?'

'I have heard of Hannibal,' confirmed Fidelma, wondering at the abrupt change of subject.

'Have you heard of the creature called an elephant?'

'I have heard of this strange beast, for one of the Caesars brought them to Britain, which neighbours my own land, in order to awe and conquer the people there.'

'Then let me tell you a story. As Hannibal was encamped here with his elephants on the eve of the Battle of Trebbia – his first victory over the Roman legions – it is said that three local men went to examine the beasts because they could not understand their neighbours' descriptions of them. You see, these three men were blind. One went to feel one of the beasts around the leg. "The elephant is like a tree trunk," he declared. Another felt the beast by the trunk and declared that an elephant was like a strange snake. The third managed to get hold of the ear of the beast and claimed the elephant was like a great winged creature.'

Fidelma waited in silence.

'What do you learn from the story?' invited Aistulf, still smiling.

'That they were all wrong.'

'Of course. And why?'

'Because they could not see the whole creature.'

'Exactly so,' cried Radoald triumphantly.

'You are going to tell me that we all have separate pieces of information and that if we put them together, we might see the whole. Very well. Let me sum matters up. The former King, Perctarit, is trying to overthrow your King, Grimoald. He has entered this country with an army supported by the Franks. To be able to face your King's army he needs supplies and reinforcements. The easiest way that he can acquire them is through the port of Genua. From that seaport there are two valley routes that lead to his army. You guard one and Grasulf of Vars guards the other. Grasulf is a mercenary. All Perctarit has to do is pay him to raise his men and take over control of both valley roads.'

'I would say that Perctarit did not trust Grasulf so he arranged for his agents to bring the gold to this valley to be paid only when Perctarit was ready to move his army and when he needed the supply lines to be opened.'

'That is logical enough,' agreed Radoald.

Fidelma smiled briefly. 'Indeed, the gold that is meant to pay Grasulf is already at the abbey and has already caused several deaths.'

'How do you know the gold is here?' demanded Radoald.

'Because the Venerable Ionas and I have seen it this very morning, and that is why I came here. I believe the chief conspirator has already gone to inform Grasulf, the Lord of Vars, and that the abbey will be attacked any time now.'

'And do you know who this chief conspirator is?' demanded Aistulf.

'I do.'

'And you said that Brother Eolann was involved?' Suidur asked.

'I said that he was not the chief of them. There was a stronger force than him at the centre of this intrigue.'

The door suddenly swung open and Wulfoald entered. He encompassed everyone with a single glance and saluted Radoald. He clearly brought important news.

'The Lord of Vars is on the move,' he said. 'We must prepare our men.'

'How far off?'

'He could reach us before the day is over.'

'Then let us first hear what Sister Fidelma has to say. She was about to tell us who the conspirators are.'

'This mystery has its origins in the story of the *Aurum Tolosa*,' she began.

'We have no time for myths!' grumbled Radoald.

'That's a tale told by old men around the hearth at night,' sneered Wulfoald.

'Let us hear her out,' rebuked Aistulf, with a frown at his son.

'As you should know,' Fidelma continued, 'I came here to see my old master, Brother Ruadán, who I was told had been beaten by those opposed to his teaching; he lay dying. We don't have to go into all that, which is entirely misleading. I believe that he was beaten and left for dead because he had discovered where the gold to pay Grasulf had been hidden. A wagon filled with gold. He did not know what it really was. From what he said on his deathbed, he believed he had found the gold of Tolosa according to the legend. "That which was taken from a watery grave must be returned to it." I did not know what that meant until Venerable Ionas pointed out the connection. The *Aurum Tolosa* gold had been retrieved from a lake. Brother Ruadán took a few coins, I think to consult Venerable Ionas. On his way back to the abbey he encountered little Wamba, and in a moment of unwise generosity, I believe he gave the boy two of the coins.

'Where things went wrong was when Wamba bought one of the coins to the abbey to use it to purchase things for his mother. The coin was recognised as being from the hoard and the next day someone from the abbey went in search of the boy. From Wamba that person found out who had given him the coins. Then he killed the boy, found Brother Ruadán and beat him to death, or so he thought. Brother Ruadán was strong and he reached the gates of the abbey and was taken in. When the killer heard he was still alive, he checked with Brother Hnikar. The apothecary felt he had not long to live and so the killer was not worried. The old man was raving, so he thought, and would be dead soon. So the killer thought there was no need to attract further attention to himself – until, that is, I came along.'

'Then what?' Radoald demanded. 'What had *you* to do with it?'

'Because of me, Brother Ruadán's death had to be brought forward. He had to be killed before he could talk to me. He was smothered to prevent that. It was then I made my first mistake. Instead of keeping my own counsel, I thought I could trust the *scriptor* Brother Eolann because he was from my own kingdom and spoke my language. A silly, arrogant mistake. I mentioned to him that Brother Ruadán had spoken of coins. Brother Eolann was a clever person, and being part of this plot, he sought to distract me by preparing a false trail, providing me with false clues about the *Aurum Tolosa* – the gold of *Servillius* Caepio. He persuaded his fellow conspirators that he could keep me busy running after shadows until I eventually decided to leave. Maybe I do him an injustice. Perhaps he did it to prevent his partners from killing me also.'

'But you did not leave,' pointed out Radoald.

'Worse. Still in my arrogance, I asked Brother Eolann to be my translator when I went to see Hawisa, the mother of Wamba. Brother Eolann was put in a difficult position. But the person controlling him suggested to Brother Eolann a cunning ruse. He told him to go with me and translate what Hawisa had to say in such a way that it increased my suspicions about Wulfoald and the abbot.'

'But he knew he would eventually be found out, giving this false information,' put in Aistulf.

'Maybe he thought that the conspiracy would be over by the time it came out. Or maybe he was told to get rid of me on the mountain. On reflection, I suspect he might have attempted to kill me by leading me to a dangerous place where I could have fallen to my death. However, he did not have the heart to let this happen and saved me from falling. Perhaps Brother Eolann was not so evil, after all.'

'But he had the heart to kill the small boy, Wamba, and old Brother Ruadán,' objected Wulfoald.

'I do not believe that was Brother Eolann. I think it was those with whom he was in the plot – his fellow conspirators. But he was possessed of a devious mind. Not killing me brought about another idea in his head: he knew we were going to spend the night in the sanctuary on Mount Pénas. I was surprised when Brother Eolann built a large fire. He made an excuse that it would be cold. It was not. But the fire attracted, as he had hoped, the warriors of the Lord of Vars. The next morning we were captured.

'His plan was to leave me as a prisoner of Grasulf. However, Brother Eolann was unable to see Grasulf until he arrived back from a boar hunt the following morning. He doubtless told Grasulf what was going on. As prisoners, I noticed a slight change in his attitude. He had already lost interest in books through which he was trying to mislead me. I found a copy of the same book that he claimed pages had been cut from. At Vars the page was intact. I pointed this out but he was not particularly interested. That made me suspicious. What Brother Eolann had not counted on was that we would be rescued by Suidur.'

'You say that Brother Eolann was just one of the conspirators – but why?' Aistulf asked. 'He was a stranger, an Hibernian like yourself.'

Fidelma suppressed a sigh. 'That is why I had no suspicion. He told me he had come from my country to the Abbey of Gall and then from there he had spent two years or so in Mailand. It did not register with me that it was in that city that Perctarit ruled. When Perctarit was forced to flee, Brother

Eolann came to Bobium with two other conspirators, determined to prepare the way for Perctarit's return to his kingdom.'

'But Brother Eolann's motive?'

'The same one you ascribed wrongly to Magister Ado.
Eolann was a staunch defender of the Nicene Creed. So was
Perctarit – and perhaps that was reason enough to cause
Brother Eolann to support Perctarit against the Arian,
Grimoald.'

'So why was Brother Eolann killed, if he was one of these
plotters?' asked Suidur.

'Because, having confronted Wulfoald, who I wrongly
thought had been lying to me, I asked Brother Eolann to
come and bear witness when I went with Wulfoald to see
Hawisa. Brother Eolann told the other conspirators. He was
advised to stage a fall so that he could not accompany us
and be found to be a liar. At the same time, to ensure the
truth did not come out, one of them went by night to Hawisa's
cabin. He killed the old woman, and set fire to the cabin.'

'The rider on the pale horse?' queried Wulfoald.

'Indeed. A pale horse just like your horse. When Brother
Eolann learned this, it was his turn to make a mistake. He
was responsible for condemning Abbot Servillius.'

'How?' demanded Wulfoald. 'True, the abbot was at Hawisa's
cabin that day to offer some compensation for the coin Wamba
brought to the abbey, but the abbot would not know any more
about the conspiracy when confronted by Brother Eolann's
mistranslation.'

'When we were looking for Brother Eolann, Venerable Ionas
said, "I have not seen him since he said he was going to the
abbot to make confession". Venerable Ionas, not knowing
the circumstances, thought he meant the usual confession which
is part of the custom here. But Brother Eolann's confession

was of the part he had played in this conspiracy, because that voice of conscience was hard to stifle in him even for his belief. Whether he told his fellow plotter or whether that person overheard the confession, both men were condemned to die.'

'So Abbot Servillius and Brother Eolann were killed by the same person?'

'That is my assessment,' confirmed Fidelma. 'Wulfoald has just informed us that there is now movement. I believe that the agents of Perctarit are about to hand over the gold to Grasulf and that he will soon make a descent on this valley with his men.'

'My sentinels have already reported that Grasulf's men have been arming and moving along the Staffel River,' Wulfoald confirmed.

'It means that Perctarit's army is ready to move from Mailand to meet Grimoald.' Aistulf's expression was grim.

'Importantly for us, it means Grasulf is heading into this valley,' Wulfoald responded.

'That is true.' Fidelma gave a weary nod. 'The gold is at the abbey where the agent of Perctarit hid it. Venerable Ionas and I saw it in its hiding place.'

'In the abbey? Are you sure?' Aistulf demanded.

'It was hidden in the necropolis – in the new tomb being built for the Abbot Bobolen.'

Sister Gisa's face had suddenly paled. She was staring at Fidelma with wide, bright eyes.

'Poor Brother Ruadán tried to tell me where he had found the gold,' went on Fidelma. 'He mentioned about evil being disguised in a mausoleum. I thought he meant something about corpses. He meant that it was where he had found gold coins. Maybe they had been dropped outside when the wagon was being put into the tomb. Something made him check inside. The wagon had obviously been brought there during the building of the sepulchre, disguised as one of the wagons filled with marble.'

'Did no one notice it being placed there?' demanded Radoald. 'What of the workmen?'

'They were undoubtedly Perctarit's men,' Fidelma pointed out.

'But a member of the abbey was in charge,' Wulfoald observed quietly. 'And it was not Brother Eolann.'

'That person was Perctarit's chief agent. The person overseeing the building of the mausoleum for the abbots was . . .'

CHAPTER TWENTY

'Faro!' Sister Gisa screamed the name. 'It cannot be!'
Wulfoald seemed the only one who did not express
astonishment. 'Everyone knew he was in charge of the
building of the tombs. Didn't he complete Abbot Bobolen's
tomb just before you left for Genua to meet Magister Ado?'

'I refuse to believe it. I *will* not believe it,' sobbed the girl.

'He told us that he had been a warrior during the war
between Perctarit and Grimoald,' Fidelma gently reminded
her. 'A little investigation might have shown that he had
served in Perctarit's army. He came to Bobium two years ago
after Perctarit's exile, about the same time as Brother Eolann
came from Mailand. Not only was he supervisor of the
building of the mausoleums, but Sister Gisa told me that he
had suggested the design of Bobolen's tomb and secured
the workmen to raise it.'

'A charitable work . . .' Sister Gisa began.

'Not so. His workmen were also Perctarit's men, and it was
there that the gold was brought under cover of the building
work. It was stored to await the day when Perctarit was ready
to make his move. Even worse, Faro is undoubtedly the man
on the pale horse who pursued and slew Lady Gunora and

would have done the same to Prince Romuald. He was the same person who was seen, still in his religieux robes, stealing Wamba's box from the cairn put up by Hawisa. He climbed down, but someone saw him and he dropped the box, which I later found. He had left his horse on the track below. It was the same breed and colour that I have seen Faro ride. The person who witnessed this event has not been seen recently. Let us hope there is not another death to be accounted to him.'

'You claim that he also killed the old woman, Hawisa, and set fire to her cabin?'

'I do.'

'Are you saying that Faro killed the boy, Wamba, Brother Eolann and Abbot Servillius?' asked Aistulf.

Fidelma shook her head. 'He might have killed Wamba – I am sure he did. But I believe there was a third conspirator. Of his identity I have a good idea but cannot say for certain. I believe I can do so only when I return to the abbey. The immediate problem is to safeguard the abbey and the gold from Grasulf's attack.'

Sister Gisa was still sobbing softly.

'You must face the facts, daughter,' Suidur said gently as he placed an arm around her shoulders.

'I will not believe it until Faro tells me directly,' cried the girl through her tears.

Fidelma regarded her sympathetically. 'If it is any consolation, I think he does care for you. Last night he warned me to leave the valley and, if I saw you, to give you that warning as well. He said the storm was coming.'

'That storm might come sooner than anyone thinks,' Wulfoald observed dryly.

'I agree,' Fidelma said. 'I believe Grasulf will attack either today or tomorrow.'

'Then we must protect the abbey and retrieve the gold at once,' Radoald declared, rising from his seat.

As the others followed his example, Fidelma added: 'I am now certain that Grasulf will have been informed that the gold is at the abbey and he is on the way to seize it. We must ride back and warn the brethren.'

'It will take me a while to gather sufficient warriors,' Radoald said with a frown.

'We have Grimoald's two warriors and four of my men who are good bowmen. I could take them and accompany Fidelma,' Wulfoald suggested. 'The abbey can be defended. We might be able to hold off any attempt to take the gold until you gather the rest of the men.'

'I'll come with you,' Aistulf announced with enthusiasm. '*Fortes fortuna iuvat.*' Fortune helps the brave.

'I thought you had renounced warfare?' Radoald said to his father.

'There comes a time when one cannot stand by with indifference. This is as much my valley and my people that Grasulf is attacking,' replied Aistulf. 'Have no fear, my son, you remain Lord of Trebbia. I am merely a hermit but I have a right to fight for the peace of this valley as much as anyone.'

Sister Gisa also insisted on accompanying them in spite of her distressed state. Wulfoald, with Grimoald's two black-cloaked warriors, rode ahead with Fidelma and Sister Gisa followed, then four more warriors came behind them with Aistulf at their head. They rode purposefully, without talking. Fidelma was worried. Her mind was still running over all the evidence, since in spite of her assurance of Faro's guilt and Brother Eolann's complicity, there was a nagging in her mind about the identity of the third conspirator. She suspected who it was but could not be sure. There was something that she was missing.

It was late afternoon when they finally crossed the hump-back bridge. Another of Wulfoald's warriors had appeared, riding towards them from the direction of Travo. He met them by the bridge. The exchange was rapid and brief.

'Grasulf and his warriors have already crossed into the valley downstream and are heading in this direction,' Wulfoald shouted to Fidelma. 'We have little time to alert the abbey and township.'

The party did not delay but crossed the bridge and galloped up to the gates of the abbey. Brother Bladulf had apparently returned from Mount Pénas, for it was he who opened the gates. Venerable Ionas and Magister Ado were already in the courtyard and came hurrying across to greet them.

'You are about to be attacked by Grasulf's men in the name of Perctarit,' shouted Wulfoald, as he swung down from his horse. 'I would gather as many people into the abbey as you can for safety, then shut the gates and be ready to receive them.'

Venerable Ionas was about to ask a question when his eyes alighted on Aistulf. He was shocked.

'My lord Billo,' he began. 'What—?'

Aistulf brushed him aside. 'Explanations can come later. You have no time before Grasulf attacks.'

'It is so,' Fidelma said. 'Brother Faro is behind this conspiracy. Is he here?'

'He has not returned since this morning,' gasped Magister Ado. 'I cannot believe it.'

'There is no time to debate the matter,' Fidelma snapped. 'You must prepare.'

Wulfoald was already ordering his warriors to take positions on the walls above the gates of the abbey.

'We cannot fight against Grasulf,' Magister Ado protested. 'This is a House of God, of peace. Our brethren are sworn to peace.'

'We will do the fighting for you,' Wulfoald said tersely. 'Just pray for us.'

Venerable Ionas stared at them in dismay. 'How can we defend ourselves with just these few warriors?' he demanded.

'Lord Radoald is coming with a larger force,' replied Wulfoald. 'They should be here soon. Please, sound the alarm bell of the abbey before it is too late.'

Brother Bladulf was waiting nervously, but when the order was relayed to him, he went to the watch-tower and, untying a rope, began the warning peal on the abbey bell. The courtyard became a sea of confused figures, with members of the brethren running this way and that. Sister Gisa had ridden off to the house of women in the township to rouse the Sisters who, with others, began flooding towards the abbey gates, some of them even herding their livestock with them. Magister Ado had become galvanised into action as he saw the panic of the brethren and the people. He was shouting instructions, trying to make himself heard, commanding, explaining, and trying to create some order in the confusion.

Fidelma now turned towards the pale, anxious figure of Venerable Ionas.

'Did you do as I asked?' she said.

He was distracted and she had to ask again before he confirmed it.

'It is all moved and the lock secured again?' she pressed.

'It was done exactly as you suggested.'

'And no one else has been informed?'

'No one saw us and I swore those who helped to silence, as you told me.'

The panicking townsfolk, including members of the female community, were now pushing in through the gates. Above the cacophony they heard the discordant sounds of war horns blasting, harsh and angry, further down the valley.

'The attack!' cried Venerable Ionas. 'We are lost!'

'We are not!' came the sharp tones of Wulfoald. 'We must hold here until Radoald arrives. The gates must be shut at once.'

Venerable Ionas stared at him for a moment. There were still people struggling to get through the gates, some with squawking chickens, others dragging goats or hauling reluctant pigs. For a moment Fidelma thought the elderly scholar would refuse the order, but then it seemed he realised there was no other choice. With his mouth drawn into a grim line he seized a passing member of the brethren. It was the fat cook, Brother Waldipert.

'Shut the gates. Go, get others and help Brother Bladulf. Tell those who cannot get into the abbey to run and hide as best they can. We can't shelter everyone. The gates must be shut now!' While the cook hurried off on his errand, calling on some of the passing brethren to follow him to the gate, Venerable Ionas joined Magister Ado in trying to organise the brethren, getting the horses into the stable.

Fidelma followed Wulfoald up the short flight of stone steps leading to the walkway above the gate. Aistulf had already organised the warriors into position, with their bows strung and arrows at the ready. Fidelma realised that the few bowmen would not keep any serious attack back for very long.

By this time, Brother Bladulf and Brother Waldipert, with the help of others of the brethren, had pressed the gates home against the unfortunate people left outside. They were now dispersing in all directions, wailing and crying in fright. Inside the abbey courtyard was a small crowd of townsfolk adding to the panic of the brethren. Fidelma, with a sigh of relief, saw that Sister Gisa had returned safely among them. She felt a moment of sorrow for the girl who had to face the terrible truth about the man she obviously loved. A few moments later, Sister Gisa with Magister Ado and Venerable Ionas joined them on the walkway overlooking the gates.

As they looked anxiously across the Trebbia, the sound of the war horns came again, and this time from much nearer. Now they could hear the advance of horses, crunching on the stony path and splashing in the shallows. The war band came suddenly into sight with banners waving. They rode up the lower slopes, coming to a halt outside the abbey walls. The people from the settlement who had remained outside the abbey walls had now miraculously disappeared into the undergrowth and forests.

'Not as large a party as I feared,' muttered Wulfoald with some satisfaction, examining the opposing force.

'Large enough to break in and destroy us,' Venerable Ionas replied pessimistically.

Fidelma viewed the enemy warriors below them. They had drawn up before the abbey gates, waiting for the order of their leader. Fidelma had already recognised the black-bearded Lord of Vars. Next to him she could see the large form of his steward Kakko, a battle-axe in his hand, carried as if it weighed no more than a hazel wand.

'Oh, look!' the cry came from Sister Gisa. 'Look!'

A warrior of youthful appearance had ridden forward from Grasulf's side. There was something familiar about his manner although not his clothing, with its burnished breast-plate and warrior's accoutrement and helmet. He halted his pale grey horse, removed his helmet and stared up arrogantly at them.

'Brother Faro!' Magister Ado breathed through clenched teeth.

Fidelma nodded slowly. 'There is the leader of this evil conspiracy that has caused all these deaths. "Behold a pale horse: and the name that sat on him was Death".'

Magister Ado was still shocked. 'But Brother Faro was my pupil! How came he to this treachery and evil?'

Brother Faro had caught sight of them looking down and moved his horse nearer.

'We are come to take something that belongs to Grasulf, Lord of Vars, and soon to be Lord of Trebbia.' His face was fixed in a triumphant smile. He turned and pointed to the necropolis. Two of Grasulf's warriors detached themselves from the rest and rode swiftly into the burial ground, their horses trampling through the graves towards the mausoleums of the abbots. Everyone waited in silence as they heard metal striking on stone. Faro sat relaxed on his horse, still gazing up at them.

'I suggest that you open the gates. We would sooner take the abbey peacefully than come against it with weapons and fire.'

Venerable Ionas looked nervously at Wulfoald. The warrior said, 'Stay firm. Radoald will be here soon. He must!' The old scholar nodded and stared down at Brother Faro with distaste.

'You know that you come against a House of God, Brother Faro. What has happened to your vows that you betray us and come in arms against your own brethren?'

'I took a stronger vow to my King long before I disguised myself in rough woollens,' was the reply. 'I am Faro, Lord of

Turbigo.' Then the young man caught sight of Sister Gisa and his features seemed to soften. 'Gisa, I am sorry that you had to find out this way. Believe me, what passed between us was not false. Now I give you my protection and offer you my companionship. Leave your drab associates and join me.'

She had been standing shivering as one caught in a cold wind. Suddenly she seemed to erupt, her face contorted with anger as she faced the truth. 'Companionship?' she cried, though her eyes were swimming with tears. 'The companion-ship of a murderer?'

'The companionship of the Lord of Turbigo, Commander in the army of Perctarit, the rightful King of the Longobards!' Faro replied.

They heard a cry of rage from the direction of the necrop-olis and one of the men who had been despatched there came riding back at a swift canter. There was a quick exchange with Faro which those on the wall could not make out. Faro looked up at them.

'So, you have found that which rightfully belongs to Grasulf? I suggest you hand it over without further delay.'

Grasulf, overhearing this, had edged his horse forward alongside Faro and there was a sneer on his face as he gazed up at them.

'Have they stolen the gold?' His voice was loud. 'Well, we will fire the place in any event,' he said. Then he caught sight of Fidelma. 'Well, well, all the little birds are gath-ered, and among them is the Hibernian princess. Don't worry – if you are taken alive, a princess ought to be worth a ransom from someone. Especially from slavers.' Then he glanced at his companion. 'Come, Faro, we cannot afford to waste words. They have our ultimatum. The gates are to be opened immediately or we start the attack and will burn this place down with everyone in it if they don't surrender.'

Faro sat back with a shrug. 'You hear what the Lord of Vars says?' he called. 'You have a choice. Open the gates or we shall fire the abbey.'

'Open the gates, open the gates!' a commanding voice began to cry from inside the courtyard. They turned in surprise to see Brother Wulfila, the steward, hurrying towards them. Brother Bladulf, so used to receiving commands from the steward, was already moving, swinging the bar away from the gates.

'Our third conspirator,' Fidelma cried. 'I should have warned you. Stop him!' But the noise of the voices from those inside the courtyard were rising too loudly for her to be heard. She turned to Venerable Ionas. 'You must stop him. Wulfila is Perctarit's man.'

While Venerable Ionas hesitated in bewilderment, it was Wulfoald who almost leaped from the wall and, running towards the gates, threw himself at the steward. Wulfila turned; he already had one of the heavy wooden bars in his hands, and wielded it with ease like a trained warrior. The blow caught Wulfoald on the side of the head and brought him crashing to the ground. Then Wulfila was pushing through the now unsecured gate.

Above the cacophony there came the sound of more war horns, long clear blasts, and a large band of horsemen were galloping across the river, banners flying as they swept towards Grasulf's war band. Faro turned to face the approaching danger and suddenly his helmet was replaced and his sword was drawn. Grasulf gave out a curse in a great roaring voice.

'Radoald!' shouted Aistulf in triumph.

Fidelma, concerned with Brother Wulfila, saw that he had

passed through the open gate and was running towards the war band of Grasulf, now in disarray. He was shouting to them and continued to run forward, one hand outstretched.

Those on the wall could hear him cry out: 'Wait! It is I, Wulfila. Wait! I am—'

One of Grasulf's men turned, a bow already strung in his hand. The arrow transfixed itself through Wulfila's throat. Without a sound the former steward of the abbey measured his length on the ground outside the gates and lay still.

They had little time to register the fact, before Radoald's warriors crashed into the bewildered and confused horsemen of Grasulf. The conflict was not longlasting, although it seemed an eternity to Fidelma. Soon the enemy war band was fleeing down the valley, leaving many dead and wounded behind. Among them, she recognised the body of the Lord of Vars.

Sister Gisa stood at Fidelma's side staring at the bodies, tears streaming from her eyes.

'He escaped,' she said flatly. 'He has fled with the others down the valley.'

It was a week later that Fidelma found herself standing on the quay of the port of Genua. She was at the foot of the gangplank of a ship whose crew were making ready to set sail. Sister Gisa and Wulfoald stood by her side.

'I cannot say that I am sorry to leave here,' she announced.

'However you feel about us, lady,' Sister Gisa said softly, 'we shall miss you.'

'All has ended well, lady, and that is something we can all be grateful for,' added Wulfoald. 'Grimoald has driven Perctarit and his rebels back into the lands of the Franks. The conspiracy to fund Grasulf's uprising to take over the strategic valley routes has been thwarted and the Lord of Vars has been slain, his power broken.'

Fidelma nodded absently. 'And the abbey is richer by a gift of gold from Perctarit. But has it ended well? So many deaths. Poor Brother Ruadán, little Wamba, his mother Hawisa, Lady Gunora, Abbot Servillius . . . so many deaths – and for what?'

Wulfoald raised a hand to his forehead where there was still a slight scar where the steward had caught him with the wooden bar.

'Wulfila . . . there is someone for whom I cannot feel sorry. His blow still pains me. Tell me, did you know he was the third conspirator in this matter before he declared himself?'

'I suspected, and foolishly did not say so before. The facts added up. I should have challenged him but could not make my assertions before Venerable Ionas and the *magister*. The very moment I arrived at the abbey I saw an exchange between Brother Faro and Wulfila that was not one between a steward of an abbey and a member of the brethren. On seeing Brother Faro wounded, Wulfila rushed forward like a servant and was sharply rebuked by Faro. I learned that both men came to the abbey two years before, after Perctarit went into exile. Both, I discovered, had previously been warriors.'

'Faro made no disguise of that,' agreed Wulfoald.

'But it was not revealed that Wulfila had served Faro, who was one of Perctarit's commanders. Aistulf later told me about the Lord of Turbigo whose reputation he had heard of when fighting in the wars two years ago. Faro was a brilliant commander. A good strategist. Faro and Wulfila joined with Eolann at Mailand and came to Bobium to plot Perctarit's return and campaign against Grimoald.'

ᴘᴇᴛᴇʀ ᴛʀᴇᴍᴀʏɴᴇ

'So it was Wulfila who murdered poor Brother Ruadán?' queried Sister Gisa.

'It was. Wulfila heard me say that I had found Brother Ruadán lucid and that I was going to talk to him again. He had to make sure that it did not happen. Wulfila smothered him with a pillow. He had not realised that I had already spoken to Brother Ruadán only minutes before. Brother Hnikar then mentioned that it was Wulfila who had come to tell him that Brother Ruadán had died in his sleep. I knew that not to be so. Wulfila had also to have been outside Lady Gunora's chamber when she left the abbey with the prince. He alerted his master, Faro, who chased after them and killed Lady Gunora. Finally, Wulfila lied to me when he said Abbot Servillius was in his chamber and would see no one. Wulfila had already killed him.'

'But why?'

'He advised Eolann to stage an injury to prevent him accompanying me to see Hawisa and revealing that he had misinterpreted what she had said. He did this just in case Faro failed in killing her before we got to her cabin. The weak point among the conspirators was Eolann. He was a scholar, acting for his beliefs against those he saw as Arians. But he was not a cold-blooded killer like his military-trained co-conspirators. The fact that he could not let me fall to my death on Mount Pénas demonstrated that he still had scruples. He was worried about the lives that were being taken. His Faith could not support it and so he went to confess his sins to Abbot Servillius. We can never be sure how Wulfila found out, or whether Eolann told him what he intended. At that point Wulfila decided that both Eolann and Abbot Servillius had to die. Faro and the conspiracy had to be protected until the time was ready.'

'You worked it out brilliantly,' Sister Gisa said in appreciation.

Sister Fidelma frowned with irritation. 'Not I. I did nothing but allowed myself to be misled by Eolann through my sheer arrogance. I should have known about Wulfila long before. I regard this as a failure of all my training and faculties. I am ashamed.'

'You are too hard on yourself, lady,' murmured Sister Gisa. 'A stranger in a strange land. You discovered the hiding-place of the gold and had it removed for safety into the abbey. That delay allowed Radoald's men to arrive in time.'

'When all is said and done, it was nothing but the same old story,' observed Wulfoald. 'The search of kings for power and all the bloodshed such ambitions bring with them. I suppose that search will be with us until Judgement Day.'

Fidelma regarded him with mild appreciation. 'There is the making of a philosopher in you, Wulfoald.'

He grinned. 'I have no such aspirations, lady. I am a warrior, so I am part of that search for power.'

'Well, remember, my friend, that force without good sense falls by its own weight.'

Wulfoald chuckled. 'I too have read Horace, lady. *Vis consili expers mole ruit sua.* It is a lesson that Perctarit has learned by now.'

'So you do not think your people have need to fear Perctarit again?'

'I do not think any such thing, lady. While he is alive, Perctarit will always try to return to what he thinks is rightfully his. Perhaps he will . . . one day. In the meantime, Grimoald rules fairly and allows both those who follow the Creed of Arian and those who follow the Nicene Creed to dwell in peace, if not in harmony, with each other. Perctarit may, however, find peace in Frankia or Burgundia and not bother our kingdom again. Who knows? I am a cynic and I follow the way of Epicurus. *Dum vivimus vivamus.*'

'While we live, let us live,' Fidelma echoed. 'Let us hope that Perctarit and his followers allow that.'

Sister Gisa had been silent all this time and now she stirred herself.

'There is little in life for me without Faro,' she sighed. 'I hate him for what he has done, and yet . . . All is blackness for me. I don't understand myself.'

Fidelma felt compassion for the girl. 'You think it now. Time is a great healer.'

'Faro,' breathed Sister Gisa, ignoring her. 'Did Faro survive that great battle against Grimoald? Has he followed Perctarit's flight to Frankia? He fooled me – he fooled us all. But he was . . .'

Fidelma smiled and laid a comforting hand on the girl's arm. 'Let me pass on the advice of Ovid in his *Remedia Amoris*: *res age, tute eris.*'

'The remedy for love is, be busy and you will be safe.' Sister Gisa's voice was tight. 'Ah, all well and good that you give such advice. How do you know how painful love is?'

For a moment Fidelma's jaw hardened and her eyes glistened. She was thinking of a young warrior, Cian, with whom she had fallen in love when she had been a student at Brehon Morann's law school. She had been only eighteen years old. Cian was a few years older – tall, chestnut-haired, a warrior in the bodyguard of the High King. She had been in love with him and he had merely dallied with her, using her until his fancy was taken by someone else. It had been a bitter pill to swallow. It probably had been the main reason for her willingness to accept the advice of her cousin, Abbot Laisran of Darú, that she should join the religious of Cill Dara, than any intellectual consideration about the Faith.

'I know how painful love can be,' she answered firmly. Yet even as she was saying it, she found a new image coming into her mind. She was no longer thinking of Cian but of the Saxon religieux she had so recently met and who had helped her resolve the murders at the Synod of Streonshalh and, more recently, in the Lateran Palace. Brother Eadulf of Saxmund's Ham, whom she had left in Rome and whom she might never see again. Why was she thinking of him? Perhaps if he had been with her, with his quiet support and questioning, she might not have been drawn down that blind road, her thoughts filled with the *Aurum Tolosa*, the mythical gold, and the connection to Abbot Servillius. Magister Ado had once accurately assessed her weakness: an over-confidence amounting to arrogance.

She was suddenly aware of one of the sailors at her side. He raised a hand to his forehead and said, 'Excuse me, lady. The Captain says that the tide is turning. We must be away at once. Will you come aboard?'

Fidelma assented and turned to her companions.

'I hope your valley is able to maintain the peace that it has now achieved. May Bobium thrive, so that Colm Bán's establishment will grow and its name become renowned throughout the civilised world.' She smiled at each of them in turn.

'Safe home, lady.' Wulfoald grinned. 'We have much to thank you for.'

Sister Gisa nodded her agreement, smiling at Fidelma through the brightness of tears in her eyes. Impulsively, she moved forward and embraced the girl.

Fidelma then stepped away and walked up the gangplank.

She turned and looked down at them as the crew began to haul in the plank. She heard the sound of bare feet on the deck and the crack of canvas as the sails unfurled. The ship's timbers groaned a little, almost protesting, as it slowly eased away from the quayside. Then the tide caught the vessel. The figures of Sister Gisa and Wulfoald began to grow smaller. She raised a hand to them before the ship turned to catch the wind and they vanished from her sight. For a moment she felt a strange sense of isolation, of missing them, and then the salt air stung her cheeks and she breathed in deeply, lifting her face up towards the sunshine.

She was going home at last. Home. Home to Muman. Home to Cashel. What was the old saying? There was, indeed, no hearth like one's own hearth.